M000310123

Raven's Way

Kerry L. Marzock

ReadersMagnet, LLC

Raven's Way
Copyright © 2021 by Kerry L. Marzock

Published in the United States of America
ISBN Paperback: 978-1-955603-63-8
ISBN eBook: 978-1-955603-62-1

All rights reserved. No part of this publication may be reproduced, stored in a retrieval system or transmitted in any way by any means, electronic, mechanical, photocopy, recording or otherwise without the prior permission of the author except as provided by USA copyright law.

The opinions expressed by the author are not necessarily those of ReadersMagnet, LLC.

ReadersMagnet, LLC
10620 Treena Street, Suite 230 | San Diego, California, 92131 USA
1.619. 354. 2643 | www.readersmagnet.com

Book design copyright © 2021 by ReadersMagnet, LLC. All rights reserved.
Cover design by Ericka Obando
Interior design by Mary Mae Romero

CALL ME WOLF

To those who have no choice
but to howl at the hungry moon.
A rabid, howling moon reaches out to
grab my strangled throat with
craving, hungry claws, intensity of
lunar midnight now driving me insane.
Fingers curl into nervous, anxious paws,
the curse of being once bitten
by infected teeth bathed in angry,
yellow-hooded wolfs bane.

Searing pain shrieks violently through
skin and bone while beseeching
moonbeams scratch and rip away
all straggling shreds of lost humanity.
The sharp echo of altering joints
with a scream of stretching sinew
blend together as call of the wild howls
a sad farewell to society.

Nostrils widely flared in anticipating
delight, as hunters golden eyes search
for wary prey, ears twitching forward
at the mewling cry of frightened
beasts now cowering in the night.
Oh..I can feel the dizzy rush of desire
for the taste of hot, sweet blood
from torn flesh once vibrant and alive.

The ravenous moon has called my
name once more as I stand in regal
silhouette on grizzled hillock, bathed
within the glow of silver moon glow.
I toss my head skyward, gleaming fangs
snapping angrily at grinning stars
lost in heavens angry roar.

A growl of primal terror builds to
soulful lament as man and wolf
combine to sing in lonely harmony.
The wretched mind of man now
locked inside the shadow of a beast,
to rip and claw and tear,
but to forever cry and pray
for everlasting peace.

Chapter 1

There was death in the air. Pure evil!

Other than the occasional nervous chirp of an anxious cricket, the loudest sound in the restless air was the wayward call of a lonely owl echoing off the bleak darkness. A silky whisper of brittle leaves warily danced across the forest carpet, adding a peculiar spookiness to this scene ripped from the pages of any first-rate horror novel. However, this was real and hell was near.

It was obscenely quiet! Danger grabbed the night in a strangle hold of ominous ferocity. Animals that normally romped by day now huddled shivering in their tiny dens this very night, and not from the bite of winter winds, but rather the heart-stopping scent of death within their midst. Creatures that usually hunted underneath the veil of darkness knew enough to stay safe and not to venture out for fear they would become prey themselves.

And so the deadly quiet persisted!

Moonlight slithered through small cracks in the sheltering canopy above this quivering world. Sporadically, a piece of moonbeam would reflect off two feral, yellow ovals – eyes of the beast. It could easily be said this was not just any beast. The creature that stared with unblinking gaze was beyond the ken of human thought. Legends had been created about monsters that prowled underneath a full moon. Frightening tales whispered around flickering campfires, nightmares for those who believed in them, sheer terror for those who did not. For these nightmares to become reality then death would surely ensue. There were no enemies this insidious creature had to fear for he and his kind were the ones to be frightened of. Its world was the underbelly of humanity. His prey; those foolish enough not to believe in monsters and the cast-offs that society had all but rejected.

But under tonight's moonlit spell, this obscene creature itself was the prey. Harried voices broke the nighttime stillness, mingled with the frenzied baying of scent hounds whose bravery alone came from the manic urges of the pack and that of a firm master's hand. Scathing beams of flashlights, like an army of drunken Cyclops, sliced through the haunting, inky darkness. This frightened search party sought an unknown killer with a sickening picture of the mangled bodies of two young boys still etched horrifically upon their minds. Their slaughtered innocence had been discovered by a startled jogger in Fairmount Park beneath a sobbing moon. The beast they searched for was a destroyer of unspeakable savagery whose killing fields lay below a shivering heaven. Sadly, these brave men truly had no conception of what horror lay in wait for them, only the stark realization they could be slaughtered next.

A low rumble erupted from the beast's massive chest, enough to cripple with fear the staunchest of men. And, if someone was unlucky enough to hear this menacing growl, it would most likely be the next to last sound they heard before listening to the snapping of their own bones amidst a final death rattle.

The creature suddenly moved and slid like a mysterious shadow into the swirling fog. Death had now entered the arena and there was not a prayer to be spoken that would prevent it from happening. No weapon in their puny arsenal, or faith and belief in a higher power, could help them this night. Blood would be shed because they dared search for a creature from their darkest nightmares.

In a spastic eruption, the dogs suddenly went berserk as they were assailed with the scent of a most dangerous prey. Quickly, barks of anxiety became cowardly whimpers and yelps of terror. Two frightened beagles broke free from their long tethers and sped off, hoping to see another sunrise, their master yelling obscenities and threats, but to no avail. Tango, a very misguided coon dog surged forward though, either extremely brave, or just too stupid to realize what lay in store for him. His older brother Charlie just stood his ground and growled a tepid warning, tail no longer wagging as nervous slobber dribbled from his quivering jowls.

Tango rushed forward and charged into the brush, anxious to please his handler and claim bragging rights. He stopped quickly, nose pointed to the ground, nostrils flaring as he picked up a scent never encountered before. But deep down, passed on through generations of hunting dogs before him, his brain registered danger while his fear screamed wolf. With his frantic barks and mournful baying now ceased, the stillness was even thicker than before. Lonely crickets no longer chirped. Wary, observant owls were too alarmed to hoot a warning from their lonely lookout posts. Frightened dogs had completely lost any desire for the hunt.

Well, all but for that crazy Tango.

"Tango, Tango, hey boy," his handler yelled, followed by a sharp whistle.

"You crazy coon dog, whatcha' got boy?"

Tango knew he had possibly heard the voice of his owner for the last time as he raised his head and stared at two bright yellow, murderous eyes. The coon dog's head dropped low as he curled his tail securely between his legs, falling to the ground in what he hoped would be a life-saving sign of submission.

It didn't work! The dark shadow with the ferocious glare moved at breathtaking speed. With a mighty swipe of massive claws the monster severed the coon dogs head, sending it sailing through the moonlight like a spinning football heading for a game winning field goal. It landed no more than three feet in front of Nestor, Tango's handler, and then rolled awkwardly to lie at the quivering toes of a frightened Charlie.

"Holy shit!" Nestor screamed out loud, both in shock and rage. "Oh my God, Tango. It killed my Tango."

A roar of unspeakable horror split the night, sending icy shivers up and down the spine of every policeman. Nestor couldn't pull his eyes away from the severed head of his beloved Tango. He felt his arm yank up and back, his hand releasing the other leash. Charlie knew enough to turn and tear ass from whatever creature was out there. Nestor, however, was not that smart.

Hearing another roar and then a wild thrashing of brush, he glanced up and came face-to-face with a heart-stopping vision of evil. A mouth full of slavering fangs and fetid breath was no more than six inches away from his very frightened face, the beast staring at him with maniacal hatred and a monstrous need to kill.

Nestor, with warm urine pouring down his pant leg, had but a few seconds to whisper "Dear God, forgive me for I have sinned …." before his throat was savagely torn out and death viciously yanked him away.

Suddenly, the night erupted with frenzied shouts of nervous policemen, followed by a rapid volley of panicky gunfire. Flashes from urgent rifles lit for a second the terrified eyes of each shooter. Bullets whizzed and crashed against innocent trees, with an occasional scream of pain when one impacted soft, human flesh, jellied from fear.

"Hold your fire! Damn it, stop shooting," yelled a frenetic voice.

Echoes repeatedly bounced around like a soccer ball as Captain Ganz tried desperately to minimize the damage from friendly fire being inflicted by his own men. As the crescendo died down the only sounds Ganz heard were the rapid breathing of Officer Leightman to his left and the unsteady pounding of his own slightly damaged heart. He figured this was not good therapy for the newly inserted stents that now resided in two of his arteries. Suddenly, he was startled as a frightened coon dog nearly bowled him over, Charlie racing by to follow the paw prints of his deserting beagle brethren.

"Nestor, hey Nestor, you okay? Can anybody out there see where Nestor is?"

Getting no response from his good friend was not the answer Ganz had hoped to receive. Then he heard a startled voice and glanced to his right.

"Captain, over here ….. holy shit," followed immediately by loud, rapid heaves resulting in the violent eruption of an earlier dinner of chicken pot pie and mashed taters.

Ganz grabbed Leightman by the shoulder and, after pushing the officer's rifle away from his own face, moved towards the direction of where the vomiting was still coming from. He thought this night was just becoming more and more of a nightmare. What kind of unspeakable hell were they stalking? Lord, for that matter, what now monstrously hunted them?

He felt Leightman stumble and fall forward. Ganz immediately swerved and pointed his flashlight toward the ground. Quickly, the cheeseburger and fries he had eaten around seven o' clock almost roared back up his throat.

Leightman lay sprawled across Nestor's savaged body, his flashlight beam shining garishly upon dark blood still spurting wildly from two evenly severed carotid arteries. Off to the right, with tongue lolling from the side of an open mouth, stared the black, unseeing eyes of Tango. Ganz felt himself reeling backwards before he was held up by someone closely behind him.

"Jesus H. Christ, what did this? What kind of monster is out there?" whispered Captain Nathan Ganz. He had spent nearly thirty years on the Philadelphia police force and had never in his entire career been this terrified of anything in his life. But he clearly knew that what they now faced was not taught in any classroom at the academy, or faced on any street corner with some gun-wielding assailant. Monsters like this were not ever meant to exist outside of nightmares and movie screens.

With a silver moon glittering off the tranquil, black water of a peacefully meandering Schuylkill River the distinct, savage howl of a rapacious wolf vibrated the stark Philadelphia skyline. Captain Ganz instinctively made the sign of a cross as he stared down at the mutilated body of Nestor Shirreck and the head of his beloved Tango.

Thank God tomorrow was Sunday because he desperately needed to talk this one over with the big guy upstairs, along with Father Joseph who thought Nathan was a little crazy anyway. Especially since wolves, or monsters, were not supposed to exist in his wonderful City of Brotherly Love.

Chapter 2

Time they say is supposed to heal all wounds. At least that's what he continued to hear over and over again. They were completely wrong though, not when pain sliced this deep, and near impossible when the loss was so life altering.

For Johnny, the early morning hours were always the worst. It had been their special time, that graceful part of day when the magic of night waltzed romantically into early dawn. When he and his mate Samantha could feel and hear the forest come alive from nighttime slumber. Eyesight so sharp they could see the slightest movement from a nervous rabbit a hundred yards away. A sense of smell so acute they could be warned of danger, or detect a dead carcass, from several miles. Hearing so adept a male deer could be heard scraping its antlers against a rough tree under the rutting moon, sexual urges driving the buck crazy in his desire for a doe in sweet estrus. The autumnal movement of deer had always been their favorite time to hunt. More meat than they could ever hope to consume, a veritable feast to be savored.

Hours ago he had violently kicked off several warm blankets from the bed, his own body heat driving him crazy. Reaching out he let his arm fall across Samantha's trim waist, pulling her to him. She aroused him like no female ever had, causing him to act like a young pup on the prowl for his first piece of tail. His father had told him, "Johnny, get it out of your system early because when your mate finally appears like a vision, you'll be enraptured forever." The day he met Samantha at the spring gathering he remembered instantly what his father had said. His heart was simply enslaved that very day by her beauty and a wild streak in her that captivated his desire.

Johnny opened his eyes to gaze at her beautiful face and saw nothing but blood. He yelled and kicked savagely to pull away, suddenly tumbling to the floor. His heart was beating so loudly he could not hear the rain pounding against the window. Pulling himself up to his knees he glanced at the bed. It was empty!

He leaned against the mattress and put his hand gently on the frigid, barren sheets. He shut his eyes tightly and thought, just another friggin' nightmare! Would they ever mercifully stop, or at least would there come a day when he could come to grips with her being taken so violently from his life? Probably not, for this was his contrition, his hellish penitence for leaving her alone that snowy night three years ago.

His rock-hard body glistened with cold sweat as he slowly rose from the floor. There were no more tears to be shed, replaced now with angry pangs of guilt and yearned for retribution. And always, always the ever present need for revenge. To find who killed her and make sure they paid with their miserable lives. To know as well that his unborn child would finally be avenged. No matter how many stood in Raven's way.

Very lightheaded, he moved towards the door in his shadowy bedroom. Stumbling, he banged his toe on the bedpost and let loose a tirade of angry words that would've made a nun turn scarlet. Limping slightly he went to the bathroom sink and turned on the tap. Leaning down he cupped his hands and splashed ice-cold water onto his face several times. Letting the water drip into the basin he realized that, in fact, he must've been crying after all. He missed his mate terribly and the emptiness he felt inside would surely never be satisfied again.

Moving to the shower he turned on the hot water until a thick blanket of steam enveloped him like a shroud. He pulled the curtain closed behind him and let the burning water attempt to cleanse him of his sorrow. Johnny realized he had to get a grip on reality for he had lost his bitter edge. To do battle right now with Samantha's killers would be his downfall. His strength, cunning, and unique abilities needed to be razor sharp because his enemy would not be burdened with the kind of grief and guilt which now voraciously consumed him.

After toweling off he pulled on a pair of faded jeans and grabbed an ice-cold beer from the fridge. The rain had finally dwindled to just a misty shower as he stepped out onto the porch. There was a damp freshness to the air, like the world around him had been absolved of all sin and made to feel whole once more. A feeling he felt would never touch him again.

Johnny sat down on the top step to let the cool, misty spray coat his face. Closing his eyes he took a long swig of beer. Thank God for alcohol he thought. Since his body would reject any type of drug, whether prescription or illegal, massive amounts of beer (thankfully his system would not allow him to cultivate a beer gut) and a bucket full of empty whiskey bottles were all that put a numbness on his loss. Taking another healthy gulp of cold brew, he angrily tossed the empty can into the darkness where it struck a sleeping tree, breaking up the unearthly stillness.

Now that most of the intense storm had passed, a fractured moon began to creep through the broken cloud cover. He let the silky glow embrace him like a satin sheet. His blood began to boil and his skin started to itch with that maddening growth of thick, black fur. Using his mind to suppress the change he stood and stared into the night. He took note of the fluttering wings of a crow, freeing itself from icy rainwater. A lonely, haunting hoot from his confessor, a great horned-owl, echoed off the dripping trees in the thick Maine forest. Johnny glanced up and saw its white eyes blink with forgiveness.

Smiling, he murmured, "Thank you my good friend, but not just yet. Soon though, it will be very soon."

A slight rustle from bushes off to the left drew his attention. Appearing like a mystical apparition, a large, gray timber wolf walked effortlessly into the muddy clearing. He continued to warily glide forward, stopping five feet in front of Johnny. Their golden eyes met in a moment of total understanding and compassion. The scene was plucked from a dream, a wolf who was the supreme predator in his violent world and a man who was more than a man, a creature that humanity only had nightmares about. He slowly extended his right arm, turning over and then opening his hand. A tantalizing piece of red meat lay there, inviting the huge gray wolf to come forward. Head held low, steam slowly escaping from an open mouth he stared hungrily at the small morsel and then inquiringly at the face of this man/wolf who peacefully sat before him, ultimately dangerous, yet friendly.

"Big boy, you gotta' come and get it or I'm gonna' eat it," and with that said Johnny slowly began moving the piece of meat to his own mouth. A low growl escaped the wolf's chest as he took two quick, but tentative, steps forward.

"That's the idea. You know there is nothing to fear from me other than I'm the alpha in these woods and you know that, don't you?"

The wolf extended his long neck and snatched the piece of meat from Johnny's palm, then turned and trotted about ten paces away where he turned, the chunk of meat already swallowed. Erupting moonlight glinted brightly off his golden, predatory eyes. This awesome creature lifted his head towards the fast moving storm clouds and howled, long and mournful, this song of the wild echoing off leafless treetops, his way of saying thank you for the little treat. And then like magic he was gone.

Johnny smiled and stood, raising his right hand to lick off any lingering blood from the chunk of meat. "Give me a little more time my friend, we'll run these hills together soon," he whispered to the night.

He turned and entered the cabin. His small, rustic haven was snuggled deep in the Maine woods. It had been his only salvation after Samantha and their unborn child were slaughtered. Going on a terrifying rampage after her death, his father and older brother searched him out, only to discover him in a mountainous cave, almost near death. After all, what was life without his mate, the only true love he had ever known?

However, his father slowly nursed him back to this land of tortured souls, trying to make him understand he needed to honor her life and that of his unborn son. So his father brought him here to this cabin on a massive piece of land that had been in their family for generations. Where his kind could run and breathe, not like within the soiled, dingy city streets that was normally his kind's habitat.

"When you're ready to avenge Samantha, and only then, you come to me. We will hunt them down together. No manner of death will be harsh enough."

Johnny felt that moment was drawing close. He filled a large, slightly chipped mug with strong, steaming black coffee and dropped his wiry body into the only chair he had in the living room, a large, overstuffed recliner where he ended up sleeping more often than not. Grabbing the remote he clicked on the tube, more for sound than anything. This time of the morning it was nothing more than re-runs of idiotic sitcoms, or inane infomercials. Hell, as far away from civilization as he was the only reception his weak pair of rabbit ears picked up was a couple snowy channels out of Bangor. Leaning his head back he closed his eyes, hoping the caffeine from the thick coffee would perk him up a little bit and appease the headache scratching inside his head.

No such luck!

Since it sounded like a re-run of the late news he kicked up the volume a little. A late-night anchorman, with what appeared to be a two-bit hair piece and obviously an orchestrated voice, was droning on about something happening down in Philadelphia.

"...... and now let's cut back to Christie Omar down in Philadelphia where early this evening a jogger made a very grizzly discovery. The bodies of two young boys were found in what appears to have been a very horrifying condition along the banks of the Schuylkill River. Christie, are you there?"

"Yes Don, I'm here just outside the emergency room of Temple University Hospital where the bodies of two young, teenage boys were discovered by a jogger a little after 6:00 o'clock this evening. Obviously, the names of these two young men are being withheld at the moment until next of kin can all be notified. However Don, I can tell you from a source inside the hospital that the condition of both bodies was extremely distressing. This source confirmed that, in their opinion, both boys had been savagely attacked by what appeared to be some form of animal, like a wild dog or possibly something larger. There have been sightings in the Fairmount Park area of the city in the past of wild dogs, but nothing ever this gruesome came as a result of them.

Don, just a second, it appears that something else is happening ....." Johnny was actually wide awake now as he put his coffee cup on the floor and sat forward in the chair. If the bodies were as mauled as the reporter seemed to allude to, then he knew it was no wild dog. He had actually been waiting to hear about such an incident, hoping that the killer, or killers, he so desperately sought would make a stupid mistake and lead him to them. "Don,

I'm back and there seems to have been another major incident out along the Schuylkill not more than an hour ago. A large group of police officers were searching the banks of the river for whoever had attacked the two boys when they were attacked themselves. It appears that a search dog, along with the handler, was killed tonight. One policeman, evidently extremely upset, said he clearly heard the howling from a large dog of some kind " His rage and excitement building, Johnny Raven walked to the edge of the porch. He knew in the morning he would be heading to Philadelphia. A wild and savage instinct for the hunt told him if his prey was not still there, then for sure there would be a fresh trail. But right at that moment he needed to run and feel the ground quake under his pounding paws, to feel his long, thick, black fur blowing in the frigid, nighttime air. Most of all though he needed to feed as the tantalizing taste for hot blood and sweet meat filled his urgent hunger. He quickly stepped out of his jeans, and moved into the muddy clearing. Storm clouds had moved along to ravage the country farther north as now a huge moon spread its welcoming arms out to him.

Burgeoning sounds from the dense Maine forest which surrounded his cabin became hushed as the sleek body of a massive black wolf disappeared between the trees. A supreme predator was now on the loose in their midst. It was time for unsuspecting prey to be on their highest alert for something would surely die tonight.

Chapter 3

The sky out west towards Lancaster and Pennsylvania Dutch country was painted in a deeply thick, gunmetal grayness. Freezing rain, and possibly light snow was being predicted to hit sometime late Sunday evening by all the local news channels. Nathan pulled his collar up around his neck and wondered if the forecasters would at least get half of it right this time. Of course, the typical army of early storm shoppers was already out and stocking up, creating agitated lines at grocery stores for milk, bread, lunchmeat, toilet paper, and other particularly important staples like pretzels, ranch dip, and cherry crumb pie. He had already stopped at the beer distributor Saturday morning to purchase his customary two cases of Coors Lite. What the hell, doctors told him to stop drinking after his heart problem but he figured he would capitulate and buy Lite beer instead, even though he hated it. It was better than that damn near beer they told him he could have. At 62 years old he was not going to give up everything he liked. Life was too damn short for that and besides, he needed to release the stress somehow.

He tossed the last piece of delectable chocolate-glazed donut into his mouth and licked his fingers clean of any revealing evidence while coasting off the zoo exit of the Schuylkill Expressway and then down to West River Drive that ran parallel with the river. A crisp, overcast, late-October Sunday morning was shocking enough citizens as they read the front page of the Philadelphia Inquirer, which screamed in large black letters, "TWO YOUNG BOYS SLAIN", with a smaller by-line "Police Attacked, Two More Dead". He hated the news and the sensationalism cast upon every story.

After coming to a slippery stop on the gravel shoulder of the road he pulled his substantial bulk out of the front seat and walked over to stand in front of fluttering yellow crime-scene tape which had been stretched around a wide area of the park adjacent to the river. He nodded to a few officers milling around with chilly hands inside their jacket pockets as he ducked under the tape and strolled slowly before stopping along the high bank at the waters edge. Last night the river had been so smooth, nearly like mirrored glass. Now this morning, with a harsh breeze roaring in from the impending storm, the Schuylkill was choppy with an angry attitude.

"Here Captain, looks like you need this," said a soft, sexy voice behind him.

Turning, he gazed at the attractive, smiling face of Detective Kathleen Morello. Reaching out gratefully, he curled a beefy hand around a steaming cup of coffee swimming in plenty of cream and sugar just the way he liked it. His wife Margaret always scolded him, saying that he like coffee in his milk and sugar. The heck with what the doctors kept telling him. At home his wife made sure he ate healthy, if not boring. Give him a dripping Philly cheese steak on a fresh Italian roll any day of the week. He sighed as he took a couple long swallows of the sweet elixir.

"Hello Detective, welcome to my nightmare. I suppose you've been brought up to speed on what's happened?" Nathan inquired.

"To a certain degree, I suppose. Each of the officers I spoke to were more than just a little upset. Kavansky kept murmuring over and over about hearing a wolf? I told him that it must've been just a large dog he heard, but then he looked at me with these haunted eyes and said it was no dog, more like a wolf from hell," she said slowly, shrugging her slim shoulders. "I guess you can give me another slant on what happened."

"Follow me," as he started walking across the road, stooping underneath the yellow ribbon and trudging up a small hill to the tree line. He stopped three feet away from two large, dark maroon stains on the grass. They both stood very still for several minutes staring down at the ground, a sharp breeze blowing Morello's long, dark auburn hair across her face. She pulled it back and reached around to pull up the hood on her jacket.

"Damn, it's just too cold this early. I think it's going to be a really brutal winter," Kathy said, just trying to break the tension oozing off him.

"So Morello, you think a wild dog could do that? Sever another dog's head, throw it about thirty feet, and then nearly decapitate a man as strong as Nestor was?"

Kathy moved in front of Ganz and knelt down beside the blood-stained grass. Looking to the line of trees she stood and walked over to some of the crushed bushes. She had to admit that whatever did this was no dog, or even a pack of dogs.

"Cap, did anybody see anything? There was nobody close enough to Nestor that saw him get killed, or could get a shot off?"

Nathan grunted slightly as he moved up to stand beside Morello. "Everybody was so spread out. Nestor had moved to this side of the road I suppose because his dogs got the scent of what they were tracking. The two young beagles broke loose and I heard him cussing them up one side and down the other. He must've let Tango go because I heard him yell out as if the dog had gotten hold of something. Then there was a quick yelp from the dog and a startled scream from Nestor. Seconds later, I swear to you Kathleen, the night just erupted with a roar like I had never heard before. I'm not embarrassed to say that I nearly pissed my pants." He paused for a moment, trying to calm down his pounding heart. "Then we found him when Leightman tripped over the body."

Morello reached into the bushes a little to the right and pulled away a dark clump of something. Holding it gently with her gloved fingers she placed it in the palm of her left hand. Damn if it didn't look to her like animal fur.

"Whatcha' find Detective, something interesting?"

"Not sure Captain, but it appears to resemble some really dense hair from an animal," as she reached into the pocket of her coat for a small plastic bag. "I'll drop it off at the lab and see what they can make of it. Were there any footprints? Wasn't it raining pretty steady last night? I was out like a light early and slept like the dead."

"Yeah, it was pretty dark last night," Ganz replied. "Then the rain came down hard, really nasty. We searched the bushes and trees up and down the park for quite a ways. Believe it or not, the only prints we saw back there in the woods were what appeared to be those of a very large dog."

He shrugged his wide shoulders as she turned and looked directly at him. "I know, I know," holding up his hands, "but that's it. They poured casts of what they found, measured the distance between the prints. It's all in the report which you can check out when you get back to the precinct."

Tapping her back and then clutching an arm, he led her away until they were out of ear shot from the other policeman milling around.

"Look Kathleen, I have no idea what we're dealing with here. I do know this however. Whatever is running loose in our city, I don't believe it's anything we've ever encountered before. I have men combing both sides of the river looking for anything that can help us. Damn newspapers are going to have a field day with this so we need to come up with answers and soon. Because of the dead boys, the Mayor and City Council are going to be demanding results and fast. Whatever is out there doing this killing, we've got to stop him," he paused dramatically. "or maybe I should say IT."

Detective Morello stared deeply into her Captain's eyes and knew for certain that he was not only confused over this case, but worried as well. Whatever he had witnessed last night would stay with him for a very long time.

Suddenly, a loud voice calling for Ganz drew their attention back down to the road.

"Captain Ganz, we need you over here sir," yelled one of the patrolmen. Ganz and Morello walked quickly over to where the patrol car had pulled to a screeching stop next to where he had parked his silver, slightly dirty, Toyota Rav-4.

"What's up Officer ... Jackson?" asked Ganz, checking the name tag.

"Yes sir, one of the men spotted something that you and Detective Morello need to see right away. It's up near the Falls Bridge at the end of the Drive. Uh, Captain, you just gotta see this. I mean it's really weird," the officer said firmly, but with a slight treble to his voice.

Ganz shook his head and mumbled something that was more for his own ears to hear than anybody in particular, "Christ, nothing about this nightmare would surprise me right about now."

Five minutes later Ganz and Morello half climbed, half slid down the bank to where the water lapped angrily at the muddy ground. There was already a small group of interested bystanders on the bridge staring down, some sitting on wafer-thin bike seats, their garish, neon-colored biking outfits screaming advertisements, painting a weird mosaic on this gray, dismal Sunday. On the far bank stood a growing crowd of gawking, Sunday morning amateur detectives, the scent of death and mystery mingling with their whining dogs and whispered concerns. Ganz tripped on a rock and went down in a splatter of mud. Kathy reached back to help him stand up.

"Shit, Margaret's going to kill me when I get home. These are supposed to be my Sunday-go-to-meeting pants. Think I've worn them one time." He raised his voice to a screechy falsetto and chirped, 'Oh Nathan, I told you to change clothes before going out there – yada, yada, yada', I can just hear her now," he grumbled.

"Your wife's only concerned for your welfare Captain. How have you been feeling anyway?" Kathy politely inquired.

He stared at her and tried wiping off some of the mud. "Why the hell does everybody keep asking me that? I had a minor heart attack and I'm fine, okay?"

Kathleen held up her hands to ward off his vociferous attack. "Hey Captain, no problem, just worried about you. Nothing wrong in that you know."

Morello moved off and stepped gingerly over the rain-soaked ground. She stopped where three policemen stared down at something which appeared to hold their complete attention, murmuring to each other about monsters of all things. She took her hand and roughly split two of them apart in order to get a better view.

At first she wasn't sure what she was looking at. It obviously looked like several animal prints, probably from some large dog like a German shepherd or a mastiff, something huge. Then she let her gaze slide ahead and had a very uneasy feeling crawl up her spine. There seemed to be a clear area free of footprints, followed by what appeared to be a slightly agitated spot of dirt and mud. Then, not more than two or three feet beyond that, was a human footprint. Not from a shoe either, but like a human footprint, albeit a large one with five toes. And beyond that footprint lay another one and then a few more before they disappeared directly underneath the bridge.

"What the .....?" she murmured under her breath, moving slowly along the river bank to where she stopped and stared up about twenty feet to the steel bridge.

"Hey Jackson, make sure this entire area is cordoned off and do it now. We don't need these prints screwed up by curious assholes, and that means us as well."

"You got it Morello. You heard her guys. Let's move back and get some tape up here real fast," Jackson ordered, with more false bravado than he was actually feeling.

Kathy heard somebody stumble over to where she stood quietly, lost in her own troubled thoughts. Glancing back she noticed Ganz was trying to keep his large body from falling down again. He'd probably rip his pants next time he fell and Margaret would be even more pissed off.

"Captain, I'm not sure what we have here, but I think what you said earlier is eerily accurate. It seems we sure are dealing with something we've never encountered before. This case so far is really weird. I mean howling wolves, large animal footprints merging into shoeless human prints and then disappearing completely, bodies being torn apart. Hell, I need a drink and something a lot stronger than a cup of coffee."

Nathan Ganz laughed in a low rumble that rolled from his heaving chest. "I'm all for that Kathy. Wish I knew whether we should ask for help from animal control, a zoo keeper, a psychic or a priest."

"Maybe all four Nathan, maybe from all four," she whispered back.

Chapter 4

The small bedroom was really dark. Pitch black in fact, all but for the bleeding red numbers on the digital clock perched precariously on a night stand by his un-slept in bed which glowed 7:32 a.m. He could never get used to a mattress so he either slept on the floor, or slumped in the chair. It was the way he liked it, especially after an exhilarating night when his beast filled the midnight sky with blood and death. He needed this special time to unwind and he found the darkness cleansed him more than anything else ever could.

Ominous rumbles of thunder rattled the window panes that were shielded by drawn blinds and covered over by thick, dark-brown woolen blankets. He hated the light the day after his beast ran free. Many times the creature stayed with him long after human thought and physical persuasions took over. Like now, when he could still taste the sweet fear in those frantic eyes of that simpering dog. Sneering, he shook his head and reached for the nearly empty bottle of Jack Daniels. Humans were so stupid, having no idea what they faced until it was far too late. Their instincts became bottled up in fear until they were completely helpless. And that sorry example of a man who weakly whispered a prayer to an unhelpful God before his throat was neatly slit with his own claws, like praying really mattered at all.

Closing his burning eyes he finished off the bottle in several long swallows and let it drop to the floor where it clinked against another empty soldier. He still could feel how he had blended in with the shadows, becoming one with the night, and then hungrily glared at that old, fat cop who at one point stood no more than ten feet away from him. Most humans lacked even the barest of instincts which could warn them of danger and death in their midst. He thought how thrilling it would've been to sink his claws into that quivering mound of flesh, ripping through that thin, white skin and seeing those internal organs spill out onto the ground. Seeing a pulsing heart still frantically beating during the last few precious seconds of life. How he thirsted at the urge to let his fangs sink into a throbbing throat, and feel that puny human's life force fill his hungry stomach. How he ached for the power which possessed him when the moon sang out his name.

Slamming his hand against the wall he lowered his head. But, he was sorely aware that he also lacked control. He hated his inabilities when rage built up like this and then consumed him voraciously. He despised the fact he was so much more than just a mere human, yet less than those of his kind who were full-blood. The moon was both his secret paramour and his arch enemy. When he ran as the beast, total power controlling all of him, he was free to truly live. Still, being less than those of his breed, he was destined to walk the earth during daylight hours and underneath moonless nights. Unable to caress the feral thrill of the wolf until the lunar mistress, his moonlit lover, called forth his beast and let her sensual glow envelop him.

After filling the bath tub with steaming hot water he stood in front of the mirror admiring his body. Muscles rippled underneath sun-browned skin, but he was not what you would call muscle bound. Those body builders with their sculpted arms and corded backs could not even compare to his strength. As he lowered himself into the steaming water he submerged completely for several minutes. He loved the feel of being completely alone, totally on the edge of life and death. It was the way he had lived now for over one hundred years and yet nobody would think him older than twenty-five. It was one of the beautiful traits he had acquired after being bitten by an infected creature.

Oh, he could age albeit a very slow process. However being less than full-bred he was looked down upon, or so he felt, for all these years. His segment of the breed was what the legends of myth and horror were constructed from. Those of full-blood were hardly ever detected since they had abilities far beyond that of a normal werewolf. That is where his anger came from because he yearned so much for those abilities and yet knew they would never be his. So he roamed the land, infecting and killing to try and assuage the pain that consumed him on a daily basis.

He had watched the early morning news and was elated at the stories about a demonic killer on the loose. They would never find him simply because he would move on once the next phase of the new moon took over. He had left a bloody trail of dead bodies littering so many city streets. Whatever clues remained had police departments completely baffled as to who, or what, they were tracking.

As he poured a glass of pure orange juice and grabbed a large apple from the bowl on the table, there was a knock at the door. He stiffened immediately because he had no friends, no acquaintances, or anybody to hold him to one place. Who the hell could this be, as another soft knock echoed throughout the apartment?

Placing the shiny McIntosh apple back in the bowl and swallowing the rest of the orange juice he moved gracefully to the door. Standing there he listened closely and could hear the faintest of heartbeats on the other side. He also detected the very powerful scent of a female who had recently had sex, stirring his hunger for the same delight.

"Who's there?" he growled, hoping to scare her off.

"Hello, is somebody there? I'm Sharon from the apartment next door," purred a sweet, high pitched voice.

"What do you want?" he snarled back.

"I was just wondering if you had any milk, skim or regular, doesn't matter. I was going to have a bowl of cereal, but I hate to go out in this weather just for a carton of milk. I can give it back to you later today after I go to the grocery store," Sharon asked.

His hand closed around the door knob and then stopped. Instinct told him not to do this, but his male desire urged him on. Gripping the knob hard, he turned it and slowly opened the door. He squinted quickly as a grayish burst of daylight slithered into the dark recesses of his apartment.

"God honey, it's really dark in there. Don't you believe in lights? Like a damn cave. So sweetie ..... you have a cup of milk I can borrow? I need to eat something, especially after last night. I mean to tell ya', what a hangover I have this morning. Think I passed out for maybe two hours," she chuckled.

He moved aside and let her wiggle on by making sure though there was barely enough room and she had to brush up against the front of him. She did have a nice ass in those skin-tight pants, he thought. The top of her white blouse was left unbuttoned and gaped open, clearly advertising the top edge of a lacy, white bra enclosing very ample breasts. As she moved into the shadowy living room he licked his lips, his stomach growling loudly. Startled, she turned around and smiled at him.

"What the heck was that?" she giggled.

"Nothing to worry about Karen, I just haven't eaten breakfast yet," he replied in another low growl, not to frighten, but rather to entice her.

"That's cool, but my name's Sharon. I don't believe you've told me yours yet?" she asked demurely, tilting her head to the side.

"You're right, I didn't, but if I did I suppose I would say it was Quentin."

She chuckled at his mysterious evasion and moved off to where she thought the kitchen was, opening the refrigerator and finally letting some light into this dark, surreal world she had entered. Damn she thought, how could somebody live like a mole? Letting her gaze scour the contents of the fridge, she almost laughed out loud, but suppressed it, not knowing how this very strange man would react. Bending over a little more just to give him a nice full glimpse of her ample derriere she took a quick glance at him underneath her arm as she reached forward. Mmmmmm, he stood there upside down and she marveled at his body. Wow, she had never seen a chest or arms like that before. Seemed like most of the jerks she always seemed to connect with were druggie-thin, or more concerned with how much they drank than how often they worked out. She had noticed him walking into this apartment day before last, but he had been wearing jeans, a flannel shirt and an Eagles zipper sweatshirt with the hood up. Even then, she could see the features of his face and got quite a sexual stir. He was well over six feet, probably closer to 6' 5", or 6' 6". Hot, very hot, she thought. She certainly had plenty of food in her apartment, so had decided to make up this story to get a better glimpse of him.

"So, where's the guy who normally lives in this apartment? I think his name is Frankie or something, but that's only because I heard somebody call him that one day. Never really talked to him that much, other than to say hello and how are you. Besides, I think he's gay anyway and wouldn't be interested in me. You two know each other?" she said, pausing slightly. "Oh damn, I mean, if you're gay I didn't mean anything by that remark."

In the shadows he smiled at her being uncomfortable and decided to play along for just a little while. Frankie had the very unfortunate luck of making his acquaintance night before last and was now very deeply buried as pieces throughout Fairmount Park. Rummaging through the dead guy's valuables he was able to find this apartment and since Frankie had a key, then the apartment was now his by rights of 'finder's keepers'.

"Frankie and I are just friends and he had to leave town for about a week. So he asked if I'd stay here and look after things. Of course, he neglected to tell me he had such a cute neighbor."

She looked at him and smiled, then turned back to concentrate on the refrigerator.

"Hey, you don't have much food in here. What's the reason for all the eggs? You got six dozen eggs in here, a big chunk of cheese and two cartons of milk," she murmured, loudly enough for him to hear.

"Don't you know that eggs are the best form of protein?" he asked, moving closer while she was bent over, her head burrowed completely inside the open refrigerator.

"Not really, I mean I like eggs, but I'm not a fanatic like this. Hey, since neither one of us has eaten breakfast how about if I make us a nice big cheese omelet?" she asked, standing up and backing directly into him. She knew he was standing there and did it on purpose, hoping her teasing action might lead to something else.

As her backside made contact with his groin, she felt a noticeable bulge that excited her quite a bit. "Ooooh, I didn't realize you were so close to me," she purred.

His arm encircled her waist and brought her tightly up against him, almost lifting her from the floor, bending over and letting his face sink into her curly mane of blond hair. His wolf moved hungrily deep inside him and a long, low growl escaped his chest.

Startled, Sharon grabbed his arm and pulled free, moving over to stand in front of the stove. Damn she thought, sounded like a dog or something, but she didn't see or smell any animal when she came in. Hell, in this shadowy darkness she wasn't sure of anything anymore. She opened the stove and looked inside, hoping to maybe see a frying pan to cook the eggs in, or maybe use as a weapon.

"So Quentin, you have a frying pan so I can make us some eggs?"

He moved closer to where she was backing up against the stove, towering over her small frame. "Don't need a frying pan. A raw egg is the densest form of protein you can eat, plus it's fast and easy. Just crack it into a glass and drink. Want some?"

She laughed warily and tried to move around him, but he blocked her escape.

"Hey, look, I think I'm going to head for the grocery store after all," she said meekly, quickly slipping underneath his arm and escaping towards the front door.

"I thought you came over for some milk and I do have some in the fridge," he asked her in a very deep, excited, wolfish voice.

"Nah, that's okay, I think my blood sugar is getting too low so I probably need something sweet pretty quickly. Maybe a few glazed donuts" she replied.

"Low blood sugar, what's the deal with that?" Quentin asked.

"Oh, I'm a type-two diabetic sweetie and I can always tell when my blood sugar is getting too low, especially after I drink so heavily the night before."

He stood back and let her open the door, squinting once again at the invading light. Infected, disease ridden, let her go he thought. Damn, but she was delectable that's for sure.

"So honey, maybe I'll catch you later, okay?" as she slipped out into the overcast Sunday morning, but at least it was daylight and safety she thought.

"Yeah, you have a nice time at the grocery store," he muttered as she quietly closed the door, engulfing him in darkness once again, just the way he liked it.

Lowering his head he tightly opened and closed his massive fists. He could feel the tell-tale thickness of hair still on the back of his hands and forearms. Moving to the fridge he opened the door, grabbed a container of eggs and took them to the counter. Taking a large glass from the cupboard he cracked open a dozen eggs, tossing the shattered shells into the sink. Without even stirring up the gooey mess he put the glass to his lips and swallowed the contents in several long gulps, wiping his mouth with the back of his right hand. He belched as he placed the unwashed glass into the sink and then moved towards the front of the apartment, grabbing a jacket on the way.

Damn, that bitch had really aroused him so he needed to run off some of his aggression. Maybe take a jog down to where he spent last night and take in some action from the Keystone Kops.

Chapter 5

The massive black wolf stood on top a distant hill, his thick fur covered by a light blanket of snow. Crazy to have the white stuff fall in late October, but it really exhilarated him. He shook his tall, wide body and let the thin coating of flakes spray off him. From another hill he heard the howl of several wolves he had run with last night. They had all taken down a large buck and gorged themselves. His stomach was definitely full. He let his long tongue slide along the outside of his muzzle, licking up the final drops of dried blood still stuck there. Throwing his magnificent head to the sky he howled his thanks and good-bye to his wild brethren. Trotting off, he entered the tree line and followed a well worn path to the clearing in front of his cabin. He hated the thought of releasing his wolf, but he knew the urgent need to leave at first light for Philadelphia. He closed his golden eyes and made his personal moon disappear, thinking strongly of human skin and bone structure. His mind exploded in reds and yellows, the shifting inevitably attached to some amount of pain which of course always was worse when he went from wolf to man than changing the other way.

His nude body, crouching now in the mud of early morning, stood slowly as he stretched, trying to minimize the stiffness. The change from wolf was easier than say raven to man, mostly because of size and body structure. In the beginning, a young pup always had its share of pain until he or she learned to control the severe alteration of bone, muscle and skin. Many problems resulted early on in some very comic situations. He smiled as he remembered once, when he was thirteen, how he had tried to bring on his wolf and ended up crouching over on two legs, but with four paws and two flapping black wings. His father and mother laughed for quite a long time and truly enjoyed bringing it up over and over again when in the company of friends.

He moved silently into the warm confines of the cabin. He wasn't hungry, but the change always made him thirsty so he grabbed a large glass container of orange juice with flying geese painted on the side and held it to his lips, chugging it and then swishing hot water around before putting it in the tray to dry. Grabbing and popping a beer he moved gracefully down the hallway towards the bathroom.

He realized he needed to leave yet he stayed tightly enwrapped in the hot mist and water of the shower. Keeping his head directly under the gushing shower head, he closed his eyes and immediately could see Samantha like it was only yesterday. Her beauty was the thing of legends. Chindu, the powerful alpha leader from a neighboring pack, had come that season to the spring gathering which was being held on his family's property. She was Chindu's youngest daughter and was actively being pursued by close to a dozen of the strongest, fittest, most determined young males of the surrounding packs. Their bond seemed to be linked almost from the moment their eyes met. Still, he needed to fight for her and he did with a wild abandon.

The vicious fighting went on for three days and by the end of that period he was undoubtedly the victor. He had proven to all competition he was the strongest and toughest of all the wolves out to claim her as a mate. He paid a price though with a wild array of scratches, gouges and bites taken from his hide. His father was so proud, strutting around with his head and tail held high.

The union between Johnny and Samantha would unite the two largest packs into one. Their fathers would lead their respective packs, but overall his father was the premier alpha of all the clans in the area.

Johnny's wolf name was Jarress while hers was Sashine. She took it upon herself to comfort him and to lovingly tend his wounds. Their breed heeled fast to be sure, but she had more important things in mind for him and needed him very healthy and virile for that undertaking. In a few days when he was stronger they mated for the first time and through that magic was created a seed for a son.

He slipped out from under the scalding water and turned the faucets off, stepping gingerly out of the shower stall and grabbed a large white towel. His eyes were still wet after drying his face and he realized that tears could still flow freely when he thought of her. Angrily he tossed the towel in the basket and strode to the bedroom where he quickly slipped on jeans and a thick, checkered flannel shirt.

He didn't need much in the way of clothes since he would be spending much of his time out of human body so to speak. Hell, for that matter he really didn't even have that much of a wardrobe anyway. Jeans (mostly faded and worn), flannel shirts, a few sweaters and sweatshirts frayed at the elbows, boots when he did wear shoes of any kind. He had one decent, dressier outfit which he stowed in his small satchel figuring he might have to blend in to get some valuable information.

Making sure everything was turned off in the cabin he stood in the center of the one main room. Having spent most of the last several years here, it was to some degree like leaving home, but someplace he would rather bury all those distressing memories. Somehow he knew he might not be returning to this cabin for awhile, if ever. He certainly wasn't sentimental anymore, that side of him being destroyed when Samantha was killed. But there was a sense of accomplishment in this remote place in the wilderness. After all, he had fallen far into the depths of hell and as it turned out, it was the solitude and peacefulness of this land that had saved him in the long run.

Moving onto the porch he closed and securely locked the front door. When he turned around the large gray wolf was standing there with a sad look in his golden eyes. Johnny moved off the porch and knelt down in front of this magnificent beast.

"So my old friend, are you going to miss me?" as he put his own strong arms around an equally strong neck, placing his head beside the wolf's left ear. And then he whispered, "Thank you Rasha for helping to save this lowly creature. I'm not sure if I'll return to this place too soon, but if I do then we will race these hills once more."

The great wolf whimpered and then licked the side of Johnny's neck, backing away slightly and then reared up on his hind legs where he placed his massive front paws on Johnny's shoulders.

"Yes my friend, you are truly the alpha in this forest, not me. Now go run and lead your pack for I have to leave."

With that said the wolf turned and loped off into the trees, glancing back several times as Johnny threw his bag onto the passenger side of the seat and then jumped in. The truck roared to life interrupting the early morning stillness. He steered out of the clearing and began the slow traverse down the old, rutted logging trail. Looking out the side window Johnny noticed that Rasha was racing along the hilltop and then stopped abruptly, tossing his head high into the air and yipping his good-bye.

Smiling, Johnny took his time at first, but once he got below the snow line he sped up until he made his way to a paved road. He figured driving straight through would take about ten to eleven hours before reaching Philadelphia. Once he got there he was a little unsure of what his course of action would be. He planned on stopping around Bangor to fill up and get a bite to eat. There he would phone his father and tell him of his plans so that Johnny's arrival in Philadelphia could be expected by the area clan. He knew the local full-bred pack would not have done the killing that was reported on the news. It had to be a were-rogue and Johnny was quite sure they were most likely looking for this deranged killer as well. However, he desperately needed his father to advise the alpha of the pack(s) around Philadelphia that Johnny wanted first crack at who could possibly be his wife's murderer, or give him a strong lead as to who was ultimately behind it. They could track, trail, search out and maybe discover, but in no way were they to destroy it. That would be Johnny's privilege and not before he obtained some answers, no matter how vicious he had to become in order to get them.

He figured after his short stop in Bangor and talking to his father he would jump on Route 95 and follow it all the way south through New York and New Jersey to Philadelphia, a city he had never been in. He strongly sensed the thrill and anticipation of the hunt begin to course through his veins once again. His anger, bordering on rage, began to take over. But he had learned to temper it this time. He knew the terrible loss he felt and subsequent destruction he had loosed upon so many unsuspecting humans after finding Samantha slaughtered, was not the way to avenge her death. He was wrong and he knew that, but he was like a were-rogue himself. Nobody could've controlled his beast. Death would always be the final answer. After leaving an ungodly number of dead bodies in his wake, both human and lycanthrope, he had escaped to the wilderness and literally collapsed inside the cave, hoping to die and join his Samantha.

This time he would channel his rage and aggression into a more positive approach. He knew whatever enemies or demons he was about to do battle with would not be chained to the same sorrow and blinding revenge that had consumed him several years ago.

The black pavement, white stripes and green road signs whistled by while he thought of nothing but Samantha. About the few precious years they had spent together and returning home that snowy December night to find his home destroyed and her body lying spread-eagled to the ground in front of their cabin, the body of his unborn son removed and stolen away.

Loud honks of a blaring air horn from a distressed trucker brought him thankfully back to reality. He had drifted carelessly into the passing lane while a large semi was barreling up on his left to pass him. Yanking the steering wheel hard to the right he drove the pickup off the road, gravel churning wildly from his spinning tires. He finally stopped halfway up a small rise, his head banging angrily against the metal molding at the top of the windshield.

He had a quick thought as to why it was important to wear seat belts, reaching up to his forehead and feeling a trickle of blood.

After the dust cleared he pulled the pickup slowly off the hill and coasted about a hundred yards down the shoulder of the highway to a wider rest area. Once safely away from the busy highway, facing an open field and a few lonely trees, he leaned his head back and covered his eyes with two very shaky hands.

"I miss you so much" he whispered, knowing her spirit was forever part of his life which had just possibly saved him from being crushed by a Mac truck.

Chapter 6

Actually, Quentin truly was his real human given name, Saunders being his family surname. Nobody could trace him anyway and more often than not whoever he revealed his name to would conveniently end up dead. So, like the lovely Sharon, he didn't much care who he told. He had been born in London to poor, but loving parents, back in 1880. Born the youngest of four siblings, both his parents worked tirelessly to ensure that he received a good education. After graduating from the university he worked as a young and upcoming barrister for a prestigious law firm with a very bright and prosperous future ahead of him. He planned on making sure his parents would be well taken care of in their golden years. That is, until the night he was on his way home from a victorious post-verdict party thrown at the firm. Until that tragically fateful night when he was attacked by a monster and infected, thus changing his life forever.

Now standing upon the metal bridge that crossed the river and connected Kelly Drive with West River Drive, he stared down with a modicum of mild interest at police standing around with hands in their pockets, or drinking hot coffee in an ongoing parade from the local convenience store across the street.

He stood almost shoulder to shoulder with an athletic, but extremely thin, young biker sitting a top an even thinner bicycle seat, dressed in a loud neon-yellow outfit with blue stripes and green shorts advertising some cell phone company. Quentin chuckled to himself. Humans were so silly in their attire, not caring how idiotic they looked. This entire area along the river on both sides with its wide paths for joggers and bikers was like a living, breathing mosaic of bright, stark colors that blended garishly in with the cascading carpet of soft red, yellow and orange leaves of fall. Even under this overcast sky of sordid grayness from another approaching storm, there was an array of brilliant color. Like a black and white photo with brief, but quick, flashing aspects of brilliance to startle the eye.

On his left side however stood a rather tall, very attractive blond, her hair pulled back in a pony tail, clad in a powder blue jogging suit, accentuating her amply endowed breasts. On her side, secured tightly to a short leash, was a large, male golden retriever.

While all the people were gazing down at the activity on the ground, or spreading wild innuendoes about what might have happened, the dog stared warily at Quentin.

She turned and saw him checking her out. Smiling she said, "Hi, so what do you really think happened here last night?"

"Haven't you heard the news this morning?" he asked in a very casual, but interesting drawl. He certainly didn't want to scare her off with his normally deep, gravely voice, which sounded more wolf than man.

"Not really. Scoots and I came out before six, walked down to the Art Museum and back, saw all the commotion on the other side of the river and decided to stop here to snoop around a little."

He displayed a very nice and engaging smile, turning more to face her and letting his broad back brush the shoulder of the skinny guy perched on the bike.

"Didn't you even hear the late news last night? Don't you own a television?" he said, feigning shock and playfully holding his heart in pain.

She laughed, a very soft and throaty, sexual sound which aroused him greatly.

"I had to spend most of the day yesterday in the office with a few of my colleagues preparing a brief for tomorrow morning. After a late dinner with a friend I just came home and crashed. Wanted today to be free and just unwind. So to answer your question of shock and dismay, yes I have a large, wide-screen TV that I hardly ever use, and no, I did not turn on the news when I got home last night."

"Well then let me bring you up to speed. Seems like a few young boys were killed last night and then the police were attacked later down the river a piece. Not sure how many, but I think somebody got killed there as well," he told her, displaying as much horror in his voice as he could produce.

As he talked to her he began to inch a little closer and that's when Scoots issued a very low, warning growl, stood up and lunged at Quentin's left hand. Everything happened so fast. He hoped her dog would eventually make some kind of protective lunge at him. Quickly grabbing his injured hand with the other he backed up, nearly toppling biker-man into the metal fence that ran the length of the bridge.

"Oh my God, Scoots stop, bad boy," she scolded, trying to desperately hold the barking, snarling dog away from Quentin.

"Does he do that often? I thought golden retrievers were a friendly breed," he said, still trying to sound startled at the savage attack.

"No, he never does that. He's hardly ever even growled at anybody before. My God, I'm so sorry. Are you hurt badly?" she asked with a shaken and worried voice. After all, she was a lawyer and instantly concerned about a prospective lawsuit.

Quentin removed his right hand from the back of his left and saw two shallow puncture wounds that had begun to bleed. Inside though, he was elated since this is exactly what he was hoping to have happen, but outside he displayed a little more concern.

"Well, it seems that Scoots broke the skin, but I think it'll be okay," as he took out a white handkerchief and wrapped it around his injured hand.

"Once the bleeding stops it should be okay. I probably should go to the emergency room though and have them look at it, get a tetanus shot. Are his inoculations all up to date?"

"Oh Lord yes, rabies and everything are all current. I'm so sorry, my God, he's never done this before. I don't know what came over him."

"Well, he certainly is a very good watch dog and protector, that's for sure. I'm usually very good with dogs, but maybe it's just all the commotion and excitement that has him on edge," Quentin replied.

"Maybe that's the case. My car is right down the street, can I take you to the hospital and get that hand checked out?" she asked him, concern very high in her voice.

"Actually my car is nearby as well. I hate to ask this, but since it's a dog bite I'm sure the hospital personnel will want to know all the information so if you wouldn't mind giving your address and phone number to me then I can pass that along. I'm sure that everything will be okay and you can rest assured I won't pursue any kind of legal action. It was just an accident and I know that Scoots didn't really mean anything by it," he said, trying to reassure her.

Holding Scoots back was getting harder so she decided to walk back to her car and put him in the rear seat while she wrote down her information on the back of a business card. She reluctantly handed it to him, her hand shaking slightly with concern. After all, she didn't really know this guy, certain that when he went to the ER they would want this information. He did seem somewhat trustworthy, but you just never knew about strangers any more.

"Well, good luck. That's my phone number on the back and I'll be home tonight if you have any problems, or want to let me know how you are," she stated in a soft, shaken voice.

"For sure, I'll do that. Thank you for this," he said, holding up the card, "And please, don't worry. The wound seems rather superficial and since Scoot's has had all his shots and is obviously a very well maintained pet, I'm sure all will be well. But, I'll give you a phone call if it's okay because I know you'll probably sit at home and worry all day long."

She laughed nervously and said, "Yes, you pegged me right, I will do exactly that. Again, I'm so sorry for what happened."

He smiled and started to walk away, then stopped and spun around.

"Oh, by the way, my name is Quentin," he started to laugh. "We were never formerly introduced," extending his right, uninjured hand.

"Yeah, I guess Scoots took care of any proper formalities. My name is Colleen Frye like it says on the card. Good luck to you Quentin and maybe we'll see each other again along the river under much more pleasant circumstances."

"I most definitely look forward to seeing you again Colleen," he laughed, starting to walk away again before spinning quickly around. "Oh, by the way, just so you know, it appears that the people who were killed last night were attacked by some animal like a large dog. Just thought I'd mention that fact in relation to what happened on the bridge. I mean, there were some startled bystanders there when your dog attacked me, and what with all the cops around, you never know what people will say. Anyway, talk to you soon."

Quentin turned and walked away, a big smile spread across his face, knowing if he turned around she would have a very startled and worried expression on her own pretty face. Of course, he had no intention of ever visiting any emergency room. The wound itself would be healed completely within the hour so he would merely stop at a pharmacy, purchase some gauze bandages, wrap it up real nice so when he unexpectedly dropped in later tonight to visit her, she would feel better that he had attended to the wound.

As he opened the door to his car and slipped in, he began to get aroused at just the thought of spending a delightful evening with such a young, beautiful, healthy, professional woman. A night of good conversation, leading to more he was sure.

He'd have to do something though about that damn dog. He didn't see any apartment number in her address so he was hoping she owned a home and good old Scoots could be put outside. If not, then good old Scoots (short for Scooter he presumed) would learn very quickly who the real alpha was. In fact, lovely Miss Colleen Frye would become very intimately involved in that realization as well.

As he pulled away from the curb and made a hard u-turn to head back towards Ridge Avenue, he flicked on the radio. After checking a few stations he left it on some pre-game show for the Eagles/Chargers game. He had become a huge fan of American football and since he had to travel quite a bit to escape his deadly visits, he was able to take in quite a number of local professional and college games. He loved hockey as well, the speed and violence giving him a rush. Perhaps if he hurried home he could catch the second half of action on Frankie's large screen television.

Chapter 7

Traffic wasn't nearly as bad as Johnny had expected it would be upon entering the city limits of Philadelphia. He made the decision to jump onto the Jersey Turnpike and that ended up being way too congested for his solitary way of existence. Of course, it was early evening on a Sunday and the only real traffic seemed to be coming from the Eagles game that had left out around four o'clock or so. He had listened to most of the contest on the radio while driving through the Jersey State. What an ending with the Eagles falling behind in the score and then blocking a field goal attempt that could've iced the game away for the Chargers. With a perfect bounce the blocked kick was run back for what ended up being the game winning touchdown. However, to add a little drama to the San Diego drive after they got the ball back, an Eagle defensive back stripped the pigskin from a wide receiver for a fumble that would've put the Chargers in range for another game winning field goal try. Talk about snatching victory from the hungry hands of defeat.

Driving over the Ben Franklin Bridge he squeezed onto the Vine Street Parkway with all the other frustrated drivers. He didn't plan this trip too well, but at least he was finally here on this gray, dismal October day. Then again, it was not like he really had any other place to go, or a job he had to be at in the morning. In fact, he hadn't worked at anything accept living or dying the last three years. His family had more than enough wealth amassed over the centuries and after his father brought him back from the brink of death he made sure that Johnny had enough funds each month to survive while hiding away from life in the Maine wilderness.

Hell, money was no big issue to Johnny anyway. He made two trips a month into the nearest small town just to stock up on the barest of staples and, of course, plenty of whiskey and beer. When he was really hungry there was always more than enough fresh meat around to satiate his wolf nature. In fact, there were times when he awoke early in the morning only to find Rasha, along with other members of the pack lying around in the clearing in front of his cabin, protecting the carcass of either a large, freshly killed deer, or maybe even a moose. When he allowed the change to come over him they all uneasily backed away, growling at first, their heads held low, golden eyes wary and nervous, never truly getting used to witnessing the alteration of form from human to wolf. After several very testy minutes of smelling each other, Johnny (Jarress) made certain that Rasha knew there would be no hostile take over of his pack. There needed to be this standoff each and every time so that Rasha could continue to maintain his standing as alpha leader in the pack hierarchy. Then, when all the pleasantries were taken care of, they immediately set to the welcome task of greedily devouring the fresh kill.

Johnny had pulled over in Bangor and called his father after filling up the gas tank and devouring a very rare cheeseburger, soggy French fries and a large glass of skim milk. He smiled to himself remembering the look he got from a middle-aged, blond waitress behind the lunch counter.

"Okay sweetie pie, how would you like your burger cooked hon?"

"Well, I imagine the cook has to throw it on the grill because he can't give it to me raw, so just tell him too barely darken each side and let the blood squish out when he presses down with the spatula, or whatever else he uses. And please, don't ruin it by adding any rabbit food. Just throw it on a roll along with a full bottle of ketchup. I do like lots of ketchup, reminds me of blood," he teased her, seeing that she had stopped writing and stood staring at him.

"Baby, what are you, some kind of wild animal?" she laughed, her eyes wide with surprise.

Looking at her name tag, he smiled and replied, "Peggy, don't you know that all men are wild animals, just in varying degrees? Some like their meat overcooked and then some of us like it raw and juicy, like our women."

Swinging the order pad to her face, she began to quickly fan herself. Then she began to chuckle and shake her head, realizing he was joking.

"Well, raw it is my beastly friend. But for a man as good looking and rugged as you, I guess the picture fits," she said, walking away and swinging her delightfully plump backside. "You are kind of weird though big guy."

He left her a nice tip and blew her a kiss as he walked over to the pay phones to call his father. She winked suggestively and told him to come back anytime.

"Hey dad, it's me," hearing the welcoming sound of his father's voice.

"Where're you calling from son? Didn't you get some snow up there last night?"

"Yeah, it wasn't really very much. I'm actually in Bangor heading for Philadelphia. Did you happen to see any of the latest news?" he asked.

"Sure did and wondered if you had also watched it. Listen Johnny, be very careful, it may just be a rogue and not connected with Samantha at all," he replied.

"I realize that Pop. Listen, can you contact the alpha in Philadelphia and let him know that I'm coming into town. I don't want to shake a bunch of tails you know."

"Sure, no problem, I'll call him now. His human name is Victor. From what I remember, he's very honorable and should help you out a lot. Once you get there though, remember the laws. Don't go running wild through his territory and make sure he knows that he's the leader. Once you get settled in then call me. Oh, we also have some relatives you can stay with just north of Philly, up around New Hope I think. I'll check it out. And, if this turns out to be Samantha's killer, or can lead us to who that person or persons are, just let me know and we'll be there the next day."

"I will father and I'll be careful. I haven't come this far to screw it up and I know it won't do Samantha's memory any good by my crashing around like a rogue again. Talk to you soon, love ya Dad."

"Love you too son, take care and be extra careful."

Johnny pulled off at a rest stop right before exiting the Jersey turnpike where he gassed up, grabbed a large black coffee and a local map of Philadelphia. From the news he remembered the area of the Schuylkill River where the two dead boys were found and knew that the police search party was attacked farther up river. He wasn't yet sure what his plans were other than to drive around the area, get a lay of the land, find a place to park, maybe catch some dinner and then shift, or shift and then run down some dinner. As a wolf, he could move much more stealthily and pick up signs he might not be able to notice in human form. He would most definitely have to be careful of the lingering police presence which still patrolled the west side of the river near the expressway, so the later he went out hunting the better.

After eating a hamburger without the bun just to get something in his stomach, he parked his truck on a side street and started walking casually towards a stretch of dense woods. Glancing back he wondered if his truck would be okay when he returned since it didn't appear to be such a great neighborhood. He had more important things to worry about at the moment though, like locating a somewhat secluded place where he could securely hide his clothing and safely bring forth his wolf.

A narrow foot path presented itself on his left so after a quick glance around to see if anybody might be observing him, like a curious cop or some inept criminal, Johnny disappeared. If a poor soul had been looking his way, then that's the way it would've seemed, leaving them most likely rubbing their eyes. His race of shape-shifters had that unique ability. To not only blend in with the surroundings as if they were not even there, whether it be wilderness terrain or city streets, but to appear and disappear when the need arose. This talent had become handy numerous times in his life.

As a young pup, he and his siblings had many a fun time playing games and conjuring up tricks against their parents. Of course, playing these jokes, especially against mother, had resulted in being punished numerous times. But she could never stay angry with any of them for very long. The closeness of their pack life and unity of family love was always prevalent. As youngsters they had many things to learn and knew when to listen closely and then when to have fun. They were the ultimate predator, but at the same time their existence was always filled with dangers, especially if they were not careful. It was the rogue wolves that gave their breed a bad name, the ones who were bitten and never had the ability to be a full weregune.

About fifty feet inside the tree line Johnny quickly took off his clothes and covered them up with some loose leaves near a very large tree that he would mark after the change. Fully nude he knelt down on one knee, lowered his head and closed his eyes. For the full-bred such as Johnny, the change could be brought on at any time, day or night. The pain associated with the shifting became bearable over the years and, of course, the older you were the easier it was. That is unless you happened to be one of the true elders of his race. As it was with humans, age became a problem and the true elders many times preferred to stay completely as wolf, their true nature, rather than endure the pain of change. But these individuals were many hundreds of years old and even his father, who was nearly two hundred fifty years young was not yet considered an elder.

There were several ways to alter shape, especially when shifting from human form to wolf, at least being somewhat in line physically. Bringing on his raven or hawk was much harder and Johnny only performed that ritual when he absolutely needed to. The beauty of that alteration though was the ability to soar in the clouds above the earth which always gave him such a feeling of exhilaration. Damn wings were always a problem though, very painful springing out from the back. It took him years to perfect that routine, not to mention a very sore spine.

Concentrating solely on bringing his personal moon to bear within his mind, it erupted in a kaleidoscope of colors. He felt the pain of stretching limbs, fingers and hands that turned into paws and claws. The facial and head structure was the most painful with the human nose and mouth elongating to the muzzle and pointed ears of a large wolf. Afterwards, when back in human form, it was his mouth and gums that usually hurt the most for up to a day, mostly because of the human teeth withdrawing and being replaced with much larger fangs, along with the tongue growing over two times its human length. Oh yeah, the curvy, fluffy tail was always the most fun with kind of a popping and ripping sound, then the feeling of it growing and growing.

The shifting actually only took fifteen seconds or so. Johnny also had the ability to alter just parts of his body which many times came in handy.

Standing now on all fours, this massive black wolf, over six feet long and well over two hundred pounds was by far larger than its natural brother, the timber wolf. The weregune had been decimated in large levels a hundred years ago when man had nearly eradicated the wolf from the northeastern United States. Even though his breed was extremely difficult to find and kill, death was still a definite possibility if they were careless, or sadly in the wrong place at the wrong time. Their natural wolf brothers were slaughtered to near extinction and Johnny's race had moved out to only the farthest parts of the wilderness, staying clear of populated areas. Many had relocated across the borders to Canada and Mexico. That is also when pack leaders obtained large tracts of land in states which had thousands of uninhabited acres, either mountainous or dense forests.

For Johnny's father and his clan, they not only survived, but multiplied as well, and when Wisconsin began to reintroduce the wolf population, his father relocated the pack there, but retained the large tract of land in Maine. Over the years before they moved, and later when they were gone, the gray wolf carefully traversed a frozen St. Lawrence River each winter from the woods of Quebec in Canada. In addition, upon their land lived some of the elders who were rarely seen, thus insuring their longevity and keepers of breed history and lore.

Johnny had from time to time met with one of the elders by the name of Zhendar, a very old, grizzled and sage weregune, his black coat mostly faded to shades of white and gray, having long ago lost that beautiful luster and thickness. He had no idea how old Zhendar was, but he thought it was somewhere near six hundred years. Johnny would hunt down a large deer and they would feast, the balance of the meat stored away in the deep pocket of the cave where the elder lived peacefully. Never appearing in human form, Johnny and Zhendar would walk slowly together to the cliff above his cave where they would sometimes just sit and bask in the warm sunlight. Their breed did not need to be in human form to converse having developed a sense of telepathy that transcended all verbal sounds. At times Zhendar's mind would just float off and Johnny knew that one day the elder would just pass on naturally, the time to exist having come at last. Or there was always the possibility he would become neglectful and suffer an attack from either younger wolves, or possibly a very large, angry bear. Johnny would miss this old one very much.

After stretching aching muscles and lifting his muzzle to capture a wide array of strange and enticing scents, he lifted his tail to mark the tree where he hid his clothes. Silently moving off towards the river he was alert for any dangerous situation. He simply would be searching for any signs of the rogue wolf, not only where the young boys had been killed, but in the vicinity of the attack on the police search party as well. Somewhere beyond that Johnny knew this creature had to have changed to human form at some point in order to cleanly make his escape. Most likely there was a car near where the change originally took place, or for that matter, he might even be living in the area.

Fortunately it was late, near midnight, so there were not many people jogging or riding bikes. The immediate problem he had though was his need to get across the river and the only way without swimming, which he was not averse to doing if need be, was the steel bridge. Lying in between two large bushes he waited a few minutes until there seemed to be no traffic and then very quickly arose to start crossing the metal structure. As he was nearing the other side a car suddenly turned the corner. The driver slammed on the breaks and blew the horn wildly. To the motorist it was simply an extremely large dog, but one that he would certainly tell others about over a couple of stiff drinks. The proverbial fish story, only this fish had four legs.

Once on the other side of the bridge, this totally unbelievable, majestic beast danced inside the grace of shadows with the instincts of a predator that really had nothing to fear from anything, man or beast as long as he was careful. Moving eastward along the river he definitely picked up the scent of another wolf, yet he still preferred to move towards the site of where the two boys had been slaughtered. About ten minutes made that possible as he slowed down, fell to the ground and let his golden eyes scour the surroundings.

Yellow police crime scene tape was still up and he noticed a purring squad car parked along the curb, but off the road. It appeared to have two occupants and the wolf could detect the odor of cigarettes and stale coffee. Moving with the utmost care he stopped where a massive stain of blood still coated the ground. Sniffing he could sense the fear and realized how easy it would've been for this rogue werewolf to come across and overtake two young, innocent boys out for some fun along the river. His anger rose inside him at the insidious nature of this rabid beast. At no time did Johnny's full-breed ever kill innocent children and avoided with the utmost care, women as well. Yes, they needed to feed and wilderness game was always a staple, but many of the packs lived near and within large cities because of the dense population of derelict and destitute individuals. Those that would not be missed by anybody and if they were, their disappearance would simply be written off to the dangers of their everyday life.

Suddenly a beam of light began to inch across the ground and came shockingly close to where the wolf hugged the ground. In a split second he was gone, but not before one of the officers had gotten out of the car to take a look around and notice the barest movement of a shadow.

"Hey Chuck, get on out here. I think I saw something move over there," he said aloud, reaching for his service revolver. The closing of a car door signaled that Chuck had heard and was joining him.

"Where did you see something? Was it a dog?" Chuck whispered.

"I don't know, but whatever it was, it wasn't human. Let's go, just be careful."

The wolf had already disappeared and was heading back up river the way he had come. Let the cops look around and, either report to a superior, or chalk it up to nothing more than taut and frazzled nerves.

Moving along slowly, but at a steady pace, he suddenly stopped and lifted his muzzle. He detected the unmistakable scent of at least one other wolf, possibly two, and it seemed to be close by. It was not the killer though, Johnny was sure of that, probably just a member of the local pack who was out searching for the rogue like he was.

Another hundred yards brought him to a complete stop and he dropped, hugging the ground. The slightest rustle of bushes to the left captured his attention so he waited, sensing the arrival of a predator, not sure of how much danger there really was. Minutes slipped by, the black wolf hardly expelling any breath, eyes unmoving, riveted to the spot where he had detected the motion.

Then a simple, but urgent question touched his mind.

Is it you Jaress? thought Veltar, Alpha of the Philadelphia clan.

Yes Veltar, it is Jaress, son of Mandhar. My apologies for not contacting you upon my arrival, the black wolf answered.

The bushes parted as an extremely large, powerfully built, dark brown wolf the color of sable emerged and was closely followed by an equally massive weregune that was both black and several shades of gray. Jaress rose and met the two wolves in a clearing safely shielded by a small copse of trees.

By weregune law, Jaress should have contacted the local clan first before shifting, but he felt there was precious little time and he needed to catch what signs might still be around. He would've searched and found the local alpha leader before the sun was up however. It was diplomatic and courteous to show servitude and respect, unless it became more of a power play. So Jaress pulled his tail between his back legs, lowered his magnificent head and waited for the upcoming rebuff.

A very deep and ominous growl erupted from the chest of the black and gray wolf now positioned behind him, before a lunge was made and sharp, stiletto like teeth bit into the hind quarter of Jaress. He pivoted and stood with hackles raised to face this threat, their muzzles pulled back, white fangs ready to do battle. But there was no fighting necessary. It was customary to show the new arrival just who was in charge.

A deep, rumbling laugh erupted from Veltar's massive chest.

That's enough Bharak, leave our visitor alone. My son is merely defending my honor. He means you no harm, thought the local alpha leader. *Though looking at the two of you, it would be one hellacious battle and would be interesting to see who won.*

By this time, the two younger wolves had dispelled their ferocity and began simply smelling each other, making sure that in the future, if the time arose, they knew what type of foe they would be facing.

No apologies needed Veltar. I'm sure you are extremely proud to have such a warrior as a son, but something tells me you can handle yourself quite well also.

That is so very true Jaress. Now, come along with us and we will take you to our home. You can wear some of my son's clothing since you're about the same size. After we've spoken and had something to eat, he will bring you back to get your vehicle.

As the moon grinned down and glittered brightly off the Schuylkill River this haunting, primal scene of three awesome wolves merging into the woods of Fairmount Park within the city limits of Philadelphia was purely one of fairy tales. For after all, wolves just simply did not exist in the City of Brotherly Love. Or did they?

Chapter 8

Kathy weaved her slightly battered, partially soiled, red Ford Bronco off the Belmont Avenue exit, crossed the Green Lane Bridge and traversed a very windy Summit Avenue towards the small house she had been renting for a number of years now. Well, an older home that had been converted into two houses. She scowled at the burgeoning golf complex sprawling on her left, envisioning a garish glow from harsh, glaring lights bleeding over the trees once it was open for business, as well as on the right side of the road which used to be a beautifully wooded area for deer, now scarred by a growing apartment complex. She had originally moved here because of the beautiful landscape. It had been, and for the most part still was, a wonderfully wooded area that still desperately clung to the edges of the city limits, yet seemed so rural. However, with the dust and noisy construction on the hill across from her house, she had regrets of no longer seeing small herds of deer galloping majestically across the rugged terrain.

Bouncing into the driveway she caught a glimpse of her dog Rain peeking through one of the long, narrow windows on each side of the door, excited that her mommy was finally home. Kathy was prepared to be lovingly mauled as she struggled to maneuver her way through the front door.

"Okay girl, yes, mommy loves you too," Kathy cooed, as Rain stood up on her hind legs and performed the begging routine with her front legs. There was no choice but to grab the dog's paws and lean forward so they could touch heads. She loved this beautiful shepherd/chow mix that was now a very frisky two and a half year old. After her previous dog Sheena of the same unique mixed breeding had passed away from a stroke almost seven years prior, she had felt there was just no way to replace her. Until the day she discovered a litter of puppies for adoption placed on an internet site at a shelter located all the way down in Ridgley, Maryland. And yes, to answer an obvious question, she received her name Rain because the day they went to pick her up, there just happened to be a driving rainstorm. Ever since, this beautiful reddish-brown dog had two nicknames, 'Rainstorm' when she was bad and 'Rainbow' when she was good. Kathy felt the jury was still out on which name she used most often. Loving this dog so much, she grabbed the thick mane around her neck and hugged Rain tightly, kissing her on the top of the head.

It was late and her dad was sound asleep in his recliner. Kathy gently admonished Rain for being so boisterous, placed her purse and briefcase down on the chair, and they went back outside. It was going to be another raw, bone-chilling night and with the sky-rocketing price of home heating oil going through the ceiling, she still resisted turning on the furnace. It was always easier to bulk up with a heavy sweater or sweatshirt and crawl underneath a plush blanket or two. Far from being cheap, she just hated paying the oil companies. The heater would most likely get plenty of workload over the coming winter.

Rain, ever since she was a puppy, loved to play this game where she lunged and tried to bite Kathy's feet. Sometimes the dog would get too cantankerous and bite down harder than Kathy appreciated. After a short period of this game, Rain turned and bolted into the leaf strewn yard, chasing both real and imagined predators that dared trespass on her turf. The dog definitely could detect every single new scent upon the grass, whether from a stray dog or wild critter. At night it was quite possible to have raccoons, ground hogs, squirrels, and rabbits invade the yard, along with the occasional skunk or fox.

"Come on girl, do your business and let's get back in the house. You hungry?" she asked, her voice echoing through the trees.

Kathy looked up at the sky, somewhat overcast with the moon trying to break through the covering clouds. Hard to say if the storm would just clip them as many fall or winter storms did when they came from the west, or pound them. For now she just pulled the collar up around her neck and waited for Rain to finish scouting the ground in her inquisitive, protective nature.

The day became a re-run of unexpected surprises, grizzly crime scenes, confused assumptions and horrifying possibilities. She remembered that grim, haunted look in the eyes of Captain Ganz out along the river, the hushed and frightened undertones from normally brave and dependable police officers, anguished tears from distressed parents making identifications at the morgue of two slain boys, Jason Tierney and Dave Splain. But most of all she was concerned over the feelings of dread she had in her own mind about this case. She realized what Capt. Ganz meant when he said it was most definitely 'some thing' they had never come across before.

It was Doc Starling, the medical examiner, who had really muddied the waters for her though. She had stopped back at the precinct and sat pondering at her cluttered desk for an hour before heading over to the lab. Johnson, the laboratory technician on duty, took a quick glance at the hair Kathy had clutched from the bush and thought it possibly looked like fur from a large, long-haired dog, but he promised to have an answer for her come morning. Or sooner and call her on the cell.

Walking up the drab, green hallway Kathy sadly observed Mr. Tierney holding his wife closely, looking like he needed somebody to support him as well. Kathy hated this time, when the ID's were made and loved ones broke down like this. There was never much to say other than "thank you for coming in" and "I'm so sorry for your loss".

She found the doc huddled over the extremely mutilated body of young David Splain, talking quietly into a microphone that hung down from the ceiling. Quietly Kathy moved around the foot of the silvery-cold, austere metal table and stopped, wishing that she had grabbed a mask for her face. It wasn't really the odor that got to her, but the sight of the wounds on his neck, shoulder and down the middle of his chest. She was happy at that moment she had not eaten anything recently.

Looking up, Doc Starling glanced at her and smiled. "Detective Morello, haven't seen you in quite a while. So you're on this case I see?"

"It seems that way Doc, it surely does." She hesitated before going on, "So what can you tell me about who, or what, did this?"

Starling stood, pushed the microphone out of the way and leaned back against the empty table behind him. Kathy watched as he stared at the nude body of the young man, most definitely more distraught than she had ever seen him. Shaken up could easily describe his mental state at the moment.

"Kathy, in all my years on the job I've never seen anything quite like this and you know I've seen a lot. In my analytical way of thinking, I'm trying to stay clear of letting my mind dwell on mystifying possibilities. But it's rather difficult not to. These two young boys were most definitely killed by an animal of some kind. I say 'some kind' because logic says it must be a very large dog, but the radius and depth of the bite marks signify something much larger than any domestic breed I'm aware of".

"Can you tell for certain about that?" Kathy asked.

"Sure, eventually we'll know what, or who, the prints are from. When was the last time you saw a bear or a wolf running through Fairmount Park?" he asked her.

"Actually never, but there have been the occasional black bear running amok in the suburbs and don't forget those tigers that escaped from that rescue place in Jersey a few years back. Plus, a number of officers on duty last night along the river still swear up and down they heard the very unmistakable howling of a wolf. Right or wrong, the prints I saw on the ground were extremely large," Kathy informed the concerned doctor.

"All very true detective and until I'm done with measuring these wounds and then doing some comparisons we'll have to wait in order to be certain. There's always the possibility that an owner's hybrid got loose."

"You mean a hybrid-wolf? Yeah, it's a very distinct possibility, that thought had crossed my mind. So when will you be finished here?" Kathy asked, naturally like any detective wanting the information yesterday.

The M.E. laughed and walked over to the refrigerator where he grabbed a large beacon of yellowish liquid and took three large swallows. Smacking his lips and sighing, he replaced the beaker back in the fridge and turned to face her. Seeing the ghastly expression in Morello's eyes he began to laugh.

"Don't worry my dear I haven't gone off the deep end yet. However, would you believe me if I told you it was only apple juice?"

"No, but whatever you need to steady your nerves then I'm all for it Doc. In fact, I could use a little 'apple juice' myself right about now after the day I've had," Kathy countered.

"Would you like a glass?" Doc asked her.

Kathy chuckled and politely declined, moving over to where she had placed her purse. There was just something very unappealing about drinking something yellow from a large laboratory decanter.

"You'll call me just as soon as you have some results then?" she inquired.

"Yes Ms. Morello, I'll do that. I also have a very close colleague that specialized in animal forensics and specifically wolf patterns and habitat. If there's anybody in this city who can give us the straight scoop it'll be him."

"Okay, night Doc and thanks," Kathy said, as she headed back to her car and her drive home.

Rain broke her train of thought by suddenly barking at a noise coming from the wall of dark woods across the street.

"Hey girl, be quiet, it's too late for barking. You'll wake up all the neighbors," she admonished the dog.

However, Rain continued to bark shrilly, the ridge of hair on her back and shoulders standing straight up. Kathy grabbed the large dog by the caller and started tugging her towards the porch.

"Hush up, be quiet. It's probably just a deer or a fox. We sure as hell don't want it to be a skunk. Come on," as she pushed, pulled and tugged the frantic dog through the door into the living room. Standing on the porch Kathy turned and stared across the street. She could feel that something was there and it certainly was no squirrel or chipmunk, something much, much larger.

Kathy went inside, closed and double locked the door, glancing back through the blinds. Too dark to see anything clearly, she flicked off the porch light.

Suddenly she felt ravenous, not having eaten anything substantial since a little before lunch when she had a large blueberry muffin and a pint of skim milk.

"Come on sweetie, you hungry? Did Pappy feed you tonight?" she asked the grinning dog, maneuvering her way to the kitchen, where she suddenly heard the loud squawking of Romeo, her six year old Moluccan cockatoo. Even under the blue cloth which covered the large cage, the beautiful white and apricot-colored bird knew Kathy was home and demanded immediate attention. Rain looked up anxiously, wagging her bushy tail.

"Okay girl, let's say hello to Romeo and then we'll all get our treats before we go to bed," she said softly, trying not to wake up her father.

"Hello, pretty boy," sang Romeo, as Kathy smiled.

If she had possibly waited another minute or two she just might have detected the rapid blinking of two, very large, extremely yellow ovals and then possibly noticed the movement through the dark shadows. Nothing more, just sinister, disappearing shadows.

Chapter 9

Earlier in the evening Quentin sat in the car outside the small house owned by the very lovely Miss Colleen Frye. His hand neatly bandaged up to signify that he had made a phantom appearance at a local emergency room, he debated on calling her first, or just merely knocking on the front door. Picking up the cell phone from the seat he decided to call instead.

"Hello?" Quentin immediately got aroused at her sweet voice.

"Hey, hi there Colleen, this is Quentin from earlier today. You didn't forget about the dog bite did you?"

"Of course not, how could I ever forget that? I've been wondering how you made out. I'm still so embarrassed. Are you doing okay?"

"Sure, everything's fine. The ER doc and nurses couldn't have been any nicer. Hey, I was wondering if I could stop by for a few minutes. I have something for you," he asked in the most appealing voice he could muster.

"Gee Quentin, it's kind of late and I really need to be in the office early tomorrow. Besides, I'm still working on this brief we have to submit in the morning and I have papers strewn all over the living room."

"I promise Colleen I won't stay long. Besides, I'm actually sitting outside your house right now and like I said, I do have something for you."

In a slightly surprised voice she asked him, "You're outside my house right now? How did you find where I live?"

"Well, don't forget, you gave me that business card with all the information in case I needed it at the hospital for the dog bite. Hope you're not mad. Honestly, I'll only stick around for a few moments and you have absolutely nothing to worry about," he stated, trying to allay her obvious nervousness.

"Well, I suppose so, but only for a few minutes if that's okay," she replied.

"That's great! Oh, yeah, I forgot about the dog. Do you think you could put Scoots outside, or possibly in a closed room? Hopefully nothing would happen, but I'm a little leery and nervous about what he might do," "Sure, that might be a good idea actually seeing what happened. Though I must admit after you left and we came home he settled down drastically. Very strange, don't you think?"

"It is strange. Maybe it's just my size and I intimate him, especially with all the commotion that was going on. So, you'll put him away for a few minutes?"

"Yes, just give me five and then come on up," she said, her voice still containing a strain of apprehension.

Seven minutes later Quentin softly rapped on the door which was quickly opened by Colleen. My God thought Quentin, this woman is absolutely stunning. Tall for a female, her honey-blond hair was pulled up and back off her face to reveal strikingly high cheekbones, soft blue eyes a person could fall into, and lips he could just devour. She was wearing a thick, plush gray and white sweater overtop a long black skirt that sensually accentuated her hips. Quentin was slightly disappointed he couldn't see her legs, but then that part would come soon enough.

"Hello, how are you? How's your hand?" Colleen asked, showing the utmost concern.

Quentin held it up between them, pure white bandages shining brightly under the garish glow of the porch light.

"It's really nothing. A few stitches, a tetanus shot, that's all. It'll be fine. In fact, I told them I saw a rabies vaccination tag on your dog's collar and you assured me all his shots were up to date. I told them you were also going to self-quarantine the animal for a few days and you were more than agreeable in every way."

"Thank you Quentin, anything I can do to help. I'm still so mortified. He has never bit anybody before," Colleen said in a somewhat mystified tone.

"Honestly, don't be upset. Oh, here, this is for you," he said, bringing from around his back a large bottle of white wine. "I thought maybe we could just have one small toast together. Consider it a peace offering for what I put you through."

She laughed brightly in the most beautiful, lilting sound. "What you put me through? You're the one who got bit. I should be giving you the bottle of wine. But it really is getting late Quentin and I have so much more work to do."

"Please? One small drink, some light conversation just to get to know one another a little better. Please?" he begged, realizing he could simply over power her but wanting instead to pursue his prey a little more in order to prolong the game.

"Sure, just for a short while. Where are my manners?" Colleen said, moving back and letting him step fully into the hallway.

"Let me go get a couple glasses and a cork screw. Have you eaten anything?" she asked over her shoulder as she moved gracefully away from him. What an alluring walk she possessed, arousing his desire for her all the more.

"I got a small bag of chips and a candy bar from the vending machines when I left the hospital earlier."

"God, then you must be hungry. What hospital did you end up going to?"

"Roxborough Memorial I think the name was," he answered.

"Hey, that's right in the neighborhood," he heard her muffled response from the kitchen.

"Yep, right down Ridge Avenue actually. It was the closest one to where I'm living," he replied while strolling into the living room, noticing an array of pictures in frames, but interestingly enough, devoid of any men and just her with that damn mutt. There were also a few where she was hugging another very attractive woman.

After a few minutes she walked in with a tray holding the bottle of wine and two frosted goblets, along with some sausage, cheese and crackers.

"Wow that really looks great. I didn't realize how hungry I was until now," he told her. "Here, let me have that bottle and I'll open it."

"But your hand, how can you do that?" she asked in surprise.

He chuckled. "I'm an old pro at this. I broke the same hand a few years ago and got very adept at being one handed for a few months."

Quentin sat down, placed the wine between his legs, inserted the corkscrew and like magic the cork popped loudly and white, icy mist escaped the bottle's neck.

Pouring the wine, she asked, "So, you said the hospital was close by where you're living. How close?"

"I'm staying at a friend's apartment while he's in Europe for awhile. I'm a writer and just needed to get away for a bit, so he made the offer to stay at his place for a month. I just got into town a few days ago actually."

"That's really cool, a writer. You've certainly had your share of excitement so far and don't tell me you write horror novels," she said, smiling and handing him a glass.

"Actually I do," he said, laughing as they touched glasses in a comical salute to friendly dogs and some that weren't. They proceeded to talk for the next hour, easily polishing off the wine, along with every crumb of food on the tray as well. He had been really hungry, but was becoming more ravenous for her by the minute.

Wearing more than a slight buzz, Colleen glanced at her watch.

"Oh my Quentin, it's really late and I do have to get some sleep. I'm afraid all this wine has gone to my head. There is just no way that I'm getting this work finished tonight. But I really did have a wonderful evening. I'm glad you stopped," she said, standing up and teetering precariously to the side. She giggled which made his wolf want to howl at every moon he had ever gazed at.

He seemed to move without appearing to move and firmly grasped her shoulders. Suddenly he was completely overpowered by her sweet femininity. He easily pulled her forward and placed his lips onto hers. She struggled for a few seconds, unaccustomed to the feel of a man's lips, before succumbing to his power. Placing her hand behind his head she reciprocated, opening her mouth and allowing his long tongue to explore her. Colleen was now completely captured in his spell. She was now his, pure and simple.

He licked the lingering taste and aroma of wine and sausage from her luscious mouth. With eyes closed, she moaned and collapsed against his broad chest. Even though Colleen was tall he picked her up like she was a mere feather. Moving towards the staircase Quentin heard Scoots growling loudly and scraping at the basement door.

Under his breath, but loud enough for the dog to hear, he growled back, "I'll deal with you later mutt. Right now though, your mommy is about to experience the night of her life. Something she obviously hasn't felt before."

Locating the bedroom he placed her softly on the bed and then hungrily gazed at her awesome form. Tenderly and somewhat ritualistically, he removed her sweater and skirt. Not surprisingly she had not been wearing a bra or panties. She lay upon her bed, legs spread wide for only him. She was now his possession for not only tonight, but perhaps forever. He quickly undressed and covered her body with his, devouring every square inch of her exquisite form. Both man and wolf let their primal urges run wild in a night like they had not had for quite awhile.

Sometime in the early morning hours while darkness still imprisoned the night, Colleen's neighbor John, who drove a bread truck, could've sworn he heard a loud howl and then saw what appeared to be a very large black figure, almost like an animal on two legs, leap from his neighbor's rear bedroom window and then quickly disappear.

Damn he thought shaking his head and rubbing his eyes, it had to be the residual effect of one too many joints last night with his buddies. But still, the weirdness of it all made him reach for his cell phone and dial 911 anyway as he walked towards her front door to see if all was okay.

Chapter 10

Victor was true to his word, or his thoughts for that matter. Johnny had followed the two large wolves to their home where they shifted back to human form. Victor's son, Barton, supplied him with a clean pair of jeans and a Flyer's sweatshirt.

Dawn had just started to creep over the horizon. It had taken a few hours getting to their home. Besides avoiding traffic, they ran down a small doe in the park and feasted well. All Johnny had eaten Sunday were the two mostly raw burgers and some very strong coffee.

There was something completely primal to the scene of three massive wolves consuming their fallen prey under fractured moonlight. Very few creatures dared to stir with the likes of these three awesome predators about. The pulling of meat from the carcass and crunching of bones for the marrow blended with their muzzles stained a bright red with fresh blood, a tapestry of ferocity. In a way, it was horrifically comical.

Not unlike a Norman Rockwell setting, the three weregune sat relaxed on the front porch in human form feeling the sun rising. Victor held a steaming cup of green tea with Splenda between his massive hands. Johnny and Barton had each loudly popped a can of beer. Who said never drink before noon? Not a weregune, that's for sure.

Victor broke the silence first.

"Your father told me some of what happened with your mate and the reason you're here. I'm sorry Johnny. We will help however possible. Believe me, I know how insane I would be if I lost my Tabitha in the same manner," as he reached for the hand of his beautiful mate who had just at that moment walked onto the porch carrying a tray of fruit and cheeses. She leaned over Victor and softly nuzzled his neck.

"Thank you my love, but some would say that you're a little bit crazy even now," she goaded him.

He jumped quickly out of his chair as she ran off the porch towards the nearby woods, giggling gaily the whole time.

"I'll show you just how crazy a wolf I can be," he growled teasingly, shedding his clothing as he raced after her.

Johnny and Barton sat on the porch, smiling and enjoying the antics of the elder couple.

"They seem to really love each other a great deal," Johnny stated. "How long have they been mated?"

Barton unwound his large, impressive frame from the chair and moved to lean against the front railing, continuing to watch the trees where his parents had disappeared, their growls of pleasure quite evident.

"Father lost his first mate nearly a hundred and fifty years ago. They had been together for only five or six years up to that point. For the next thirty years, Victor was quite lost, at least from all the tales I've heard."

Johnny slowly got up and joined his new friend at the rail.

"How did she die if you don't mind my asking?"

"She was caught in a trapper's steel trap. Unfortunately she could not change and the only way she could free herself was to chew through her own leg which she did. On three legs and in great pain his mate, Sashar, traveled over mountainous terrain for nearly five miles. Quite often she stopped and howled to father, calling for him to come and save her, which he tried at his own great peril. But it was too late. From massive loss of blood she left an easy trail for the trapper to follow. He saw her limping badly at the edge of a cliff and shot her. She fell to the rocks below where the bastard never ventured. Victor found her badly mangled body the next morning."

Barton paused, obviously very moved, and finished his beer in several long swallows. Johnny handed him a fresh can which he angrily popped and took several more swigs.

"You don't need to go on. I realize how painful this is, believe me," Johnny muttered, knowing that pain only too well.

"No, I'm okay," he continued. "Father buried his loving mate right there at the bottom of that cliff and lay at her graveside for an entire week. His emotions switched from the deepest sorrow to the wildest rages. On the eighth day he rose, climbed to the top of that cliff and followed the trail to where the tracker that killed his mate was camped with ten other trappers near a waterfall. Needless to say, Victor killed them all. For that entire week and one hellish night, Victor was insane, the wildest of rogues. He slaughtered them all without mercy, their encampment filled with hundreds of animal pelts, many of them Canidae. After that he went as deep into the Rockies as he could and became for the most part a lone wolf. So Johnny, you can see that my father does know what you've been through, the rage and pain that drives you for revenge."

Standing in silence, Johnny was stunned at the story he had just been told. A tear trickled down his cheek, for not only Victor's loss, but his own as well.

"Is Tabitha your mother then?" Johnny asked.

"Yes, father came out of the mountains one day and ran into my mother's pack shortly thereafter. For his being alone all those years, he actually thrived in the wilderness and became quite strong and independent. My mother was the alpha female and seemed to have an instant attraction to him. There was a vicious power play and battle with the alpha male, her mate, which she never truly cared for. Father won and the defeated alpha left with his two sons and several loyal followers. The ones who remained formed the basis of this pack that eventually settled in Philadelphia."

At that moment Victor and Tabitha bounded into the yard like two playful puppies belying their ages and then raced each other to the porch. After nearly bowling Johnny over they crashed through the front door into the house where they quickly shifted, dressed and reappeared, completely rejuvenated after their early morning run as wild beasts.

It made Johnny quite melancholy as he fondly remembered the many times he and Samantha had roamed the forest and hills together. She was so beautiful, both in human and wolf form. Upon realizing that she was going to give birth he was elated. Unlike natural wolves, their kind could only have one child at a time. And so the birth of any child was a wonderful event, a blessed edition not only to the mated pair, but to the entire pack as well. The night they told both their parents that Samantha was with child became an epic event and so shortly afterwards they all changed and ran through the hills howling their pleasure. Afterwards, all the males got completely plastered as their frustrated mates picked up the pieces in the morning, not completely happy with the antics that had gone on, but nonetheless loving and caring. It had been a time for happiness.

"So Barton, would you take me back to my car? That is if it's still there and in one piece. I have to find a place to stay, do some snooping around during the daylight."

"Johnny, you'll stay here of course," said Victor. "We have plenty of room, either here under our roof or with another pack member if you want."

"Thank you so much Victor, but I'm better off on my own. I'll need to get into the mind of this killer in order to hunt him down. And tonight's the new full moon for this cycle. It'll be much harder to locate him them and he might move on."

Johnny firmly shook hands with the elder weregune and then hugged Tabitha tightly. As they drove away, Johnny saw the look in Victor's eyes. It was the distraught look of rage and insanity. It was the look of loss and sorrow Johnny now lived with every single, painful day.

Chapter 11

The deer appeared out of nowhere. Mary Beth had no time to swerve or even hit the brakes. The frightened animal slammed violently onto the hood of the car, the shattered windshield exploding in upon her. With the head and antlers of the dead buck lying on the front seat and the horrified young girl covered in glass, her face began to bleed profusely from several deep lacerations along with numerous other superficial scratches.

The airbag deployed in another loud bang. Now it was even more impossible to steer the out of control vehicle on a very dark and curvy Manor Road. The car hit an abutment at the entrance to an old cement bridge and then careened back to the other side where the sound of grinding metal filled the night. The road turned to the right, but Mary Beth was unable to steer the car due to her own shock and not being able to see where she was going. The car plunged down an embankment where it violently jolted to a stop. What had seemed like an eternity for her had happened in five very short seconds.

She had started working the early night shift for an insurance company as a data entry operator on River Road in August. One of her biggest fears was driving this winding road late at night when she got off work, especially during foul weather. She had always been wary that a deer or other animal could jump out and race across the road in front of her. And now it had happened.

Both she and the severely damaged vehicle lay broken in a ditch on a very dark, lonesome road wondering how long it would be until someone would come and help her. As the airbag deflated Mary Beth found herself trying to see through a white, hazy mist of dust-like talcum powder. She closed her eyes because it began to sting quite a bit. As she began to raise her right hand to wipe her eyes sharp pain ripped through her shoulder. Unable to see clearly through blurred vision she attempted to lift her left arm and found she could do so even though it seemed stiff. With her left hand she touched her right arm and suddenly was aghast at feeling something narrow and long pinning her shoulder to the back of the seat. She realized it was part of the antlers from the dead deer staring at her with the tragic question, "Why me?"

A single headlight glared into the darkness, bouncing off trees in a garish display of light. Steam hissed loudly from a shattered front end. Mary Beth fought hard to retain consciousness and was surprised there was little pain, especially her shoulder. The worst was her face as she could feel shards of glass stuck in her cheeks, forehead, nose, and felt the salty taste of hot blood rushing freely into her mouth. She slowly moved her right hand, reaching out blindly to the passenger side of the front seat for her purse. Hopefully it had not fallen onto the floor and she could obtain her cell phone. Groping desperately she finally touched the leather of her bag and sighed in relief. At least something had gone right.

Slowly unzipping the top of her handbag fingers groped inside until they touched the phone. Out and onto the seat, she touched the on button which threw a small green glow into the dark interior, very alien looking. She knew her husband would expect her home in about ten minutes having called him right before leaving the office. He always expected her to do that so he wouldn't worry. He would be calling her shortly if she was unable to dial the phone, pain starting to gnaw angrily at her right side.

From behind she heard a loud rustle, like someone falling or moving through some bushes. It continued for a few seconds, abruptly stopped, and started again. Then a strange noise that sounded like a growl. Now the pain in her shoulder plus the stinging in her face was quickly forgotten, replaced by abject fear. A wild dog or perhaps a pack she thought? Then there was silence, completely quiet, the hissing from the broken radiator fading away. Mary Beth was scared, but at least she was inside the car with the doors locked. Her husband Ron always made sure she was in the habit of locking the doors after she got in. He kept reminding her over and over about women who were molested in parking lots after getting inside their vehicles and not locking the doors fast enough.

She stared at the shattered windshield and realized that an animal or person could easily get inside. Now the fear returned. As did the sounds, only now instead of a growl it was like a sharp scratching against the rear bumper of the car. Like a nail, or a rake, being run along the metal. Then a loud thump and the car jolted as if being pushed to the side and out of the way. Mary Beth's heart pounded in her chest, black eyes of the dead deer staring directly at her in the moonlight. Tears now ran down her cheek which blended with the lingering taste of blood still inside her mouth.

A loud, thunderous growl broke the quiet. It was unmistakably the sound from a very large animal of some type, coming from close behind her on the driver's side. Completely forgetting the pain she touched the key pad on the phone, knowing it by heart as she indexed the speed dial number for her husband. She also hit the speaker since it was hard to get the phone to her ear.

"Hello? Mary Beth, is that you?" a voice asked through the silence.

She moved the phone as near to her face as she could, the antler stuck in her shoulder limiting motion.

"Ron? Ron it's me. I've crashed on Manor Road. Honey, I'm really hurt," she cried out.

The sounds she had been hearing stopped when Ron's voice came out of the phone and she had begun to talk. Now they returned much louder, scrapping on the side of the car before the tense, night air was split apart by a horrendous roar.

"Mary Beth? Mary Beth, what was that?" she heard Ron's voice from the phone.

"Honey I'm so scared. There is some kind of animal ....," but she could not finish her words.

The rest of the windshield crashed in on her and a huge black, hairy, clawed hand reached inside, grasping her by the neck and chest. Like she was nothing but a rag doll it yanked her forward, the seat belt restraining her. She screamed and screamed as the cell phone slipped from her hand and fell to the floor.

"Mary Beth? Mary Beth, what's going on? What is that?" the harried and frightened voice of her husband echoed wildly in the darkness.

Suddenly the seat belt ripped free and Mary Beth was yanked screaming in terror from the seat and through the broken glass. She found herself dangling in the air unable to feel anything, not pain or fear, just knowing that she was about to die staring wide-eyed into the pure face of evil. All she saw was a mouth full of teeth moving towards her and then felt a pulling, a ripping and tearing. She wondered what it was and realized it was her throat.

The last thing she remembered before darkness took her was being swung back and forth as Ron's voice kept calling her name and then fading to silence.

The phone hovering precariously on the nightstand jangled harshly. Kathleen awoke quickly, always a light sleeper. It came with the job. She heard Rain moan with displeasure as she reached to turn on the light and grab for the annoying contraption.

"Yeah, hello, who is this?" she mumbled, glancing at four thirty a.m. glaring in bright orange on her clock radio.

"Detective Morello, this is Ganz. All hell is breaking loose," she heard her Captain's voice crackling in and out on the phone.

"Captain, your phone is really breaking up. What the hell's going on?" she asked, now sitting up on the edge of the bed, completely alert.

"We have two serious situations Kathy. One is off Ridge Avenue near the high school, and the other somewhere on Manor Road. I'm pulling up to the scene on Manor now. I need you to meet your partner at the other scene. Damn, this is bad Kathy, this is really bad," he said, giving her the address on the street off Ridge Avenue in Roxborough. It was only ten or twelve blocks from where she lived and Manor Road was not far away either.

"Okay Cap, I'm on it. I'll call you when I get there and have a handle on things. Anybody dead that you know of?" she inquired, already out of bed and slipping out of her pajama bottoms, but her superior had already hung up.

Rain immediately jumped off the bed and began to vociferously wag her tail, smiling at the thought of going outside. She leaned hard up against Kathy's leg, not wanting to lose contact with her mommy, knowing Kathy would be leaving again.

"Yes sweetie, I'll take you out for a minute while the car's warming up. Mommy has to go to work though and I need to get dressed," she cooed in baby talk to the dog.

Her father was struggling to get up out of his easy chair. The telephone call had jolted him out of a deep sleep and he always hated that. The air compressor was humming and chugging as it normally did. Over the past year, Kathy had gotten used to the constantly droning sound as her father began depending on oxygen more and more.

"Dad, take the tube from around your neck before you walk away from the chair. You'll strangle yourself one of these days," she said, hitting the dining room floor already in constant motion.

"Who the hell was on the phone in the middle of the night?" her father grumbled.

She laughed. "Who do you think? Captain Ganz and it seems we have lots of trouble out there tonight. It also appears to be right here in Roxborough too."

She had pulled on a sweatshirt knowing it was going to be cold and slipped into her hooded coat. Grabbing her purse she leaned down and gave her father a quick kiss on the cheek.

"Don't worry, I'll be fine. I'll call you just as soon as I get a free minute. And for God's sake, please go upstairs and lie down in bed for awhile. Come on girl," she said, exiting the house and trotting to the car.

As it warmed up she stood at the end of the driveway staring across the street to where she had heard the sounds when she got home last night. Remembering how crazy Rain had gotten she began to wonder if there was any connection to what had happened in other parts of the area and what was apparently hiding in the woods.

"Hey girl, come on, back in the house. I gotta' go to work," leaning down and giving the dog a big kiss on the head. "I love you. Now go inside and protect pappy."

Leaping into the front seat, she pulled out of the driveway and hit the gas pedal hard, heading up the hill towards Ridge Avenue. She barely paused at the stoplight and sped down a nearly deserted street only braking slightly as she flew by a small shopping strip on the right, a deserted grocery store on the left, and then speeding through the light at a comatose high school. She made a hard left and saw police lights flashing and bouncing off houses. Opening the window she held out her shield and was motioned through where she came to a screeching stop half way down the block. She immediately saw the old, battered Honda of her partner, Tommy Darnello, pulled partly up on the sidewalk. She wondered if any of them had a nice car.

Jumping out of her vehicle she walked briskly across the street to the house where all the activity was. An ambulance was already parked in front of the place waiting for somebody, either alive or dead. She stopped beside two officers and smacked one of them on the shoulder.

"What's up Roberts? Is Tommy inside?" she asked.

"Hey Morello, they really called out the big guns on this one. Christ detective, what a mess we have here, but at least the 'vic' is alive, barely," he responded in his loud, somewhat obnoxious voice.

"Is there anybody dead?" she inquired.

"I think just a dog, pretty mangled from what I understand. Quite frankly, I haven't been inside and have no desire to either. Had pizza and lots of beer last night if you know what I mean," he laughed.

Yeah, she knew what he meant. She had upchucked a few dinners in the past as well. She ran up the steps to the porch slipping her rubber gloves on as she went. She could smell the blood and could tell this was not a scene she was really prepared to see. Even though she had been privy to many terrible crime situations, it just never got any easier. At least not for her and it probably never would.

Everything seemed okay as she entered the house other than too many cops milling about. As they moved aside for her she was then able to see a narrow strip of blood coming down the steps from the second floor and going down the hallway to the kitchen. She thought it definitely looked like prints of some type in the blood trail.

"Okay you guys, out of here, now. There are way too many in here to screw this crime scene up. Officer Leightman, get them all outside now and don't let anybody else in here unless you check with either Tommy or myself. Got that?" she said grimly.

"Yes ma'am. Let's go guys, outta' here now. Come on."

Just at that moment she noticed movement at the top of the steps and looked up. The EMT squad had brought the stretcher to the upper landing and was preparing to convey the victim downstairs. At least she noticed the sheet was not covering the entire body so she breathed a heavy sigh. Something was going right anyway.

"Hey, be careful up there guys," she warned them as one of the techs took a step backwards and lost his balance. Of course he slipped on the blood and went down hard to one knee, balancing his end of the stretcher at the same time.

"Shit," he yelled out in pain.

Standing up, he got his balance and they began very carefully to traverse the steps, trying their best not to step in the blood and contaminate the scene. Impossible really, it was already contaminated to some extent.

"Hey Kathy baby, is that you?" she heard the deep voice of her partner.

"Yep, it's me Tommy. What the hell have we got here?" she asked, happy to see him back after his two week vacation in Cancun, but she would never tell him that.

"I wish I knew Kat, I wish I knew. She's pretty torn up, but surprisingly alive. How I haven't the faintest idea. Been down in the basement?" he asked her.

"Not yet, just got here. What's up down there?"

At that moment the stretcher arrived at the lower landing and Kathy got a good look at the victim. Holy shit, what a mess she thought. Blood was splattered all over her face and blonde hair, but it didn't appear there were any wounds she could see on the head and face. However, there was an angry, gaping wound on her left shoulder. Kathy asked them to stop for a second and she lifted up the sheet very carefully. Her mouth opened and for a second nothing poured out. For her to be speechless took an awful lot.

"What the hell are those marks across her left breast and stomach? Jesus, they look like long slash, or claw marks?" she asked in a throaty whisper, looking up at the EMT tech.

"Exactly detective, that's the first thing I thought. Whatever did this is either an animal or somebody with very long fingernails," he threw back at her.

But at least she was still breathing, albeit very laboriously. Tommy was right though, how in God's name she was still alive was beyond the scope of reason.

"Be careful guys. Was she ever conscious at anytime since you got here?"

"Hey Morello, you can see her, would you be?" asked the nearest EMT, the one who had slipped at the top of the steps, his right pant leg completely blood-stained.

"Probably not by the looks of her," she answered, "How bad is she besides those ghastly wounds?"

"Massive blood loss obviously and lots of other smaller wounds that appear to be bite and claw marks which you've now seen," he said, laughing aloud just to settle his own nerves. "Someone, or something, enjoyed gnawing on her."

Kathy moved aside, not really knowing what else to say. She watched the guys take the stretcher outside to the ambulance and then looked up as Tommy joined her. He put his arm around her shoulder and steered her towards the kitchen and the basement area.

"So did you miss me, huh? Come on, just a little bit?" he joked with her, if for nothing else but to ease the tension.

"Why Tommy, have you been away?"

He laughed as they got to the top of the basement steps. They stood there silent for a moment. Kathy did not want to go down there, but at least it was not a human being. The stench of death, blood and who knew what else was overpowering.

"Tommy, have you been down there?"

"Well, I went half way down the steps, stopped, took one look and came back up before I lost it. Figured I'd wait for you to give me support," he said.

"Yeah right, well no time for the weary, let's check it out" she answered.

The only light in the basement came from a light bulb that was nearest the steps. Blood appeared to be everywhere and worse than that, there also appeared to be what looked like body parts lying on the floor. As Kathy got almost to the bottom of the steps she stopped and let her eyes take in the most insane sight she had ever seen. And she had seen many including terrible traffic accidents and multiple murders. But this was worse, far worse. Only a madman or something more evil could've wrought this devastation.

Obviously what had been a large dog was literally torn limb from limb. The floor and walls in the basement were splattered with blood and long brown fur. All four legs and the head were lying separately and all Kathy could think about was that cootie game she played as a little girl where plastic legs and the alien head were separate pieces from the body of a bug. For just a few seconds she had to keep the bile down that had traveled nearly up her throat.

She whispered, "Tommy, what the hell happened here? What could've done this?"

"I don't know Kat, but I'm about ready to head back to Cancun. Sorry, but I'm outta' here," he said, turning and moving quickly back up the stairs.

"If the forensic guys are up there make sure they get a team down here right away," she said to his disappearing back.

She knelt down on the steps and let her gaze scour the scene. Whatever had done this had to have unbelievable strength, not to mention either a very large knife of some kind or claws that were extremely lethal. She thought of Rain and tears began to well up in the corner of her eyes. If something did this to her precious dog, Kathy knew she would temporarily go insane with rage.

Back up stairs she met Tommy in the living room.

"Kat, somebody was here and it wasn't an animal. I mean she had company, somebody that sat right here in this room eating and drinking with her. Upstairs in the bedroom, the bed was definitely used for more than just some bloody nightmare. She was nude and her clothes were laid nicely on the chair in the corner. Without a doubt there was a sexual encounter before all the blood starting flying," he said.

"Okay, forensics will get everything they can and we'll go over it with a fine tooth comb. In the meantime I'm going to give Captain Ganz a call and see how he's making out at the other scene," she said, walking out the front door.

Standing on the porch she let the crisp, early morning air fill her nostrils and expand her chest, the horrible stench of death and slaughter trying to leave her own mind. Closing her eyes she tried to settle her nerves and think straight. She had to be calm in this nightmare, and that's exactly what it was turning out to be, one helluva' nightmare.

Reaching for her cell phone she punched in the number of Nathan Ganz and let it ring. Her gaze moved over the street and suddenly stopped. Across the street, a few houses in from the corner stood a very tall, extremely handsome man. For a split second Kathy could've sworn his eyes glowed like she had seen Rain's do when lights reflected off them. They almost appeared yellow or golden for a moment, but now they looked normal. She wondered how in the world he had gotten past the officer at the end of the street.

The phone continued to ring and she decided to hit stop as she began walking down the steps and moving towards this very mysterious stranger, an uneasy feeling spreading in the nether reaches of her stomach.

Chapter 12

The early morning sky was the darkest blue Ganz had ever seen, almost black pearl, but still blue nonetheless. He stood in the middle of Manor Road and stared up at what was left of a honey-mustard moon covered with spidery tendrils of snowy, white clouds. How could a sky look so beautiful and yet cover so much death below? Shaking his head he moved his attention to the vehicle that lay smashed at the bottom of the small ravine. He had a gnawing pain in the pit of his stomach. What the hell was going on?

"Ruiz, what's the status down there? Is the woman alive?" he asked, his deep voice echoing through the trees.

"Not likely Captain. Hate to tell you this sir, but there is no body, at least of a human being. All we have down here is a very large buck, the front half inside the car and the ass end sprawled across the hood. The windshield is completely shattered and caved in. There's a lot of blood on the driver's side of the seat, but I have to tell you Captain, there is no body of any woman. All that's here is her purse and cell phone that is still turned on."

Ganz looked back up at the fading moon. Shit, what a nightmare he thought. It was definitely time to retire and soon while he still had the chance.

"Could she have gotten out of the car and staggered away, or any signs of that happening?" Ganz asked hopefully.

"Sir, both doors in the front are jammed in. We tried opening them and couldn't. The only way this lady got out of here was through the front windshield. Oh, and it appears that the seat belt has been torn out," Ruiz replied.

"Then maybe she was thrown in the collision," Ganz said.

"Possibly sir, but it looks to me like the whole window is busted in, not out. And anyway, we've checked all around here and there is no sign of a body lying anywhere. But here's the thing Captain, you ready for this?" Sergeant Ruiz asked.

"No, I'm not ready, but somehow I think you're about to tell me anyway."

"Well sir, there is a large smear of blood on the hood in front of the driver's seat. I hate to even think about this possibility Captain, but I think the woman was pulled out of the car through the front windshield," Ruiz said very slowly.

"Okay Ruiz, get up here now and assemble most of the men. We need to start a search of this area right away. Radio in and get more help out here. Oh, and who is that sitting in the patrol car with Thompson?"

Ruiz crawled up the hill and looked to where Thompson was talking to a very distressed young man.

"That's the husband I believe. She evidently called him on her cell phone after she crashed and he heard some terrible things. He's obviously extremely distressed which you would expect after hearing your wife scream bloody murder," Ruiz said emphatically.

"Okay John, get the guys and scour this entire area. I'm going to talk to the husband."

Ganz walked down the road to the other side of the bridge as Sgt. John Ruiz started barking out orders. At the same time a few more squad cars pulled up, doors opening and closing.

The husband glanced up as Nathan walked ponderously toward him. He had seen that haunted, painful stare in many victims and their loved ones over the years. It was never any easier, always unsettling, especially since he knew it only too well himself.

It had been one year ago, almost to the day in fact. As if it happened only yesterday, he remembered hearing the phone ring and informed that his son had been shot while on duty. Terry was only 27 and had been on the force for three years. After returning from performing his duty in Afghanistan he talked to his father about becoming a policeman and following in his father's footsteps. Nathan was already extremely proud of his son and relieved he had survived both the tragedy and nightmare that was the turbulent Middle East. So with great pride, and a fair amount of trepidation, Nathan helped somewhat in getting his son's new career started, though he told him he'd have to make it on his own.

While answering a violent domestic dispute Terry was gunned down by an irate husband who was high on cocaine and had already shot his wife. I suppose after killing a cop he figured what else did he have to lose since he was so completely crazed anyway. Opening the front door he came running out, gun blazing at the other officers protecting themselves behind their cars and was slain in a hail of bullets.

When Nathan arrived on the scene his son was already in the ambulance covered completely by a very stark, white sheet. He spent the next fifteen minutes sitting alone with his son, holding his hand and crying for only the third time in his life, once before when his father died and only a year ago when his shepherd Rex had succumbed to cancer.

So he knew only too well that look etched across Ron Mizerk's face. He stopped a few feet away and decided to slowly kneel down to be more eye to eye with the distraught husband. This was a painful job in itself since he had gained, whittled away and regained the same fifty pounds since the death of his son.

"Hello Mr. Mizerk, my name is Captain Nathan Ganz. I know this is a very difficult time, but I need to ask you some questions and they may have already been asked of you by Sergeant Thompson here. Are you up to it?" Nathan asked more gently than his size would've made you think was possible.

"Yes sir, I'll be fine. Please call me Ron though. Have you found Mary Beth yet?" he asked quietly.

"You've already been down to the car?" Nathan asked surprised.

"I was on the phone with her and knew she was driving home from work on Manor Road. We live close to here in Lafayette Hill." He looked up at Nathan, his eyes huge with grief.

"Captain, I can understand the accident, they happen everyday. Hell, I've been in several of them myself, but the noise from the phone is still ringing in my ears. I can't get it out," he said, raising his hands to cover the sides of his head.

Nathan let him have a few seconds and then gently placed his hand on the husband's shoulder. Ron lowered his arms and slowly raised his anguished eyes.

"I'm sorry, but the growling and the screams drove me crazy. She called me on my cell phone. Since I didn't want to lose contact with her I called 911 from our house phone and then ran out to the car and drove here. At first I didn't even know she had gone off the road at this point since I was driving so fast.

When I got to the end of Manor on River Road I realized I had missed her," he said tearfully.

"Take your time Ron. Do you need some water?" Nathan asked.

Ron shook his head and loudly blew his nose.

"No, I'm okay, thanks. I kept yelling to her on the cell phone the whole time, but after the last period of screaming I never heard anything else. I drove back up Manor a lot slower until I saw the huge gouge in the cement post at the beginning of the bridge, then the dents in the metal fence. I parked here and walked across the bridge until I saw where she had gone off the road. It was dark, but I had the flashlight so I climbed down to where the car was."

He looked up at Ganz with that frightened, forlorn stare again.

"She wasn't there Captain. She wasn't in the car. I started calling her name, climbed back up to the road yelling for Mary Beth and that's when the first police car pulled up," he said frantically. "Where can she be? How could she have gotten out of that wreck?"

"I don't know Ron, but we're searching for her now. Maybe she was thrown, or climbed out. She could've wandered off and maybe passed out. We'll find her sir, we'll find her. You said you heard growling, like from an animal?" Nathan asked.

"Jesus, yes, it was unmistakable. Very loud, it had to be a large animal of some kind. I swear it sounded like a huge dog, or a bear. I don't know really, but it was definitely growling and Mary Beth was screaming so loud. The sounds became fainter and then stopped completely. It was like the phone just went dead, but there was never a dial tone. I saw her cell phone lying on the front seat of the car so I turned mine off and called 911 again, pleading for them to send somebody," Ron said, his voice rising.

"Okay, okay son, settle down. Listen, I want you to just relax, we'll find Mary Beth. If you want to go home we'll send an officer with you so we can keep you apprised of the situation here. Or you can remain, but I need to be assured you'll sit here and stay out of the way. Let us do our job, okay?"

"I want to stay Captain so I'm here when you find her. She'll need me."

"Alright Ron, just sit here and try to relax. We'll find her, I promise. Either Sergeant Thompson, or another officer will be right here if you need anything."

With his legs groaning and heart moaning, he stood up and lumbered back to the other side of the bridge where the car had careened off the road. Something was just not right with this case. He always prided himself on being in control, methodical, a leader who his men could depend on. Nathan did not feel that way right now. He had no idea what they were looking for, either human or animal. All signs pointed towards the latter, but how could that be? What was that large and vicious to have killed at least three people, a dog, and who knows how many more? It was against all reason, yet he had no choice but to lean that way. He knew that forensics and the lab had to give him some answers and very fast because he wasn't sure when, or even how, this was going to end.

Suddenly there was some shouting in the distance and then an officer came running down the road towards him.

"Captain I think we've found her," he croaked in a labored and strained voice.

"What the hell do you mean that you think you've found her?"

The policeman was bent over, not only from exhaustion, but it appeared he was about to heave his guts all over the road.

"Sorry Captain Ganz, but I said 'think' because there's a severely mutilated body up on the golf course. Captain, it's horrible, I've never seen anything like it," he moaned and then did in fact vomit profusely over the railing.

"Goddamn it," Ganz yelled out as he started walking at a fast pace up the road to where a number of officers were stumbling out of the tree line on the left side.

None of them spoke, they just pointed. One offered his hand to help Nathan step over a narrow ditch and up a small hill. Knocking the guy's hand out of the way, he suddenly got more energy than he was capable of and leaped the gutter, climbed the hill, walked through some trees out onto a long, dark fairway. Any leftover moonlight shone down onto the open fairway of the golf course. Over the eastern horizon dawn was beginning to break on what promised to actually be a sunny day for a change. Not that Ganz would even care at this point.

"Over there Captain," an officer pointed. "On the eleventh green and you're not going to like what you're going to see. She's definitely dead sir and I mean very, very dead. I've seen a lot, but nothing like this."

As Nathan moved up the short part of fairway to the wide green he saw several officers to the left kneeling down, crossing themselves and praying. What the hell was going on, he thought? These are grown men, Philadelphia's finest, brave warriors and they were either praying, or throwing up.

Then he saw Mary Beth Mizerk, or what was left of her. He felt like crossing himself, praying and throwing up in that order as well. She lay crumpled in a heap like she was thrown onto the ground right near the solitary flag that was blowing in the breeze. It was as if her killer had just tossed her there like she was nothing but an old doll, or a used piece of cloth. Blood was everywhere, literally everywhere. The dark grass of the green was stained a dark cranberry. The young woman's throat had been ripped out. What appeared to once be a sweater now lay in tatters about her shoulders, waist and arms. Her face was a mask of blood, either from the pieces of glass still there from the accident, or what appeared to be possible claw marks. And then there was the breasts and stomach. Five very distinct, deep marks stretched from the top of her left breast, running down her stomach to where it now lay exposed to the coming dawn.

Not caring about the crime scene Nathan took off his coat and covered her body. It was sacrilege to leave this young woman lying here in the open like that. Jesus Christ, what could've done this he thought? Not a man, Nathan was sure about that. No human being could do this and those were most definitely claw marks from some very large creature.

Suddenly, there was shouting behind him. Nathan stood, turned and saw Ron Mazerk breaking free and running towards the green and the body of his dead wife. Nathan moved his hulking frame quickly to block the distraught husband from seeing what remained of his wife.

"Mr. Mizerk, stop, please. I can't let you see her, not now," Nathan implored.

Ron Mizerk stepped back and let a fist go, striking Nathan Ganz on the chin and dropping him like he was a loaf of bread. Then Mary Beth's husband ran to where his wife lay and he yanked off the coat covering her body.

"Oh my God, oh my God, Mary Beth, how in God's name could this have happened? Who did this?" he wailed, his voice echoing out across the open golf course towards the beginning of early morning traffic out on Ridge Avenue. He fell to the ground and held his wife, blood and all, crying as Nathan Ganz looked on. The word nightmare kept bouncing around in his head.

Chapter 13

Kathy Morello walked slowly towards the stranger and stopped about ten feet to his right. He was tall, very well built even under the jacket and extremely handsome. In fact, for a second he truly took her breath away.

"Excuse me sir, can I help you?" Kathy asked.

He turned his head slightly and stared at her for a few seconds. Kathy could've sworn she saw that same golden tint appear again. Then he spun his head and glanced back at the house.

"Hey, excuse me, I was talking to you. I'm Detective Morello and this is a crime scene. I need to know why you're standing there so interested in all of this. Do you live on this block?"

Kathy started moving towards him and opened her coat so she could easily reach for her gun.

Then he turned and faced her, again stealing her breath. My God, those eyes were almost feral she thought. Kathy had never seen anything like it before. This was most definitely not any normal guy, at least none that she had ever met before.

"I'm sorry Detective, just caught up in what's happening here. My apologies," he said quietly.

"And what do you think is happening here? Do you know something that the police should know? If so, we need you to either give us your statement or move on and let us do our job," Kathy informed him.

She now stood tensely only about three feet from him. Kathy was a little over five foot seven inches so not real short for a woman. Yet she felt dwarfed by his size. He was most definitely near six and a half feet and had to weigh well over two hundred pounds, but she could tell there was not an ounce of fat on his entire body. He appeared to have this lithe, almost catlike grace to him when he moved. His face was rather gaunt, but yet very chiseled with a sharply etched chin and an aquiline nose with deeply set eyes. His shining hair was black as a raven's wing and fell to just below his shoulders. He most definitely appeared to possibly be of some Native American descent, but Kathy had no idea which one. Maybe none at all, it was just his sharp features and strong, aquiline nose that pushed her in that direction. She was, in fact, quite in awe of his impressive physical appearance and calm demeanor. That didn't happen very often, but at the same time she was extremely wary of him and alert for possible trouble.

"It's not what I think Detective Morello, it's what I know. And what I know as a fact you may not wish to believe, or even be able to comprehend," he told her in a very powerful and commanding, but low voice.

She stared at him, almost mesmerized. "Tell me then," she said. "But before you do, who are you and why are you here?"

With a most engaging smile he said, "My name is Johnny Raven. I suppose I am what you would call a tracker and I've been on the trail of this killer, or killers, for several years now. They murdered my wife and unborn son three years ago outside of Tucson, Arizona in the Mt. Lemon mountain range."

"I'm sorry to hear about your loss Mr. Raven, but this is a police matter and you're not an officer of the law, or are you?" she asked him.

He smiled again. Damn she thought, she could fall right into that smile.

"I was a private detective and worked for several agencies from time to time.

After my wife was murdered I left and have not returned," he said quietly.

"Do you have any identification that I could see Mr. Raven?" she asked.

Damn, there was that smile again. She figured she'd have to tell him to stop doing that because it was interfering in a police investigation.

He quickly reached inside his jacket with one hand and she tensed.

She moved back, on the alert for trouble. "Easy, what are you reaching for?"

He held up his hands, palms out. "Hey Detective, you asked for ID and my wallet seems to be buried within a pocket that just happens to be on the inside of my jacket. I mean you no harm, believe me."

Kathy smiled back, a little more at ease. Johnny thought her smile was radiant. There was something about this woman that was bewitching, but he couldn't take the time to pursue that. More important things on his mind like finding the monster.

He opened his wallet and passed it too her.

"There's my Maine drivers license and in the sleeve right behind that is my identification from the last agency I worked at. It was tough to leave, but there was nothing to keep me there any longer."

She stared intently at the picture and then up at him. There was a noticeable difference in his appearance and yet he was still the same. The photo was definitely taken in a happier time of his life because now he possessed a shiny darkness to his eyes and a terribly gaunt, haunting look that was painted across his face.

"So Mr. Raven, this ID is ....." she began and he stopped her.

"Please Detective Morello, call me Johnny. My father is Mr. Raven, and he even hates that title, so please Johnny will do just fine."

She smiled at him and nodded. "Okay then, Johnny it is," as she handed him back the wallet.

"As I started to say, the ID from your days working for that agency is out of date so I can't let you participate in this investigation. But I do respect your past and would be welcome to any light you can shed on this situation. As well as why you feel I won't believe what you might tell me," she said.

He glanced up at the sky, feeling the moon fade in the distance. Even though he was weregune and wasn't ruled by the moon like a rogue werewolf, the different phases of the moon still commanded his attention and could crawl inside him like the fingers of a sultry lover or an insipidly, evil serpent.

"Detective Morello, you are not dealing with a normal situation here, not that any murder is ever a normal situation. You have to believe me when I tell you that this creature you're looking for is not fully human. It is nothing anyone here in Philadelphia has ever dealt with before and you need me on this, or you need to let me alone and track it by myself. More will die if I don't find him soon and," pausing to look at the sky, he continued "we only have a few more nights and then we'll lose him for several weeks, maybe completely if he moves on to another city which has been his pattern."

Kathy stared at him, back to the house, up at the sky and then back to his face again. She wasn't sure what to say.

"So, are you saying that we're dealing with some kind of wolf man, Lon Chaney type of killer?" she asked in disbelief. Well, he did say that she wouldn't believe him, but that prospect was purely laughable.

"I'm afraid that's exactly what you're dealing with. He will change according to the phases of the moon. There are actually six days in the cycle when he will alter his bodily structure, with three or four nights being extremely deadly. Then there will be a stretch of around ten days where we will lose him and the killings will stop," he informed her as kindly and yet forcefully as he could.

"Wait a minute! If I'm to believe all this crap, and the jury is still out on that verdict, I thought a man could only change into a wolf under the full moon," shaking her head. "Christ, I can't believe that I'm even discussing this possibility with you, but let's continue on this crazy path anyway."

"Oh detective, it's not only possible. It's absolute fact. This creature can change during both periods of the full and the new moons, which is twice a month depending on how they fall. You see...."

"Hold it, just you wait one damn minute," she said, shaking her head and walking away a few steps. "This can't be happening, not here, not today. I mean this isn't Transylvania you know. This is Philadelphia, PA in the good old U.S. of A. Werewolves and vampires do not exist, only in legends and nightmares."

Johnny held up his hands. "See, I said you wouldn't believe. Just let me do my thing, stay out of my way for the next few nights and maybe I can catch and kill it."

She turned angrily and stomped back, stopping right in front of him, looking up.

"Don't you tell me how to run my investigation Mr. Raven. And let me tell you something else. I'm an excellent detective and whether I believe this mumbo-jumbo or not, I'm not ruling out anything, especially after what I've seen over the last two days."

"So tell me what you've seen then. What happened in that house for instance?"

"I can't tell you, it happens to be police business," she said quickly.

He started to laugh and strolled nonchalantly away from her towards the end of the block.

"Okay Ms. Morello, you go on looking and following your leads to wherever it may take you. I could use a very strong cup of coffee right about now and some breakfast. I don't know why, but I'm suddenly really hungry too."

She ran after him, grabbed his arm and yanked him around.

"Hey buster, I'm not done with you yet. I'm the police detective here, not you, and if you refuse to answer my questions then I'll have you transported downtown and we can do it there at the precinct. One way or the other mister, you'll tell me what I want to know," she said dramatically.

Johnny put a massive hand with extremely long fingers over her much smaller one and pulled it off his arm. Kathy felt electricity surge through her body, like she was shot with some type of adrenalin, making her woozy for a few seconds. Startled, she yanked her hand out of his quite begrudgingly.

He looked down at her and smiled. "If you won't believe me, and you won't tell me what happened in that house, then what's the use? I can only tell you the truth, what you're dealing with. Detective Morello let me be completely straight and I hope you understand. You are dealing with something that you've never encountered before in your career, or even your lifetime. What you've seen on the big screen is only Hollywood's adaptation. Please try and understand you are playing with a very deadly, extremely dangerous creature and you most definitely need my help."

Just then her cell phone rang and she reached for it, thankful for the interruption.

"Morello here," she spoke into the phone.

"Kathy, this is Nathan. How are things there?" Ganz asked.

She turned and walked away from Johnny, lowering her voice.

"Nathan, it was brutal in that house. The woman's alive, but I honestly have no idea how. She was torn up pretty good and is being transported I believe to Hahneman Hospital. Also, her dog was completely dismembered and pieces thrown around the basement like they were toys. Anyway, I was just about to leave here. Tommy can handle the scene," she said. "How are things where you're at?"

There was a very distinct pause and Kathy thought she lost the connection. Then his very troubled voice appeared again.

"You won't believe it Kathy," he said.

"Try me Nathan, I'd believe anything right now," she laughed slightly.

"We have a young woman who seems to have been pulled from her wrecked vehicle and whose mangled body was found up on the golf course. No sign of the killer, but everything leads to it being either a very large, enraged man or some kind of vicious animal. If Tommy can handle the scene there then I can definitely use you here. We also have a very distraught husband on our hands as well."

"Is he involved in the killing? Was he in the accident with her?" she asked.

"I'll explain when you get here," and the phone went dead.

Kathy stood, seemingly alone, lost in her thoughts when suddenly a hand on her shoulder made her literally almost jump out of her skin and she turned.

"What the hell do you think you're doing? About scared me to death," she yelled at him.

"Sorry Detective Morello for scaring you. I couldn't help but overhear your conversation. Did you say that the woman in the house is still alive?"

"Yes, she's being transported to the hospital as we speak. Why? Is that a bad thing?" she asked him accusingly.

He stood there impassively, staring down at her.

"If I told you what I'm really thinking then you'd say I was a very callous and uncaring individual. I can only say that she may wish she had died," Johnny answered her.

"Okay, enough is enough. I need to know more about this fantasy tale you were spinning before."

He started to laugh. "Yeah, it's a fantasy tale, a fairy tale of myth and monsters.

Miss Morello, you need my expertise and special talents on this case. Take me with you to the other crime scene while there may still be time to track it."

"I can't Mr. Raven. This is official police business and it is Detective Morello to you."

He started walking away. "Okay, do your own thing and stumble through this investigation. I'm going to get some breakfast and then do my own search."

"Okay, alright then. Stop right there and come with me. When we get there, you stay out of the way and trust me that Captain Ganz is not going to be very happy that I've dragged a citizen along with me."

"I promise I'll be as quiet as a church mouse," he said quietly and smiled.

"Yeah right, something tells me you're much more dangerous than a church mouse, but I need you so let's go."

Chapter 14

Quentin awoke to find himself curled among some dense bushes off a back road which bordered the Schuylkill Nature Center. He was completely nude and, to say the least, lay shivering in the cold, early morning air. Stretching out much like a dog would do after waking up from a deep slumber he slowly stood on two shaky legs and glanced around the small clearing. There had been no pleasant puppy dreams while asleep. He knew his clothes were around some place so he began searching until he spied the cuff from a pant leg sticking out of some leaves near a large tree. It was kind of easy to detect the urine scent where he had marked the tree before the moon ripped away his humanity last night. Well, his pseudo-appearance of being a human. The humanity aspect of his life had gone on a permanent vacation many, many years ago.

There was always a period of mixed emotions in those virgin hours of early dawn. He was incredibly alive when his beast was on the prowl, insanely powerful and exhilarating, feral in every way possible. At times he slightly remembered his hellish deeds wrought during the night. Those quick flashes like you might have in a dream, or sometimes during a terrible nightmare, that can send shivers up your spine and cause you to awaken in a cold sweat. If he had just recently killed something, whether it was animal or human, then many times his hands and mouth could still be blood-stained like they were now as he ran his tongue over encrusted lips. Sometimes there were also little clues left like tufts of fur from a rabbit or deer stuck in his teeth, or those nauseating occasions when he regurgitated what he had consumed, bones and pieces of flesh that just would not stay down.

However, now he was utterly famished so he was aware he hadn't eaten anything too recently. He stared at his hands and knew it was human blood. All the news programs would be carrying what happened during the night. It was the magic of television and instant reporting so eventually he would hear about somebody dying in a terrible manner.

Back to the day his life was changed forever, so long ago now that it was almost but a distant memory, he barely teetered on the brink of sanity after realizing he had caused so much havoc and death. Paper boys would be yelling loudly on the street corners of London, "Read about another murder. Monster strikes again." Then before he realized what he had truly done, the night fell and the moon captured him once more in its vicious cycle. How could a beast, a slavering creature, be anything but insane his mind kept telling him? It took many years until he became somewhat used to his beastly side. It took him longer to embrace the creature and become one. Taking what money he had saved before his human life was savagely stolen from him, he purchased a small plot of land far out of town on the moors, with a smallish cottage where he could be alone. It was his desire to stay away from the city crowds and killing more innocent people.

In the beginning he locked himself in the basement and chained both hands and feet to the wall. Little good that did since the alteration of his body and genes gave him the strength of ten men. Plus, he would wake up only to find the manacles and broken chains clinging to his human limbs, tattered pieces of clothing still hanging on his gaunt frame. He got completely tired of buying new shirts and pants as well. In fact, the old, gray bearded guy who ran the hardware store in a nearby village was very nosy and kept asking why he needed so many chains. He also narrowed down the area of the two windows near the top of the one basement wall and installed extra wide bars. He double strengthened the door and put two very large padlocks in place, hiding the key once he locked himself inside. It held and contained him, but his basement was in such a shambles. Thankfully he was far enough off the beaten path that nobody could hear his demented raging. At least he thought so anyway.

Then one day he decided to stop at the pub in the nearest village which happened to be twenty miles away from his home. Before he knew it, he was actually having some fun with a few of the customers shooting darts and throwing down shots. However, as the night wore on he got progressively ill, continuing to bend over with severe spasms in his stomach. He realized it was near the full moon and it was at that time he became aware the change would come over a series of days, both around the full moon and the new moon.

He never made it home. Crossing an open field, trying to take a shortcut that would get him down to his basement sooner, the pain just became too intense and he fell. And where he fell was where he changed. Being far enough away from population he just roamed the deserted hills, chasing anything alive that moved and was dumb enough to stay near him. When he awoke at morning light, covered in mud and grime, he noticed his clothes were also in tatters. And so he learned, as everyone does in life, the so called tricks of the trade, how to make things go a little easier for yourself. One thing he knew for sure though. He would never spend another horrendous night in that cold, dank jail cell of a basement.

And he never did. After getting dressed he made his way across the field and crossed Hagys Mill Road to a small housing development where he had parked his car last evening. Quentin then guided the car out towards Ridge Avenue. Since there was a diner down on Umbria Street, he most definitely needed lots of strong black coffee along with something to eat. It was still early and the diner would've just opened so it wouldn't be too crowded. At least he hoped so because he was never very sociable after the change.

As he sat down at a booth in the back of the diner, a middle-aged waitress with short reddish hair brought him a stained, plastic-coated menu and a glass of water, which he swallowed right down. Well, at least he didn't lap it up like a dog.

"What would you like to drink sir? Coffee, juice?" she asked him.

"Black coffee and very strong, a carafe if you have it. If not, then just bring me two cups now. Also, I'm ready to order if that's okay," he said, his voice still very guttural. It was funny how it still sounded just like a growl.

"Give me two orders of sausage and two orders of bacon, undercooked, along with six eggs slightly cooked as well. In other words, very runny, and make sure it's undercooked, or believe me, you'll take it all back."

"You got it darlin', we aim to please here. How about toast or a muffin?" she asked him with an amused tone. She saw all kinds in this diner on her shift.

"No bread, just bring me that damn coffee," he warned her.

"Hey, okay, don't get your underpants in an up-roar, I can see you've had one helluva' night," she said, strutting off behind the counter.

At that moment the front door jingled and in walked two of Philadelphia's finest from the 5th. District. Damn it, Quentin thought, can't a wolf man even have a peaceful breakfast? The waitress had left the menu lay on the table so he grabbed it and made like he was still deciding on what to order.

"Hey Betty, how's business?" the first officer asked, a very large, out of shape Philadelphia's finest.

"Well I declare, if it isn't Starsky and Hutch, where have you two been, and why are the two of you together? Thought you brave guys worked alone here in the 5th," she replied happily over her shoulder.

"Jesus Betty Ann, what a night. I've been here in the 5th almost five years now, on the force for fourteen, and I've never seen a night like this. Hell, for that matter two of them like we've had back to back in this city," Officer Kramer bellowed in way too loud a voice Quentin surmised. At least they hadn't noticed him yet.

Betty turned around with two large, black coffees and placed the cups in front of them as they sat down at the counter. Quentin started to seethe a little bit since he had ordered first and was still waiting for his coffee. If looks could kill then she'd be popping daisies right about then.

"I echo that," said Officer Johnson, a much slimmer, African-American member of Philadelphia's finest. Terrill Johnson had only been on the force now for a little over a year so he was no longer technically a rookie, but being hooked up with Kramer this whole night, he certainly felt like one. At least that's the way his obnoxious partner made him feel. Hopefully it would only be until this shift was over and he'd be paired with somebody else that didn't belch, fart and tell bad jokes.

Betty filled a carafe with hot, black, steaming coffee and grabbed an empty cup as she moved towards Quentin's table with a smile. Always a smile even when the customers are assholes, at least that's what an older waitress had told her twenty years ago when she began working here at the diner. She loved it though, her bubbly personality being conducive to dealing with the public. It was hard putting up with jerks like this one she was walking towards, but her philosophy was always 'put up with them for a few minutes and they'd eventually be gone'. However, if they were repeat customers who happened to be jerks then she was forceful enough to put them in their place and train them to be polite and respectful. It was pretty funny how some of them became such dear friends over the many years she had been working at the diner. In fact, between Thanksgiving and Christmas she made out like a bandit with many of her steady customers either giving her nice gifts or good old, cold cash.

"Here you are sir, sorry it took so long. Your breakfast should be out shortly and I did give instructions to undercook everything, just the way you requested," she told him with one of her most radiant smiles. Her pearly whites always softened them up a little.

Quentin grabbed the carafe angrily and started pouring coffee into the cup, spilling some onto the table. Betty reached into a pocket on her apron for a small towel and he growled, "Just leave it."

"Sure honey, anything your little old heart desires," she threw back at him, turning and strutting back behind the counter. Guess there was at least one who didn't fall for her radiant smile.

None of the encounter was missed by Officer Kramer who, besides always looking to straighten out jerks like this one, had a huge crush on Betty Ann as well.

Quentin looked over top of his cup as he drank down the hot coffee and saw the policeman staring at him. Kramer nodded and smiled. Quentin lowered the cup, nodded and smiled back.

"Morning sir, you have a rough night?" the overweight cop asked him.

"Yeah, you could say that," Quentin replied. "Work was a real bitch. Busier than bees on a sugar high, the boss was on everybody the entire late shift. So some of us stopped for a few beers and then a few beers became a few more. You know how it is."

Kramer laughed and said, "I sure do. Had a few of those nights myself, but you know my friend that doesn't give us the right to be rude. You know what I mean?"

I'm not your goddamn friend Quentin thought, but he certainly didn't need a confrontation so he acquiesced, nodding back.

"I sure do officer, didn't mean anything by it," he replied, looking over at Betty. "Sorry ma'am, just a rough night all the way around. I do apologize if I offended thee."

Betty looked at both men and started laughing. "Hey guys, no problem. When you work in this diner as long as I have you just learn to deal with situations where somebody has had a rough time. Hell, I've had many a rough day and night myself," she chuckled.

"Now Officer Kramer, you just be a good old boy and concentrate on your coffee and that delicious cherry Danish in front of you. Officer Johnson, how's that new little baby boy of yours?" she asked, trying to break up the tension.

Kramer smiled at Quentin and thankfully turned his full attention to attacking the pastry rather than pursuing the argument.

"Thanks for asking Betty. He's doing great and so is Martha. He does have his days and nights mixed up though and hopefully that will change soon," he said laughing.

"Give it time dear, give it time. When you have an off day how about you and Martha bringing the little guy in here," she said, carrying two plates of food over to Quentin's table.

"I'll do that Betty Ann, thanks," Officer Johnson said with his mouth full of pastry.

The waitress put down the plates and said, "Enjoy sir, and hopefully the cook didn't over cook a thing."

The yellow of the eggs was oozing out over the plate and the meat was still pink. Quentin realized how famished he was and nodded his thanks as his stomach growled like a hungry wolf.

Betty Ann winked at him and then asked as she walked away, "You got a name stranger?"

Through a mouthful of eggs and sausage he stared at her and said, "Tom!"

"Okay Tom, you enjoy."

As the two policemen walked out a few minutes later, Kramer looked over and tipped his hat. What a grade 'A' asshole Quentin thought, but at least the cop would live to see another day.

With breakfast finally over, he sat back and finished off the coffee, his growling stomach finally silenced. Now he was content and could head back to the apartment, relax and maybe get some sleep. Possibly that sweet little Karen, or Sharon, whatever her name was could keep him busy since he most definitely felt the need for sex. Even though she was diseased with diabetes, a little romp in the hay wouldn't hurt anything.

As Quentin left a nice tip and paid his bill, two large truck drivers came through the front door just as he turned to leave. They bumped into each other roughly and the first guy pushed Quentin against the cash register.

"Hey buddy, watch where the hell you're going," the guy said.

"Excuse me," Quentin replied, "but you bumped into me."

The guy turned, at least as tall as Quentin, but a good fifty pounds heavier with a huge beer gut and scruffy, dirty beard.

"You hear that Rocco, I bumped into him. That the way you see it?" he shot back.

"Not at all," Rocco said. "In fact Tony, I think he bumped into you on purpose."

Betty Ann came around and put her much smaller hand on the antagonist's huge, tattooed bicep.

"Sit down Tony. You too Rocco, there was no problem here. What the hell is wrong with all you guys this morning? You drink straight testosterone last night? Men, I swear, none of you are worth the time God spent figuring out how to put you together."

She placed her hand on Quentin's shoulder and winked good-bye with her sweetest smile.

Quentin left as the two burly truck drivers sat down, their loud laughter echoing out the door as it swished shut. He was seething right about then, first the fat cop and now these two idiots. Too much had happened after changing back to human from his wolf state. He put fifty cents in the paper machine and ripped out a Philadelphia Inquirer, then walked to his car which faced the diner in the parking lot. He got in, slammed the door angrily and started to scour the front page, mostly looking for articles on his deadly escapades from the night before along the river. He had become so depraved over the years that there was little conscience left to be bothered by his killing sprees under the moon's direction. Besides, he always got quite a thrill out of reading the articles. For a long time he cut them out and saved them in a box but a fire at a tenement he had stayed in destroyed them all and so he stopped his sordid collection.

Looking up from the newspaper, the diner door was thrown open. Mutt and Jeff walked out yelling good-bye to the grateful waitress, happy most likely to see them leave. As they walked across the parking lot to their delivery van they bumped and pushed each other playfully. Once they got to the truck, the larger of the two goons started groping in his grimy jeans for the keys. It was time to continue unfinished business! Quentin got out of his car and walked around the front towards the truck. This wouldn't take long, he was sure of that. It was good that the truck was parked in the back of the lot almost behind the diner and not visible from the street.

"Hey Tony, did you forget this?" Quentin growled.

"What?" Tony said, surprised as he twirled around. Quentin buried his massive fist into the guy's grotesque beer gut, doubling him over, then grabbed his throat with a huge hand and hoisted the heavy truck driver off the ground, slamming him up against the side of the truck. Hearing the noise, Rocco came running around the front of the truck right into Quentin's other outstretched paw. Rocco gagged loudly as the air to his windpipe was quickly expelled. With eyes bugging out in fright he was lifted and also slammed harshly into the side of the truck. Quentin smiled at the two large men trying to breathe with their feet kicking wildly a solid two feet of the ground.

"Now Tony, tell me who bumped into whom back in the diner and who owes who an apology? Huh, can you hear me? Excuse me, cat got your tongue?" he asked, smiling at the beefy truck driver and squeezing just a little bit harder.

Choking and gagging, Tony barely was able to say, "I did, I'm sorry."

"Oh that's okay my friend. We all make mistakes Tony, but maybe next time you bump into somebody you'll say excuse me. Do you think that would be the honorable thing to do?"

Tony could do nothing more than nod slowly as his eyes bulged fearfully while beginning to turn blue. Quentin then slammed their heads together and let them drop to the surface of the parking lot like two sacks of trash. Picking up the keys to the truck that had fallen out of Tony's hands, he opened the door and easily picked up both guys, tossing them into the cab as if they were mere feathers. Pushing down the lock on the door he slammed it shut, tossed the keys over the wire fence into the junkyard next door and ambled quietly back to his car. Quentin glanced around and didn't see anybody who might've taken notice of what happened. However, he didn't see Betty Ann staring out the rear window of the diner, her mouth gaping open and shaking her head in disbelief.

Pulling out onto Umbria Street he headed home. Even though he felt exhilarated once again, he was also quite tired. He needed to retire to his 'dark cave' as the sweet Sharon had described the apartment. Maybe she would be nice enough to spread her legs and if not, well then he'd just take whatever he desired anyway.

Chapter 15

Kathy maneuvered the car off Ridge Avenue, traffic slowing down due to extremely curious early-morning drivers, and came to a stop when a uniformed officer motioned her to pull into a housing development on the left. He walked over to her and Johnny as they exited her vehicle.

"Sorry Detective Morello there is just so many cars parked along the road that we need to keep a lane open for the ambulance," he said warily, as if this sweet, attractive detective would bite his head off.

"Hey McMurphy, that's no problem. I won't hold it against you this time," Kathy said smiling. "How's your wife feeling by the way?"

Looking at her with the pained expression of somebody who's loved one is fighting serious medical problems, he smiled at her.

"She's doing okay Kathy. Thanks for asking. It's not easy, but she's a real soldier in this, a heckuva' lot stronger than I am, believe me. We're taking each day one by one and have decided that it's all in the hands of the Lord. We're just appreciating every second we have together," he told her, trying to be strong, but not doing a good job of it. His wife Rosemary had been diagnosed with advanced abdominal cancer six months previously. Kathy knew what he was going through because her father's sister had died many years ago from a massive cancerous tumor in the abdomen.

She hugged him. "Frank, give her my love and if you need anything all you have to do is ask me."

"Thanks a lot," he said, definitely a catch in his voice.

"So, what the heck is going on here and where is Captain Ganz?"

"He's down about half a mile. They have a dead, extremely mutilated body of a young woman on the golf course. I haven't seen her Morello, but from what I understand it's pretty damn ugly," McMurphy said, taking in the presence of the very tall, imposing stranger that had gotten out of the car with Kathy.

"Thanks Frank, we'll walk on down and see if we can help out."

Kathy and Johnny started ambling down Manor Road, both very quiet and reflective. There were times when speaking aloud just wasn't the thing to do. As they walked, Johnny let his nostrils open up completely to a myriad of scents lying on the chilly morning air. He could already smell blood and easily detect a dead body. There was also the very distinct, but past, presence of a wolfish creature. Whether he was allowed to help or not, his need to follow whatever spore he detected was paramount to him tracking this murderous animal down.

A few officers standing around told Morello to move onto the golf course at a certain point since it was harder to reach the further you got down the road. So the very strange couple moved onto the grass and started walking to where they could see the glow of bouncing flashlights. As Johnny moved with the intense purpose of a tracker who was intent on not missing anything, he paused and knelt to closely examine the ground.

Kathy stooped down as well. "What's up Daniel Boone?"

"He came past here for sure," Johnny said, swiveling and looking behind him, then at her. "What name did you call me?"

"Never mind, it doesn't matter. So we're definitely dealing with a man and not a creature?" she asked.

Johnny stood and they started walking towards where the body was still lying on the green. "You're dealing with a male, but not a man, at least not at this point."

"Oh right, I remember, X-files," she said, her voice almost a whisper.

He smiled at her. "Detective Morello, I think there was at least one episode where Fox and Maulder became involved in a case that dealt with a werewolf. They did a good job as some movies have done, especially "The Howling". I actually liked that movie. But I'm hoping you begin to get serious about the possibility. I hope you also let me have some freedom here in order to track this beast."

She stopped and turned. "I am serious Mr. Raven. My motor only runs at one speed and you'd best believe I won't discount anything, even fairy tales," she said, moving along then towards where she saw Nathan Ganz standing with arms folded around his massive bulk.

Johnny watched her cute behind strut towards the large man standing just off the green. He had to admit that she was attractive and he definitely loved her spunk.

"Hey Captain," Kathy said, walking up to stop beside him.

"Thanks for coming Morello. They're just about ready to put her into the ambulance. Want to take a look?" he asked, turning and noticing Johnny standing about ten feet behind them.

"No, not really, but I think I have to," she said, moving forward. Johnny began walking along behind them.

"Who's the guy with you Kathy? This is a police investigation."

"I'll fill you in later Nathan, but for now I think he might be a valuable asset on this case. Seems he's a tracker of some kind and I think we're going to need his services," she replied.

They stopped at the covered body and Kathy knelt, pulling back the sheet. There was an obvious intake of breath and she closed her eyes.

"You okay?" Captain Ganz asked her.

"Yeah, I'll be fine. It's always that first look, you know? Does it ever get any easier Nathan?"

"Never for me and I hope it never does for you either. It's what makes you such a good detective," he replied, giving her a rare compliment.

Johnny had moved up to where he stood to the left of Kathy and could get a full view of the body. His anger surged and he had to suppress the wild rage that came from within. Visions of Samantha crashed through his mind. He had to find this murderous beast and slay it, whether it was his wife's killer or not. This killing spree had gone on way too long now.

"May I get a closer look?" he asked her.

Kathy looked up. "What, this isn't close enough for you Mr. Raven? It's obvious from her wounds why she died."

He knelt down and looked at her. "I can detect things you can't. Besides I need a few moments to get its scent and then I'll be off."

She stood up muttering to herself, "Then by all means Mr. Raven, do your thing."

Johnny lightly touched the ground around Mary Beth Mizerk with his fingertips, nostrils flaring. Then he moved and gracefully slid beyond the body where he knelt again, placing his entire palm onto the ground.

"He went this way Detective Morello," Johnny said, now standing. "I have to follow this trail and I'm best at doing it alone," and then he was off.

"Hey, wait a minute Raven, you're not going to be a lone wolf on this. I'm coming along," Kathy yelled, following him quickly.

"What the hell is going on here?" asked Ganz, lumbering after them himself, but unable to follow the two figures in front of him. He realized he was too damn old for this shit and it most definitely was time for him to retire. That is if he lived through this case.

Johnny stopped suddenly, turned and looked towards Manor Road as Kathy caught up with him. "Slow down a little bit," she said, out of breath.

"I can't slow down detective. We need to move and believe me when I say you can't keep up with me," he said under his breath. "It went over there to the east, across the road and in the woods at that point," and he pointed.

Then Johnny kicked off his shoes and started loping with the grace of an animal towards Manor Road. Kathy stared down at his abandoned shoes and then at his disappearing back. She picked up the shoes and started running after him as fast as she could.

"Hey Raven, wait up, not so fast damn it," she yelled, her voice and breasts shaking up and down as she ran across the uneven ground.

By the time she had gotten to the road he had already disappeared into the woods. Officer McMurphy was standing there, shocked at what he had just seen happen.

"Hey Morello, who the hell is that and where is he going?" he asked.

"Following the tracks of who killed that woman. Give me that radio on your belt and take these shoes and my car keys. Get hold of another hand set and I'll keep you posted," she said, also disappearing into the woods where Raven had entered.

It was a flat out joke. She was a fish out of water in the thick growth of bushes and weeds around her. Yet this stranger had moved as if he were at home in this rough terrain. She struggled mightily through the brush, snagging her jacket numerous times, as well as her right hand on sticker bushes. Then she broke through the dense thicket and came to an expansive area that was just trees and where she could move a little easier.

"Hey Raven, where the hell did you go? God damn it, let me know where you are," she hollered, panting and looking at her right hand which had started to bleed.

Johnny was a good hundred yards ahead of her, crouched and letting his piercing eyes follow the footprints of his prey. It was still a werewolf up to this point and was not concerned in the least of hiding his trail. So it was easy to follow. Johnny wondered if it was too easy so he was completely wary in case the creature in either form was still around. He could also hear the struggling lady detective behind him and he smiled. Serves her right he thought so he decided to let her struggle.

Coming through the trees at the top of a rise he paused, staring down at an open field and a sequence of long buildings, one very old and the other new, like a barracks or a dorm of some kind. He studied the ground around him and noticed a few clumps of dark hair that hugged a sticker bush. He held it to his nose and realized he had smelled this scent before. His turbulent rage began to surge.

At that point a huffing, wheezing, gasping, out of breath Kathy Morello staggered up beside him and dropped to her knees onto the ground.

"Thanks for waiting you bastard. I'll get even for this," she gasped.

He grinned at her. "It seems that you're quite out of shape detective. Maybe you need to join a fitness club and hire a trainer."

"I repeat Mr. Raven, I will definitely get even with you for this. Now, what the hell's going on," she panted.

"He came this way and down through those buildings. I'm sure there are people in that long building so they're lucky this creature kept on going. I have to go," he said, abruptly standing and then moving down the hill.

Kathy jumped up and started running after him, almost falling forward on her face. "Hey, which way are you going?"

"Just follow and try to keep up. And if I were you I'd also keep my mouth shut," he said, as he moved down the hill in the loping long distance run of a wolf.

Kathy was seething inside, but she needed this grade A jerk so she just kept pursuing him. The police would've never been able to follow this trail, nor even be remotely aware that it was there. Finally, she came to level ground and crunched across some gravel and then a parking lot. Raven had already disappeared around the building and she cursed him under her breath.

She found him at the edge of the woods along Spring Mill Road which faced Hagys Mill. He was sitting back and balanced against a fire hydrant, like he was meant to do just that. Watching her stagger up to him he rose and let her sit a top the chilly hydrant.

She stared at him, her eyes bulging out, chest heaving. "Okay, now what? Which way did he go?" she asked.

"Up through that yard right there and into those woods behind the house. What is that area anyway?" he asked her.

"It's the Schuylkill Valley Center, a very large tract of land that was donated a number of years back as a wildlife conservation area," she replied.

"Okay, let's go," he said, on the move once again like a phantom.

Thinking she was going to die, she lifted her exhausted body and began following him up into the yard. At that point a man opened his front door and came out onto the small porch.

"Hey, what the hell is going on? Who are you people?" he yelled at them.

She held up her shield. "This is police business, so just kindly get back inside your house right now," as she saw the head of a large dog poke out behind him. "And do not let that dog outside whatever you do."

As she followed him, she toggled the radio and spoke, "McMurphy, you there? This is Detective Morello, over."

Loud static and then his voice, "I'm here detective, where are you … over?"

"Inform Captain Ganz I'm on the south side of Hagys Mill Road. Bring my car over here and just wait. Also, tell him to close the road in both directions as quickly as possible. Over."

"You got it Detective Morello. Hey, you sound like shit … over," he shot back as a parting remark.

"I feel like shit McMurphy. Just do what I asked you and no comments."

After moving through the bush and some open fields with long, tall grass she saw him standing and then kneeling. Joining him she knelt also, nearly falling over from exhaustion.

"What have you found now?" she wheezed loudly.

"He stopped here and changed. I smelled his scent over there against the tree. That's where he left his belongings, probably the car keys and maybe some clothing."

"You're serious aren't you? You're actually expecting me to believe that he altered his form from some animal to a man, changed clothes and then walked away like nothing had happened," she said in a disbelieving voice.

"I told you earlier detective, believe what you want to believe. If you want to find him then you'll just absorb what I tell you. I'm sure eventually you'll get lab results that will tell you that you're absolutely dealing with a wolf, but it's not like any wolf you've ever heard of or read about in school," he told her.

She stared into those piercing, predatory eyes and saw that damn golden glint again. Somehow she did believe him, everything he was saying. This case was too wild not to.

"How do you do that?" she asked.

"Do what?"

"Make your eyes shine yellow for a second or two, then change back to normal."

"What is normal detective? Are you prepared to think about what is not normal?" he asked her.

"Right about now Mr. Raven I'm ready to think that anything might be possible," she answered.

"Very cool and remember the name is Johnny, okay?"

He got up and began moving again. Moaning she rose and started following him. At least he was going slower this time. He stopped at the edge of the brush along Hagys Mill Road and moved slowly, alertly, onto the road and then paced into the entrance of a housing development. Stopping at the corner he knelt, touched the ground, looked to his right and moved with great stealth down to a spot on the street where he finally stopped. Kathy was not too far behind him since he was moving slower.

"Now what?" she asked.

"His car was parked here. He came out of the woods as a man, walked to his car, got in and drove off. End of the line," he said dejectedly.

"You can't track him now?" she inquired.

"Nope, he's left the surface of the ground. I'm sure that he probably turned around in a driveway, early enough that most people would still be asleep. He went out to that road we just crossed and then who knows which way he turned. I'll have to wait until tonight when he's back out again."

"You're sure he'll be on the loose tonight and not hiding or moving on?" she asked him.

"Pretty sure since the moon is still ruling him and he has no choice but to obey," Johnny said in a very haunting voice.

"Ah, right, the full moon," Kathy answered.

"No, not a full moon, a new moon," he told her.

At that point McMurphy pulled up in her car, followed by Ganz in his Rav-4.

"I could use a strong cup of coffee," Johnny said.

"And I could use something stronger than that. Let's fill in Captain Ganz and then I'll buy you that cup of coffee. It's the least I could do for you after trying to kill me as well" she told him, turning and walking back to where Nathan exited his vehicle, obviously extremely distressed and upset.

Johnny watched her move gracefully towards her supervisor, admiring the way she had kept up with him. A little bitching, but that was to be expected. He liked her never quit attitude and he didn't know many men that would've kept up with him like she did. He kidded her on being out of shape, but knew that wasn't the case. She definitely worked out and could tell that underneath the heavy jacket she had on was a well put together body. His beast rose like it hadn't in quite some time and he was unprepared for that.

"I'm sorry Samantha," he whispered. "I love you, but it's been so long. I will always love you."

Chapter 16

As he held the door open for her like any gentleman would, she walked into Friendly's where they were seated at a table as far back as they could get. Kathy explained to the waitress they needed to talk with some degree of privacy. She showed the young girl her detective shield and with a certain degree of nervous anticipation seated them quickly. Kathy ordered coffee, orange juice and a bagel while Johnny stared at her rather curiously.

"You should eat more than that detective. This could be a very long day and you never know when you'll get a chance to eat anything substantial again," he told her.

"That's quite okay. After seeing that poor young woman's body and then running all over field and dale after you, I don't have much of an appetite right now. If I get hungry later I'll grab a few dogs," she stated.

"Dogs, you eat dogs?" he asked her.

She started to laugh and couldn't stop. It was just really funny the way he so innocently said it, but at least his remark actually started to relieve some of the tension built up inside her over these last few difficult days and nights. So Johnny just sat there amused at her amusement over his comment.

"I meant hot dogs Mr. Raven. You know, those long tubes of shiny skin filled with stuff we never want to know about. On a roll with lots of ketchup, mustard, onions and relish, possibly even chili. I live on them," she said, her cheeks red from laughing so hard, wiping a tear from the corner of her eye.

"Don't believe I ever ate one," he replied.

"Well now, that is a shock, somebody who happens to be living in this modern era not ever having eaten a good old American hot dog. Sometime later today maybe I'll treat you to your first one. You're in for a big treat," she said.

After wiping her eyes free of tears that had fallen from her giggling outburst, she became serious once more, ever the professional, unless she was talking to Rain and then she sounded like she was talking to a baby. Well, Rain was her baby after all "Now Johnny, continue on with your story from before. What the hell are we dealing with here and no bull shit either. I'm ready to believe almost anything right about now. At least, almost anything," she told him.

He took a few sips of coffee, keeping his eyes centered upon the beauty of her face. His feelings were completely screwed up now. He had just met her today, but already there was something magical about this woman which was simply overpowering, causing his senses to seem like they were short circuiting. Realizing that it was his male, animalistic desire surging up to titillate the ends of his nerves once again after so many years, he tried his best to suppress it. You're an idiot he scolded himself for letting your silly male sexual desires sidetrack you from the important task at hand which was finding a killer, a monster, maybe Samantha's murderer, and hopefully saving some innocent lives as well.

Putting down the coffee cup, he looked deeply into her eyes, feeling that she had the depth of understanding to at least conceptualize what he had to tell her and if not, then he would avoid the most obvious, which she would probably not believe at all.

"How often in your lifetime have you said to yourself that something is just too unbelievable or too ridiculous to ever believe? That your very analytical, police-oriented mind ruled out because something just didn't quite fit into the quote "profile" of your case," he asked her seriously.

She had a few seconds to think about that as the nervous, young waitress brought their breakfast and asked if they needed anything else. Kathy thought about telling her to just leave and give them some privacy, but she only smiled and politely said no thank you. There was really no reason to be rude just because she herself was extremely nervous about this case, as well as possessing a strong physical attraction to the man who sat directly across from her hungrily shoveling pieces of almost raw bacon into his mouth. She sipped some orange juice and couldn't slide her gaze from his eyes, waiting once more to see that brief glitter of gold she had glimpsed before. It didn't materialize though, maybe because it needed something bright to shine on them, like a cats when headlights struck their eyes in the darkness. But as ruggedly handsome as this man was, there was also an obvious aura of danger about him. This was most definitely not a person to tangle with and she felt it would be better to have him on her side rather than against her. Though it was pretty evident that what, or who, they were after was extremely dangerous and deadly as well.

"Sure, there have been a few times in my career where I've hit an impasse on a case and had trouble following clues because they led me down a path I had difficultly in believing. There were also numerous occasions when I went on gut instinct and, of course, being the only woman in the department I was accused of using good old female intuition. It's just the typical male stereotyping that most women receive in a male dominated job. But this is different, this is real. I've looked on in horror at the bodies. I've seen the tracks and I've spoken to officers that heard the terrible howls on Saturday night along the river. I realize we're possibly dealing with some type of animal, or in my personal opinion, a supremely strong and demented individual who thinks he's an animal, i.e. a wolf or whatever," she commented. "But I just have a difficult time in believing this wolf man theory of yours, I'm sorry."

"No need to apologize Detective Morello, I know it sounds crazy, just a little absurd. Just like you had said earlier, werewolves and vampires, Lon Chaney and Bela Lugosi, pretty hard stuff to fathom. I'd probably think I was weird as well, certifiable in fact," he chuckled in that deep, resonating voice of his.

She smiled, "Yeah, after that trek through the wilderness I think you just might be certifiable, and me as well for following you," holding up her hand to show a few ugly scratches from all the thorn bushes she had encountered.

"And please, while we're sitting here chatting over coffee, just call me Kathy. On the street I'm Detective Morello, okay?"

He nodded in agreement while he shoveled a large hunk of sausage dripping with runny egg into his mouth. She almost said something and decided not to. Obviously from the appearance of his body underneath the clothing he didn't have a cholesterol problem to deal with. In fact, no matter what his diet was, he looked exceedingly healthy.

"Can I ask you something Johnny?"

"Sure, anything, and hopefully I can answer it truthfully," he replied.

She hesitated slightly. "How do you know so much about this killer? And are you so positive that this is the same man, or whatever, that murdered your wife and son?"

Finishing up his coffee, he placed the cup on the table and sat back. He studied her for a few brief moments, wondering just how much to tell her, deciding to be somewhat evasive at this point and see what she could, or would, absorb.

"I've followed leads much as the ones that brought me here almost a dozen times over the last two years. But he moves quickly, never staying in one spot long enough. Most often, when I'm able to hear of an incident, the current phase of the moon is nearing an end. It takes me awhile to get to some cities and of course I'm following his trail after the fact. He's extremely vicious and deadly as your city and police force have come to find out. This is also a very shrewd and intelligent individual I've been tracking and who most likely is aware that he's being trailed. He doesn't care much about leaving clues because he knows your normal type of police investigation will not locate him. By the time you get lab and forensic results he's usually long gone and then the killing stops."

"And why do you think it's the same person?" she asked him.

"I don't for sure. However I know his scent was left around the body of my wife, but he wasn't alone. He is the only one though I've been able to follow. The others, possibly up to ten or more, are very smart and evasive. I think their purpose was singular in leaving a message for me. The one I've been following, the one here in your city, I hope to finally track down in order to find out the answers I need concerning just who the others might be, as well as what happened that night in particular. Trust me, he will tell me when I find him."

She studied his face while he talked. Clearly there was extreme anger when he spoke of the killer and definitely deep anguish after all this time when he referred to his wife and her death. How much she could get out of him most likely would depend on how tactful she was and not be so forceful that she would push him away.

"What was your wife's name, if you don't mind my asking?"

"Samantha. We had only met the year before at the spring gathering of our family. I guess you would call it a reunion. It was instant attraction and we became mates shortly thereafter," he said quietly.

"You became mates? What the heck does that mean?" she asked him.

He grinned with both his eyes and mouth. The few times Kathy had seen him smile she thought it was actually very engaging and was just a bit jealous that his Samantha must have seen it so often before she was slain.

"Sorry, you would refer to it as being married. It's a clan thing I suppose. My people are very much tied to nature, the seasons, wildlife, the call of the wild," he chuckled, realizing he had to be somewhat careful in what he said.

The waitress came up then and asked if they wanted any more coffee. Johnny said yes and watched her swish away in her cute little pink outfit. You can take the man out of the wolf, but not the wolf out of the man Kathy thought as she watched his eyes follow the young girl's path.

"Your unborn son was killed also," she commented.

His eyes became dark and cloudy almost instantly at her question. He stared at her and it sent a cold shiver up and down her spine.

"Why so many personal questions detective, thought we were going to talk about who we're trying to find?" he asked her in almost a growl.

"Sorry, it seems I keep apologizing to you. I suppose it's my curious nature and belief in that I feel many times you catch a criminal by realizing the attachment that person has to others around them. You brought the death of your son up earlier if you remember," she told him.

"Our child was torn from her womb, most likely while Samantha was still alive. Is that what you wanted to hear detective?" he said bitterly.

Tossing the napkin on the table, he got up and stalked out of the restaurant leaving Kathy stunned, watching him angrily push through the door. Well, that certainly struck a sensitive chord she thought. Taking the tab to the cash register, she paid for breakfast and then joined him outside where he was leaning up against her car, arms folded, eyes hooded like those of a hawk.

"Okay Johnny, no more questions of a personal nature, at least not for right now. I didn't mean any harm by the questions, just need to get to know you a little better if I'm going to rely on what knowledge you possess, your unusual abilities, as well as depend on you if push comes to shove," she said, trying to make amends.

"Push comes to shove? Detective Morello, you folks from Philly talk awfully funny," he replied.

She smiled and nodded. "I guess we do Mr. Raven."

At that moment her cell phone rang and she flicked it on.

"Hello, Morello here, whatcha' got?"

"Detective, it's Steve Johnson from the lab. I have some answers for you on those prints taken along the river Sunday night, as well as the fur you dropped off to me."

She felt a sense of anticipation. "Go ahead Steve?"

There was a slight pause. "You want to come in here or tell you now?" he asked.

"Tell me now Steve, I have no idea when I'll be getting time to come in there, probably not till later in the day," she said.

"Okay! Well it's most definitely an animal. At first glance the prints are evidently the paw marks of a large dog, but Morello there's no dog that I know of which is that big. In doing some on-line research they are definitely from a wolf, as is the fur you dropped off, as crazy as that sounds," Johnson said in a rather unsettled voice.

Kathy looked up at Raven who stared back at her, his eyes raised.

"Thanks Steve, good job," she replied, just about to break contact.

"Oh, hey, almost forgot. Doc Starling said to tell you to definitely call him or stop by the morgue. He has some pretty surprising stuff as well. Talk to you later detective," he said, hanging up himself.

Kathy flipped the phone shut and reached for the front door of her car.

"So who was that? What's up," Johnny asked her.

"Get in the car Mr. Raven, we have to move," she said quickly.

As she screeched out onto Ridge Avenue heading back into town she wondered how much she needed to tell him. It also distressed her to know that it appeared he could be right. They sat in silence for about a minute until she stopped for a light and then glanced over at his stoic demeanor. It was a look of I told you so.

"It seems that the prints found along the river and the piece of fur I took from a bush near where Mr. Shirreck was killed happens to be those of a wolf," she told him.

Johnny looked at her for just a moment and nodded somewhat smugly. He decided not to say a word though.

"However, I won't rule out the possibility this could be a hybrid-wolf who is under the control of a seriously demented individual," she informed him.

He just nodded again, which infuriated her to no end. She couldn't stand pompous assholes, especially when she knew she might be wrong and just refused to admit it.

"That's always a possibility detective," he said, just as Kathy's cell phone rang again.

"Kathy, this is Nathan, where are you right now?"

"Coming down the Ridge past Andorra. What's up?" she asked.

"We just got called a short time ago from a waitress at the diner down on Umbria and Domino. Seems there was an altercation with a customer inside the diner and then one in the parking lot as well with the same guy. Check it out. Did you talk to Doc Starling at the morgue yet?" he asked her.

"No, but I spoke to Johnson in the lab. Seems the prints and the fur I dropped off were from an animal, specifically a wolf," she said, waiting for his response.

"Yeah, we'll see. Guess I should contact the zoo and animal control after all. Call me after you talk to that waitress," and the phone went dead.

Coincidentally, Kathy was coming up to the light at Domino so she made a hard right and sped down the hill. Johnny grabbed hold of the dashboard and she laughed at his obvious discomfort. Kathy thought there was at last a small chink in his armor.

"Don't worry, I'm an excellent driver," only slowing down at the stop sign on Umbria and taking the left hand turn hard so that Johnny placed his right hand at the top of the door before she screeched to a stop in front of the diner parking lot.

Jumping out of the car she walked briskly to the diner, leaped up the steps and through the front door. Johnny followed her closely like a little puppy with his tail wagging and tongue hanging out. The diner was actually pretty crowded at this hour of the morning and several waitresses were scurrying around taking orders, pouring coffee and banging breakfast plates onto tables.

"Can I help you?" asked an older gentleman at the cash register.

"One of your waitresses called the police a little while ago about a certain problem you had earlier with a customer," Kathy stated.

"Hey Betty Ann, the police are here. That was fast you know, she just called about fifteen minutes ago," the old guy said.

"Fifteen minutes, really? We're slipping then, should've had somebody here before this. I'll have to file a complaint," she shot back with a quick wink.

Betty Ann finished placing the coffee pot she had been carrying behind the counter on the burner and then strutted over to where they stood.

"Took you long enough," she accused them.

Kathy looked at the guy behind the cash register and smiled, raising her eyebrows with an amused look.

"Can't please everybody all the time I suppose," he said, smiling and winking back at her. She loved to banter with older men.

"So Betty Ann, you called the police. Tell us about this altercation you reported."

Betty Ann took them aside and replayed what had happened with the strange customer, both with the two cops and then the two burly delivery guys that came later.

"And, the really crazy thing is this," Betty emphasized. "I just happened to be glancing out that rear window there and saw the weirdo who said his name was Tom, though something tells me that he was not telling the truth, walk over to Tony and Rocco."

She then informed them of how he literally beat the two of them silly, picked them up like they were stuffed animals and threw them into the cab of the truck. Then he tossed the keys over the fence into the junkyard.

"You mean that white panel truck over there?" Kathy asked her.

"Yep, that's the one and as far as I know, they're still in there too. I was too damn frightened to go outside and check on them in case the guy came back. So the owner, Harry who is standing over there, told me to just call the police and let you guys handle it. Now you're here so get to work and see if they're okay," Betty Ann ordered them, about as well as any sergeant could.

"Thanks Betty Ann, you did a marvelous service," Kathy said, turning and noting that Johnny had already left the diner and saw him through the windows heading towards the truck.

She ran out and tried to catch up. He had already jumped onto the step of the cab on the driver's side and was staring inside.

"They're in there Kathy and by the looks of them, they're completely unconscious. I can see some blood on one of their foreheads, but I can't see the front of the other guy's face."

"We'll have to break the window then in order to unlock the door since we don't have the keys so step aside," Kathy instructed him, reaching out for a short pole that was leaning up against the cyclone fence.

When she turned around to face the truck however, Johnny had already opened the door and was leaning inside to check on their condition.

"I thought the door was locked. How the hell did you do that?" she inquired curiously.

"The guy must've not locked it after all because it came open quite easily. I'd call an ambulance though detective. They're both out cold and quite frankly, neither man looks to be in very good shape."

Kathy ran back to her car and radioed dispatch. Then she walked over to where Betty Ann and Harry stood together on the steps looking on.

"How are they?" Betty asked her.

"They're alive I think and hopefully they'll be okay. Can you give me a description of the guy who did this and did anybody get a look at what kind of car he was driving?"

Betty Ann gave her a fairly good physical description of his appearance. She thought the car was a Ford Focus, dark blue, possibly 2003 with what appeared to be some damage to the right rear fender. She apologized for being terrible on knowing the exact make and model of the car since she had been driving the same old 1980 Chevy Impala for over 25 years now and didn't have enough money to buy anything new.

At that point Harry walked back out the front door and handed her a slip of paper which contained the last three digits of the license plate.

"Sorry detective, I couldn't get all of the number on the plate. The guy just peeled out of here like he was going to hell in a hand basket. But I was at least able to get those three numbers there. My eyes just aren't what they used to be, you know?" Harry said sheepishly.

"Harry, this is really great, thanks a lot. We'll be able to locate him with this I'm sure. Thank you to both of you," Kathy said, looking back then as the ambulance pulled into the parking lot to take care of the still unconscious delivery guys.

Kathy then dialed Captain Ganz and filled him in on what was happening.

"I actually think we might've gotten a break Cap. Didn't one of the people in that development off Hagys Mill give a statement that there was some kind of dark blue car parked in front of their house most of the night and that they saw a tall, strange looking guy get in and drive off early this morning before it got light out?"

"Yes, they did. Okay, I'll have BMV run this partial plate and we'll see where it leads. In the meantime Kathy, take a ride over and talk to the M.E., then meet me back in the precinct where we can sort through this mess. I shutter to think we might have another night like the last two."

"You got it Nathan and let me know if BMV comes up with anything," but she was suddenly talking to a dial tone. Nathan had already hung up. He had a really bad habit of doing that and she'd have to say something eventually.

She and Johnny got into her car and then pulled onto Umbria Street heading towards the Expressway and their drive into Center City.

"Do you think it's him, the same guy that's been doing the killing?" she asked.

"There's a very strong possibility. If he did stop there to have something to eat then he would still be feeling the effects of the night and most likely would be very confrontational. So perhaps he did make a mistake after all, or then it just might be some asshole who like Betty Ann said, had a tough night at work and was not in a very good mood," Johnny replied, hoping though it was the first choice and that this beast had finally made a mistake which would take him closer to confronting Samantha's killer.

Chapter 17

The frightened doe crashed through the trees and dense thicket, picking up speed as she entered the moonlit clearing. Eyes wide and nostrils fluttering madly from exhaustion, she continued to run towards the far, welcoming tree line at the opposite end of the field. Fear of dying was the only thing that continued to propel her onward. Following closely upon the hooves of this frantic deer was the snarling, ever-present whisper of death. She was accustomed to the daily gambit between predator and prey, but the hot, fetid breath she felt blistering her fleeing back legs merged with the pungent, musky odor being released from erupting metatarsal glands. The scent was overpowering to the beast as it was merely playing with her. She was fully aware that death was but a few precious heartbeats away.

The creature was now even with her left flank, spittle from its fangs searing the doe's skin. It reached out with scimitar-like talons, raking the deer's hide and causing the panicked animal to bleat in pain and fear. She swerved quickly to the right, attempting to outmaneuver it and for a split second she did. That was all though as the beast pivoted as well and reached out with blinding speed. The frightened animal went down and before it could even think about rising to run again was completely engulfed by terror.

The first thing to be torn open was the throat as the doe's large, vacant black eyes stared up at the moon. The stomach was second to be ripped apart, unveiling a host of succulent morsels.

With blood dripping from claws and fangs this wolf creature lifted a massive head to bite harshly at a commanding moon. It sang out for victory and the thrill of the hunt. It howled to power possessed when running free as the beast. Cries of anguish consorted with empty winds amid humanity lost. The creature then plunged its gaping muzzle into the steaming hot inner sanctum of the fallen deer, partaking from the spoils of war.

Like an actor upon the stage of a tragic play underneath moonlight's glare the monstrous wolf raised and turned its head to glare ....

She sat up screaming! Nurses and doctors from the emergency room all raced to her assistance. The nightmarish vision of the wolf as it slowly turned to face her in the moonlight was just too much to comprehend. The face of the creature had been her own upon the body of that ghastly, wolfish figure, covered in blood from the deer's insides.

The first nurse in the room tried to hold Colleen Frye down and was savagely thrown to the floor. A large male attendant knocked the sliding table out of the way and put his massive hands upon her shoulders, trying to hold the screaming woman down. The wound on her left shoulder began to bleed freely again, saturating the bandages. Doctor Hastings, the emergency room physician, had finally gotten the initial bleeding stopped, not only from the shoulder but from other severe scratches and lacerations as well. They were just waiting to transport her to surgery in order to completely close the wound.

"Miss Frye, settle down. Please, you're okay, you're safe," spoke Dr. Hastings in as soothing a tone as he could muster. "I'm going to give you this sedative to calm you down."

"No, please no, don't want to sleep again. Please, don't put me to sleep," she implored, staring up at him with haunted eyes.

"We have to get you settled down so we can work on that shoulder. You came to and had a flashback at what happened. Believe me, you're safe and you'll be okay. Now, this is going to sting just a little bit."

Colleen winced for a split second and glared at him. She did not want to go back to sleep and see that monster ever again. But quickly she felt very relaxed and fought desperately to keep her eyes open. No sleep she kept saying to herself, over and over again, do not fall asleep.

In the hallway Tommy Darnello, Kathy's partner, stood in the doorway to Colleen's room. He had just entered through the ER lobby when the screaming started. Holding up his detective shield he ordered the guard at the front desk to let him in which he did. He couldn't be sure the screaming came from Colleen Frye, but something in the back of his mind said it had to be. Any woman, for that matter any individual who had survived such a vicious assault, would most likely have been screaming as well.

He stopped the doctor as he walked by. "How is she doing?" Tommy asked.

"She'll sleep again, at least until we get her to surgery and close that shoulder wound. Funny thing though, the bleeding started again when the attendant held her down and it just as quickly stopped on its own, very weird."

"So she's going to be okay then?" the detective inquired.

"She's young and strong. And besides the shoulder wound, most of the other lacerations will heal easily enough. I must admit that is one serious set of slash marks down her breast and stomach. I've never seen anything quite like it actually. We've had more than our share of animal bites and scratches, but never anything to this magnitude. What kind of sadistic monster could do something like that detective?" Dr. Hastings asked in a voice that was both troubled and confused.

"We don't know who or exactly what we're dealing with yet doctor. But we'll find him, believe me, we'll find him and hopefully sooner than later," Tommy said, staring at the sleeping young woman.

The doctor left to see other patients and Tommy moved into the room to where Colleen Frye lay completely at ease, her beautiful face at least relaxed for the moment. Tommy could only imagine what she had went through and his anger seethed inside him. He wondered what terrors she must be dreaming of right at that moment and could not keep his concerned eyes off her pretty face.

Just then an extremely distressed young woman with long, brunette hair burst into the room. She was followed closely by a tall, bearded, distinguished looking gentlemen attired in a dark, charcoal gray, pin-striped suit. Tommy stood up right away.

"Oh my God, Colleen what happened?" the young woman cried, her voice shaking and almost a whisper.

Tommy extended an arm and stopped her from reaching the bed.

"Excuse me ma'am, who are you and how are you related to Miss Frye?" he inquired, feeling that he knew already the answer.

"My name is Sara, Sara Graynor. Colleen and I work together. She's also my closest friend," Sara said, wiping tears from her eyes. "Who are you?"

"I'm Detective Darnello. She's sleeping at the moment so try not to wake her," he said, turning to the tall guy behind Sara.

"And you sir, your name is?" Tommy asked.

He produced a card and handed it over. "Jonathan Price III, senior partner at Price, Zimmerman, Kearney and Hart. What can you tell me happened to Colleen detective? Is she going to be okay?"

Sara had moved towards the bed and stared down at the beautiful blonde, gently holding one of Colleen's hands while trying her best to staunch the flow of her own tears.

"She's been through a tough time, but the doctors feel she'll recover completely.

Seems she has an extremely nasty wound to her shoulder and a number of scratches and lacerations, but she should come through it okay," Tommy answered him.

"Who did this? Do you know?" the attorney inquired, trying to keep his voice low yet forceful in that annoying way some pompous lawyers often had.

"Not yet, but we will. Evidently she was entertaining a man so I'm sure that forensics will find quite a bit of evidence so we can find him quickly. That's about all I'm at liberty to tell you at the moment. What was Miss Frye's relationship with your firm?"

"Colleen has been at the firm for three years as one of our finest, most energetic, up and coming attorneys. Miss Graynor is a lawyer there as well. When Colleen didn't appear at the offices early this morning for a meeting we obviously got extremely concerned, she is never late for anything, extremely diligent and hard working. We called both her home and cell phone, but had to leave messages so we sent one of our junior lawyers to her house. That's when he was stopped by a police officer at the end of the street and was prohibited from seeing what had happened to her. He called the office immediately and I was then able to make some quick phone calls in order to find out what had happened to her. As soon as we realized she was being transported here we came right away," Mr. Price said, almost without stopping to take a breath.

"Well sir, I'm sure you are completely aware that was done to protect Miss Frye and the crime scene. Besides, the gentleman you sent was not a relative and could not prove otherwise," Tommy shot back. He couldn't stand empirical sounding lawyers like Jonathan Price, thinking their shit didn't stink. Tommy knew otherwise.

Just at that moment Colleen opened her eyes slowly and smiled at the sight of Sara hovering over her bed.

She simply whispered, "Hi honey."

For some reason Tommy sensed Jonathan Price III had become noticeably tense.

Sara leaned down and gently pushed aside a lock of blonde hair from Colleen's forehead, then leaned down further and kissed the young woman on the lips. Sara's tears dropped upon Colleen's cheek and she lovingly wiped them clean.

"What happened? How are you feeling? I was so worried, I thought I lost you," Sara said between sobs.

Colleen pressed Sara's hand tighter and smiled.

"I'm okay, I'll be fine. To be honest I don't remember much," she said slowly.

"Excuse me Miss Graynor, but I'm going to have to talk to Miss Frye for a few moments before she goes to surgery," Tommy stated firmly, glancing at Jonathan Price as well. "Alone!"

"Come along Sara, let the detective do his job," Mr. Price said, looking at Colleen and smiling. "It's good to have you back with us dear. We'll be right outside if you need us for anything."

After they departed, Colleen looked up at Tommy. "Who are you?" she asked.

"I'm Detective Darnello, homicide. I was one of the detectives that came to your house. Can you answer some questions Miss Frye? I'll only be a few minutes, but if you don't feel you're up to it then I can come back later. The sooner the better though so we can find who did this to you."

"I guess I feel okay other than being a little tired right now. I'm not sure I remember very much, what would you like to know?"

"Are you in any pain at all right now? I could find a nurse if you are before we start," concern clearly in Tommy's voice.

"I'm fine surprisingly, other than just being sore you know? Like I was hit by a Mack truck," she giggled slightly. "I always say that when I'm sick with the flu or something. Now I can honestly say that I do."

Tommy smiled, he liked this lady. Not only was she extremely attractive, he could tell she was very personable and intelligent as well. Something in the back of his mind however told him she might not be interested in him, or any man for that matter.

"So, can you tell me who this person was? He was in the house so you obviously knew him," Tommy inquired.

She looked at him, like she was really attempting very hard to remember, but having difficulty.

"I had just met him earlier in the day, I think in the morning sometime. God, let's see, I went for a walk in the morning with Scoots, I think to the museum. I'm sorry, not sure about that," she mumbled.

"That's fine Miss Frye, doesn't matter where. What happened when you came back from your walk?"

"I stopped at the Falls Bridge because of all the commotion with the police. I think it had to do with somebody being murdered, sorry don't remember clearly. We were on the bridge and this really tall, good looking man started talking to me," she paused, confused. "Something happened, what was it? Oh yeah, Scoots bit him because he moved towards me."

"Your dog bit the guy at the bridge?" Tommy asked, very interested now.

"Yeah, I mean Scoots is always so friendly and yet for a few minutes he was like this crazed dog. Never seen him like that before. Anyway, the guy's hand was bleeding. I gave him my information because he was going to go to the emergency room, which I think he did."

Tommy leaned forward. "Which hospital, did he say?"

"I believe it was Roxborough Memorial. I remember being surprised because it was near where I live and then I found that he lived in the same general area," Colleen said, her voice a little slurred from the sedative.

"Did he say where he lived?" Tommy asked her.

"No, this is so hard trying to remember. I think he said he was staying with a friend, or at a friend's home. I'm so sorry Detective Darnello. I'm a lawyer and can't remember much of anything."

Tommy leaned forward and took her hand, squeezing gently.

"Hey, you've been through one helluva' time, it's a wonder you're sitting here even able to talk to me so clearly. Just take your time, no rush, and if you get too tired to keep talking then you just tell me and I'll come back later."

"No, let's go on while I'm able to. I know the more information you get the easier it will be to find him," she murmured.

"So did you go to the hospital with him?" Tommy inquired.

"No, that was the weird part though. He called me on the phone, it was fairly late I think. I was doing some paperwork. He told me that he was in the area and would like to stop by. I believe I told him no, but he was insistent so I agreed to him stopping. I put Scoots in the basement because of what happened earlier in the day. Oh my God, how is Scoots? Is he okay? Who's watching him?" she said, starting to get very agitated.

Tommy stood up and moved to the bed, trying to get her to calm down.

"Just lie back, everything is fine. We'll talk about your dog in a minute. What happened then?"

"That's where it gets really fuzzy and I don't remember much detective. He came in, we sat in the living room, had some wine and something to eat I think. I'm not sure, but I might've gotten a little drunk and then that's it," she said with finality, looking up at him. "I don't remember anything after that. Do you think I passed out?"

"I'm not sure Miss Frye. Somehow you ended up in the bedroom. Your neighbor was going to work and saw somebody, a man, leave your house from the back. He called 911, police were sent. They tried to get an answer from inside and couldn't. Fearing for your safety they had to break a window in order to get in. Don't worry though because the window is being fixed and your house is safe. You were found upstairs in the bedroom pretty messed up. And then you were transported here."

She just sat and stared at him, completely feeling disassociated with what her life had been like twenty-four hours earlier.

"I don't remember much, I'm so sorry," she said very softly.

"Honestly, you've done wonderful. Just one more thing, did he give you a name?"

Colleen thought really hard, closing her eyes.

"Wow, I think it started with a G, something like Gary or Greg, maybe John or Jonathan. Oh God, I know it. Wait, I think it was Quentin. Yes, that was his name," she said, almost shivering when she said the name.

"Did he happen to give you his phone number or address?"

"No, I'm sure of that. He was only going to stay for a little bit because I needed to finish up my work. But we drank the wine and all," she answered.

"Are you certain he went to the hospital?" Tommy questioned.

"Yes, or at least I think he did. He said he did and his hand was all bandaged up," she replied.

"Okay, you lay back and rest. You did real fine Miss Frye. I'm not sure even I would've been as strong as you were. Thanks so much," Tommy said very sincerely.

"Can you tell me how my Scoots is doing?" she asked, looking up at him.

He hesitated for a few seconds, not knowing how he should reply but felt she needed to know.

"Colleen, I'm not really sure how to say this, but your dog is dead. Whoever was in the house killed him. I'm so sorry," Tommy said softly, having a Labrador retriever of his own.

She had a very hard, swift intake of breath and the tears started flowing fast. He moved forward and put his arms around her, letting her cry onto his shoulder.

"What kind of monster would do something like this?" she asked him through her sobs, taking a box of tissues that he handed to her.

"I don't know Miss Frye, I don't know. But we'll find him I promise," he said gently.

At that point the emergency room doctor and several nurses came in with an attendant standing outside with a gurney.

"What's going on detective? Miss Frye, are you okay?" he asked very concerned.

Tommy looked up and nodded. "She's fine doc. Miss Frye answered some questions very graciously and then asked about her dog. She's obviously distressed right now."

"Okay detective, move aside. I think you've done enough damage right now. We need to transport Miss Frye to the O.R. and get that shoulder taken care of," Doctor Hastings said, nudging Tommy out of the way and pushing him towards the door.

"Miss Frye, let me take a look at that shoulder real quick before they steal you away from me," the doctor said gently, loosening the edge of the bandage wrap.

He quickly got a very mixed and confused look on his face.

"Well this is certainly interesting," he mumbled.

Tommy heard the remark and stopped, turned and took a step back.

"What's interesting doc?"

"The status of this wound," the ER doc replied. "As crazy as it sounds, it appears that it's healing very quickly. Let me look at these marks on her stomach. Nurse, pull that curtain further over."

The curtain then blocked Tommy's view and he waited, not too patiently either. A few minutes later Doctor Hastings walked around the foot of the bed, removed his gloves and tossed them into the receptacle.

"Nurse, we're going to transport her anyway. We may still have to close something yet," he said, moving towards the door.

"So, what was so interesting doctor?" Tommy asked him.

"I've never in my life seen anybody heal so quickly, especially from a wound so massive. When she was first brought in here we were very concerned about what appeared to be so much tissue loss and possible damage to the muscles and bone. Plus, those claw marks that run down her breast and stomach are beginning to turn pink, like they would after a few weeks of healing," the doctor said, almost in a dazed mumble.

He shook his head and walked into the hallway.

Tommy turned, looked back at Colleen Frye who was being gently helped onto the gurney. What the hell is going on here, he thought.

Heading towards his car he decided to check with Roxborough Memorial Hospital and see if they had any dog bite victims come in yesterday morning. However, a strong instinct told him that would not be the case, at least not for the monster they were after.

Chapter 18

Quentin was smart. After all, you didn't survive all those killing sprees through all those empty cities without perfecting the art of evasion. He parked the car near the ACME in the Andorra Shopping Center parking lot. Then a nice brisk walk of about twenty minutes brought him to the apartment house where he was temporarily residing. After all, the cops weren't stupid and they would find the car quickly and trail him to Frankie's apartment, and most likely barge in trying to capture him. He just needed to get inside this morning to remove what few belongings he had. In any town there was always plenty of lonely hearts hoping to find love for just one night. There would always be others like Frankie he could rely on to provide a place to stay.

Not bothering to worry about fingerprints since it wouldn't matter anyway, he bundled his scant amount of clothing into his valise and walked out, closing and locking the door securely behind him.

"Morning Quentin," a soft voice said behind him.

He turned and there stood Sharon looking like she was fresh off another all-nighter, trying to appear pleasant, but at the same time trying to hide her wariness of him.

"Hey Sharon I was hoping I'd see you. I wanted to apologize for yesterday. Was feeling a little under the weather and think I might've acted a little weird. Hope I didn't frighten you too much," Quentin said, using his most charming voice.

Smiling, she stopped at her front door and said, "Well, it was a little strange. But I forgive you and hope you're feeling better. Are you going someplace?"

He held up the small suitcase and grinned. "Yeah, well, my work calls and I need to get back home, take care of a few things. Hey, would you mind giving me a lift to the train station? I have no idea how the buses run along here and I can't stand cabs. I'll be happy to give you gas money."

"I don't know Quentin, I'm really tired," she said. "As you can see, I haven't slept yet. I have a bus schedule in here though if you'd like to check it out. They run pretty often up and down Ridge Avenue. I assume you want the station down near East Falls."

"I guess that's where it's at. Sure, I'd love to see the schedule so I'm not standing up there on a street corner too long," he said hopefully.

Pushing in the door she held it open for him. "Come on in, I think it's somewhere on top of the desk."

Sharon slipped off her jacket and tossed it on the couch along with her purse. She reached for a small lamp on the desk and started to rummage through a scattered pile of papers for the schedule. Quentin closed the door and silently locked it behind him, softly putting his valise on the floor. Then he moved into the apartment and over to where she stood.

"Ah, here it is," she said, turning around and finding that he was standing right behind her.

Startled she backed into the desk chair, almost knocking it over. Damn she thought, this guy does that all the time.

"Hey, you gotta' stop doing that, about give a girl a heart attack," smiling up at him.

"Sorry, just felt the need to be near you. I do find you extremely attractive," he told her.

"Well there are other ways to show it rather than being so damn aggressive.

Honestly honey, I find you pretty hot yourself, but I don't shadow you around like that," she giggled nervously.

Quentin raised his hands and backed away, bumping into an easy chair. He needed sex and knew she was ripe for the picking. He didn't want to overpower her, but he would if he had to. Having her receptive to his manly offerings would be much better for both of them.

"I keep apologizing it seems. Please Sharon, don't be frightened. It's not often when I find a woman so attractive," he told her.

"Well, I guess that means you're not gay then," she laughed.

He smiled back at her and opened his arms, palms out. "Nope, not gay, and what you see is what you can have. Interested?"

"Mmmmm, what time does your train leave?" she asked him coyly, her eyes shining at the prospect of getting this guy in bed.

"Doesn't matter really, I was going to purchase a ticket and just catch the next train to Cincinnati whenever that might be. It's not like I have to be back at a specific time, so I have all day and," he winked, "all night as well."

She kicked off her 3" heels and moved up against him. "Then I think we can fill up the time rather nicely, don't you? Just as long as you're a gentleman and there's no rough stuff, okay?"

He took her face gently in his massive hands and bent down, covering her mouth and letting his long tongue caress her teeth and probe the depths of her throat. She moaned and grabbed his shoulders, her legs suddenly weaker than they'd ever been.

Quentin broke the kiss and whispered, "No rough stuff, I promise, just the thrill of your life. Here or in the bedroom?"

She couldn't speak which was extremely rare for her. All she could do was point towards the dark hallway. He picked her up in his arms like she was but a tender flower and a feeling of anticipation began running through her veins. She could only look into those eyes and swear they changed different colors. But who cared as long as the most important part of him worked well.

He placed her gently on the bed and began unbuttoning her blouse to expose a bra of sheer black lace literally exploding with her full breasts. Rather than reach around to undo it he just slipped the straps down from her slim shoulders and suddenly both breasts were free, nipples standing out hard and pink, just waiting to be kissed.

Sharon lifted her hips from the bed and he slid her skirt and slip down to her ankles and then off, letting them fall softly to the floor. With her panty hose still on he lowered his head and spread her legs wide. She groaned with anticipation like she had never done before. He said she was in for the thrill of her life, but she didn't realize he meant pure ecstasy. And this was only the beginning, causing Sharon to tingle with anticipation.

He let his tongue push in the dark brown, silky material and enter her like a searching snake. She lifted her hips off the mattress to his inviting mouth and he placed his hands underneath her buttocks, letting her female scent engulf him. He wanted to howl right then.

With longer teeth than the normal man he ripped through the material like it didn't even exist.

"Hey," she moaned loudly. "Those are new."

He touched her lips with his fingertips. "Ssshhhh, be quiet, I'll buy you ten new pair. Just lie back and let yourself float free."

But she was already lost. The hell with torn panty hose because she was ready to rip them off herself. Quentin stood and slipped off his tee shirt and jeans. She gasped aloud at his erection. The only thought that went through her euphoric mind at the moment was whether she would survive being impaled with what she stared at.

She reached for him. "Please do it now, don't wait, I'm on fire."

He covered every inch of her with his body as if she didn't exist and entered her while she gasped in pain and surprise. She knew that the word ecstasy was not sufficient to describe what she was feeling right then. Sharon just closed her eyes, smiled and let his power take her to a place she had never been before. She swore she heard the howl of a wolf and could even caress the beast's luxuriant black fur.

"Your Doc Starling is quite the character," Johnny said, his eyes smiling at some of the remarks the medical examiner made.

Kathy slammed the door to her car, deep in thought and didn't hear a word of what he had said, still very troubled by some of the doctor's findings.

"And after I've turned into a wolf tonight when the moon is full, I hope to locate and kill this creature for you," Johnny countered with her silence.

Kathy looked at him. "I'm sorry, what did you say?"

"That it's actually turning out to be a pretty nice day," he replied.

"Yes it is actually. I was getting tired of all that damn rain. So what did you think of Doctor Starling?" she asked.

Johnny laughed and shook his said. "I think he's very knowledgeable actually and seems to really do his homework. Are you actually surprised at some of the things he told you?"

"A little I suppose, but not completely. These last few days have been like falling into the twilight zone or something on the X-files," she said, confusion still etched on every word.

"Ah, bringing up the good old X-files again. So what do you think Fox and Dana would do exactly if they had a case like this?" he asked her with grave seriousness.

"You're teasing me now and frankly I'm not in the mood," she hotly responded.

"No, actually, I'm being quite serious. What do you think they would do?"

"Well, Dana would most definitely be the ever pragmatic scientist and state that there were explainable circumstances in this case that would rule out certain unbelievable possibilities. Fox on the other hand would go out to get some silver bullets to fill his gun with and then wait for the moon to rise," Kathy said, starting to laugh.

"Now that's the detective I've come to know and love in such a short time," he said jokingly. "The lovely detective possesses so much wit and intelligence."

For a fleeting moment her heart stopped. Did he really say that? Nah, don't even go there Kathy thought. This guy is big time trouble, she could sense it. Keep any relationship purely professional all the way. Besides, her damn track record with men was abysmal. The last jerk she dated was nothing more than a self-centered, egotistical, beer guzzling asshole. Rain had growled at him the first time they met and Kathy should've known right then he was bad news. Obviously her dog had much more intuitive power into the male sex than she did.

"Let's not let all this mumbo-jumbo get you so confused that you fail to see the big picture. What are the facts the doctor gave you? Listing them in order: numerous animal hairs around the crime scene and on the bodies, most likely an animal such as a wolf; DNA off the dead bodies from not only a wolf, but a man as well; tracks that are much larger than any domestic dog and which fit those of a large wolf; distance of the stride appearing as if the wolf walked on two legs; radius of bite marks which are consistent with that of teeth and mouth size of a wolf; and, let's not forget the statements of numerous police officer reporting howling that sounded like a wolf, as well as the very obvious sound of a large animal growling through the cell phone to Mr. Mizerk. So Detective Morello, I ask you, if it appears to be a wolf, and it sounds like a wolf, would you then assume that it could, or should, be a wolf?"

She looked at him, not only stunned, but equally amazed. He spelled it all out for her in one basic paragraph.

"No Mr. Raven, not yet, but close," she said. "Really close. I still have not ruled out the possibility of a hybrid and a sadistic owner."

He sighed noticeably and sat back against the seat.

"So where can I drop you off? I need to get into the precinct and check in with Captain Ganz," she asked him.

"My car is still parked around the corner from Colleen Frye's house. You can drop me there and then I need to find a room somewhere. Would you have any suggestions?"

"You have no place to stay? You just drove here without any reservations? Where exactly did you come from again?" she inquired, getting more interested by the minute in this guy.

"I have a place up in Maine. Very secluded where I can be alone," he told her.

"That sure as hell doesn't surprise me. You can track all you want to and I suppose you even run with the wolves, you seem to know so much about them," she said jokingly.

Johnny stared at her very intently. She could not know what he was, but realized she was extremely intuitive without even knowing it.

"Detective Morello, you must know that all men are wolves in sheep's clothing. Some are better hiding it than others," he joked, giving her the smile that just seemed to melt her for an instant.

"Yeah, well, most men are assholes if you want my opinion, but I'm sure you don't since you are one."

He started laughing as she blended in with expressway traffic and headed back towards Roxborough to drop him off. He stared out the window at the river, like a mirror containing the images of multi-colored trees, the art museum, boat house row. He had seen how that was lit up the night he drove into town and was amazed at how beautiful it was.

"So, would you have any suggestions on where I can grab a room, nothing special," he inquired as they pulled onto the street where his car was parked.

"Depending on what you want, there are some classy places on City Line Avenue not far from here. Further out west towards King of Prussia on Route 202 you'd be able to find some smaller, cheaper places. How will I get a hold of you? Do you have a cell phone?"

"No, never needed one. They're just a big pain in the ass anyway, always going off when you don't want them too, invading your privacy. Leave me your number and I'll check in with you when I find a place," he stated firmly enough.

She handed him her card, watched him exit her vehicle and unlock his. For a brief moment she thought of telling him he could take the spare bedroom at her house but immediately thought different. Actually she worried about being so close to him, not trusting her own judgment. Besides, her father would probably bitch about bringing another stray home, and Rain would most likely kill him with kindness. Or bite him, one or the other.

She pulled away, reaching for her phone, needing to call Captain Ganz and tell him she was on her way in to the precinct.

Her gaze though was on Johnny's car as it made a u-turn and headed back towards Ridge Avenue. This was a very deep, complex, dangerous, but extremely sexy guy, and she positively knew she needed to keep a perspective on things. This was absolutely no time to let her sexual libido run wild like she was in heat. Besides, she had a killer to catch and soon.

Chapter 19

Two hours later the brain trust sat around a small conference room table adjacent to Nathan Ganz's extremely cluttered office discussing all the evidence which had been piling up over the last several days like snow from a classic nor'easter. A nearly empty box of glazed and chocolate donuts with colorful sprinkles rested directly in front of Nathan, screaming out to him in an open invitation to indulge to his heart's content. Mouth watering, he eyed them hungrily. But he had already eaten two, along with a bagel earlier. He prayed that somebody would soon place their claim to the prize in order to remove his temptation.

Kathy finished off her cold coffee with a slight grimace and started playing with a couple stirs, bending them into weird shapes. Dr. Starling, the Chief Medical Examiner, had just finished talking about the evidence he had obtained from the autopsies, some of it just too unbelievable for any of them to grasp. Kathy heard Captain Ganz talking, but was still mulling over what the M.E. had said.

"So with the evidence of hairs, footprints, bite radius and DNA," stated Doc Starling, "we can safely assume that an animal was present, specifically a wolf, or a hybrid of some kind, though from the size of those prints, it would have to be extremely large. However, this is the most astonishing thing I discovered."

He lowered his spectacles and stared at each of them in turn, settling on Kathy. He either thought she would scoff at him, or be his only believer.

"While taking swabs from the wounds and testing them, we not only found strong traces of wolf DNA, but in lesser amounts, human as well," he told them, smiling and lifting his eyebrows at the same time.

"What the hell does that mean?" barked Nathan.

"Well Captain Ganz, it means that not only did an animal create those wounds, but then a human being placed their mouth at the same location, for what purpose I don't know and quite frankly I'm afraid to make any conjectures. I get the facts and then let you arrive at probabilities," the doctor stated firmly.

Kathy spoke up. "Doc, might you be saying there's a possibility an animal could've attacked the boys, created those terrible wounds and then a man came along afterwards and proceeded to bite, or gnaw, at those same wounds?"

"Entirely possible Detective Morello," he answered in a surprised response.

"Or, speaking of other possibilities, could man and beast be the same creature?" Kathy asked, waiting for the stunned remarks.

Captain Ganz stood up with an extremely quick response.

"Kathy, do you realize what you just said, even what that could imply?"

Nathan asked her, his voice actually rising to a higher level than she had ever heard it.

"I realize it sounds absolutely crazy Captain. But if you look at the evidence, the fact of having an animal there at the scene along with somebody in the background instructing it what to do, is beginning to have less validity for one important reason, especially in light of what the doctor just told us," she told him.

"And, what's that?" he sighed.

"We only found animal tracks around the boys as well as Mary Beth Mizerk, no tracks from a man were found anywhere. However, human prints were discovered at a point further away from the bodies, like those underneath the Falls Bridge and the area off of Hagys Mill. I hate to think of that possibility too Nathan, but it's certainly leading me in that direction."

Captain Ganz smirked, made a snorting sound and let his wide body crash down into the chair, pulling his hands to his eyes and slowly shaking his head.

"Also Nathan, Mr. Raven and I have had several very interesting discussions about this killer," Kathy added.

Nathan Ganz looked up with a quizzical gaze.

"Yeah, just who the hell is that guy anyway? You never really told me."

"He's a tracker and has worked for law enforcement in Arizona. His wife and unborn son were killed three years ago and he's been tracking this monster throughout a number of cities over the last few years. This is actually the closest he's come, mostly because he was able to hear about the death of the two boys and able to get here fairly quickly," Kathy told him.

"Do you trust him Kathy? Is he some kind of fruitcake or nut ball?" Nathan asked her quietly.

"I trust the fact he believes in what he's told me and so far, with all this evidence we've obtained, it fits exactly what he's discussed with me. We could very easily be dealing with one creature, for want of something else to call it, sir" she said.

Nathan Ganz stood up and moved around to stare out the window. Why was this happening when he was so damn close to retirement he thought? Hell, he figured he needed another donut, but at that very moment Tommy barged through the door, making a very noisy entrance. He also immediately reached for the two donuts and stole them from right under Nathan's nose.

Through a mouth full of donut and sugary glaze stuck to his lips he stared at both Captain Ganz and his partner.

"Sorry I'm late Captain, but I followed up on a few things, like stopping at the hospital where Miss Frye was taken when I had the opportunity to ask her some questions," he mumbled. Ganz was still very angry this young smart ass detective had stolen his donuts, especially since he had decided they were his own property.

Tommy proceeded to inform them of the stranger the young woman's dog had bitten at the Falls Bridge and the fact this guy was at her house that night. In addition, he had stopped at the Roxborough Hospital emergency room to check records. Not to his surprise, there was no man with a bite wound from Sunday attended to, so the man was lying to Colleen about getting medical treatment on his hand.

"Plus, we found long, black hairs on her bed, as well as in the basement where the dog was slaughtered, along with partial prints in the blood that resembled those from an animal. And, get this boys and girls! The injuries to Colleen Frye, especially the shoulder which was very nasty, as were those slash marks running down her stomach, had already started to heal. The ER doctor was extremely confused, stunned in fact. I'm going to head back later this evening and check on her," Tommy finished up, dropping the last piece of donut into his mouth, smacking his lips to infuriate Nathan even more.

Kathy smiled at him. "Hey Romeo, are you sure that's the only reason you want to go back and check on her?"

Tommy licked his fingers off and held up his hands.

"Hey, as much as I would love to pursue the rose covered avenue towards a relationship with her, it seems we travel down different streets," he replied.

"What the hell does that mean detective?" asked Nathan Ganz in a huff.

"Captain, I think he's trying to be as diplomatic as possible in saying that Colleen Frye may be a lesbian," Kathy said softly.

Before Tommy could answer, there was a knock at the door. Sergeant Taylor stuck his totally bald head inside the room.

"Sorry to disturb you Captain Ganz, but we got a call from BMV on the partial plate from the diner. They've got the list comprised of overall possibilities down to color, make, model, and because the witnesses were unsure of the exact year, then covering a three year span. How else would you want it broken down?"

Nathan glanced to Kathy and Tommy, raising his eyebrows.

"For right now, single men only between the ages of 25 and 35," Kathy advised, glancing at Tommy for some additional input.

"Well, Miss Frye said the perp mentioned either living or staying at a friend's apartment or house in the Roxborough section. That could be just a pile of shit he was giving her, but just to be on the safe side, ask them to break out one side list for that area. We can work exclusively on those hits. The rest of the search can cover Manayunk, East Falls, and Andorra" Tommy answered.

"If that's the case then and this guy, or whatever, is staying with somebody else then the car may not be registered in the name of the killer," Kathy surmised, "and if that's the case, then are we dealing with two killers?"

"Okay Sergeant, pass that on to BMV and tell them to get the sorted list here to us ASAP. Also, check in with the 5th. District and make damn sure they're looking for this car in that area."

"Yes sir, I'm on it," Taylor said, closing the door.

Heading quickly for the exit, Kathy grabbed Tommy's arm and pulled him with her towards the larger room in the detective bureau. He banged his knee on the corner of her desk and swore out loud.

"Damn Kathy, I can walk myself, or do you want to put a leash on me. Ouch, that hurt," Tommy whined.

"So sorry little Tommy, but we're heading out," she said, already thinking two steps ahead of her partner.

She yelled back to Ganz, "Captain, Tommy and I are heading back to the Roxborough area. When that list gets here, especially the smaller one, call me. We need to jump on that right away."

"Yeah, yeah, okay. Goddamn it, do your job and find this monster and soon," Nathan yelled at them as they left the office.

His booming voice echoed in her ears. Find this guy? At least find the guy before he turns into some wolf-like creature tonight and kills some other innocent people she thought.

Johnny really didn't need a place to stay. He knew he'd be shifting later tonight anyway. The killer was in this particular area, he was sure of it, could smell him. With the strongest part of the new moon being over tonight, there was the strong possibility the creature would move on, or just go into hiding until the full moon phase arrived in about ten days.

He called his father and told him everything he knew.

"Dad, he's here and I'm very close. If I don't get him tonight, then he might disappear for awhile," Johnny told him.

"I agree with you. After tonight he won't be able to change fully. I wouldn't be surprised if he hasn't already moved to another location, knowing that the police will eventually trace the vehicle to whoever he has surely killed," said his father. "What are the police doing to find him?"

Johnny grunted his dissatisfaction. "The same steps most police departments usually do. Amass all the evidence from dead bodies and crime scenes, test it, question witnesses and then wait for the next killing. They're always a step behind and a day late, but there is one particular detective who is quite bright."

"Be careful Johnny and don't trust him completely, especially where you're concerned. You have to protect the sanctity of our race, as well as the local clan."

"I realize that father, and the detective is a female," he replied.

There was very evident hesitation from the other end. Johnny could tell his father's mind was churning a mile a minute.

"What's she like son?"

"She's very competent and capable of locating this monster. She's also extremely beautiful," Johnny replied.

"Son, do not tell her more than she needs to know. You can find the beast, especially if you rely on Victor's help. Let the police fuddle along like they usually do and track this killer tonight on your own with Victor's clan if you need to. Understand me?"

"Yes father, I will. I had planned on returning to where his pack is living so I could leave my truck there. Plus, I haven't slept and need to rest a bit. I'll be out tracking as soon as the sun goes down."

"Okay, I trust you Johnny, but sometimes I worry your judgment can be extremely clouded. I'm going to start planning to leave tomorrow for Philadelphia, especially if you don't catch him tonight. Tell Victor I may be coming and will have a small group with me. Your mother will remain behind however. Johnny there's something I haven't told you yet. You will be blessed with another sibling though it's too early to say yet if it will be a brother or sister. So, please be careful my son," he said.

There was a swift intake of breath from Johnny and his heart swelled with joy and pride. His parents, brothers and sisters, the extremely strong and loving pack way of life developed over many, many generations for the weregune, were the things valued above all others. He was at the same time saddened by the loss of Samantha and his unborn son. The pack mourned for a month because to lose any member is like losing one from your own family. Johnny also felt he would never have this personal sense of pride again for how could any other female take Samantha's place in his heart?

"I will, I promise, now more than ever. Such great news father and please give mother my love. Either I or Victor will call you in the morning."

Johnny drove around the Roxborough section of Philadelphia for several reasons. First, to see if he could spot the car described by Harry and Betty Ann from the diner, a long shot at best. And second, to get a feel for the territory. As a young cub, learning the ways of the hunt and tracking prey, the ones who knew what they faced ahead of time were much more successful and had a better chance to live.

He was really tired and soon found himself driving over the Green Lane Bridge into Belmont Hills towards Victor's house. Knowing he was at his best being alone, he would nonetheless welcome any help from Victor and his pack.

But he needed to stop somewhere and call Detective Morello. For nearly the entire time after being dropped off at his car, she was on his mind. He wondered what that meant. After all, he had not even had one thought towards another female since the night Samantha had been slaughtered. Now, the blossoming urges he had not felt in over three years were extremely bothersome, especially with her being a mere human. It was true there were some of his breed that fell in love with those not weregune, and though some of these relationships were very successful, many ended in disaster. It took a very special human being, male or female, to accept the truth.

Johnny stopped at a Wawa convenience store, bought a jumbo cup of coffee and then went outside to the pay phone. He dialed her cell number and waited, sipping hot coffee and staring at the traffic speeding by on Belmont Avenue.

"Yeah, it's your dime so don't waste my time," her voice came over the phone. He grinned at her sense of levity and he also felt the strange tugging inside him every time he heard her voice.

"Hello Kathy. It's Johnny and I thought I'd better check in before nightfall. What's up?" he asked her.

"Well, well the mysterious Mr. Raven. Where are you?" she inquired.

"Right now I'm standing in front of a Wawa on Belmont Avenue drinking some wonderful coffee. What the hell is a Wawa anyway?" he asked her.

She laughed. "There happens to be a town in Pennsylvania by the name of Wawa where their headquarters is located. Seems convenient to name their stores Wawa I suppose. Have you been staying out of trouble Johnny?"

"Detective Morello, you wound my pride even thinking I could be anything but a model citizen," he countered.

She started giggling in that wonderful laugh she had.

"Okay Mr. Raven, I trust you. Have you found a place to stay yet?" she asked him, more to the question than Kathy felt he knew.

"Johnny, call me Johnny, the only Mr. Raven I know is my father and he might bite you if he was called mister too often. And yes, I'm actually heading over to some friends of the family. I can stay with them temporarily. Why, did you have someplace else in mind?" he asked, raising his voice slightly.

She hesitated briefly, not sure what to say. "That's good to hear, I hadn't realized you had friends around Philadelphia. You're just full of surprises. I am at the moment merging onto lower Ridge with my partner, Detective Darnello. We're going back to the crime scenes and have another look around. I might also add we had quite a good skull session where your theory of who and what we're after was discussed."

"So detective has it been determined that I'm certifiable yet? Or is your Captain Ganz a believer now?" he asked her, chuckling at the same time.

"As hard as it is for him to understand, he's seen far too much over the past few days to discount anything. Nathan is extremely good at what he does, but the best asset he has which has worn off on me, is never to completely discount anything. Though I must admit, the thought has crossed my mind that maybe I should stop at a nearby Barnes & Nobel bookstore to look for something written by Laurel Hamilton or someone else in the horror genre," she said laughing.

"You read her novels? I'm surprised Detective Morello, you seem to be such a no-nonsense, show me the facts kind of professional," he teased her.

"I love her books, I'm a huge fan. Anyway, do you want to meet someplace in a little bit? I still owe you that hot dog remember."

He was very tempted but said, "Actually, I'm really tired right now and think I need to rest. I haven't slept for awhile and will need to be really alert tonight. The thought of having a wonderful hot dog meal with you is more than an entertaining thought however."

"For me also, believe me. The hot dogs can wait since you do need your rest. When you wake up call me on my cell phone right away and we'll touch base. And listen Johnny, I don't want you running around this city getting into trouble, do you hear me?" she said firmly.

"You have my word of honor Detective Morello. Please be careful," Johnny told her.

"You too Johnny, something tells me that we will be having another extremely chaotic night."

Johnny hesitated before answering. "Trust me detective, you can count on it."

After hanging up, he pulled his truck out onto Belmont and headed for Victor's house. He did need to sleep for a few hours and get some substantial food inside him as well. Tonight would most assuredly be chaotic, for him and the lovely Detective Morello. As much as they attempted to believe, until they actually faced the raging beast, they still had no true idea what to expect. He also felt the strong urge to protect her as well, a strange desire he had not experienced in a very long time.

The beast sat on the edge of the bed, staring down at his conquest. She indeed had experienced the thrill of her life like he told her she would. Sharon had been exactly what he needed. Last night with Colleen Frye had been different. His wolf needed to surface and let his sexual desire be sated. There was also the incredible urge to infect somebody and he was extremely attracted to her. He would have to keep tabs on her for she would surely need direction in order to make the change easier. Something he had never had the opportunity to experience, making the awakening of his wolf nature extremely difficult and troubling.

Now though he gazed upon the battered body of Sharon Farris lying on the floor, her face badly discolored and a large pool of blood spreading underneath her head, saturating into the beige carpet. It looked so dark Quentin thought. He had not wanted to hurt her. His desire was to purely satisfy a deep sexual need.

However, afterwards she treated him like he was nothing more than one of her tricks who paid her well for services rendered. He was no whore's trick and when he called her that she went ballistic, getting much too loud. Quentin had reached out, grabbing her tightly around the throat to shut her up. She kicked and scrapped his face with her long fingernails which of course really pissed him off. So he beat her with his fists, rage building up.

Since it was daylight he couldn't change, but deep inside his wolf always had control over him. He threw her around the room like she was nothing but a rag doll, his eyes dark and hooded. Even though he couldn't change completely he did become much hairier, his eyebrows became extremely bushy, nails extended to claw-like length, and his teeth became longer and sharper, sticking out from the corners of his mouth. She had gazed at him with horror, realizing she was surely about to die within the claws of a monster.

Now she lay on the floor totally dead. And, Quentin was actually morose about it. He had killed so many innocent people over the years that one more didn't matter. He knew it would never end until he himself was slain. At times he welcomed death, but that was his human side. When the wolf realized his urges, it got angry for it no way desired an end to its rampaging life.

He thought about staying here in her apartment for awhile, but decided against it. Somebody might've noticed him going into her apartment and he was still way too close to Frankie's place. He felt that very soon they would find the car, track it here, and he needed to be long gone. He also felt the need to stay in this city which he had come to like in a very short time. There was one more night to run free and then about ten days of intense longing, but only the barest hint of alteration, most of those changes within him.

Quentin checked out her refrigerator and surprisingly found an open carton of eggs minus three. He grinned at the thought of yesterday morning. She must've acquired a taste for an omelet like she wanted to cook for him and went out to buy some eggs. She also had orange juice with lots of pulp. He cracked the eggs into a glass, drank it straight down and followed with several large glasses of juice. Killing always gave him such a huge appetite.

Grabbing his small suitcase he opened the door a crack, mostly to let his eyes get used to the light in the hallway, but also to see if anybody was out there. Then he slipped out and headed for the side entrance. It was leaning towards middle afternoon and even though the moon was hours away, there was still the intense pull. Black, coarse hair had already begun springing on his arms, chest and legs. Underneath his skin he felt very intense rippling like those damn tics you could get in the corner of your eyelid. Quentin needed to find a place in the area to change and sooner the better. He also remembered staring at the beautiful detective the other night, excitement searing his loins. Her house was nestled quite charmingly within an extremely wooded area of the city. Perhaps it was time to pay her a visit tonight.

Kathy answered her cell phone on the fourth ring.

"Where and the hell were you at Kat? You gotta' answer your phone faster than that detective," Nathan yelled, slamming her mostly because he was under extreme pressure from not only the brass and the Mayor, but the parents of the two boys, Mr. Mazerk, and an ever present onslaught of reporters.

"Sorry Captain Ganz......sir," Kathy shot back (when she was upset with his attitude she always referred to him as 'sir' because it annoyed him so much), "we just came out of Roxborough Memorial and you can't use cell phones inside the building."

With a slight hesitation, he softened his tone.

"Forget it Detective Morello, I'm just up to my elbows and asshole in this case. Everybody and their mother want information yesterday. What's up at the hospital?"

"You won't believe it Captain," she said, a surprised note in her voice.

"Try me Kathy, I'd believe just about anything right about now."

"Well, it seems that Colleen Frye has been discharged from the hospital, as shocking as that may sound," she told him.

"What the hell? How could that happen, I thought she was almost dead?"

"Well, it seems when they finally got her to surgery, the shoulder wound had healed completely. There was nothing to suture up. And those ugly claw marks going down her breast and stomach were all but disappeared, just five long, pink marks like if you happened to try and scratch an itch too hard," she relayed the surprising facts.

"Where did she go, back to her house? That's still a crime scene," barked Nathan.

"We're not sure. Her friend Sara Graynor was here and they left together. Colleen signed herself out from the emergency room. We'll contact the law firm and get Miss Graynor's address, which is probably in Center City. Right now Tommy and I were going to head over to the house, see if she stopped there. By the way, why did you call me?" Kathy asked him.

"Right, well it seems the police in the 5th. District might have located the car parked up in the Andorra Shopping Center. There's a squad car picking up either the waitress or the owner of the diner to identify the vehicle as being the one the killer drove away in. So get your butts up there first and then head over to Miss Frye's house."

"You got it Captain, we'll ....., " damn he had cut her off again.

They jumped into her car and cut over to Henry Avenue which would be faster. Traffic was relatively light so they got there in less than ten minutes. In the parking lot they went airborne over a few speed bumps and screeched to a halt where several police vehicles surrounded an empty dark blue, Ford Focus.

Harry, the old guy from the diner, was standing nearby nodding his head yes to one of the officers. They both looked up as Kathy and Tommy approached.

"Hello again Detective Morello," Harry said, winking, "we have to stop meeting like this."

She smiled back. Yeah, she definitely enjoyed elderly men since they were so much more gentlemanly than the jerks she had dated recently.

"Hi Harry, is this the car you saw? The license plate has the same three numbers," Kathy asked him.

"Yes ma'am, it's the same car. I'd stake my life on it, even down to the dent in the rear bumper. It's definitely the car," Harry informed her.

She shook his hand and thanked him as he got back in the squad car to head back to the diner. Smiling, Kathy heard him ask the policeman to hit the lights and siren which he did. At the same time she hit the number on her cell phone for Captain Ganz.

"Hey Cap, it's Kathy. The car was identified by Harry from the diner. It's definitely the car so we need you to contact Warrants Division, obtain a warrant as fast as you can, not only for the car but the place of residence for the owner as well. The owner's card is missing, so once you get it then call me with the address and we'll meet you there. We may also need a SWAT team."

"I'm on it detective. Maybe we've finally gotten a break or else he just dumped it there and has moved on already," Nathan said curtly.

"That's probably the case if he's as intelligent as Mr. Raven said he is, but we need to follow everything to where it leads, you know that Captain," Kathy answered.

It had been a very nice day, kind of warm and sunny for a change, but looking out to the western sky it was getting dark once more. All they needed was another night of bad weather in trying to catch this guy, or monster, or beast, whatever the hell it was.

Chapter 20

Johnny drove to Victor's house and reviewed everything with the local alpha that had transpired during the day. After having a bite to eat, in order to get something in his stomach, he was shown to a quiet back room upstairs where he could get a few much needed hours of sleep. If he could that is, considering all that he had on his mind. Victor said Barton and another member of the pack, Raphael, would accompany him on the hunt. Even though Johnny preferred to track and work alone, he had no choice since he was in their territory and thus thanked Victor for all he had done so far.

The bed was way too soft for Johnny so he decided to sprawl out on the carpet which actually was fairly plush. Many times back at the cabin in Maine he would curl up on the hardwood floor in front of the fire place, his only cushion a thin, frayed throw rug. Since it was chilly however, he pulled a thick woolen blanket down on top of him from the bed for some warmth, especially since he most always slept in the nude. Too often during his sleep over the last three years, dreams of running wild and nightmares of seeing Samantha's dead body, could bring on the change, thus shredding more clothes than he eventually got tired of replacing.

Within minutes he had drifted off into a deep slumber and found himself racing across a large, open expanse with his thick, black mane fluttering in the wind, golden eyes shining brightly in the crystal clear moonlight. As he slowed and then loped casually towards the top of a nearby hill which rimmed a steep cliff, he felt the familiar presence of another wolf shadowing him. There was no danger though, he was certain of that. In fact, there was an unmistakable scent that brought him skidding to a stop as he pivoted sharply and stared into a wall of darkness.

"*Who is there? Who follows me this night?*" Jaress questioned the darkness.

No answer came forth and the black wolf moved closer to the tree line, his acute eyesight peering into the deep shadows. Still, he felt no danger from this shadow.

"*Jaress, it is I, Sashine. I have come to run with you one last time my love.*"

She was a pure vision of beauty as she trotted majestically from the safety of the woods. Her brilliant white fur glowed like newly fallen snow under an illuminating moon. She grinned and moved to stand in front of him, extending her muzzle to touch his. And they kissed, gliding closer together where they rubbed necks and smelled the intoxicating aroma of each other. Jaress was now on fire being this near his beloved mate. He towered over her in a position of protectiveness which he had failed to do one fateful night.

"*I have missed you so much Sashine. My life has not, and will never again, be the same without you,*" he whispered.

"*Oh my sweet Jaress, I have so much missed you as well. It is very lonely without you, but have peace in your heart for I am fine. Do not fret my love, and rest assured our son flourishes as well, you would be so proud of him.*"

The two, magnificent wolves strolled together shoulder to shoulder towards the cliffs edge and sat, silhouetted against the dark, star-filled sky with the silvery moon directly above their heads. For a while no thoughts were spoken, nor needed, just the tender closeness both of them coveted.

"Sashine, I need so desperately to hold you even if it's but for one last time."

She laid her head against his shoulder and thought, "My sweet Jaress, we cannot let this night pass without being within each others arm. I am ready if you are."

They stood as one now etched upon the hill, black and white wolf. Closing their anxious eyes in order to bring forth the moon they shared, a rainbow of lights cascaded before each of their desires. Within seconds they had changed into human form.

Jaress reached out and brought her tenderly to him where she fell into the safety of his strong arms, having missed the tenderness of his caress, the heavy pounding of his heart when she placed her head against his chest. He kissed her silken hair, her glittering eyes, her luscious breasts, and let his tongue explore to depths he may never reach again. She covered his handsome face with her own kisses of longing and let her tender fingertips trace the contour of every bursting muscle he possessed. And so they passionately made love for the last time underneath a moon that exploded with romance, a moon that for one night belonged to only these two magnificent wolves. When their throes of passion had been exhausted he held her tightly to his massive chest, so frightened to let her go for he knew it would be forever this time.

"I must leave you now my love. I have brought you terrible nightmares and my nearness to you will continue to do that," she whispered against his neck.

"I cannot lose you again Samantha. The dreams and nightmares are that which bind us as one. You are all I have left, the memories of what we had together. If I lose those, then life for me will no longer be worthwhile," he told her gently, tears breaking free from his haunted eyes.

She slipped slowly from his grasp. Upon her knees she looked down at his face.

"You must not let me interfere with finding the right mate in the future. I know you will find love again and it's what I wish for you. It's what you would want for me if I had been the one left behind. The dangers you now face are great my sweet. Please do not let your strength be diminished by the pain of losing me," she told him, her face beautiful in the moonlight.

He let his long, rough fingers caress her silky skin and knew that she was right.

"I will never love another like I have loved you Sam. You are my life mate and how could I ever love another as strongly as I do you?" he implored.

"But you will Johnny, trust me. Yet I know whoever that lucky female is to have you as a mate, you will never forget what we had together, even if it was for only a short while. But it is time for me and our son to move on to another plain of existence. However, know that I will always be near, to protect and guide you. You may not always be aware that I'm there, but trust in our powers and know that I will be close, watching over you, as well as whoever you finally select as a mate," she said softly, kissing Johnny endearingly one last time. Kneeling before him she closed her eyes as she shifted back to the magnificent white wolf.

She rose and walked to him where Johnny stroked her luxuriant fur and laid his face against her muzzle. With golden eyes shining only for him, she lifted her head and howled in the most elegant symphony, a song of love and longing. Turning quickly, she loped towards the trees where she stopped and turned around.

"Good-bye my sweet Johnny and my soul-mate Jaress." Without looking back, she disappeared from his view through a veil of tears that ran before his eyes.

"Good-bye Samantha, my eternal love Sashine," he whispered.

Johnny awoke with a start, jumping up from his place on the floor. Victor had entered the room and barely touched his shoulder.

"I'm sorry Johnny, but you were having a very intense dream. Are you okay?" he asked as gently as he could.

Johnny lowered himself to the floor and crawled back slowly until he struck the wall where he sat for a minute holding his knees tightly, head buried within his thoughts, before he raised his eyes to Victor in a pleading gaze.

"Barton told me of how you lost your mate. How did you survive? How did you finally give her up?" Johnny croaked.

"I've never given her up completely. I'm sure as Barton told you I was quite lost for many years, a very crazy, dangerous rogue who was not fit for life in any pack, or to be around civilization. Sashar was my life and I had failed her. I should've been with her that night and instead chose to run with my pack brothers. So I blamed myself for her being alone, suffering the pain from the trap and the terrible fall from that cliff after being shot by the trapper," Victor said, his eyes holding a steady gaze onto Johnny's, but still containing an angry, haunted look after all these years.

"How did you give her up? I failed Samantha as well. I should've been with her the night she was killed and I can never forgive myself Victor."

"But you can, you will and I think you have. If your dream is what I think it was, then your Samantha came and said her final good-bye as did my Sashar. Life goes on Johnny and I found my love again in Tabitha. Samantha wants only the same for you. You must avenge her death and then you will be free to move on and hopefully become as happy as I am," Victor said, standing and reaching down to help his friend to stand.

"Johnny, another thing that will end all the pain and torment for you will finally be achieving the revenge for Samantha that you have pursued. I tracked that trapper for days until I found him. After slaughtering all that was in his camp I had saved him for last. And believe me, he told me all that I needed to know about that fateful day and then some," Victor said with animosity filling his voice. "It wasn't just the fact she got caught in the trap by blind luck then?" Johnny asked him.

"No my friend, there was underlying currents to why Sashar was away from the den area that day. Getting caught in the trap was a mistake, but her death was not. I have lived with that secret for a long time," Victor whispered, his voice very low and troubled.

"I hope you finally come to peace with it and if I can help I will," Johnny said.

"Thank you and I honestly think you may be able to do the same. Now, get some clothes on that magnificent body before my Tabitha sees you. I'd hate to have to fight you," he joked, giving Johnny a rough push on the shoulder.

Johnny smiled. "Thank you Victor, for everything."

The elder weregune only nodded and walked out of the room. However, Johnny saw from the droop of his wide shoulders, he had never fully given up Sashar and carried with him a terrible burden. Johnny knew that he would also never give up Sashine, his Samantha, for the same haunting reason.

Johnny slipped into a heavy sweatshirt with holes in both elbows and his oldest pair of jeans. He wouldn't have them on that long anyway. Walking into the kitchen he saw Tabitha at the counter cleaning dishes from dinner.

She turned. "Hello Johnny, there's fresh coffee on the counter and still some apple pie if you'd like a piece."

"Thank you Tabitha, but I'm still quite full from dinner though I'll take you up on the offer for some coffee. Oh, may I use your phone?" he inquired.

"Of course, it's in the hallway. I'm almost done here and then you can have some privacy," she said smiling.

After she had left the room, Johnny grabbed the phone and dialed the cell number for Detective Morello. On the second ring she answered.

"Where the hell have you been? I need to get you a cell phone Johnny. We found the car that the killer was driving and we're in the process of surrounding the apartment house that belongs to the owner of the vehicle," she said gruffly.

"Sorry detective, I needed some sleep. Where are you at?"

Kathy gave him the address and told him where to park. She would instruct the officer at the road block to let him in and get there as fast as he could. Johnny said he would and hung up.

Pouring the coffee into the sink he grabbed his keys from the table near the front door and walked quickly out onto the porch. The light was just about gone and Johnny knew that this night could very well produce some results at last.

"Victor, I just spoke to Detective Morello. They have the place surrounded where this murderer could possibly be at. I need to leave right away, but I'll call you so stay near the phone," Johnny said, trotting to his truck.

"Take Barton with you Johnny, he could be of help," Victor yelled after him.

"No sir, it would only confuse the issue with the police. Detective Morello knows and trusts me. Just be ready for my phone call," he said, slamming the door and revving up the cold engine. He raced out of the driveway, bumping onto the street and then down the steep hill towards Belmont Avenue. It would surprise him completely if the killer was still in the apartment.

Johnny was sure he had moved on already, especially since he had left his car far enough away from where he was staying. But he could get fresh spore to follow and that would be invaluable.

Johnny knew that maybe finally tonight Samantha's death would be avenged.

Chapter 21

He knelt down with Kathy behind her car in the grocery story parking lot. Driving here quickly was no problem. Getting in was much harder than Kathy had said it would be, but mission accomplished. He had a certain way of persuasion about him, another one of his many gifts so to speak.

"What took you so long Mr. Raven? The party's about to start without you," Kathy said, in a low, throaty, truly sexy voice.

"You didn't have to tell me I'd have to park over four blocks away detective," he replied, looking around. "So where is the guy supposed to be living?"

"You look in pretty good shape to me so walking four blocks after running through the woods last night like an animal shouldn't be much of a problem for you," she tossed back at him.

"That's true. I was just pulling your chain," he said, winking at her.

"You're quite incorrigible. The address for the owner of the car is in that apartment house across the street. SWAT is nearly in position. Then we'll go and introduce ourselves at the front door with a warrant," Kathy informed him.

"How can I help detective?" he asked, staring over at the apartment house. This is all too easy he thought.

"You're a civilian so you'll stay right here. I thought it was right you should be notified since you've been tracking this guy for so long. If he is in there and gets away, your skills will come in handy. I'll signal when you can come up," she said, standing and motioning Tommy and a few police officers to move forward.

"Detective, what's the guy's name, the owner of the car?"

"Not sure that it matters to you, but Frank Sanchez, why?" she asked him.

"You realize of course that he's most likely dead, whether in that apartment or not. I think you are also smart enough to know that this guy we're looking for won't be in there either," Johnny said, looking up at her.

She half smiled, half smirked at him, like he was a blooming idiot.

"Yes, but we need to move on the side of caution Mr. Raven. Just stay here and I'll call you up as soon as I can," she instructed him.

"Be careful Detective Morello. Wouldn't want to see you get hurt by accident."

"Just you be a good little boy and stay put," then she was off, Tommy at her side, heading for the front door of the apartment building.

The apartment itself was on the second floor, half-way down the hall. With guns drawn they moved into position, Tommy to the left and Kathy to the right of the door, backed up by four police officers and several SWAT team members. The rest of SWAT was positioned on the outside of the building in case the 'perp' tried to get away. Kathy nodded to Tommy who then pounded loudly on the door.

"Sanchez, Frank Sanchez, this is the police, open the door now," Tommy hollered loudly.

Not a sound came from inside the apartment so Tommy rapped hard again.

"Mr. Sanchez, this is your last chance. We have a warrant to search the premises. If you, or anyone else that may be inside the apartment, do not open the door we will be forced to break it in," Tommy yelled out.

No response meant that's exactly what they did. A large, burly police officer holding an assault rifle moved in front of the door and kicked hard, the door splintering and blowing inward. Tommy and Kathy, in a crouch with pistols in the assault position, moved into the dark interior. Flashlight beams crisscrossed the room.

The living room and kitchen were clear. Kathy motioned for the police officers to head down the hallway to where the bedrooms appeared to be.

"Tommy, pull those damn blankets down from the windows and somebody hit the light switch," Kathy said, voice completely under control.

Suddenly the small amount of daylight still remaining outside streamed throughout the empty apartment. The ceiling light came on a second later. The place was empty as both Kathy and Tommy thought it would be.

Putting down their guns they started to look around, searching for anything that might give them a clue to who the killer was. Five minutes later Kathy remembered that Johnny was still outside so she made her way out the front door where she found him leaning against a post.

"Are you relaxed Mr. Raven?" she asked him.

"Not bad actually, so was anybody home?" he inquired.

"You knew he wouldn't be so why should you act surprised?"

"I'm not, so can I go up and have a look around? I promise not to touch anything."

Together they went back up to the second floor and entered the apartment. Johnny walked around, his nostrils flaring, trying to pick up any scent that he could, or see any little thing the police might have missed.

"He's taken everything with him. He would have very few clothes, possibly just a very small suitcase or a duffel bag. But he was here Kathy and not too long ago, hours in fact," Johnny told her, moving out into the hallway.

She followed him and suddenly bumped into his back.

"What the hell did you stop so quick for?" she accused him.

"I smell blood. There's somebody dead on this floor," Johnny said, moving to several of the apartments and standing by the door, until he got to Sharon's.

"In here Kathy. I think you have probable cause to go in without a warrant," he told her, moving back.

After calling Tommy and the other officers out to the hallway, Kathy knocked hard and hollered to anybody inside that might be hurt. With no answer coming, the door was kicked in with the police entering once more with guns drawn and in crouches. With no body in the front of the apartment or the kitchen, they moved down the hallway until they got to the end bedroom.

Sharon lay bent and twisted in the middle of the floor, her blood saturated hair lying askew across the carpet.

"Shit, why the hell would he kill her?" Kathy whispered aloud.

"He most likely needed sex after his rampage last night and the confrontations at the diner this morning," Johnny said, standing directly behind her. "She most likely got frightened of him, became loud and he shut her up. To this beast, killing means nothing. He's been doing it for many years."

Tommy looked at him quizzically. "Many years, how old could this animal be?"

"You wouldn't believe me if I told you detective. Just know that killing to him means nothing more than you swatting a fly or crushing a spider. Life means absolutely nothing to it, especially human life," Johnny answered him.

Outside the apartment house darkness had fallen. Lights from numerous police cars echoed and bounced off telephone poles and neighboring buildings, almost appearing like a side show. Johnny walked to the sidewalk and stood with hands in his pocket. Kathy came up and stood beside him.

"Johnny, what the hell are we dealing with?" she asked in a nervous voice.

"You're dealing with hell Kathy," he said, lifting his head and smelling the air, suddenly looking around intently.

She felt him stiffen and searched his face for signs.

"What's wrong Johnny?" she asked.

"He's here somewhere, nearby, and he's watching us right now," Johnny said ominously.

"Are you sure? Can you tell where, or who it is?"

"No, but I can smell him. Kathy I need to move and I need to do it alone. That's how I work, you will only slow me down," he told her, starting to walk away.

"Johnny, take this other cell phone and keep in touch with me. I also cannot vouch for your safety, especially with so many edgy police that will be searching the area tonight," she told him.

"I'll be careful and will have no need for a cell phone. I wouldn't be able to take it with me anyway. I will contact you though," he said, moving quickly and gracefully away from her.

He stopped then and turned to face her with a very concerned look.

"Detective Morello, if and when you confront this beast tonight, please do not hesitate to shoot first. He is a killer and if you see him, I promise you that you will not see a man."

Kathy smiled and laughed nervously. "Should I have silver bullets then?"

Without smiling, Johnny answered, "It's good to have a sense of humor Kathy, but not right now. From your legends, silver will kill it for sure. But you don't have that at your disposal right now so if you see it then shoot directly for the brain or the heart. And shoot it more than once, empty the entire clip. Any other direct hits will slow it down but not kill it. Kathy, avoid contact with it at all costs. Do you understand that?"

"Yes, I understand you Johnny. Shoot first, ask questions later, and shoot it in the head or the heart," she replied.

"The brain Kathy, make sure it's the brain and more than one shot to make sure it's dead," he replied sternly.

She nodded that she understood as he moved away once more. Kathy thought he had the movements of a wild, predatory animal and knew there was a lot of mystery to this strange but intoxicating man. She looked away for a second and back. Damn, he was gone already. She wondered how the hell he did that.

The high pitched sound of an ambulance could be heard coming up Ridge Avenue. Before this evening was over, Kathy felt safe in assuming there would be many more sirens screaming through the night. She turned and went back inside the apartment house to find Tommy.

At the same time Johnny had gone to his truck and drove down the street on which he had driven up to Ridge Avenue, then pulled off to the side and parked. Moving with stealth and quite invisible from prying eyes he slipped into a wooded area, undressed, hid his clothes, and shifted to his wolf form in less than fifteen seconds.

The large black wolf shook his radiant fur and lifted his head, smelling the air for the scent of his enemy. Staring up at the awakening moon he howled, preparing for the hunt.

As Kathy and Tommy walked out the front door and headed for their car, they heard what sounded like a wolf howling into the night. They looked at each other and shook their heads, nervous fingertips scratching up and down their spines.

Chapter 22

The beast glared through blood-thirsty eyes at the police as they scurried around like scalded ants. They couldn't find the hole in their asses if their lives depended on it, he growled to himself. There was that pretty detective he watched the other night. Beside her, standing out in the open so he could be seen, was the weregune who had been following him like a shadow for the past two years. He knew who it was too, the mate of that weak, whimpering female who had her stomach torn open by his own claws. The one whom he took the greatest pleasure in as he ripped out her throat and watched the last glimmer of life fade from her eyes. He had been the one to remove the unborn child. He hadn't intended to, but the others came after him so he did it for protection.

Now he glared with venomous hatred. This Raven had never been as close to confronting his wife's killer as he was now, no more than a hundred yards away. Yes, he and this weregune bastard would most assuredly meet under an angry and harsh moon. And he longed for it, either to free himself from the shadow that had been haunting him from city to city, or escape this life of monstrous slaughter.

The creature watched as his enemy walk away and then just as quickly disappear. It was obvious why he had left for he knew that the beast was in his midst. The weregune would change and that is what he must do for he felt the searing pain of the moon's teeth biting into his brain. Black hair had already begun to creep and crawl out of every pore in his body. Ripples of altering muscles were felt just underneath his burning skin, like a thousand termites eating hungrily at what humanity still lingered.

The beast turned and ran through peaceful backyards and past loudly yapping dogs. Not even stopping to look, it charged out into traffic along Henry Avenue, adeptly avoiding screeching cars until he disappeared in the trees on the other side, heading towards the temporary safety of the Wissahicken Valley. Several drivers were not as lucky as the grinding of metal filled the night.

As frustrated drivers stood around staring at their mangled vehicles, waiting for the police to arrive, they all turned as one person and listened to the haunting, bone-chilling howl of a large beast. A werewolf was loose once again on the streets of Philadelphia.

Jaress moved among the shadows, unseen, unheard. He blended in with the darkness like it was a layer of his skin, the only visible attribute a pair of glowing, golden eyes that occasionally blinked. Standing behind several trash cans along Ridge Avenue the wolf stared at the dwindling police presence, proceeding to search the area for a killer upon the loose. Leaning up against a vehicle were two humans that he knew, especially the female. His desire stirred, even as a beast.

When Jaress altered his form he still retained feelings and human thought, but it was minimized somewhat by that of the animal he embraced, whether it be wolf or bird of prey. He was keenly aware of who she was, his will to protect her very strong, but a much more pressing need was paramount. The creature he followed must be found and destroyed if possible, but not before he obtained the truth in regards to Sashine.

Like a whisper of black silk he moved across the street, nose to the ground and sought the trail of a killer. Not far, near the back of Shop Rite, he located what he hoped to find. His lips pulled back in a savage grimace revealing fangs that could easily tear through any skin and bone, animal or human. A deep, thunderous growl emerged from his massive chest. The hunt was now fully engaged.

He moved among the shadows with the grace of a cat, the fearless nature of a predatory wolf, and the acute awareness of a most dangerous bird of prey. In effect, he had no equals. The only thing that could kill him was a very unlucky stray bullet that was a direct hit to his brain, or having his heart removed by another member of his race. That would only happen if he was on the verge of death anyway.

The trail was strong and he could tell the creature was still in human form, but not for long. Jaress glanced at the moon as he moved through back yards and empty side streets. Avoiding detection was paramount to a weregune for if he was detected then most times the individual seeing him would end up dead. No witnesses so to speak. Since a weregune was most adept at killing whether in beast or human form, many unsolved deaths could be attributed to his kind. It was not the philosophy of Jaress however, but there were times nonetheless when he also had killed to protect their existence.

He stopped behind some trees and took note of the traffic accident. The werewolf had come this way and then moved into the dense forest across the road. Like nothing more than a swift breeze that blows your hair, he was across the open area and safely among the trees. After a few minutes he picked up the trail. Jaress could also tell that the spore was changing to more of a wolf and was acutely prepared for a dangerous confrontation. Taking on a rogue werewolf was perilous because they fought with frenzied passion, their only emotion a despicable hatred of the human race and all weregune.

With ears pitched forward, eyes slanted and intense, his senses at the highest alert, he moved through the darkness with but only one mission. To locate and confront this killer who had taken his Samantha. Jaress was very close and the time was near.

As Jaress moved with great stealth, his nemesis Quentin raced headlong through the trees, limbs and bushes battering him with hateful accusations that made him even angrier, a forceful moon reaching inside his body to bring forth the beast. Pain was excruciating and he moaned in agony as he ran, bending over more and more until he collapsed. His face began to change into a quasi-human/wolf appearance, ears growing longer into pointed lupine shapes. Drooling fangs began to replace smaller human teeth. His spine cracked and bowed like the snapping of a thick pencil as the creature threw back his head and angrily howled at the moment of this perversion to the flesh. In less than a minute he had changed completely into a crazed and ravenous beast, a killing machine. It was a predator of unspeakable horror.

Looking around, his muzzle open, moonlight glinting off long, sharp fangs he turned and detected the presence of the weregune that trailed him. Similar to those of full-breed he retained some of his human traits, but not as many. He was more pure, ravenous, hellish beast at this point. He could not teleport his thoughts and any sense of logic or conscience was gone.

He tore off the last remaining tatters of cloth that still remained on his limbs and crouched, moving further behind some thick brush. His senses were now keenly alert for the appearance of the weregune, this Raven who had been dogging his trail for several years. The creature was actually thankful that tonight would be judgment day. It was not prepared to die, but it also did not fear death for in effect he had died a hundred years ago when he first became infected.

"Kathy, let's move. A large traffic accident just happened a few minutes ago on Henry Avenue. The people involved are raving about a wild, hairy man running out onto the road. Sounds like our guy," Tommy yelled, already jumping into a patrol car with Sgt. Ruiz and went screeching down Ridge Avenue.

Kathy was right behind him. Her mind was split on following this killer and where Johnny had disappeared to. Something strongly told her that he had also went in that direction and she hoped he would not be taken for the killer. All police were on the highest sense of alert tonight. She felt that anything even resembling an animal tonight would be shot on sight.

They pulled up onto the shoulder and ran to the front of the mangled mess. After some quick questioning and fingers pointing to the direction the hairy beast had run, both Kathy and Tommy pulled their weapons and crossed over Henry Avenue into the woods on the other side, followed by six police officers. Kathy held up her hand and they all crouched down.

"Okay guys, listen up. This killer is extremely dangerous and most likely is so deranged that he will not be able to listen to any of your commands to stop and give up. In fact, he will most likely attack before you even get a chance to yell anything at it. Some of you have seen the man that was with me on several occasions, Johnny Raven. He's a tracker and should be ahead of us somewhere. Don't get too trigger happy and shoot him by mistake. The monster we're after thinks he's a wolf so be prepared for anything. Understand?" Kathy asked them with extreme intensity.

Murmurs were all she received, but they were ready, at least she hoped so. She wondered if she was as prepared as she told them to be, and if they all would survive.

"Okay, let's spread out, but try and stay within eyesight of somebody. If you see something then yell out so we all know what's happening. Stay alert and let's try to end this tonight without anybody else getting killed. Let's rock and roll," she told them.

While the small group of nervous policemen began their cautious but intense search through the dark woods, Jaress stopped about ten feet from a small clearing and dropped to the ground. The beast was here, hidden in the trees on the other side of the open area, waiting for him to make a mistake and reveal himself. He was way too smart for that, but he also knew the creature was aware he was there. Crawling forward slowly, his eyes moved quickly in every direction, prepared to counter any attack from the beast. He also heard the noisy stumbling and bumbling of the police behind him, detecting the scent of the female as well. They were still far enough behind to not be in danger as yet. He needed to end this now and quickly.

Moving cautiously along the edge of the clearing, the massive black wolf stood erect, head held low towards the ground, beady eyes peering towards the direction where he knew the creature hid. And then it appeared, emerging like a grotesque vision, looking more like a wolf, but standing bent over on two legs. Its arms, more like smaller front legs, reached towards Jaress, hands now paws with claws where fingernails used to be. Slobber dribbled from its mouth amid a deepening, ominous growl that sounded like he was saying "Jaaaarrressss".

The two creatures circled each other, prepared for the other to strike while waiting for the perfect opportunity to go for the kill. The weregune sank low, coiling his back legs to spring. With an ear splitting roar it leaped towards the werewolf, striking the creature chest high and sank his fangs into the rogue's shoulder. The beast screamed in pain and began raking the back of the massive wolf which now propelled it towards the trees. They fell to the ground, rolling and tearing at each other. Blood, fur, and skin flew in all directions. This was a battle to the death for one of them, but Jaress knew he could not kill this creature until he found out the truth.

Suddenly the beast clutched Jaress in a crushing embrace and then flung the wolf across the clearing where it slammed into a large tree. Lying there, dazed and in pain, the black wolf felt the werewolf grab one if his rear legs and start dragging him towards the trees on the other side of the clearing. Extending his neck forward, the massive black weregune sunk its teeth into a leg of the creature, pulling it back on top of him. Under moonlight's glare, two nightmarish beasts fought to slay each other.

Kathy was the first to set eyes on this unbelievable sight. It was truly something out of a horror movie yet it was real and destroyed in one second all of her thoughts on myth and legend. She remembered what Johnny had told her, to shoot first and not question the decision. It was evident the creature that hardly resembled a man anymore was grappling with a large wolf. She hesitated ever so slightly to make sure it was not Johnny that the creature was fighting with and then yelled before firing her gun.

The creature turned its horrifying face and roared his displeasure at this mere human having the nerve to confront it. Jaress took the slight hesitation on the beast's part to sink his fangs into the werewolf's neck. At the same moment Kathy began to fire, not really sure where the bullets would strike. Shoot for the brain or heart, Johnny had told her, but in her panic she just began shooting.

Some of the bullets missed while a few hit their designated targets. Both creatures were hit and roared defiance at this additional onslaught. The werewolf rose up and turned towards Kathy, towering over her. It was a nightmare in real life, one that she never imagined she would encounter in her police work.

Dropping one clip from her gun she immediately slammed another one in place. The werewolf had moved so close she could feel its hellish breath raining down upon her. The monstrous creature swung a brutish hand at Kathy who felt the cloth of her coat tear away violently.

She moved a step backwards as the huge black wolf leaped on the creature's back, flinging it to the side, ripping and tearing wildly, the animal's only intention to finally kill its despised enemy. Gunfire erupted from several directions as Tommy and another police officer came upon this grizzly sight. The werewolf was hit numerous times, knocking it backwards where it disappeared into the trees. The black wolf lay on his side, bleeding from numerous wounds inflicted by the werewolf as well as several gunshots from Kathy's blazing gun. Tommy and the police officer followed the beast as it continued to crash through the brush, trying to get away.

That left only Kathy and the wolf in the clearing as she moved cautiously forward. After all, this beast had saved her life, but she was still extremely wary with her gun pointed towards the animal. She suddenly froze as the wolf raised its head and stared at her through intense, golden eyes. Eyes that she had seen before and her heart began to beat harder. As if in a dream, the air rippled around the wolf that was still lying on the ground. Kathy could not believe her eyes and for a second the thought of insanity entered her mind. What she saw was not possible, yet this entire night was not possible. The wolf changed shapes and Johnny

Raven, totally human and bleeding from numerous wounds, stared at her with those same yellow eyes.

"Please don't be frightened Kathy, I won't hurt you. I need to change back to my wolf in order to heal, for I will die if I stay in human form. The creature will get away and I need to track it until morning when it will turn back into a man. It is mortally wounded and I need to talk to it in order to get answers. Then I will kill it, but you have to trust me," he said to her in a calm, soothing voice.

"How is this possible Johnny? What in God's name are you?" she asked, on the verge of losing it completely.

"I will answer all your questions, but believe me, if I don't turn back I will not survive and I need to leave now," he said, as the air rippled around him until he was once again a huge black wolf glaring back in her direction.

The beast rose and towered before her as she lowered the gun. The wolf suddenly disappeared leaving Kathy completely alone in the clearing doubting her own sanity and belief in what was real and what was not. She lifted her eyes to the dark purple sky and stared at the moon, realizing that monsters truly did exist.

Chapter 23

Jaress moved cautiously through the trees, closely following the blood trail of the rogue. It wasn't long before the police were left far behind so it was just the two vicious creatures once again. His injuries healed as he walked in wolf form. Daylight had begun to creep over the eastern horizon to spread its fingers into this secluded world that was Wissahicken Creek. Jaress knew the werewolf had changed and was most likely lying somewhere mortally wounded.

As the black wolf moved around a small curve in the creek he spied Quentin lying half in, half out of the water. He growled deeply and the werewolf turned-man lifted his head slightly to look upon his death sentence at last. He laughed in a guttural sound from a neck wound that still gaped open and a lung shot from that crazy woman detective.

"My shadow Mr. Raven, we finally meet. I wish it were you lying here and not me," he said painfully.

Jaress continued to walk slowly through the stream until he stood five feet from his enemy. His golden eyes glared a hatred he thought could never be felt for another living thing as he changed from wolf to man, standing overtop of Quentin.

"You're about to die, but I need questions answered first. If you don't want to experience more pain than you've ever felt, I think it would be in your best interest you tell me what I want to know," Johnny instructed him, a threat he was prepared to backup.

Quentin stared at his nemesis and grinned. Did this weregune really think he feared death? After a hundred years of killing, he almost welcomed it even though his destination was most likely hell.

"Pain means nothing to me, you should know that, and I fear not death. If you want answers my tortured friend, then you must sweeten the ante, or just kill me," he snarled back.

Johnny grabbed the monster by the throat with one hand, shutting off the wind pipe, his fingertips digging into the open flesh. With his other hand he pressed with all his strength on the shoulder he had torn apart, feeling the bones crunch. Quentin winced in pain and sneered back, trying to breathe and failing to do a good job of it.

After a minute Johnny released his grip and let the human beast fall back into the water. To kill him would give Johnny only gratification for avenging his Sam's death. It would not find out who was behind the killing for Johnny knew that this creature would not have done this of his own volition.

"Tell me what I want to know and then we'll talk. That's your only recourse, otherwise you die now," Johnny growled ominously.

Quentin pushed hard with his feet, sliding like a worm out of the water onto the muddy bank. The deep wound on his neck gaped open so much that Johnny could see the windpipe shuddering with each intake of air.

Sneering at Johnny, Quentin croaked, "And what can I tell you that you don't already know, my friend?"

Johnny reached down again and picked his limp body up with both hands cupped around his chin, legs dangling like a puppet.

"I'm not now or ever will be your friend. You're a monster that has killed for way too long, and that night you attacked my wife, you wrote your own death sentence," Johnny growled, throwing Quentin further into the stream and then wading in after him.

Quentin sputtered to keep his head above water just as Johnny reached him, bending over and pushing his entire face under the cold water. The creature kicked and beat against Johnny's hips for over a minute before he was suddenly yanked from the water and thrown back onto shore.

Coughing and gasping for breath, he choked, "No more, what do you want to know? Then just kill me if that's what you plan to do."

Towering over the wretched creature, Johnny snarled, "Who ordered you to kill my Samantha? Who else was there that night?"

Quentin chuckled, "What makes you think I didn't run across that sweet mate of yours on my own?"

Johnny kicked the beast savagely in the ribs bringing forth a grunt of pain.

Quentin laughed, "Okay, okay, can't you take a joke? You have enemies far more powerful than me Mr. Raven, you and your entire pack of curs."

Reaching down, Johnny yanked Quentin half off the ground.

"Tell me who and why? Then you may get your wish and die," Johnny snarled loudly, squeezing the badly injured shoulder once again.

"On second thought," Quentin grimaced, "maybe you should ask your father who may have ordered me to kill your lovely wife."

Johnny brought the beast's human face closer to his own and looked venomously into Quentin's eyes.

"You bastard, what does that mean? How does my father figure into this?"

Grinning up at Johnny, Quentin's laugh echoed through the trees.

"Your father has a deep, dark secret Mr. Raven and your wife was just the beginning of revenge because of that secret. It is true

I was ordered not to attack your wife, but believe me I jut couldn't resist, I did so enjoy ......"

But Quentin never got the rest of his confession out of his evil mouth as Johnny was viciously attacked from behind by an unseen enemy, knocking him ten feet away. Turning his head, he stared into the murderous head of a huge, grey wolf. Johnny immediately closed his eyes and shifted to his own wolf form in order to do battle with this new assailant.

Leaping to all fours, Jaress turned and moved to the side, growling and snarling at this new, unexpected beast before him. Stunned, he sensed who it was and roared in anger. The two massive wolves circled each other, waiting for just the right opening. In a blur they struck out and extended their open mouths, searching for an opening in order to lunge at the neck and bring their enemy down. They both hit their mark. Landing loudly in the in the icy waters of Wissahicken Creek they splashed loudly and roared, trying to tear out the others throat.

Rapid gunshots were suddenly heard coming from high on the bank. Johnny felt the beast he was fighting quickly go limp and fall away. The gunshots continued to ring out as the shooter continued coming further until the clip was emptied and only a clicking sound echoed in the early morning light.

Kathy stood ankle deep in the creek, the muzzle of her flashing gun choking in anger. Ejecting the spent clip, she deftly inserted another one and squeezed off two more direct shots into the brain of the dead weregune as she had been instructed by Johnny.

Jaress got up and moved to tower over the dead wolf. As he stared down, the other weregune shifted back into human form. Jaress realized it was Barton, Victor's son, and was temporarily stunned. Why had he attacked Johnny? With blood pouring from the dead wolf's destroyed head, Jaress turned and glanced at the bank. Quentin had disappeared, obviously taking advantage of the situation to make his escape. Then Jaress slid his gaze further behind him to see Kathy Morello standing in the water, her gun leveled directly at him, at the living, breathing, blood-covered beast standing before her.

"Run Johnny, run!" she croaked. "Get the hell out of here now before other police get here. Leave while you can and we'll meet later. Go!" she said urgently.

Jaress turned and scrambled up the other creek bank, turning only once to look back at this disheveled, but still beautiful, woman standing in the freezing water, her gun still leveled at him, but who now glanced down at the nude and bloody body of Barton. Then Jaress disappeared, more confused than ever now. What did Victor and his father have to do with Samantha's death? More answers he was most definitely going to find.

Chapter 24

Tommy moved up to stand beside Kathy and put his hand on the gun she now held pointing downwards at the body lying submerged in the creek. Gently he pried her vise-like grip loose from the cold metal and pocketed her gun. Putting his arm around her shoulder he guided her out of the frigid water.

"Jesus Christ, what happened here? Is that the killer?" Tommy asked as gently as possible so not to startle her even more than she was.

In a daze she gazed hauntingly up into Tommy's eyes, bewildered and stunned.

"That's one of them. The other one got away, but he's mortally wounded I think," Kathy droned.

Concerned, he asked, "Are you hurt Kat?"

She shook her head, "No, I don't think so, why?"

"Because your left arm is all bloody from the shoulder to the wrist. Come on, we need to get you out of here and get treatment," Tommy said, keeping his arm around her.

"Okay, I didn't even realize it. I don't remember getting hurt," she groaned, the magnitude of what had happened this night beginning to weigh her down from sheer exhaustion.

"Hang on Kathy. I think you're going into shock. Officer Hentzl, get over here and help me with Detective Morello. Sergeant Gracey, radio in and get an ambulance out to Henry right away. Also, have your men search the area and be very careful. One of the killers evidently is still on the loose, but it's badly hurt."

Trudging carefully as possible through the thick woods under a gray, dismal cover of another early fall morning, Kathy moaned some words that were unintelligible. Tommy could barely detect 'wolf', 'impossible', 'raven'. He was deeply afraid she was about to pass out so he picked her up in his arms, carrying her the rest of the way towards the flashing lights on Henry Avenue.

"Kathy, hang in there honey, just hang in there. I can see the ambulance and you'll be okay," Tommy said soothingly.

Several EMT techs met him as he broke through the trees, placing her on the stretcher and wheeling her to the back of the vehicle. They sliced open the sleeve on the one side of her coat so the wound on her arm could be checked out. It was nasty looking! Five long, very deep claw marks that had obviously been inflicted by some beast, but the only body lying in the water happened to be in the form of a badly mangled man. Tommy stood back and intently watched the technicians hook her up to an IV and apply a temporary wrapping to the entire length of her arm.

Before they closed the back door, Tommy got inside the ambulance and sat as close to her as he could for he was not about to let his partner out of his sight. She had been through enough already and seen something extremely horrible and frightening, more than the rest of them could maybe ever comprehend.

Jaress had stopped when he achieved the safety of the trees and turned around just as other police arrived to span out, their guns drawn. He watched a man come over to the woman, place his hand on hers and then remove the gun. The wolf then caught a glimpse of her injured arm and his heart felt remorse, if a wolf's heart can feel that emotion. The creature must have bit or clawed her. For a rogue werewolf to infect another it could be done by either fang or claw. Jaress knew he'd be seeing her again soon, to talk about what she had seen, as well as badly needed help in realizing what had happened to her.

There were too many police congregated around the water for the wolf to pick up the trail of the creature he came so close to killing. But they would meet once more and Jaress would not fail again. Instead he crept upstream like a misty shadow to find a safe place he could cross the stream. Being virtually invisible when he had to be was what allowed his breed to slide through the human populace so easily.

He crossed Ridge near the apartment house to the sound of screeching brakes. He heard an elderly man ask his wife if she had seen the dog that had run in front of their car.

She yelled, "Damn old fart, you can't see anything anyway, so just keep your eyes on the road."

Ten minutes later Johnny was dressed and pulling away from the spot where he had parked the truck. His mind was in a complete turmoil over what the werewolf had told him concerning his father. What was this deep, dark secret and how did it result in Samantha's death?

He had only felt sick in his stomach once before when he had mistakenly consumed some poisoned meat left out by a wary farmer to ward off hungry predators. Johnny felt like he had been poisoned and gut shot at the same time.

He drove around aimlessly for an hour not knowing where to go or what to do. Kathy had been hurt by the creature and that alone was very bad. She had at this time no idea how her life had changed in a split second. He would need to talk to her soon, but knew she would be extremely fearful of him now that she was aware he was a monster as well, at least in her eyes. Yet he would have to make her understand what was in her future and what options were available.

First he needed to find an out of the way place to sleep for the night. Second, he needed to contact his father to see if they had left for Philadelphia. Third, he would have to scout around Victor's house, but he was certain he would find nothing. Victor was too smart to stay once he found out his son had been killed. Knowing that Johnny would come looking for him would, by itself, make him move away. At least temporarily until a proper attack or defense could be planned.

Johnny found a small twenty-unit, flea-bag motel along Rte. 202. Once in the room he fell backwards onto the bed and shut his eyes. It had been a long night and he was very sore, not only from wounds inflicted on him by the rogue and Barton, but several of the gunshots he had received. The wounds had mostly healed, but the torn muscle tissue was still very painful, at least for another few days. He had dispersed the bullets like foreign matter as the gunshots healed. It was the way his race was able to avoid metal poisoning from stray gunshots. Fortunately, Kathy had not meant to hit him, or at least he hoped that was the case.

Johnny made a call to his father and found that he, along with two siblings and four other pack members, had left during the night. His mother asked if everything was okay and he told her most of what had transpired during the night. She was as worried for her son's welfare as any mother would be.

"Mom may I ask you a question?" he inquired, not sure she knew the answer, or if she did, would tell him.

"Of course Johnny, you can ask me anything, you've always known that. What is it?" she asked back.

"Do you personally know this Victor that leads the pack here in Philadelphia?"

"No, can't say as I do," his mother answered. "I know of him, but we've never met. He wasn't always from Philadelphia, but I'm not sure from where or when he moved his pack there. Why do you ask?"

"Just curious is all. Do you know how long ago he and father might have been friends?" he asked her.

There was a slight hesitation before she answered.

"I had to think for a second, but I don't know that they ever knew each other, at least as long as your father and I have been together. Where is all this curiosity coming from? Did something else happen there?" she asked, worry now edging her voice.

"Nothing really mother, don't worry. Hey, on a bright note, congratulations. Father told me the good news when we talked yesterday. I'm very happy for you both."

"Thanks sweetie, you'll have a new brother or sister in the spring."

After a few more casual pleasantries he hung up, yet still retained the nagging concerns over what he was told relative to his father. When he arrived in Philly, at some point shortly thereafter, Johnny felt he would need to confront him and find out the truth behind Samantha's death, or possibly a reason for it.

Sleep escaped him and so he left the room around noon, grabbed a quick burger and coffee, and then headed back to the Roxborough section of the city. While he drove down the expressway thinking of Kathy, he realized he needed to take a detour to Victor's home. Johnny needed to make certain that the Philadelphia Alpha was not there and if he was, then he would find out the truth no matter what he had to do.

Colleen Frye was awake very early while ominous darkness still covered the city in a chilly shawl of foreboding. Standing by a shadowed bedroom window overlooking a virtually empty Market Street far below, she allowed her gaze to drift upwards to stare at a magnetic, intoxicating moon. Horrible dreams, stark nightmares in fact, plagued her last night like they had briefly in the hospital. She could not rid herself from that frightening image of the wolf turning its head with a bloody human face – her face. Placing a shaking hand on her shoulder she realized something was drastically wrong, big time wrong. The doctor told her how terrible her injuries had been when she was brought into the emergency room and yet other than something resembling a newly formed scar and five bright pink scratches running down her left breast and stomach, it was all completely healed. She had some fleeting memories of that night, remembering a very dark stranger who was both handsome and frightening at the same time. But she had somehow fallen under his magical spell, aided by the amount of wine she had consumed. She never had been a very good drinker, becoming quite tipsy and flirty after two glasses.

But now, she felt completely different, like her life had been suddenly ripped apart, drastically altered in some horrifying way. Colleen moved quietly back to the bed and stood looking down at Sara. She loved her so much, but felt that Sara was now in possible grave danger somehow if she stayed near her, at least for the moment anyway until she understood what was happening.

As she started to turn in order to go and wallow under a hot, scalding shower, somehow hoping to cleanse herself of fears which had been raging inside her, Sara groaned slightly and opened her blue eyes to see Colleen standing there.

"Hey honey, what's up? Wow, it looks so dark outside," she moaned softly, tugging the blanket tighter underneath her chin.

Colleen leaned over and kissed Sara on the forehead then lightly on the lips.

"I couldn't sleep sweetheart, I was just going to take a hot shower. You go back to sleep. I think I'm going to go back home early. The police should be gone by now. I just feel so restless and don't think I'd make very good company right now," Colleen whispered in Sara's ear, now able to smell so much more of her enticing aroma, more than she had ever been capable of detecting before. It was like a vast, new array of senses were now open to her, abilities like sight, sound and smell so keenly sharp.

"No Colleen, please don't go. Or maybe I'll go with you, okay?"

"I really need to be alone for awhile honey," Colleen said, kissing her partner again. "Just go back to sleep beautiful."

Sara threw back the covers and moved around the bed, sexy as hell in her long black nightgown. Colleen felt like burrowing her face so deeply between those luscious breasts that were so damn inviting.

"Then we'll take a shower together. If you're leaving for a little while then I want to spend as much time with you as I can," Sara said, starting to cry. "Colleen, I thought I lost you last night forever and I just couldn't bear that. Tell me you'll never leave me."

Colleen held her tightly and let Sara sob for a few minutes against the shoulder that had been supposedly injured so badly, rubbing Sara's back and neck with a loving, circular touch. She had not been this happy in many years and meeting Sara had been nearly the best thing to happen in her life. Colleen had never been involved before in a lesbian relationship, but the closeness between the two women at work brought them into many situations where they were together, both at the office, in the courtroom, and during their personal time as well. Sara had always been cautious of letting her sexual tendencies known to anybody in the law firm, feeling it would be tantamount to dismissal, or she would become ostracized in some way by the managing partners.

Yet one night after grabbing a veggie pizza and watching a few romantic movies in Sara's apartment which followed a particularly difficult day in court, she opened up to Colleen about her sexual preferences. At the same time she subtly made it known to Colleen how much she cared for her, not only as a good friend, and that she knew Colleen was not a lesbian and there was definitely no pressure on her to respond.

Colleen was not surprised for she had never known Sara to date, or even been intimate, with a man. Hell, Colleen's personal sexual life was a disaster any way, a demolition derby of egotistical, self-centered guys that only desired one thing from her. Many of the guys she dated were law students and eventually young, anxious, do anything to get ahead, lawyers who thought more about their own careers than forming a loving relationship with anyone.

Sara had not been that way though. She was a very sweet, loving and caring woman who Colleen felt extremely relaxed and wonderful around. A week later, one night after doing some shopping, they became intimate. Just a few wonderful kisses and heavenly embraces, but it was a start. Colleen became captivated with Sara's charm and tender heart, enchanted by her sensuality and willingness to please her. That had been a year ago and it quickly became evident to other members of the law firm that these two young women had more than a working relationship between them. Some of their co-workers had no problem with it but others did, making their displeasure known in a variety of different ways. But Colleen and Sara knew they would be leaving the firm shortly, already having made contact with a law group that was much more open to their sexual preferences, desiring only to have capable and dedicated attorneys on board. Both women were extremely excited about the upcoming move.

After a very intimate shower together, Colleen got dressed and kissed Sara good-bye, holding her very close. For some reason she felt a dread forming inside her, that somehow Sara was about to depart from her life and Colleen felt crushed by that prospect.

The drive home on the nearly deserted streets did not take long. In fact, she drove slowly past a still sleeping art museum and then down Kelly Drive. There were already rowers putting their shells in the water, well before the sun broke the horizon. She loved this area and had come here often with Scoots to jog. Just the thought of her beloved dog not being in her life anymore brought a large lump to her throat. Tears began to run wildly down her cheeks. Thank God she was practically the only driver on the road for several times she went into oncoming lanes on the sharp curves.

There was still yellow crime scene tape up around the front of her house. She angrily ripped it away. Screw the police, this was her house and she was okay. Unlocking the door she was assailed by sudden memories that nearly caused her to pass out. Holding onto the door jamb she let the dizziness pass and entered the foyer. Closing the door the silence was overwhelming. Tears began to flow once again as she realized that her loving dog had not bounded from another part of the house to excitedly jump on her, tail wagging with a big doggie grin.

Colleen dropped her keys in a tray on the small desk just on the inside of the living room, draped her coat over the chair and walked out into the kitchen to heat some water for a cup of tea. Her eyes staring down at the tiles on the floor she reached for the light switch. When the lights came on she was startled to see Quentin sitting at the table, splattered blood still clinging to his face, eyes dark and sunken.

With a frantic gasp Colleen turned and raced out into the hallway, trying to reach the front door and possible escape. She didn't make it as Quentin's massive hand grabbed her by the shoulder and literally threw her into the living room where she slammed into a chair, her momentum spilling her and the chair crashing to the floor. Before she even had a chance to scramble away he was upon her.

"Don't move," he snarled, glaring through eyes that bordered on insanity. "I don't want to kill you, but I will."

Colleen's heart pounded frantically and yet surprisingly she sensed a kinship to this wild, insane man. She laid there not moving until she felt his fist release the hold on her shoulder and he stood up. Then he did a strange thing by extending his hand in order to help her up. She put her smaller hand in his and he hoisted her like she was a soft flower. He then gently guided her to the couch where she sat down, not knowing what next to expect.

"Don't be afraid of me Colleen. I didn't quite no where to go so I came here. As you can see from my appearance, I didn't have the most enjoyable evening. I just need a place to stay and clean-up a bit," he told her as gently as he could, not wanting her to be frightened.

"What did you do to me Quentin? I should be dead and yet I'm nearly healed. I can see, and hear, and smell in much greater clarity than before. What are you?" she asked him, voice bordering on hysterics.

"There is enough time for explanations Colleen. Just know that you are now so much greater than before. I have given you a gift that you will either love or hate me for. Only you will be able to determine that," he told her, his eyes peering into her soul.

Suddenly Colleen shot up from the couch and launched herself at him, screaming, kicking and pummeling him as they spilled to the hardwood floor.

"You monster, you killed my dog, I hate you. I could never love you," she screeched, angrier than she had ever been in her life. So angry she could kill.

He let Colleen have her way for a moment in order to release all the pent up anger and hostility inside her as he grabbed and held her tightly while she cried hysterically.

"I'm sorry Colleen, but the dog had to die. Eventually it would've attacked me and I would've had to kill it anyway. I'm afraid your dog would not have accepted you as well," he told her firmly.

Getting up he helped her to the couch once again.

"Now, I need to clean up and know that you'll still be here when I'm done. Colleen I don't want to tie you up or silence you, but I will. Do you understand that?"

She didn't answer, just nodded her understanding. Her eyes were filled with hate, but she would bide her time for revenge.

"I also need some food Colleen and then I need to rest so I can let these wounds heal. Thankfully none of them are fatal, but it will take me awhile to mend. Can I trust you?" he asked intensely.

Colleen only stared at him, not knowing what to do, but yet aware he would most assuredly kill her and she needed to buy time. So she nodded yes.

"Tell me Colleen, don't just nod. I need to hear your voice," he snarled.

"Yes, I'll be a good girl for now, but know in that dark heart of yours, if you even have one, that I hate and despise you for what you've done. For now, just take a shower and clean up. You actually stink and happen to be extremely disgusting to look at. I'll fix you something to eat and then I need some questions answered," she told him in a very low and ominous threat.

"That's my girl," he said turning towards the hallway.

"I'm not your girl and never will be. Don't ever call me that again," she growled.

He turned and smiled. "Oh yes my dear, you don't know how connected we are now, but you will find out soon enough," leaving to climb the steps to the bathroom.

Colleen didn't know what kind of a monster he was, but somehow she was frightened with the horrifying sense her own life had been changed in such a way that she might welcome death rather than continue living.

Chapter 25

Kathy entered the house followed closely by her father. The pain in her arm had surprisingly diminished to nothing more than a dull ache underneath the skin, mostly because the muscles had been slightly torn according to the attending physician. He had placed a few sutures where the wound gaped open, but commented later upon her release from the emergency room that it seemed to him it would heal nicely. At least muscle damage appeared to be minimal, but that would become stronger as well. He also could be heard muttering under his breath, "Hell, it seems like it's mostly healed already."

Tommy realized as he hovered over Kathy that it was the second time he had heard the same comments. Something very strange was happening, far beyond the scope of his limited understanding. He was just very grateful his partner would be okay. He had watched with great trepidation as Kathy got into her father's car and pulled out of the parking lot, her tired but haunted eyes glancing back at Tommy.

Now as she slowly removed her coat Rain sat in her bed eyeing Kathy suspiciously. The dogs head was down, almost as if she didn't trust her mommy.

Kneeling down, Kathy said softly, "Come here girl, what's wrong. I need a big hug and kiss right about now."

Rain got up and slowly came forward. Then the oddest thing, Rain lay down in front of Kathy placing her head in her paws in kind of a submissive pose.

Kathy started to laugh. "Hey what's wrong with you? Mommy's okay, I'm home safe and sound."

Rain got up and moved forward where Kathy put a big hug around the dog's neck.

From the kitchen came another voice.

"Hello....pretty boy," sang the high pitched voice of Romeo.

Kathy laughed. "Somebody else wants to say hello and I'm suddenly very hungry. Come on girl."

Getting up and moving into the kitchen she spoke over her shoulder, "Dad, you hungry? Want some lunch?"

"Yeah, that would be nice, but you should go upstairs and lie down. You need to rest that shoulder. I can fix us some hot soup and turkey sandwiches," he said, following her into the kitchen where Romeo started squawking, spreading his large wings, bobbing and weaving like he was in a sparring match with an invisible opponent.

Kathy went over to the cage and opened the door, putting her hand inside. Romeo suddenly screeched and backed away to a perch further back.

"What the heck's going on with these two? They almost act like they're afraid of me. It's so weird," Kathy said surprised.

"Maybe it's the hospital smell, disinfectant, medicine, whatever. Animals are very sensitive you know," he replied.

"Yeah, maybe you're right. You know, I am kind of tired so think I will go up and lie down. I could use some tea and an English muffin though," she hinted, giving her father a big hug and a peck on the cheek. "I love you so much dad."

Returning the hug he answered, "I love you too. I worry so much about you Kathy. Wish you'd give up this job because one of these days you're not going to be so lucky."

"I know you worry and I promise to be careful. This case is just very dangerous. After I take a nap we'll talk about it, okay?"

"That's fine, but only if you need to talk. Now go up stairs," he said, giving her a light smack on the ass.

Kathy laughed and moved towards the steps just as her cell phone rang.

"Hello, this is Detective Morello, what's up?" she said.

There was a slight pause then a familiar voice spoke into her ear.

"Detective Morello, this is Johnny. Are you okay?"

"Yes, I'm okay it seems. How did you know I was hurt?" she asked him, concern lining her words. The last time she had seen him he was a large, black wolf with bright, golden eyes and blood staining his muzzle, dripping into the Wissahickon Creek.

"I stopped behind the trees and watched for a few minutes as your partner and other cops came up. That's when I saw your arm. How are you feeling?"

"Surprisingly pretty well considering any other possible consequences I suppose," she said. "Where are you Johnny?"

"I'm actually nearby at a McDonald's. I needed some hot coffee and a few burgers. You know, those double cheeseburgers aren't bad and they're only a buck," he chuckled, "Though I threw the rolls and pickles away."

"Yeah, I don't think a wolf is used to eating bread and pickles too much," she retorted.

There was a pause and then, "You'd be surprised what a wolf can eat when it's pretty hungry."

Kathy started laughing hysterically, trying not to hyper-ventilate.

"Johnny, everything I've known up to this point has just been thrown out the window," she said quietly after the giggling stopped.

"I know Kathy. Are you too tired to talk right now?" he asked.

"I'm very tired to be honest, but I know sleep will be impossible. The doctor gave me some very strong pain pills and if I take them I'll be completely in lala land. I can't afford to be so zonked that I'll be no use to anybody," she replied.

"Can I stop by? I promise not to stay long," he said.

"Yes. I really do have a ton of questions though I'm not sure you'll answer them."

"I'll be as honest with you as I can Kathy, but I don't know if everything I have to tell you will be very well received," he said.

"Try me Johnny. Two days ago I would've told you all this bullshit was fantasy, right out of a Stephen King novel. Now today, I might be able to write that book myself. I'll be waiting for you," she told him.

She watched Quentin wolf down half a dozen eggs, sausage, three glasses of orange juice and four cups of black coffee.

"Guess you were hungry. I suppose killing and tearing apart innocent people can give you a voracious appetite," she told him.

He grinned. "Yes my dear, you don't know the half of it. But you'll be finding out shortly, trust me."

Colleen stared at him, that ominous feeling of dread returning to burn her stomach like she had experienced at Sara's apartment earlier that morning. He had done something terrible to her and she was extremely frightened to find out what it was.

She got up from the table and angrily grabbed the plate out from under his face, egg dribbling down his lip.

He growled, "I wasn't done yet bitch."

"Oh, you're done asshole because I want you out of this house and away from me as soon as possible," snarled Colleen in a voice she wasn't used to hearing.

Quentin violently kicked the chair behind him and rushed towards her like the unholy creature he was. He pressed her back against the sink, crushing her breasts and then putting his massive, hairy hands on hers, blocking any escape.

"No my dear, I am not going anywhere. We have a bond between us now. You belong to me," he whispered with ominous intent against the side of her face.

Colleen struggled, trying to release her hands from his cold, steely grip and then spat in his face. Quentin didn't release his grip, but relaxed just enough for her to push up from the cold metal at her back. She had just enough space to bring her knee up into his groin with as much force as she could. Letting her hands go he roared in anger as she pushed him hard away from her. As he crashed against the kitchen table she ran for the hallway and escape.

Hot breath virtually singed the hairs on the back of her neck as he caught her before she unlocked the front door. His arms securely locked around her shoulders, his right hand clamped on her throat, he dragged her backwards into the living room. Quentin fell back onto the couch, his possession still imprisoned within his monstrous embrace.

"Settle down you little hell cat. You can't get away, and if you try again I will most definitely kill you. Do you understand me?"

"Yes," Colleen croaked.

"Good, that's my girl. I'm going to release you, but you'll stay lying right here against me because I love the feel of you," he moaned in her ear.

His hand came away from her throat and she coughed for air. His arms unlocked from around her shoulders and she did as she was ordered, especially now that both his hands had moved to cup both her breasts.

"What did you do to me? I can feel that something is wrong," she asked him.

"It depends on how you look at it my sweet Colleen. It's true that I am a man, but so much more than just a mere man. You are a woman, but now so much more than a woman. I have infected you Colleen with my own wolf blood. In the beginning you might think it poison, but you will come to welcome the change like the sweetest wine," he told her.

She couldn't move now, terror gripping her heart like she had never felt before. Infected! What the hell was she to become now she thought, some crazed, insane woman who bayed at the moon, wolfing down raw meat and lapping water out of a bowl?

"I don't understand Quentin. Please elaborate," she asked, her voice barely a whisper.

"Your life will now be utterly ruled by changing phases of the moon. You will experience incredible alterations when both the new and the full moon look down upon you. At first you might become incredibly nauseated with what you may do, but you will come to embrace your wolf as I have," he told her reverently.

"That's bullshit. You're insane and if you want to howl at the moon and chase rabbits on all fours then so be it. There are padded rooms for people like you, but I won't play your silly games," she warned him.

Quentin started to laugh and released her, getting up from the couch. Standing over her he let his face contort into a monstrous grin.

"Silly games you say, chase rabbits? Then watch my beautiful protégé," he told her, removing his shirt to reveal a massively muscled and hairy chest.

Colleen sat there too frightened to move, not knowing what to expect next. She believed him completely when he said that he would kill her and without even batting an evil eye. She suddenly felt extremely frightened as he came closer to hover over her.

"The moon is down and this new phase is over. But the pull is still intense and I can still alter my appearance even during the new and full moon's song. So my sweet Colleen, just watch and see what your future will be like," he warned her.

He closed his eyes tightly, but she was too panicked to move an inch. With his hands clutched tightly into fists, the muscles in his forearm began to bulge. Suddenly the hair on the back of his hands began to grow out and was followed by a much larger expanse on both arms. She heard a ripping sound, the creature's fingernails creeping forward and becoming sharp talons. Colleen looked up and stared at the monster's face where she saw faint rippling underneath the skin, his teeth beginning to jut out of his mouth. In horror she watched the faint extension of his face growing into a muzzle.

She passed out colder than a moonless night in January.

Quentin knew he could never bring his beast out completely, not without the full moon's presence. But between the two major phases, especially on the cusp of each, he was able to drastically alter his appearance when he needed to frighten or overwhelm somebody. Like he had done for Colleen to give her a flavor for what kind of power she now possessed. There was more truth to the Jekyll-Hyde legend than most people could ever believe.

Yes, Quentin knew only how terrifying it was. In an instant, your entire life was uprooted and torn asunder. Every single value and dream a person had before becoming infected was now destroyed in a moment of tragic fate. But given time, what was lost was then replaced with something better, more powerful, greater than your imagination could ever perceive. To live as a human, albeit tortured, and then become a creature that most people only had nightmares about. Certainly his life would've been so much better if he had been born weregune which is something Quentin had desired for years after he had been infected and then acquired knowledge of this secretive race of shape-shifters. But he had no shot, though to change from rogue to weregune was possible. Not for him because it mostly happened to infected females, and not very often.

He leaned over and picked Colleen up easily. She needed to rest so he carried her upstairs and gently laid her on the bed. He would be there when she changed in ten days. Not something to do on your own and unprepared like he and so many others had to suffer through. She was lucky to have him Quentin felt for he would help her to understand her full potential. He would also deeply covet his new mate because the loneliness in his life had been overwhelming.

Sitting on the edge of the bed he held her hand in an affectionate gesture, something he had not done in well over fifty years. The last female to hijack his heart was Nadyia whom he had great hope for. Sadly though, she could not get used to the rage in her beast and the killing that transpired. Threatening to go to the authorities and reveal his secret he had to silence her forever, vowing then he would never allow his feelings to taint his judgment where love was concerned. Until the day he met Colleen, when with one vicious bite he turned her life to darkness where only creatures rule.

Chapter 26

Victor slammed his hand against the wall so violently that a lamp fell over and some plaster from a crack in the ceiling came raining down. Tabitha sat quietly, sobbing. Three other weregune stood stoic and silent in the middle of the room.

"My son is dead and you did nothing to prevent it?" Victor questioned in a low, snarling accusation.

"Victor please, I couldn't do anything," pleaded Reuben, "Barton told me to stay hidden in the trees. That he wanted Raven for himself in order to appease you. I didn't notice that woman come into the stream from further down until it was too late. I'm sorry," lowering his head.

Victor turned slowly, his eyes darkly hooded, ripples of anger emanating in a deadly aura from his entire body. His oldest son was dead and he needed to know why before handing out the appropriate punishment. His two younger sons, Walker and Constantine flanked Reuben, making sure he had no way to turn and escape. Victor walked over to his mate and placed his hands lovingly on her shoulders.

"You are weregune and yet you couldn't detect the presence of a lowly human, and a female no less. Her powerful scent alone should've alerted you," Victor said.

"I'm sorry sir, but the wind was very strong and she was downwind. I did notice her, but by then she was close with her gun drawn and it was too late. By your own directive we were not to harm the police in any way," he nervously whined.

Victor quickly moved in front of Reuben, his hand whipping up and knocking him to the floor where he was then grabbed and yanked back to his feet in the strong grasp of Victor's two sons. The elder weregune moved to stand inches from Reuben's face, his breath angry and tortured.

"He was my oldest son and you let him get shot," screamed Victor, the venom from his words stinging Reuben deeply. "You stayed hidden like a damn coward and let Barton get his head blown off. You slunk behind some trees while he was killed."

"I'm sorry, you know how close Barton and I were, but as she stood there with her gun raised I wasn't sure who, or if, she was going to shoot at all. Then I heard a number of police coming up from behind me. I would've had to move quickly at that point in order to stop her."

"So you shivered like a weakling and let her shoot him," Victor declared.

Reuben shook his head, trying to get free but couldn't, securely ensnared.

"If I would've attacked her then she would've died. There would not have been enough time to get away before the other police arrived. Besides, after she shot Barton the strangest thing happened," Reuben cried out.

Victor stood there, his eyes inches from Reuben's face, waiting for anything that could've substantiated a reason for not killing the female detective when he had the chance. There had been nothing to this point but now he waited, his patience balancing on a very thin thread.

"What happened that was so strange you let Barton get killed," Victor growled.

"It was almost immediately that she began shooting, emptying an entire clip into both Barton and Raven. She quickly replaced the clip and moved forward towards Barton only and then shot him twice in the head. Victor, she knew exactly where to shoot him," Reuben said in a coarse, broken voice.

"How could she know something like that?" Victor asked, backing away.

"After she shot Barton she then leveled her gun at Johnny like she was going to shoot, but then stopped. He looked at her and she told him to run, to get away. Victor, she knew that the wolf was Johnny Raven," Reuben said, his eyes worried, but hoping he would not feel Victor's total wrath.

"So, she has been working with Raven on this case, but somehow knew that he was the wolf. Interesting, but I highly doubt Johnny would've told her about us. It's probably more like she had some stupid female intuition or something."

"And then he was gone Victor, as was Quentin who took the opportunity to get away while the fighting was going on," Reuben said.

Victor turned and grabbed Reuben's throat, cutting off the weregune's breathing, lifting him off the floor which was no easy feat since Reuben weighed well over three hundred pounds.

"Your mistake was not striking right away when you had the chance. My directive on not harming the police did not apply in this instance Reuben. It was my son she killed, my oldest son, the future of this clan and you let it happen. There is not a pack member that could ever trust you again, least of all me. We could've handled the minor death of one insignificant, female detective, but I can't handle the loss of Barton," Victor coolly replied before ripping Reuben's neck from his shoulders as easily as tearing off a stalk of celery.

Almost in slow motion Tabitha looked on as Reuben's headless body slumped to the floor, Victor still holding the weregune's head and neck firmly in his huge hand, blood pouring from the broken carotid arteries. Reuben's eyes blinked and his mouth moved wordlessly for nearly ten seconds before being released and dropped to the floor like a spoiled melon.

Victor violently kicked the head which bounced against the door and then turned to look at his two younger sons. "Get this piece of shit out of my sight and then come back here immediately. Also, get the pack together in front of the house and be prepared to leave here within the hour. Go now," Victor barked out, his rage not this intense since he lost his first mate.

Turning he walked over to Tabitha and sat softly beside her on the couch, grabbing her hand and bringing it to his mouth where he kissed it lovingly. They sat there for ten minutes, holding each other, Tabitha silently sobbing against his shoulder. He felt like crying as well, but his anger was too intense and he needed to show strength and leadership even though Barton had been killed.

"Victor, why did Reuben say that Barton attacked Johnny in order to appease you? I thought you liked him. What's going on and why is our son dead?" Tabitha said, trying to hold back her tears. She had cried enough and needed to be strong if the pack was moving out of here for whatever reason. And she would find out the real cause.

Victor got up and walked to the part of the floor where Reuben's blood stained the carpet. He wasn't sure how much to reveal to his mate, but knew with their son's death he would have to be as honest with her as possible.

"Please Victor, there is something I don't know and somehow my son has died because of it. Tell me," she said in a whisper.

He turned and moved to stand in front of her, his gaze hard as steel, but loving.

"My dear, there is a past before we met that ties Johnny's father and I together. Barton found out and I believe felt compelled to try taking matters into his own hands. What happened to our son was not suppose to happen, but it did and I feel devastated about that. Trust me, I did not know he was going to attack Johnny," he tried to assure her.

"But you obviously knew that Reuben was there and so you must've known that Barton was there as well," she said defiantly.

Victor reached forward and grabbed her shoulders, bringing her closer to him.

"Tabitha, I am always aware that where Barton went so did Reuben. It was only logic that they were together last night and I was obviously correct. Harming Johnny Raven was not what I wanted to see. His father hurt me many years ago and revenge will be mine, but on my own terms," he replied, embracing her tightly.

"What did he do to you?" she asked him.

"That is between us my dear, but someday you'll know the whole story. For now though we have to move from here, so please get together what we need," he told her.

"Why do we have to leave? If Barton attacking Johnny was not your fault, then what are you afraid of?" she asked.

Victor turned to stare at her, his eyes dark and smoldering.

"I said enough is enough. Do you hear me?" he yelled loudly. "I will not stand for anymore of your insolence. I am Alpha and you will listen to what I say. I love you Tabitha, but I will not allow you to question my authority."

She stared at him, wanting to shout back and scream at him for somehow getting their son killed, for she was positive her mate was behind it. Instead she turned and went about amassing the things they would take with them. There would be time to find out the truth later. In the meantime she had to mourn her oldest son and be the subservient mate, but not forever.

Johnny pulled up in front of Kathy's house and sat quietly for a few minutes. He wasn't sure how to handle this whole situation. Ordinarily he wouldn't care in the least about a human, other than a child, being infected by the rogue. But this woman was no ordinary human. Almost instantly he had acquired a strange affectation for her and yet he knew the feelings were not staged. He sensed stirring emotions not felt since he held his beloved Samantha. He could tell this woman was strong, but he had seen far too often what happened to those who could not comprehend or accept the existence of their beast. In order to explain how her life was now changed he would have to reveal everything about himself and his race, something that for the most part they could rarely do.

Walking slowly around the front of the truck he started up the steps to the porch when the door opened and she walked out. Behind her he could see a dog with coppery red fur going crazy, jumping against the window that ran the length of the door.

"Hello there, any trouble finding the house?" she asked him.

"No, it was pretty easy. Sounds like your dog is trying to protect you," he said.

"Well, she gets pretty crazy at times when somebody comes around. She'll kill you with kindness though, she just loves people," Kathy informed him.

"However, as brave as she seems to be," Kathy laughed, "she's been traumatized by our neighbor's cat, Shadow, who attacked her. So now, even though she may have the heart of lion, she's been scarred for life when it comes to domestic cats, poor baby."

"I can understand that since I'm not too wild about cats either. Most dogs aren't," he chuckled at the inside joke. "What's her name?"

"Rain and she's a shepherd/chow mix. The day we went to adopt her there was a driving rainstorm so I thought it appropriate to name her Rain. Plus, I had just seen a program on the Animal Planet about a German shepherd who was a war dog in Vietnam I think and that dog was named Rain. I thought it was cool and since it was raining that day, it was a natural choice," Kathy replied.

"Nice name and an interesting story, I like it. So, do we go inside, or would you just like to walk for awhile?" he asked her.

"Let me get my coat and gloves since it's kind of chilly. We can take a walk down to the Tow Path along the river. It's really nice down there, I love it."

Johnny stood with hands stuffed deep in his jacket pockets. Looking around he noticed how beautiful the area was, a thick expanse of woods where leaves had fallen and trees stood like an army of lonely skeletons. He could get used to this area, near enough to the city, but yet the type of landscape where his beast could run safely, or at least most of the time anyway.

He heard the door open and turned around. She was absolutely stunning Johnny decided. Wearing a beige knit scarf and a dark brown suede jacket, her deep auburn hair fell softly on her shoulders. He knew something was happening with his feelings towards this woman and was totally unprepared for whatever the consequences would be.

"You ready? I'd bring Rain along, but she demands too much attention, and all she does is stop and sniff. Besides she'd probably never let you alone," Kathy laughed.

They walked down the hill towards the old arched and cracking bridge which only now held up silent railroad tracks.

Neither of them said anything of substance. Johnny mentioned what a nice area it was and she agreed, saying that she had lived here now for almost ten years. Kathy talked briefly about how so many deer used to run over the hill across from her house, but the darn construction of town houses on the hill kept them from coming around much anymore. Both of them were avoiding as long as possible discussing the events of last night.

Crossing the railroad tracks they passed the closed and run down Septa station and walked carefully down a short, winding cobblestone road. There really is a yellow brick road Johnny thought with amusement. Then the Schuylkill River spread before them as they stopped and watched a few ducks swim in the cool water.

As they started walking down the Tow Path, Kathy spoke first.

"I suppose we should get past the small talk and face the problems we have here. Would you agree?" she asked, looking up at his darkly handsome, strongly chiseled face.

"There are definitely questions you have which I must answer and I have things to tell you that may be quite troubling," he replied.

"Then let's start by the obvious question. Just who and what are you Mr. Raven?" she asked, stopping in front of a large, gutted shell of a building which had been a water treatment facility that operated well over fifty years ago.

Johnny cleared his throat and lifted his eyebrows, a nervous grin tweaking the corners of his mouth. Reaching down he grasped a small rock and tossed it toward a large tree where it cracked loudly in the silence, echoing across the placid river.

"Well, you see me now walking, talking, smiling, and what you saw last night was my beast. Kathy, I am both human and wolf," he told her quietly, "amongst other things. You would most likely understand the word shape-shifter. That's what we are."

Kathy made a grunting sound, somewhere between a nervous laugh and a frightened gasp. She crossed her arms trying to ward off a chilly breeze, or was it more an irritating itch of fear scrambling up her spine like a frenzied bug?

"You mean you're a werewolf like in the damn horror movies?" she questioned. "I don't know for sure the black beast I shot and stared at last night was you Mr. Raven, but something in those golden eyes told me it was. How can this be Johnny? You weren't walking bent over on two legs. That was an animal, a very large, wolf."

As they continued to slowly stroll along the path, sometimes pausing to let the unbelievable reality sink in, and at other times pacing steadily because the exercise helped defray their anxiety, Johnny began to tell her about his race and who he was.

"Detective Morello, I am weregune. We are a race of shape-shifters that has lived among humanity since life first began to walk this earth on two legs. We are not those which make up your legends of werewolves. They are a scourge that lies between weregune and human, thus infected by a rogue only to then infect others. We are the wolf, bear and large cat that hunt amongst you. We are the hawk and raven who soar upon the winds searching for prey. You will not see us as a beast unless we allow ourselves to be seen. The moon does not rule us like a werewolf even though she is our Goddess. Able to live as beast or man has given us the ability to walk among you and exist undetected. You saw my beast last night who is called Jaress. You killed another weregune by the name of Barton, also known as Bartho. And you were attacked and injured by the rogue werewolf who slaughtered my wife Samantha."

A full minute passed as they stood with hands on an old wooden fence which bordered a rusty, abandoned lock which had allowed water to once flow into the canal. Years of trash from raging storms had piled up like a small mountain of tree limbs, crushed boats, splintered docks, pieces of swept away lawn furniture and children's toys. Geese, mallards and a host of other ducks swam together upon a surface of tranquility.

Kathy moved away and started to laugh.

"You have got to be kidding. This is such a pile of horseshit, a nightmare story you've chosen to weave and hope I'd fall for. There is always a realistic answer for everything and what you told me is not believable. Next you'll have me thinking that vampires exist as well," she said, backing slowly away from him.

He didn't answer, preferring to pick off some large splinters from the rotting wood, tossing them into the water. Turning he smiled, as if not answering the question had in effect relayed the truth.

Kathy started to laugh hysterically, tears rolling down her cheeks. After a minute she stopped for fear of hyper-ventilating and passing out like she had done once before.

"Okay, werewolves and vampires, yeah right. You really expect me to believe that? There is a logical explanation for this," she said, following up her laughing spell.

"Kathy, if I told you vampires did exist then you obviously wouldn't believe me. However, my not telling you it's true doesn't preclude the reality that in fact they do and right here within your own city," Johnny answered.

She started walking along the path underneath a large outcrop of weathered rock just shaking her head, but at the same time touching the shoulder that had been injured and was now surprisingly nearly healed. Kathy spun around to face him.

"Okay, so I believe I saw two wolves last night. I believe that the creature we were trailing and what attacked me was a beast that very much resembled a wolf on two legs, and then watched in disbelief as the wolf I killed turned into a man right before my eyes. So what is there not to believe I suppose? Every value I once possessed, every faith I ever learned, every lesson I was taught is now no longer of any use to me. Nothing will ever be the same as it was," she said, her voice rising with each stated fact.

"You're right Kathy. Nothing will ever be the same. Your life will never again be what you've known," Johnny said staring at her, not knowing what reaction to expect.

"But I wasn't bitten. What I've seen in the movies and read in books is 'the bite of a werewolf' makes you turn into a beast. I was clawed, not ravaged by fangs. Isn't that the way it goes?" she asked.

"Not really I'm afraid. With a werewolf, both the fangs and claws can infect someone. There is only a small fraction of time when possibly the infection can be removed, but not by your medical knowledge. A weregune can suck out the disease, but only within the first hour which almost never happens because we are most often not around. I'm sorry Kathy, but you have been infected and will begin to feel your body change when the next phase of the full moon approaches."

She jumped at him, screaming, punching, slapping, and clawing. Her rage was so intense that he fell against the rotten fence and crashed through. Only a mere two feet of ground separated him from the canal lock and he fell into the water, getting entangled in the debris. Completely submerged he tried to rise and felt his foot jammed in between two large tree limbs. The water was murky since the splash had awakened layers of sleeping silt and river bed. He reached down blindly to locate his ankle and free himself from his entrapment.

Suddenly there was another large splash and Kathy was there beside him. She reached for his entangled foot and began to pull at one of the limbs while he grabbed the other. It was like a vise, but between the two of them they managed to pull the trap apart far enough to free his foot. They both pushed up to break the surface. Sputtering and coughing they managed to get to the bank and climb out of the water.

Two guys on bicycles had stopped and stood calling down to them.

"Are you all right? Give us your hands and we'll pull you up," yelled one of the bikers, now on his belly and reaching down.

Johnny grabbed Kathy and picked her up as if she was a leaf where she grabbed hold of the guy's hand. She was then pulled up and leaned against part of the fence that wasn't broken. Johnny simply leaped to the top effortlessly causing the one cyclist to widen his eyes in disbelief.

"What the hell happened? You two have a lover's spat or something?"

"No, we were leaning too heavily on the wood and it gave way. I fell and she jumped in after me to help," Johnny said, hovering over Kathy who was still coughing up dirty river water.

"Damn, you two are lucky. That water is freezing. I have a cell phone, let me call for an ambulance," the one biker with a flaming orange outfit said. "No, don't call," Kathy coughed. "I live very close. We can walk there and change clothes. We're fine," she said, looking at Johnny, "I think."

Johnny slowly nodded. "True, we're okay, just a little shaken, very wet and extremely cold right now. Thanks so much for your help. We'll call someone to fix this broken fence before somebody else falls in and drowns."

The cyclists rode off, looking back and shaking their heads, enough excitement for one day on what was supposed to be a nice, leisurely ride to Valley Forge and back.

Five minutes later, without a word spoken the entire way, Kathy unlocked her front door to the frantic barking of her spastic dog.

"Rain, get down girl. Move back, go lay down," she ordered.

Her father jumped up. "My God, what the hell happened to you two? It's a little cold to be going swimming."

Kathy laughed, shivering. "Yeah, we had an accident down on the Tow Path, leaning against the fence and it broke."

"Damn city, we're going to sue their asses for this," her father said loudly, handing them towels from the basket that he had just brought up from the basement.

He glanced over at Johnny and extended his hand. "Hello there, I'm Carl, Kathy's father. And you must be the infamous Johnny she's spoken about."

Johnny took the elderly man's hand. "Yes sir, I hope you didn't hear anything too dastardly about me."

Carl chuckled, "Nothing too bad, at least nothing I can't repeat. You're a pretty big guy and I think I have something that will fit you until your clothes are washed and dry. Kathy, take the young man upstairs, show him the bathroom and I'll heat some water for tea, or would you rather like some coffee?"

"Tea will be fine with me unless you have coffee already made, stronger the better," Johnny replied, trailing Kathy up the steps and followed extremely closely by a sniffing dog.

"You're a man after my own heart. I like it strong enough to curl the hairs on your chest but Kathy doesn't. So coffee for us and tea for the lady," Carl could be heard muttering as he walked into the kitchen.

At the top of the steps Johnny bumped into Kathy who had stopped.

"Sorry, I was keeping an eye on your dog. He seems very intent on trying to determine if I'm a threat or not," Johnny said, smiling at her.

"She's very protective and you might have insulted her when referring to her gender," Kathy said reproachfully.

Rain growled low when Johnny reached down to pet her.

"Hey girl, I'm sorry. I'm no threat to you or your mommy and I'm on your turf so you're the boss," he said, scratching the nervous dog behind her ear.

"She likes you Johnny. Maybe it's just a dog thing, you know?"

Johnny looked up and smiled. "Yeah, maybe later I'll shift and we can lick each other," he said in a low chuckle.

He stood up and faced her. She did have fear in her eyes, he could see it, but she was strong and Johnny hoped that somehow she'd survive all that he had told her plus what else she faced.

"Are you okay?"

With a nervous laugh, she said, "Oh sure, isn't everyday that a girl gets told that she's now a werewolf," tears beginning to form in her eyes.

He reached out to hold her, but Rain started to bark and nipped at Johnny's leg.

"Rain, stop that, go down stairs now," she scolded the dog, but Rain continued to growl, a ridge of hair down the middle of her back standing straight up.

Johnny put his hand up to silence Kathy and knelt down in front of the dog. As he did his eyes suddenly turned to a bright golden color. Within a few seconds Rain had settled down and was now half sitting, half lying on the steps looking straight up at Johnny, nothing more than a soft whine being emitted.

"How did you do that? What did you do to her?" she whispered behind Johnny's back.

"Basically I just told her she had nothing to fear from me, this was her territory and you were safe. It's a canine thing," he softly chuckled, standing up and facing her.

"A canine thing my ass Mr. Raven," she laughed. "Rain is completely safe and you are not. Come on, I'll give you something to wear so you can get out of those wet clothes. Then we'll have something to eat. I think we have more to talk about."

An hour later after some strong coffee, hot soup and thick ham sandwiches, Johnny came downstairs back in his own dry clothes. Kathy was already sitting in the corner of the couch, her legs underneath a warm blanket with Rain lying in front of her, eyeing every move that Johnny made.

"Well you look nice and warm now," Carl told him. "Johnny, you can sit here in my chair. I think I'm going to go upstairs to finish watching this movie and hopefully take a nap. Very nice to meet you young man and I hope next time it's under better circumstances."

"Thank you Mr. Morello, it's been my pleasure to meet you. Hopefully you'll enjoy that nap," Johnny replied.

Kathy's father bent down towards her and said softly, "Don't stress yourself out honey. You've had a really tough twenty-four hours and you need some good rest. Take a few of those pain pills, they'll put you out."

"Thanks Dad, I'll be up soon. Johnny and I need to still discuss a few things though. I love you," she said, kissing her father on the cheek.

"Love you too doll. Come on Rain, let's leave these two young people alone. Come on girl," he coaxed.

Rain stood up slowly and kept her eye on Johnny as she walked to the steps. A golden glint in Johnny's eyes caused the dog to scoot quickly up the steps and head straight for the safety of Carl's bedroom.

"Peace and quiet at last," Kathy said.

Johnny smiled, "Yeah, at least for awhile anyway."

"So do you think this rogue creature is going to disappear now?" she asked.

"The recent phase of the new moon has past and he can't completely change now. So he'll find a place to hold up, lay low, or might even leave the city. I'll do my best to track him from the woods he was in last night, but if he managed to find a car then I'll lose him until he strikes again."

Kathy was silent for a moment. "Johnny, I'm afraid, really afraid and I've not been this frightened ever in my life."

Johnny gracefully stood and moved to the couch. "Come here," he told her.

Kathy sat up and slid over so she was closer to him. He put his strong arm around her, feeling the tenseness in her shoulders and back. Shivering a little he put his hand against the side of her head and gently brought her face to his chest.

"Just relax, everything will be fine Kathy. I'll be here to help you through this," he said, the silky feel of hair against his lips.

She pushed away from him and sat straight up.

"Okay, no more bullshit damn it. If in ten days I'm going to howl at the moon then I might as well be dead now because I won't let my life fall apart or destroy the lives of innocent people. I swear to you right now I'll pull the trigger myself," she said, her voice rising and tears welling up in her eyes.

"It won't come to that Kathy. I won't let it," he assured her, reaching out his arms which she knocked away, standing.

"You won't let it, like you're some friggin' God. It's your kind that did this to me so why should I trust you?" she asked him, moving to the other side of the room and lumping onto a small settee.

"Not my kind Kathy. You were infected by a rogue, not a weregune. However, I can fix that even though it might not be pleasurable," he told her.

"And just how do you propose doing that? You can cure me completely? I thought my life was ruined now," she said angrily.

"Kathy I'm sorry, but you'll never be able to return to the life you knew. I can infuse you with my blood. You can become weregune and your life will be so much better," he said, trying his best to assuage her fears, yet unable tell reveal everything.

"Jesus Christ, I can't believe any of this. Johnny, get the hell out of my house. Leave right now," she said, pointing to the door.

"Listen Kathy, it will be okay, trust me."

She lowered her head into her hands and whispered, "Get out Johnny, please. I'll be okay, I won't do anything foolish. I just need time to think and let this all sink in. I promise I'll call you before I pull the trigger. Now please, just leave."

Johnny got up and walked to where she sat, Kathy noticeably flinching when he placed his hand on her shoulder. Grabbing his coat he opened the door and left. Once in the car he sat alone for a few minutes hating what he was and what had happened to her. He would watch over her and somehow she would come around.

Suddenly he straightened up, hearing his father's voice inside his head.

Johnny, we're here in Philadelphia. If you hear me come to Valley Force Park and look for the large church on the right hand side as you drive through. We're in the woods behind the church.

With extreme trepidation he started the truck and drove away from Kathy's house. He caught her looking out the curtain as he pulled away. She was very frightened and Johnny knew that any blood letting was far from over. Now that his father had arrived he had many questions to be answered, the primary one being what connection his father and Victor had which would've resulted in Samantha's death.

Chapter 27

When Colleen awoke it was like she had been drugged. Her mind felt as if it was languishing inside a laundry bag with all kinds of dirty, seedy thoughts. She lay there within the shade of early morning and tried to get her head to stop spinning. As a wave of nausea struck she very quickly threw back the blanket and ran stumbling to the bathroom where she draped herself over the toilet. Five minutes later, with both her stomach aching and throat burning, she turned out the light and shuffled back to the bed where she found Quentin propped against a pillow smiling at her.

"Good morning love. That's quite normal I'm afraid, but it will pass in time. I guess you could consider it morning sickness," he said, chuckling in a very low, throaty growl.

"Get out of my bed you monster. I may be forced to have you stay here, but I will not sleep with you. Get out, now," she said, her voice rising.

"Monster you say. Look who's calling the kettle black, my dear," he said, beginning to laugh as he stood up.

Colleen sincerely prayed that nothing had happened during the night. Even though he was extremely sexy in a completely masculine way, he none the less repulsed her as she felt another wave of nausea engulf her. Turning she raced to the bathroom, getting there just in time for more volcanic eruption.

When she returned to the bedroom he had thankfully left. She felt slimy, so damn filthy and ashamed. A shower was desperately needed. Undressing in the bathroom, letting her clothes fall to the floor, she gazed at her reflection in the full length mirror on the back of the door. Her fingertips caressed the almost completely faded marks on her shoulder, breast and stomach. She did feel completely different, like everything just buzzed around her, standing in the bathroom with the shower running, steam billowing out from overtop the glass shower door. She could hear Quentin rummaging around in the kitchen on the first floor and smelled the delightful aroma of coffee being brewed like she never had before.

Colleen stood straight and let her hands feel the hardness of her stomach, obtained from a brutal regimen of weekly 'ab' workouts. She let her anxious hands trace their way up her body until they stopped to cup perfect breasts, letting fingertips titillate the nipples until they became red and rock hard, to the point of bursting. Moving one of her hands down to rest between her legs she closed her eyes, caressing in a circular motion, moaning in sensual bliss. A vision of Sara appeared behind her closed eyes as tears began to squeeze out from darkly shuttered eyelids. Her precious Sara would no longer be in Colleen's life, she knew that now for sure. Before achieving orgasm she stopped and shuddered, feeling it was sacrilege to enjoy that heavenly cascade of emotions while not holding on to the woman she loved.

Opening the shower door Colleen stepped into billowing waves of steam to let the hot, scalding water nearly burn her skin. Moving underneath the pounding water Colleen started to cry, rocked by severe spasms of guilt and hatred. She looked up at the shower caddy and reached for her shaver. No way could her life rush into a monstrous unknown. She would become a beast like Quentin and she could not allow herself to kill another human being, other than maybe the creature who had infected her.

Placing the shaver against the inside of her left wrist Colleen began to hack back and forth, shredding the skin and severing an artery. Moving the shaver she performed the same chaotic surgery on the right wrist, dropping the shaver so it bounced off the tile floor of the bathtub. Crimson water pooled around her feet as Colleen stared at her mangled wrists. It was better to die while she was still partly human and not a ravenous beast. She lowered herself until she sat on the bathmat, her back against the cold starkness of the pink porcelain finish. Feeling dizzy, almost euphoric, Colleen smiled and realized she would escape Quentin after all.

"Jesus Christ woman, what the hell do you think you're doing," Quentin yelled as he slid back the shower door. He had almost instantaneously smelled the overpowering scent of fresh blood and raced upstairs to the bathroom. Turning off the water, he reached for her as she frantically beat back his hands.

"Don't touch me. Let me end this nightmare Quentin. I will not be a creature like you, I'd rather die," she hissed at him.

Quentin slapped her hard, not once but three times, Colleen's head rocking back and forth against the tiled wall. In a daze from the blows and loss of blood she ceased resisting. He picked her up and placed her on the plush, wall-to-wall carpet of the bathroom. Leaning over he took her left wrist in his hands and began to lick up the blood, allowing his tongue to close the wound. Then he did the same with the right wrist.

Her blood tasted so sweet, turning him on like nothing had in such a long while. Then he took his own forearm and sliced it open. Taking Colleen's head he tilted it back and open her mouth.

"Drink Colleen, you need to replace the blood you lost and mine will revive you with new strength. You will feel more alive and intense than you ever have before," he informed her.

She coughed and sputtered as his life force filled her mouth, coursing down her throat, splattering on her cheeks and spilling over her lips. Colleen opened her startled eyes as she began to kick and scream, knocking him from a top her. She jumped up and moved to the toilet, trying to gag the blood from her body. But she couldn't. Glancing down she noticed that the open gashes on her wrists had completely healed. She fell to the floor on her knees and began to wail, rocking back and forth.

Quentin moved and knelt beside her. Placing his huge hands on her shoulders he held her while she cried, deep and racking sobs which lasted nearly ten minutes. Finally it subsided and she gently pushed him away. He handed her a small towel to wipe her face which she also used to blow her nose. She flung it angrily across the room against the far wall. Quentin extended an open hand which she accepted as he helped her rise.

"Let me get dressed Quentin. I'm fine, really. I know my life is lost now so please go. You don't have to worry. I realize you won't let me take my own life. I'll come downstairs in a little bit."

"Are you sure you're okay? I can sit in the bedroom so I'm close if you need me," he said.

She turned and started to laugh. "I think you've been enough help already. Just please go, I don't need a babysitter to get myself dressed. I'm suddenly hungry so I'll be down in a few minutes."

He left and she moved slowly into the bedroom, reaching for a warm, pink and gray jogging outfit. She was really cold to the point of shivering uncontrollably. Sitting on the edge of the bed she wrapped her arms around herself until the shaking subsided. At least on the outside because inside she still shook in fear. Fear over what her life had become, a life of such promise now shattered against a future of despair.

Kathy had been napping when her cell phone sang out loudly. After Johnny had pulled away from the house everything just seemed to come crashing down upon her. Mentally she was a wreck and physically her arm had begun throbbing even though the wound itself had closed completely, since some of the muscles had been torn resulting in lingering pain. She did in fact pop two pain pills and even though she was not suppose to drink alcohol she felt a small glass of red wine couldn't do much damage. It helped her nod off quite quickly.

She reached for the phone and flipped it up. It was Captain Ganz.

"Hey Nathan, what's going on?" she asked a little groggily.

"All hell is breaking loose detective. Everyone's down my back, from the Chief's office to the Mayor to the news reporters and all the way down to every crazy little animal protection group. It's been a damn nightmare and Kathy, believe me when I tell you, after this case is officially over I'm retiring," he said gruffly.

"Animal protection groups," she said laughing, "there was no body of any animal they could protest about. Now I could understand maybe some monster protection group harassing you."

"Yeah, that's for damn sure, but evidently word got out from some unknown source, I love that crap about unknown sources, whereby you shot and killed a wolf. So they're demanding to see the body and throwing out shit like endangered species, cruelty to animals," Captain Ganz replied. "It had to be a cop that released info like that. I'll sure as hell find out who it was and have their balls swinging over an open fire."

"But Cap, there was no body of an animal and to my knowledge I was the only one there in the creek. The others didn't come up until seconds later."

"Doesn't matter Kathy, a wolf was mentioned and it could've been a damn cat, dog or bird and they'd still be all over us," he replied.

Pausing for a second Kathy continued, "Nathan, any ID on the guy I shot?"

"Not as yet. His fingerprints are not on file in any database. Hell, the guy was naked as a jay bird and you nearly shot his head off. You're going to really have to come up with a good explanation when you go in front of the review board, especially since there were no weapons found around him."

"When's the review board?"

"Well, that's one of the reasons I called. They said if you're up to it, then tomorrow morning, but only if you're okay Kathy. I can stall them a little longer if you need me to."

"No, that's fine. Actually I was thinking about coming into the precinct anyway" she said.

"Absolutely not detective, you're on official sick leave as we speak. So just sit back and rest that arm. Lord only knows what you saw out there young lady, so I don't want to see you for at least two weeks. I've mentioned to the Chief, the Mayor's office, as well as to the press that the killer has been found. So for the moment there's some time and I don't want you coming back here until you're ready."

"Thanks Nathan, but I'll go completely stir crazy with nothing to do. Besides, I told you there seems to be two killers and that one got away," she told him.

"Yes you did, but at least all concerned for now are pacified and it will give Tommy and the rest of the department time to sort everything out. Hopefully there will be no more killings and maybe if there was an accomplice, killing alone is not his style. But I have a number of officers combing the woods up and down Wissahickon Creek for any clues, as well as going back over all the crime scenes. In fact, I believe that Tommy is going to be heading over to Miss Frye's house to see how she's doing and ask her some more questions," Ganz said.

Kathy laughed. "Yeah, I'm sure he has no ulterior motive behind that move."

"Knowing Tommy, he probably does, but if she likes her toast buttered on the other side, it won't do him any good. Damn guy thinks he's God's gift to women," Captain Ganz replied, also laughing.

"Tommy's a good cop, we all know that. He just loves the ladies, that's all there is to it. Plus, the guy does have a heart of gold. Sometimes I think he's too much of a softy to be chasing criminals, but I'd want him backing me up no matter what."

"Yeah well, I agree with you on all counts. Kathy, rest and get your strength back. If I need you then I'll call you, but for now just get your story ready for the review board tomorrow. And I mean Detective Morello, that's an order, do you hear me?"

"Yes sir, I hear you. I'm actually exhausted and still very sore," she said.

"Hey, by the way, I meant to ask you last night at the hospital. Whatever happened to that crow, hawk, raven, or some type of bird name? He was supposed to be this super duper tracker and I didn't even hear his name mentioned at all," Nathan asked.

"Don't know actually. He showed up briefly at the apartment house and then left, I assume to do some tracking. But I never saw him in the woods or around the creek at all. Plus I haven't heard a peep from him either," Kathy said, obviously lying.

"Well, if he does come around you tell him that I want to talk to him and right away," he told her.

"You got it captain. Will I see you tomorrow at the review board?"

"Yes, my presence has been requested as well. Take some more pills and go back to sleep Kathy. You're going to need all your wits about you tomorrow.

These guys are like sharks, always ready to nail a good cop over something."

"Thanks Nathan, I will," and she hung up.

Leaning back against the couch she closed her eyes. Her arm really ached, but it was bearable at least. She would really have to stretch the truth at the review board. They would think she was certifiable if she said she had been attacked by a werewolf and thus infected, as well as shooting a wolf that turned into a nude man. Yep, most likely they would rule on a psychological leave for her. Tommy would most likely show up sometime later in the day and she'd discuss with him as much as she could.

Obviously the part about her being infected was not anything she wished to discuss with anybody other than Johnny. She wondered where he had gone. He had to get a damn cell phone and next time they talked she'd remind him to get one. She also regretted kicking him out like that, but it was all just too much to handle. In fact, it was still totally unbelievable and she couldn't imagine that in ten days or so she'd be changing into some ravenous beast. But he said that he could help her so their next conversation would be much more in depth and she would not let her emotions take over.

Kathy stood and reached for the leash. Rain immediately got excited, standing on her two hind legs like she loved to do. Normally Kathy didn't put a leash on her just to walk up the street, but this time she thought she'd head back down to the river. Grabbing her coat she opened the front door and the dog bounded out, grinning and happy to be going for a walk. After the leash was on her, Rain grabbed part of it in her mouth and started to walk away, as if she were taking Kathy for a walk. The dog had been doing that ever since she had been a puppy and it never failed to make Kathy laugh. But at least for now she had way too much on her mind, least of all what would happen in ten days underneath a full moon.

Tommy parked in front of Colleen's house and sat there for a few reflective moments. He wondered why he was really there to see how she was doing. Especially since it was evident she was a lesbian and very much in love with her friend Sara. But there was something about this woman that completely had cast a spell over him and he just couldn't put his finger on why. Preferring to be a player and not let any woman tie him down for too long, he couldn't stop thinking about Colleen. Besides, he honestly did feel she was in danger. There was the nagging issue of how quickly her wounds had healed as well as the fact that Kathy told him in no uncertain terms that the guy she shot was not the creature who attacked her and probably Colleen as well.

He peered at the windows as he climbed the few steps to the porch. Knocking on the door he stood and waited, almost hoping she wouldn't even answer the door. But she did glance out the curtain so he waited for her to open up. There was almost a shocked glaze to her eyes at the sight of him.

"Detective, why are you here? I've told you everything, there is nothing more to say about any of this," she said, startled by his presence.

Instinct told him something was terribly wrong. She looked worn and haggard, not only upset that he was standing on her porch, but frightened of something as well.

"I just thought I'd stop and see how you are. Find out if you're going to stay in this house. Detective Morello did shoot one of the killers, but we're pretty sure another one is still on the loose. He may come back here Colleen and you should be aware of that possibility. I can take you someplace else that would be safer if you'd like," he told her.

"Thank you, but I'll be okay. I might go back to Sara's apartment later. Just needed some time alone to think over a few things, get some clean clothes," she said nervously.

"May I come in for a few minutes?" he asked.

Her evident hesitation told him volumes. Something was wrong and he had an idea what it might be. Getting inside the house was paramount right then. He opened his jacket in order to reach for his gun faster if it came to violence.

"I suppose, but just a few minutes. I'm really tired and was just about to go upstairs and throw a few things in an overnight bag," she replied.

Tommy smiled. "Okay, just a few minutes. So, how are you feeling?"

Colleen stepped back and decided to keep him in the foyer near the front door. She was sure Quentin was completely aware another person was in the house. She only prayed he would stay out of sight. Her fear was high that this nice detective would get killed if he stayed in the house too long.

"I'm fine actually. I can't explain why the wounds healed so fast, but I've always been a fast healer and bounce back from injuries quicker than the normal person," she answered.

"Well, I think you must admit it was like a miracle. I mean, I'm religious to a certain degree, trying to make Mass on Sunday mornings when I can, go to confession once in awhile so our parish priest doesn't get too angry at me," he said smiling, "but the way you and Detective Morello healed was astonishing."

Colleen looked at him, stunned at what he had just said about his partner.

"Detective Morello got bit as well? Oh my God, when did that happen?" she asked, startled.

"Late last night down in Wissahickon Creek, but she's okay. We had the bastard too, but he got away even though she was able to shoot another guy who was somehow connected to the killer we've been tracking. She actually didn't get bit, I think just severely clawed. Very nasty, but it's almost healed as well," he informed her.

"You think there were two killers? Now you do have me nervous. I think I'm definitely going to grab a few things and head back down to the city. Thanks Detective Darnello for stopping by," she said, reaching for the door knob.

"I'll wait until you pack and make sure everything is okay. It's no problem at all and I'd feel better knowing you were safe," he tried to assure her.

Opening the door completely now, she said, "I'll be out of here in five minutes detective, honestly. Nothing's going to happen that quickly. Besides, if you want to wait in your car I'll be right outside."

Tommy smiled and turned to reach for the storm door. Suddenly there was a muffled thud that came from somewhere on the second floor. Spinning, Tommy's eyes darted up the steps as he reached for his gun. He felt almost immediately upon entering the house that somebody else was there. Now he was positive and extremely wary.

"Move aside Colleen. Is it him?" he said, his voice strained, trying to get her behind him.

"Yes it's him, but he's extremely dangerous detective. We should just leave now and you can call for back up. He'll kill you if he gets the chance," she said in a throaty whisper.

"I want you to go outside right now where you'll be safe. Take your cell phone and call 911, tell them there's an intruder in your house. Go now," he said, pushing her towards the front door with his free hand.

"No, I can't leave you. Just please, come with me," she pleaded.

Tommy was at the foot of the steps now, his gun pointed forward and up towards the landing. Halfway up the stairs he stopped and listened. Even though there had not been any other loud noises he could feel the ominous presence of something dangerous. With heart pounding amid an adrenaline rush he moved up the steps slowly, eyes ever alert for the killer to spring upon him from any direction.

"Detective, please stop and come back down," Colleen whispered, also moving halfway up the steps.

He motioned for her to keep quiet and to go back down the steps. She didn't listen to him. If there was a way she could alert him before Quentin attacked then she would. Her hate for this creature was so blinding she only wanted him dead no matter what the consequences she might suffer.

At the top of the steps Tommy crouched, listening for any possible noises. There was nothing. He glanced down the hallway towards a closed bedroom and the bathroom. The thud sounded like it came from the left side of the house so in a half crouch he slid against the wall, gun held in front firmly in both hands. The first door was slightly ajar as he used the toe of his foot to nudge the door open further. Quickly he slid in along the wall, moving the gun back and forth. The room was empty.

Back in the hallway he went to the next door which was closed. Grabbing the knob he turned slowly and then pushed it in fast, moving in low and hugging the wall as much as possible. Tommy's heart was pounding in his head. His throat was completely dry to the point of coughing, but that was a definite no-no. This was an opportunity to either catch or kill the beast and he couldn't blow this chance.

Moving further inside the dark room he let his eyes scour as much of the area as possible. Could he have been mistaken about the sound? But Colleen had confirmed the fact somebody was in the house and alluded to it being the killer. No, somewhere this creature was hiding, waiting for the opportunity to kill it.

The opportunity came faster than Tommy had anticipated from behind.

Before he could turn, Quentin's arm went around Tommy's throat, yanking him back and literally off the floor. He gagged as his feet flailed wildly. Unable to breathe Tommy began moving his gun to point behind him, ready to shoot at no matter what was there. He hoped Colleen had stayed downstairs. But his gun hand was painfully grabbed by strong fingers and bent backwards. Tommy tried to yell but couldn't, the loud snap of his wrist echoing in the shadowy room. The gun fell to the floor as Tommy realized he might die.

"Quentin, please don't kill him. There have been too many die already. Let him live and I'll go anywhere with you. Please, do it for me," Colleen pleaded.

"And why should I do that? He'll only call for back up as soon as he's able to. I don't need to be watching behind my back," he growled, strengthening his hold on Tommy's neck, virtually cutting off all air flow.

Colleen grabbed his arm tightly and held on. "No, he won't. He's almost unconscious now, ready to pass out. I have a place outside of town we can go. Nobody will find us there," she told him, but not revealing that Sara knew where their special house in the country was.

Quentin twisted harder until Tommy blacked out completely and then released him to fall heavily to the hardwood floor. Quentin kicked him viciously in the center of the back and stood, glaring down. He hated most everybody, but he really hated cops.

If it weren't for how much he cared for Colleen then this asshole would be dead already.

"Okay my love, I'll grant your wish this one time. Do not ever again plead for the life of something so insignificant. Gather together your stuff and let's leave before he comes to. I wouldn't want to go back on my word and have to kill him," he snarled, leaving the room, slamming the door violently shut behind him.

In ten minutes they were in her car and steering towards Ridge Avenue. Her secret haven was about an hour away in Washington Crossing, up near New Hope, nestled snuggly right along the beautiful Delaware River. It was very secluded and comfy, her and Sara's little love nest. It would give her more time to think about the situation. Possibly he would settle down and at some point avail herself an opportunity to slip away. She wondered if Detective Darnello heard her mention where they might go before he passed out. He was a smart guy and hopefully would realize that Sara might know where the country house would be. If he didn't hear her say where they were going then Colleen would just have to use her own savvy to make an escape, or kill the beast she was now connected to in such nightmarish ways.

It was easy finding the old, imposing stone church located on a winding Route 23 in the vast expanse of Valley Forge Park. A large memorial built to commemorate the fallen from George Washington's Continental Army beginning that fateful Christmas of 1777. A brutally cold and snowy winter where over two thousand soldiers out of approximately twelve thousand had succumbed to a variety of illnesses such as typhus, typhoid, dysentery and pneumonia just to name a few. Harsh conditions of blowing snow and freezing temperatures nearly defeated, without a shot being fired, the army that Washington quartered there, brave soldiers comprised of children as young as twelve years old and then ranging up to elderly men in their fifties and sixties. All exhausted, poorly fed, ill-equipped with most of them wearing nothing more than rag tag uniforms and thread-bare shoes. But through their strength of spirit and perseverance, along with assistance from the local populace of Philadelphia, along with reinforcements and supplies, they survived to move out towards New York in June of 1778 and on to victory against the British.

Johnny parked his truck in a far corner of the parking lot and nonchalantly began walking out onto an open field towards a large area of trees nestled quietly behind the church. His father said they would be somewhere in the area so Johnny would just walk until they came together. Of course, he would be totally aware of their presence long before he saw them, as he was certain his father already knew he had arrived.

Even though it was during mid-afternoon an ugly, overcast sky did little to spread any light through the thick ceiling of naked treetops. Wildlife indigenous to the area like squirrels, rabbits, foxes and chipmunks hid in the safety of their small dens and nests. The singing of birds was mysteriously silent, though most humans would never detect its absence. But Johnny knew why they preferred to nervously just stare down at such an unnatural sight. Wolves were present and who knew if they desired a nice little morsel before conducting their beastly plans.

As Johnny entered a small clearing he suddenly stopped and waited. Silence was complete, not a squeak, a peep, a twig breaking, a leaf blowing. Tension was nearly at the breaking point, like brittle ice on a newly frozen pond. The first thing he spied was five sets of golden, unblinking eyes surrounding him. Like magic their bodies quietly appeared, five majestic and massive wolves, one jet black, two a dusty gray, and the other two

249

a combination of white and gray fur. The large black wolf moved forward and slowly circled Johnny, sniffing and growling slightly. It was a pretense of superiority that Johnny hated every time it occurred. After all, he was quite aware his father was the supreme alpha and his subservience was expected. But shit, he was his son and you might've thought his father could just greet him warmly.

After about fifteen seconds of making sure Johnny was safe, as if his father had to worry about anything, the other four wolves came closer and brushed against him in acceptance, giving him their welcome.

"Hello father," Johnny said quietly, "should I shift and join you as wolves, or do we talk as humans for awhile?"

The huge black wolf lowered his head, growling deeply in his massive chest. Then he sat and closed his eyes, searching for his personal moon to alter shape. In less than a minute all five wolves had changed to their human bodies and stood around Johnny, pushing and slapping him on the shoulder and arms. It was quite comical really. Johnny stood there in his plaid flannel shirt, black leather jacket and faded jeans while his father, two younger brothers, an uncle and cousin proudly displayed their nakedness for the entire world to see. Modesty was not something a weregune thought much about.

"Father, you'll catch your death of cold," Johnny said smiling, moving forward to embrace the senior weregune he so admired since he had been such a mischievous pup.

After making the appropriate greetings, which of course would've been quite the eerie tale discussed around many midnight campfires, Johnny and his father moved off to speak in confidence.

"So you've had a tough time of it sounds like," his father said.

"Yes sir, it's been quite interesting to say the least. We almost had the rogue caught last night, but some strange things occurred and he got away."

"Fill me in son so that we know what we're dealing with.

Johnny told him how they found the apartment where the rogue werewolf had been staying and then finding the body of the dead woman next door. For the moment he left out what Quentin had told him in Wissahickon Creek, preferring to jump ahead and convey where Detective Morello had come into the creek, shooting anything that moved, killing one before he and the rogue got away.

"Who did this detective kill? Another rogue?" his father asked.

Johnny hesitated slightly. "No sir, another weregune."

His father stood up and stared at Johnny, puzzled at this answer. "How could this be? Did she shoot him in the heart or head by accident?"

"No sir, Detective Morello knew exactly where to shoot because I told her," Johnny said.

"You did what? It's against our law to tell a human about our race unless it's absolutely necessary and if such a necessity occurs then it can only mean one thing," he said, looking intently at his son for an answer.

Johnny walked away from his father to look back at the clearing where the other four had reverted to wolf state and playfully wiled away the time by snapping at each other, jumping and tumbling like puppies on the ground. Yes, it had been a necessity for Johnny to tell Kathy about himself. Not only to protect her from the rogue, but to save her from herself now. He turned and faced his father.

"Yes, there is something between the detective and myself. It happened almost instantly and I have no explanation as to why since I wasn't expecting anything to happen. She was also wounded last night by the rogue and lived. You know what that means father."

"I smelled her scent on you. It's been a long time since Samantha was killed and it's nice to see your emotions coming to the surface again, but a human female. Why?" his father asked him.

"Who's to say why when it comes to the heart. You taught me that. There is just something extremely enticing and compelling about this woman. If she would not have been infected then I wouldn't have opened up to her. Father, there's only one way to save her now. She must become weregune," Johnny said emphatically. "With or without your consent, I will do this, unless she of course refuses. Then I have no idea what I'll do at that point, but I won't desert her."

"I will stand behind you son. I always have and always will."

Johnny hesitated, looking up through the leaf-bare tree limbs toward a grayish-

white sky. "Evidently not always father since the weregune that Kathy killed was Barton, son of Victor, who I believe you've known for quite a long time."

"Yes, Victor and I have known each other for awhile, but not before he came to Philadelphia. I have no idea where he came from prior to arriving in this city, just that he brought a small pack with him and developed it into a very strong and honorable clan. Why do you question me about this?"

Johnny turned and faced his father. "Because the rogue told me before I was attacked by Barton that you and Victor had a long, tragic history and it was because of you that Victor's previous mate had been slain. You still deny knowing him?"

Silence filled the woods. Even the four playful wolves stopped and sat on their haunches as if their servitude and obedience was needed at this time. The elder weregune turned to face his son.

"Long before I met your mother I was young and wild. There was a female I had gotten completely intimate with from another pack and we met frequently in secret. Her mate was not very nice, to the point of being cruel and abusive. She was planning on leaving him and we were to meet the following evening to go off and form our own pack. I was there waiting at midnight and she never showed. I searched for her nearly a week, finally locating her pack which had moved on. I found out only then that she had been slain by a trapper. As it turned out, she had been killed on the last night we were together. I was extremely distraught and went off myself for awhile to be alone with my troubled thoughts and broken heart. But Johnny, her mate's name was not Victor. It was so very long ago, but I believe his human name was Edward."

"Then I believe he changed his name before forming the pack that came here to Philadelphia," Johnny said, hesitating before going on. "Father, he was evidently behind Samantha being killed, some insane reason for revenge, though I believe he must've been after me. Since I was far away that night, he wrought his vengeance upon Samantha by using the rogue, Quentin. I also think that's the reason Barton attacked me last night, to try taking me out once more and getting back at you."

His father looked Johnny in the eyes and grabbed his shoulders.

"Jaress, my beloved son, I knew nothing about this. The fact that Sashar was murdered by the trapper was a cruel mistake. Possibly if she had been more alert and not thinking of our plans to leave together the following evening then she would have noticed the danger and avoided injury. I did not meet your mother until almost thirty years later. At no time during that period had this

Victor, or Edward, ever faced me on the issue of Sashar. Johnny I'm so terribly sorry if this is in fact the truth and not something that was babbled by the rogue to save his own miserable life. You know that I loved Samantha like she was my own naturally born child. It rips my heart right now at even the barest thoughts to know my own frailties and mistakes from so long ago could've been the result of her death."

He leaned back against a large tree and slid to the ground, his head bowed between his bare knees. Johnny had only seen his father show tears three times in his entire life. Once only three years ago during the burial of Samantha and their unborn son. The first time was when his oldest and first born son, Bhetar, was taken and tortured at the hands of Roberto, the Master Vampire in Seattle, during the great werewolf/vampire wars of nearly one hundred years ago. He searched long and hard over the next ten years attempting to rescue Bhetar, but to no avail. One night Johnny happened to come upon his father in wolf form at a clearing overlooking the great Cliff of Souls. He was mournfully baying at the moon, seeking forgiveness due to his inability with finding his son and bringing him safely home. His father was completely aware that his oldest son might be forever lost, even if he still lived. Roberto would have changed him into one of his murderous horde and only the Moon Goddess had any idea if he still lived, or had any memories left about his family.

With Jaress secretly looking on, his father turned his head revealing tear-filled eyes the color of dampened corn silk, exposing the haunting pain he lived with each day as a result of not being able to save Bhetar.

And the third time Johnny saw tears was now. Kneeling down he lifted his father's head. Without saying a word he put his arms around his father and they both sobbed quietly for several minutes. Yes, male wolves cried, especially at the loss of their beloved females. They hoped to mate forever and when she was no longer there a vast emptiness was created until at a future time another one might capture their heart.

"Father, I don't blame you. You had no idea this evil Victor would've tried such a terrible thing and you couldn't possibly have known that Edward changed his name and moved here. He evidently enlisted several rogues to help with his dirty work. I would have much preferred him to be honorable, at least in revenge, to attack me. Even though Samantha was very strong and a good fighter, she would've been more concerned with protecting our son and not fought with the intensity she normally would have."

"Thank you son, it helps a little to know you don't harbor blame against me. But it deeply crushes me to know Samantha and my grandson were slain because of my weakness. Do you know where Victor is now?"

"No sir, he moved on. He also now has lost a son though it was at the hands of Kathy. Father, she will be a target now and we must protect her. Victor has moved the clan and we all will have to be on the highest alert for attack. You will also have to bring in additional help for it's my understanding his pack is quite large now and very strong."

His father rose and placed his arm around Johnny's shoulder, walking toward the clearing.

"We have relatives around New Hope who will join us. I will also call your mother a little later and have her speak to Samantha's father. There will be others here before midnight tomorrow. What are your plans for protecting Kathy?" he asked.

"I'll go back to her shortly. She needs to know the seriousness of this situation. I will try and hopefully bring her to where you'll be at in New Hope tonight."

"Good, now let us run for awhile. We haven't eaten for many hours and will need all our strength for the coming days."

Jaress and his father knelt and easily changed shapes. A small pack of six wolves now trotted into the clearing as darkness fell. They stopped and stared at the rising moon. Throughout the air blanketing Valley Force Park, a haunting blend of wolf voices froze anyone in earshot. For after all, wolves could not possibly exist in Philadelphia.

Chapter 28

Sara got out of her car and leaned back against the door. Colleen had not returned any of her phone calls all morning and with each unanswered message she had grown progressively more worried. She felt the insidious creeping feeling that something was terribly wrong. Obviously after surviving such a horrific attack, Colleen had not been her normal vivacious self. But she was different now, almost possessing a new edgy personality, intense and almost wild, at least that's what her love making had been like last night. Sara tried to assuage her partner's fears and wished for Colleen to stay with her longer, but to no avail. Now she stood on the front porch inserting her key into the front door. Upon entering the house the first thing Sara noticed was a thick, ominous silence. The temperature had been turned down and it was extremely cold inside these quiet walls. That worried her instantly for she knew intimately how much her sweetheart loved to be warm.

"Colleen, are you here?" Sara called out in a strained voice.

Nothing! No response, no answer as Sara glanced warily into the living room. Empty! Moving down the hallway towards the kitchen the first thing she noticed was a partial pot of coffee with the machine still turned on. Colleen would've never left the house without turning it off and scrubbing out the pot. Also, soiled dishes were still stacked in the sink. That was very much another no-no where Colleen was concerned. Now Sara's worry heightened.

"Colleen honey, it's me, Sara, where are you Baby?"

Silence permeated the cold stillness. It was so quiet that Sara's footsteps echoed throughout the house like ice dripping in a cavern. Ascending slowly to the second floor, Sara's heart was thudding loudly inside her ears. At the top of the staircase she moved towards the bathroom where the door stood slightly ajar. Gently pushing it in Sara stared at an extremely messy sight with several towels littering the floor, droplets of blood staining the carpet and further examination revealed Colleen's shaver lying on the bottom surface of the bathtub in a small, stagnant pool of rust-colored water.

"Colleen?" Sara called out, her voice rising hysterically.

She moved out into the hallway and suddenly stopped. There was a soft, low moan coming from the master bedroom. Sara rushed down the hallway and pushed the door in. Lying on the middle of the floor was a man, his back to her, yet he appeared to be somewhat familiar. Putting her right hand up to cover her mouth to suppress a startled gasp, Sara moved slowly around the body until she faced the man. With a noticeable intake of breath she knelt down and placed her hand on his shoulder.

"Detective Darnello, what happened? Where is Colleen? How badly are you hurt?" The questions came tumbling out.

Tommy groaned as his eyes fluttered open, still clouded over by a curtain of unconsciousness. He murmured something, but she was unable to hear him clearly. Moving forward she knelt closer and tried to help him turn over on his back. From his throat nearly being crushed by Quentin he was barely able to croak out words that made any sense. Sara mistakenly grabbed hold of his broken wrist and he moaned in pain.

"I'm sorry detective. What can I do? Who can I call?" she asked him.

In barely a whisper she heard him say cell phone as he weakly pointed to his jacket pocket. Finding the phone and turning it on, she held it closer to him. With his good hand he hardly had the strength to press a few buttons, but he finally did and pushed it towards her. Sara held it up to her ear and listened to the ringing.

"Hello, this is Captain Ganz. Tommy, is that you?"

After a slight hesitation, Sara replied, "No sir, my name is Sara Graynor, Colleen Frye's friend. Captain Ganz, I'm calling from her house and there's a serious problem here. Your Detective Darnello is badly hurt on the second floor and Colleen is missing. There is blood all over the bathroom, too. The detective really needs an ambulance and very quickly."

"Miss Graynor, you stay right where you're at with Detective Darnello, there will be police there within minutes. Is the downstairs door unlocked?"

"Yes sir, we're in the main bedroom upstairs. Please hurry," Sara told him.

Kathy was sleeping, dreaming of woods and hills, smelling the intoxicating aroma of live prey. She could hear their frenzied heartbeats while loping silently along the narrow trail, head held low as she followed the fresh scat deposited by the relaxed deer. All of these senses caused her to feel so incredibly alive, feral and beastly. Yet as she moved gracefully through this dark forest that was clearly her domain, thoughts were not only that of a creature, but human as well. A confusing dilemma as she rounded a small curve in the path and then stopped immediately, dropping to the ground and staring ahead at a clearing where four deer stood munching on fresh, succulent grass.

Stealthily she slid towards the bushes on the right until she was out of sight. The buck raised its head, his jet-black eyes staring at the now empty trail they had traveled not long before. White tail twitching alarmingly back and forth, his mate glanced up with nervous anticipation. The two younger deer continued to snack, somewhat oblivious to the dangers that nature presented to them on a daily basis. The deadly scent of predator the buck picked up was something it was not used to around the safety of these woods, but he still was completely aware of danger now within their midst.

Kathy moved to the edge of the clearing, her eyes zeroed in on one of the younger fawns closest to her. Warm saliva dripped from her open jowls. She was incredibly hungry and anxious for a kill. The buck made a mewling sound and now all four deer were extremely alarmed as the male and female moved quickly to prod their young away from possible death. The beast tensed, power in her hind legs preparing for a spring into the clearing, the scent of blood and fresh meat utterly intoxicating. As she leaped, the startled deer bolted towards the safety of the forest on the other side of the clearing.

The telephone on the nightstand rang and rang. The beast stopped, alarmed, viciously angry for the ugly ringing in her pointed ears. The huge wolf turned and stared where the annoying sound was coming from.

Kathy sat up in bed, her heart thumping wildly, sweat drenching her t-shirt, skin glistening, eyes startled. The telephone continued to jangle obnoxiously and she realized it was her cell. Angrily she reached out to the table and grabbed the phone, flipping it up and saw it was Nathan Ganz. She let it ring two more times, trying to let her heart slow down from the nightmare she had just been through.

"This better be good Nathan, what the hell's up?" she said groggily. "I was in a deep sleep, or something, not sure what it was actually."

"Sorry to wake you Kathy, but you need to get dressed. Tommy has been hurt and he's at Roxborough Memorial in the emergency room."

Kathy was already out of bed and reaching for her jeans. Tommy hurt, not good she thought. What the hell was happening in her neighborhood?

"What's up Captain, I'm already getting dressed?"

"It seems he went to Colleen Frye's house to see how she was doing. I can't tell you what happened to him as yet, but I got a call from her friend, Sara Granger, telling me that she was at the house, Tommy was in the bedroom on the second floor hurt badly and it seemed that Miss Frye was missing. I'm on my way to the hospital now so I'll meet you there. Get moving Kathy," he instructed her.

Turning off the phone she peeled off the wet t-shirt and threw it in a basket of dirty clothes. Running into the bathroom she tossed cold water onto her face and then stared intently at herself in the mirror. The unsettling dream, or terrifying nightmare, was so vivid it still had her heart revving like a formula one race car. My God, she was so keyed up she felt as if she truly was that large, feral wolf ready to pounce at those defenseless deer and slaughter one. She shuddered, but felt strangely exhilarated.

"Move Rain, mommy has to leave, I gotta' go to work," she said, scratching the excited dog behind the ears.

Leaning down she kissed her beloved friend on the forehead. "I love you, come on I'll take you outside real fast before I go."

Running quickly down the steps she found her father just coming awake from a deep slumber in his comfy recliner.

"Hey honey, who was on the phone?"

"Hi Dad, it was Nathan. Tommy is at Roxborough Memorial, he's been hurt and I need to run over there right now. You feeling okay?" she asked, bending over and kissing him of the cheek.

"Yeah, just tired, like usual. Don't worry about Rain, I'll get my coat on and take her out after you leave. Just get over there and be with Tommy. Call me when you get a minute," he said, hugging her.

"Okay, I'll call you. Hey, if Johnny stops by or calls, tell him where I'm at or call me on my cell phone. I know I can't use it inside the hospital, but at least I'll know that he knows I'm there."

"Do I detect a slight note of admiration for that young man?" her father asked.

"Yeah, sure, like my track record with guys lately has been any good," she retorted laughingly. "But you have to admit, he's pretty damn good looking."

"He is that, but you have more important things to worry about right now. If he calls or stops, I'll tell him where you are. Just please be careful Kathy."

Grabbing her keys, coat and bag she headed for the front door. However, she was blocked by an obstinate dog who desired to go along.

Kathy laughed. "Move girl, I love you too. We'll go for a long walk soon, when I get home, okay?"

A few minutes later she was speeding up Shawmont Avenue and over to Henry where she could make better time. She was upset over being injured and couldn't be with him when he went to Colleen Frye's house. That's what partners were for, to back each other up. She knew that Tommy felt terrible he was not beside her when she got clawed by the beast and that it had gotten away as well. Tommy was impulsive and should not have gone to the Frye house alone so she was angry at him for doing that also.

Her thoughts equally rested heavily upon Johnny Raven. From the very first time she saw him, there was an immediate physical attraction. But now, with all that had come to pass since her injury, there was an unexpected pull, an intense desire that burned beneath her skin. Kathy also knew she was not the same woman as before, something was happening inside of her. Fear and exhilaration were equal emotions, along with staring into the unknown. Right now she had to worry about Tommy and then find the killer. In the end, however, she had come to a firm decision. She would in fact take her own life before turning into some ravenous creature that bayed mournfully underneath a full moon and then rampantly slaughtered the innocent.

Taking the corner sharply into the ER parking lot she slammed on the brakes nearly in front of the entrance, generally where rescue vehicles backed into. Darn place was packed, though she would move it as soon as she knew Tommy was okay. She still left enough room for an ambulance to back into.

"Excuse me Miss, you can't park your car there," said the elderly guard who started to stand.

Kathy held up her detective's shield. "Don't get your underpants in an uproar. This is police business so please open the door now. I'll move my vehicle as soon as I see my partner. Now open up the damn door."

A whoosh of air followed her frantic voice as the double doors opened, the guard knowing when to back down. She saw several police standing around one of the rooms and ran down the congested corridors. The place was packed with patients lying on gurneys in the hallway and others sitting in chairs. She figured a 'No Room at the Inn' sign should've been posted outside so incoming patients would prepare for a long wait.

"How is he?" coming up to the first officer standing at the door.

"Hey Morello, not sure yet, the doctor's in there now with a nurse and they shoved us out into the hallway. He's alive though and conscious so that's good. Also, I didn't see any blood so that's another welcome sign. From what I gather he was taken from behind and almost strangled so there's definitely severe throat damage. I think he has some broken ribs so he must've been kicked when he was down. Oh, and I think a wrist is broken as well."

Damn Kathy thought as she moved into the room and walked to where the curtain was pulled closed. She peered in just as the doctor looked up.

"Don't you people listen? Can you wait outside please? I'll be done in a minute," the doctor told her.

"No sir, I won't go outside. This is my partner and I'm staying. How is he?"

Anger clouded the doctor's eyes for a moment and then he glanced back down at Tommy, mumbling something that Kathy was sure she did not want to hear.

"He's stable and we've just given him a sedative. He was quite agitated when they first brought him in. We're going to transport him in a few minutes for x-rays. He has severe trauma to the throat and larynx, most probably from strangulation. It also seems from a closer examination that at least three vertebrae might be cracked, some ugly discoloration on the right side of his back. It appears his wrist might be broken also. We need to get him to x-ray and then we'll know for sure."

"Is he able to talk at all?" she asked the doctor.

"Don't you people ever give up? The guy is badly hurt and needs to rest. How much plainer can I make that?"

In barely an audible whisper, Tommy said, "sssss okay doc.... my partner."

The doctor moved back with arms crossed against his white coat, not happy in the least his patient was being taken from him for even the slightest moment. Kathy gently nudged the nurse aside and leaned over the bed.

"Hey Tommy what the hell happened? Seems I can't let you out of my sight for a minute. Just because I got hurt doesn't mean you have to do everything I do," she said smiling down at him, softly brushing some stray hair from his forehead.

"Had him Kat," he croaked. "Bastard was there....came up behind me....very strong....smelled really bad....how's Col...leen?"

"She wasn't there. Her friend Sara found you and called it in. You'll be okay and we'll find her. Just rest," she tried to say soothingly with emotions roiling inside her.

"Talk....to....Sara....she may....know....where....." he stopped, no longer able to speak.

"That's it detective, move aside. We need to get him ready for x-ray and he must not talk any more."

Kathy leaned over and kissed Tommy on the cheek. "Hang in there partner. You'll be fine and don't worry sweetie, I'll find her and the guy who did this."

"Out, right now detective or I'll call security. I don't care who you are, this is my patient."

Not wishing for an altercation she walked out into the hallway at the same moment Nathan Ganz barged his way through the double doors. Kathy turned to the same officer she had spoken to before.

"Where is Sara Granger, the woman who was with Tommy and who called in the emergency?" she asked.

"Not sure, but she was suppose to be sitting out in the waiting room. We told her not to leave, that she needed to be questioned further by a detective," he said, moving down the hallway.

"How is Tommy doing Kathy?" asked Nathan.

"He's okay, they're going to take him to x-ray in a few minutes. Hard for him to talk, but he managed to tell me that the killer was there and to talk to Colleen's friend. She may know something about where they went," she told him, moving towards the double doors and the waiting room.

The area was packed with no Sara Granger in sight. Kathy turned, hands on her hips, eyes blazing and stared at the officer.

"Where the hell is she?"

"I don't know Morello, she was here earlier," he said, looking around.

"Officer Jenkins, get this straight. It's Detective Morello, you got that? Who did she talk to earlier and did she give a statement?" she said angrily.

"She talked to Ruiz standing outside….Detective Morello," he replied, miffed at Kathy putting him in his place.

Kathy moved through the outer doors where Ruiz stood smoking a cigarette.

"Those things will kill you Officer," Kathy said.

"Yeah, well, so will everything else on this damn job detective. What's up?"

"Fill me in on what Sara Granger told you and did you see her leave?"

"Nope, thought she was still in there, but then I just came out here a few minutes ago," as he started to relay to Kathy what the young woman had told him. Nothing much really, that she had come looking for her friend because she was worried. Went upstairs, found the bathroom, heard Tommy moan, used his cell phone to call Captain Ganz and that was it.

"Tommy managed to tell me to talk to Sara Granger, as if she knew more. Did she happen to say where Colleen might've gone?" Kathy asked him.

"She did say something about Miss Frye having a house up around New Hope and that's a possibility, but she didn't tell me exactly where. I assumed that she would give more details when you guys spoke to her."

"Yeah, well, that's a moot point now since she's disappeared. Thanks Ruiz," she said, moving towards Ganz and spying Johnny walking up towards her from the street. She noticed how he moved, with the grace and finesse of a wild animal, a beast.

"Captain, we need to locate Sara Granger and also find out about a house she owns up around New Hope. That may be where the killer took her. Seems that Tommy heard it mentioned before he blacked out, like Colleen was hoping he would hear."

"I'll do that right now. You staying here?" he asked her.

"Nothing much I can do here at the moment. I'll come back later when Tommy is admitted to a room. If you find Sara Granger hold her and call me. That girl has some explaining to do about taking off like this. I'm worried that she may be heading there on her own which would be a deadly mistake," she replied.

"I agree. I'll find out what she's driving, put out an APB and inform the police around New Hope to be on the look out for her. We should locate that house by checking Miss Frye's records."

"If it's not too late for both ladies," she muttered, moving away from Ganz and walking towards Johnny who stood leaning up against the back of a parked vehicle.

He watched her move towards him and felt desire build like a bursting wild flower in morning. God, she was so beautiful he thought. How that lustrous auburn hair cascaded like a wave around her slim but strong shoulders. Usually she had it swept back in a couple barrettes, but now it just flowed free. He wanted nothing more at the moment than to run his fingers through that thick mass of hair, to gently frame her face with his hands and let his lips softly caress hers.

"Hey, what's up," she said, breaking his sensual reverie.

"Oh, nothing much I guess. I called the house and your father told me you were here. Thought you might possibly need me, or I could help in some way. How is your partner doing?" he asked, trying to suppress the need to possess her body.

"He'll be okay hopefully. Won't be talking too well for awhile since this creature nearly strangled him to death. Have no idea why he's even still alive," Kathy said, perplexed.

"You're right, he should be dead and most likely that was the creature's intent. Possibly it was Colleen Frye that staid his murderous purpose. She would have a strong connection with him now and it's possible he merely bowed to her request. Any idea where they went?" he asked.

"No, somewhere around New Hope I think, but we don't know exactly where. Sara Granger does, but she's taken off. Bunch of shit really, he just seems to be staying one step ahead of us," she replied.

"New Hope is where my father is heading to stay with relatives. We'll have some help in the area once we know exactly where the place is at. How are you holding up?"

"I'm okay. Just tired but alive at least, you know what I mean?" she asked, looking up at him, staring deeply into his yellowish eyes for an answer.

"Yes, I certainly know what being alive means. You ready to get out of here?"

"Yep, how about buying me a cup of coffee? There's a diner right up the street."

"Absolutely, lead the way detective. Coffee and booze are the only things that keep me going sometimes," he replied, smiling.

"So you're saying that you're a junkie for caffeine and a drunken lush as well," she threw back at him.

"Among other things," he said, placing his arm around her shoulder.

She realized it was a feeling she liked, the heavy press of his hand and arm in a protective embrace around her body. Her emotions just flew around inside her, screwing up her thoughts with abnormal desires. There had never been a man affect her like he had. But then, this was not just any normal male, a fact she was completely aware of.

Chapter 29

Sara turned slowly off Taylorsville onto a road that ran peacefully along the Delaware River, her thoughts troubled as to the welfare of Colleen. The police would've been extremely angry once they realized she had snuck out of the emergency waiting room, but she felt the more time that went by then the greater danger Colleen was in. Sara placed her hand inside the pocket of her jacket in order to touch the pistol that hid there. It had been in the glove compartment of her car where it had mostly stayed ever since she received the permit to purchase it. After a very nasty altercation with an irate client, combined with the fact she was a lawyer that brought her into contact with equally detestable people, she was granted permission to obtain the gun for safety reasons. Colleen had refused to get one, having a dislike for weapons of any kind. That was ironic in itself because she was an excellent shot with either a pistol or a rifle, her father having been a career Marine and instructing her at an early age how to handle weapons. She always said that if it weren't for the abundance of guns then crime would certainly be a lot lower. Sara agreed, but for the first time there was at least some relief she had possessed the foresight to acquire it.

She didn't travel far before pulling into a deserted parking area set before a small strip of closed businesses. It had gotten progressively darker as she sped up Route 1 and I-95. Now she stood staring across a large open field which separated her from their small getaway home set serenely beside the river. Running cautiously across the open area she then wound down a narrow path that led into some sparse woods to the right of the house. When she came to the clearing they generously referred to as a yard, Sara knelt and tried to observe any movement. She could hear the soft gurgling whoosh of the river to her right. Colleen's car was parked in front of the house, but no lights glowed inside that she could see.

Sara moved quickly in a somewhat half-crouch until her back caressed the cold exterior wall near the back door. Holding the gun up against her chest in one hand she reached for the door knob and as gently as possible tried turning it. Nothing, it was locked. Placing the same hand inside her jacket pocket she grasped the keys and then took a quick glance inside the curtained window. Seeing no movement within the kitchen she knelt and placed the key in the deadbolt lock, turning it as softly as possible. They only locked the back door using the deadbolt and rarely locked the inside of the door knob. It actually was a pretty safe area to live in.

Quietly replacing the keys in her pocket she took a few seconds to try and calm her frazzled nerves. Sara was truly scared, but even more frightened for Colleen as she silently prayed her partner was still alive and well. Very slowly turning the knob she opened the door barely enough to slip inside and then as gently closed it behind her, trying to make as little noise as possible.

The house was deathly quiet until she heard the sound of muffled voices coming from the second floor. Moving quickly, Sara's back kissed the wall until she reached the small staircase leading up to the bedrooms. Six steps took her to the landing at the end of the hallway. Glancing quickly around the corner she found the area lit only by a small lamp perched atop a narrow table midway down. Sara could definitely hear Colleen's voice accusing somebody of something and Sara breathed a little easier. At least the woman she loved was still alive for the moment.

Tiptoeing as softly as possible down the hardwood floor she stopped beside the bedroom door, heart thudding so loud she was afraid the killer inside would know she was there. Holding the gun up before her face she realized how afraid she was, but it was Colleen inside their bedroom and Sara knew she would surely kill to protect her. She took a moment to say a small prayer before barging in.

Inside the room, Colleen was angry. "You are nothing more than a monster. How many innocent people have you slaughtered over the years?"

Quentin laughed. "Too numerous to count my dear, but then sweet Colleen, I didn't kill them, the beast did as you will find out in due time."

"I would rather die first. You've already ended my life with the poison you put inside of me. Now I will have to do the physical taking of that life since you won't," she spat at him.

Quentin moved to where she sat on the bed, towering over her. "I have not killed you, rather I have given you life, more powerful than you could ever imagine," he said, but then turning to stare intently at the closed door.

Holding up his hand for her to be silent he moved quickly to stand against the wall on the opposite side where the door would open. Colleen realized at the same moment that somebody was definitely in the hallway. Her senses had come alive and she could literally here the frightened beat of another heart. Suddenly and with great fear, Colleen realized it was Sara, but too late.

The door flew open as Sara ran in, gun held out in front of her, moving it back and forth. She saw Colleen sitting on the bed with a startled look of surprise on her face. It was a split second before she heard the deep growling voice behind her.

"Well, well, well, if it isn't the brave little lesbian girlfriend. Happy to make your acquaintance Miss Granger," Quentin said, moving towards the middle of the room.

Sara spun and pointed the shaking gun towards him. "Get away from us...now...or I'll shoot," she said, her voice wavering.

He laughed, holding up his open palms.

"But see, I'm defenseless, what harm can I do to you? You've got the weapon."

Sara kept her gaze on his imposing figure and asked, "Colleen, are you okay? I was so worried."

"I'm fine Sara, why did you come here? You've put yourself in serious danger," Colleen said, rising and moving to stand beside her.

"Ahhhhhh, now isn't that sweet. Yes, you definitely do love each other. Hey, I have an idea, why don't I just sit over there and watch you two make love. What a turn on that would be. Then maybe I can join in later in order to show you both what a real man can do," he said, his laugh a deep rumble that filled the room. "Screw you Quentin," Colleen hissed. "Sara, give me the gun. He won't hurt you with me here."

"Oh, don't be too sure of that my fair Colleen. I told you already when I let that damn detective live, you're quite out of options now. I will most definitely do whatever I wish. And, you have only yourself to blame for your lover standing here right now. If I would've killed him, then Miss Granger would not have thought about coming here. So whatever happens to her will be on your lovely shoulders," he answered her very nonchalantly, but with malice nonetheless.

"That's where you're wrong," Sara said, "I would've come here anyway the first chance I got. This is our place and I would've showed up for sure."

"Oh, that's right," Quentin said, raising his eyebrows and smiling an evil grin. "This must be your little love nest. But now it's mine," he said, moving with uncanny speed, grabbing the gun from Sara's grasp.

However the gun went off as her finger squeezed the trigger. The bullet entered his right side just below the rib cage, temporarily knocking the wind from him and sending him reeling backwards where he fell into a chair. Reaching down with his hand he brought up bloody fingers before he looked up smiling. Then he put them in his mouth and sucked on them.

"Yummy, that's good. Well Colleen, your little love bug has a sting it seems. Ouch, that hurts a little bit you know. I suppose I'll just have to remove her stinger my own way," he said, getting up from the chair, the side of his shirt already saturated in blood.

Colleen moved to stand in front of Sara. "Stay away Quentin, she didn't mean to do that. If you would've stayed where you were I could've gotten the gun from her."

"Maybe so my dear, but I hate having guns pointed at me, especially by hysterical females. Stand aside, I don't want to hurt you as well," he said, moving forward.

Pushing back, Colleen held one arm behind her around Sara's waist and one warding off Quentin.

"Stay away or I swear as God is my witness, I will kill you if you harm her in any way," Colleen hissed.

He started to laugh which then grew to an ominous growl. "God has forsaken you dear Colleen. You're a spawn of the devil now, don't you realize that? You're a monster now just like you call me. A beast and you won't kill me because I've given you life."

Colleen had been slowly steering Sara towards the door. "Run Sara, get out of this house and call the police. Run now," she whispered, shoving her frightened partner towards the open doorway.

Quentin was much too fast however. His one arm swung up and sent Colleen reeling towards the far wall where she crashed and slid to the floor. The other arm reached out and grabbed Sara underneath the chin, literally hauling her off the floor.

"No Quentin," Colleen screamed. "Please, let her be. She was only trying to save me and had no idea what kind of creature you are. Please Quentin, I beg of you. She'll leave and I'll make sure she doesn't contact anybody."

"But my dear, you told her to call the police. What the hell do you really want Colleen? Make up your damn mind. Besides, this little hell cat will not rest until you're safe. So, do I kill her, or just infect her?" Quentin asked Colleen, so innocently. "Eany, meany, minie, mo, do I bite her now and let her live? Or do I tear out her throat and let her go?"

Colleen raced across the room and lunged at Quentin, hitting him with enough force to knock him against the open door, slamming it shut. He fell to the floor, still clutching Sara in his strong hand and trying to ward off the blows from a crazed Colleen.

Quentin reached out and grabbed Colleen's hair, spinning her around and then enclosed his arm around her throat. For a few seconds the only sound heard was the gasping for air from both females. He lay with his back against the door shaking his head back and forth. The bleeding from his side had all but stopped already.

"What a revoltin' development this is. Here I am, shot and bleeding all over your clean floor and holding two struggling, out of control women at the same time. Most men would love to be in this situation, but probably not the bleeding part. So Colleen, what am I going to do with you two? I hope you realize I can't let her live, and I can't kill you either. Something has to give and I think you have to finally realize just what and who you are now.

It's your decision my dear. If Sara lives she will become like you are now. Or she can die, knowing that you love her very much."

"Let her live Quentin, please, but don't infect her. She was only coming to protect me. She had no idea what kind of danger she was in. Please, I love her, don't harm her," Colleen pleaded, tears of anguish raining down her cheeks.

"But I've already told you, I granted your wish to save one life which was that worthless detective. You pissed away your chance to save the woman you love on a piece of shit policeman. Now, when you could've used that wish to save your lovely Sara, well my sweet I'm so sorry, but you're quite out of wishes, only dire choices left. Does she live or die Colleen? You have a fifty-fifty choice, die as a woman, or live as a beast. What will be the fate of the sexy Miss Granger?" he asked her.

Colleen realized with horror that whatever option she selected then Sara's life was over and she couldn't bear that. At least if she let Sara live for now, it would give her more time to figure out how to kill him later. Then, at some point, she and Sara could end their lives together, and so she now wept openly.

"Let her live Quentin, I couldn't stand her death upon my hands."

Tightening the grip around Colleen's neck he closed his eyes and envisioned his right hand turning into claws. The moon was still strong enough for him to alter his hands or teeth. Without opening his eyes he slid three of the claws across the velvety soft skin of Sara's throat. She had already been faint from having her windpipe crushed by his hand, but in startled gaze her eyes flew open. The pain was not intense, but she could feel the skin ripping apart. A gurgling sound reached Colleen's ears and she began to struggle harder, trying her best to get free. The metallic scent of fresh blood assailed her nose and she realized immediately what he was doing. The bastard had lied again.

Sara tried to talk, but couldn't. She felt pressure from the creature's claws and could tell her throat was being ripped open, but there was nothing she could do other than lie there and let death take her. Tears burst from her eyes realizing she might never know the warm hugs and tender kisses from her Colleen ever again. She would allow the peacefulness of death to possess her. It had been a good life up to now, too short though, so much left undone. Strange there was no pain she thought. However, there was a soft caressing up and down her throat, almost to the point of being sensual. It was Quentin's long, snake-like tongue passing on his healing powers.

"You bastard," Colleen screamed, as she broke free of Quentin's strong arm. "I asked you to let Sara live and instead you've slit her throat. I'll kill you for that."

Colleen sprang for the discarded gun, wheeled on one knee and aimed. The first shot took Quentin in the left shoulder and the next one struck him on the left side of his neck. She was very good, keeping her shot radius from striking Sara. Quentin roared his defiance and left Sara fall to the floor, struggling to rise and defend himself. Colleen's next shot exploded in the enclosed, slightly lit room and took him squarely in the pit of the stomach. Quentin flew backwards against the wall as he leered at her.

"You fucking bitch, you can't kill me. Don't you realize that?" he growled, trying to bring forth any possible change he could still achieve, but he couldn't.

Colleen stood up with Sara's gun held before her in a tight, two-handed grip. She moved slowly forward, worried about Sara's slumped body, but more afraid to take her gaze from the beast lying before her.

"You'll die now Quentin. There are two bullets left and I know exactly where to put them. Your reign of terror is over as of tonight. I told you to let Sara live and you defied my wishes. I suppose this here bitch was more than you expected," she hissed.

He spread his mouth into an evil grin, looking at her through clouded eyes, blood flowing freely down his lips and chin from his nose.

"My reign of killing may be over, but yours my dear has just begun. Go ahead sweet Colleen, end my nightmare now, but welcome yours," he requested, "and let me be your very first kill".

The gun exploded in her hand, the first shot taking him in the middle of the forehead and the second one tearing through his heart. The beast was finally dead.

Colleen dropped the gun and ran to where Sara lay slumped on the floor. She knelt and lifted her sweetheart into her arms.

"Sara....Sara....can you hear me? Honey, please stay with me," Colleen pleaded, tears rolling down her face. "Don't leave me alone, please don't leave me alone."

Sara's eyes fluttered open as she broke a slight grin.

"Hey baby," she croaked, "is it dead?"

"Yes, he's dead. Can you move? We have to get out of here before somebody calls the police."

"Sure, but I don't think I can walk. I'm really not in much pain, just so very weak," she whispered.

Lifting Sara in her arms, Colleen rose and moved to the door that had opened up when Quentin slammed against it after being shot. He lay there in a quickly expanding pool of blood. He was most assuredly dead. Colleen carried Sara outside and placed her lying down in the backseat. Then she ran back inside, grabbed her purse, two throw blankets from the couch and slammed the front door behind her. After covering Sara up so she'd stay warm, Colleen was quickly peeling away from the house. Her very acute hearing now picked up the distant wail of police sirens. Some neighbor had for sure heard the volley of gunshots and called it in. Racing down towards the light at Taylorsville Road and Rte. 532 she had to pull off to the side of the road as two police cars with lights flashing made sharp turns and sped down the road towards Colleen's house. All they would find was a dead killer lying on the floor in a deep crimson pool of his own worthless blood.

Colleen realized that soon there would be a search for her and Sara as well. Somehow she had to get them away, at least to have time for Sara to heal. But getting away from the police was pushing them towards an unknown future of terrifying proportions.

Chapter 30

Johnny held the cup of steaming coffee up to his lips and stared at Kathy. He never thought he would become so enraptured by another female after forming such a tight, loving bond with his Samantha. It distressed him because of the strong feelings of love he still held for his dead mate and realizing he was somehow cheating on her. But Samantha had told him within several dreams she did not wish for him to live his life for only her memory. They had their special time together and it was beautiful. But she wanted him to find another mate and be happy, to have the children he had always yearned for. Now he looked upon this beautiful human who was now infected by the rogue's werewolf blood. He knew that Kathy was strong, but yet so vulnerable right now. Plus, she still did not even begin to realize what had to be done in order to save her.

"Penny for your thoughts?" she asked him.

"What? You need a penny from me?" he replied.

She laughed. "Where in the world have you been hidden away from society Johnny Raven? If I didn't know any better I'd swear you were an alien from Mars, or some other world. It's just an expression we humans use. In other words, what are you thinking about?"

"How beautiful you are. And I was also thinking about Samantha," he said softly.

"You still miss her terribly, I can tell. She must've been a very special woman."

"Yes she was, very much so. We had our whole lives ahead of us and these last three years for me have been pure hell to be honest. I've had no direction, no will to live, only an insane revenge in my heart. I always thought that when her death was finally avenged, and if I still lived, I would just go back to Maine and spend my days there. In fact to be honest, I thought I would just surrender to my wolf and live the rest of my life running with the pack," he said quietly, his eyes almost staring through her, seemingly concentrating on something Kathy could have no way of knowing, at least not yet.

He placed his coffee cup down and sat back. "But then I met you in this whole mess and my emotions are just racing in circles," he said, looking straight at her.

"Johnny, we just met. With all that's gone on and my future unknown, I'm not asking anything of you. I just want to find this killer and end this murderous rampage," she told him. "Whatever happens after that is beyond my control, or at least most of it."

"And just what does that mean?" he asked her, knowing the answer already.

She hesitated, playing with remnants on her plate from a piece of cherry pie.

"Johnny, I've decided that I won't live as a beast. If what you say will happen can in fact occur when the next full moon arrives, I will not be around to experience it."

He stared at her, knowing completely that she meant suicide. It was a very common decision for those who had been infected, especially the ones who were smart like Kathy. To live as a rogue werewolf was no true life and Johnny knew he could not do it as well. He remembered how crazed he was the year following Samantha's death, lashing out at anything that moved. But he was weregune which was a completely different existence. He still had time to discuss the future with her and explain what her world could be like, hopefully a life with him where they both could experience the love they so craved.

"Did I shock you?" she asked, glancing up from her plate.

"No Kathy, not really, but please know there are still many things for us to discuss and after that, if you still feel the same, then I won't stand in your way. All I ask is that you give me a chance and listen to what I have to tell you, nothing more," he requested, hoping he would still be alive to help her.

"I suppose I can do that Mr. Raven. But right now," she said, sliding out of the booth and standing up. "I have to go check on Dad and Rain. Do you want to come with me, or should I take you back to your car?"

He grabbed the check and stood up, helping her on with her coat.

"I'll tag along if you don't mind," he said, placing his hands on her shoulders, allowing the intoxicating smell of her to arouse him even more.

Kathy turned and smiled. Clutching onto his arm, she replied, "Sure, let's get over there. If Dad fell asleep then Rain must be going bonkers about doing her business."

"Going bonkers? Doing what business?" he inquired with a confused look.

She laughed, "Never mind silly, not important, just follow me."

They paid the tab and walked down a side street where her car was parked. Kathy started the engine and turned to see if anybody was driving up the small street before she pulled out. Her gaze rested upon Johnny who was sitting on the passenger side just staring at her. He raised his hands and gently cupped her face, the thrill of having his strong fingertips brushing against her cheeks set her veins afire.

"Do you realize just how beautiful you are Kathy? How much I've wanted you?"

She didn't answer him. She couldn't say a word, just looked into his eyes like she was a star struck school girl and sat there awaiting his next move. Leaning forward he ever so gently placed his lips on hers, drawing every sweet taste of her lips into his mouth. Kathy closed her eyes and succumbed to this magical spell he had cast upon her. Never in her entire life had a man swept her away like this. She opened her mouth and let his tongue explore the inside of hers. My God, she was soaring, spinning, falling out of control. Her heart pounded behind her anxious breasts, wanting him to just devour her. She never wanted this kiss to end. But it did.

He pulled slowly away from her and smiled. "So, should we go check on your father and Rain?"

"Ah, sure, I guess," she said breathlessly. "I mean, I could just call him I suppose and we could maybe go somewhere else."

"And where would that be? Do you have a secret place in mind?" he asked, a mischievous smile forming on his face.

She punched him in the shoulder. "No, but you're staying somewhere aren't you? How far are you away from here, unless you're sleeping as a wolf under the stars?"

"Oh, I'd say I'm at least a good half hour away, and no I'm not sleeping in the woods though don't knock it if you haven't tried it. Kathy, I'm not rushing you. Without a doubt I want to sleep with you very much, but we need to know when the time is right. Unless of course you feel the time is right now. I surely wouldn't be disappointed."

"I don't know anything about being right. I just know I've never felt this way about anyone before. You drive me completely crazy. I can't even think straight when you're around me. Let me call my father and see how things are at home before we make a decision," she said, reaching for her purse with quivering hands.

As she grabbed the cell phone she decided to check her messages. The last call she had received was from her father and only about ten minutes ago. Damn, why had she not realized the phone was turned off?

"My Dad called while we were in the diner. Let me call and see what's up," she told Johnny.

Dialing the number she heard it ring and ring. After four rings her recorder picked up and she hit the end call button.

"I don't know why but I feel really strange. I mean, he could be outside with Rain, but why do I have this deep sense of dread Johnny?"

"Let's go, follow your instincts. We're not far from your house and if there is something wrong its better that we get there as quickly as possible," Johnny told her, already worrying himself. If somebody was searching for Kathy they wouldn't care if she was home or not, they would just barge in. She hit the gas pedal and they screeched down the side street, hoping their fears were not valid ones.

Rain sat very still and tense, staring with apprehension at the door, a low and deep, guttural growl rising from her broad chest. Something was clearly outside her house. She could smell the sinister danger of it. The dog got up and cautiously walked to the window on the side of the front door, moving the white, gauzy curtain aside with her nose. Suddenly she started barking wildly, the hair along the ridge of her back standing straight up like it did when she got really agitated over something.

"What is it girl? Somebody walk past the house again? Come on Rain, stop that barking, it hurts my ears," Carl said.

But she didn't care about that, only protecting her turf and getting at what was outside. The dog began to paw at the small window panes, her claws making heavy clunking noises on the glass. The barking became more insane as the scent of something she was unfamiliar with assailed her nostrils.

"Hey, hey, that's enough. What the hell's rousing you up like this?" Carl asked her as he limped to the window. Damn feet and arthritis always gave him a problem when he got up from his recliner.

He stood curiously at the window and parted the curtains, staring out into the dark evening illuminated only by a street lamp and glow from a silver moon. Nothing was there that he could see, but he continued to watch anyway. He wished that Kathy would return his message, though when he had called for her a few minutes ago it was just to see if he could find out how Tommy was doing. Now it was a completely different story.

A few cars drove past the house, their headlights casting a garish brightness onto the porch. It was then that Carl saw a shadow move and he immediately thought prowler.

"What the hell was that girl? Did you see that?" he asked the shrilly barking dog who no doubt saw it, but sensed extreme danger as well.

From the inquisitive glow of the street light hanging on the telephone pole at the end of the driveway Carl saw another shape move and damn if it didn't look like an animal of some kind slithering across the concrete for a brief moment. He reached down and grabbed Rain by the collar, trying to pull her back from the window.

"Stop that barking Rain. Something is definitely out there, but I don't know what it is. It might be a stray dog, a raccoon or even a skunk, so I can't let you outside, no telling if it's mean or rabid. Move away so I can open the door and take a look around. Come on now, move away from the door," Carl said, using his left leg to push the yapping dog backwards.

Carl unlocked the door and struggled to keep Rain inside. Shit, it was cold so he just stood there shivering with the inside door closed and holding the screen door halfway open. The sound of clanging metal came from around the side of the house.

"Who's there?" he called out, thinking just maybe it was the wind knocking something against the cyclone fence in the backyard.

No answer from whomever, or whatever, was slinking around out there. Suddenly Carl heard what sounded fully like a growl, deep and menacing. Quickly with his heart beginning to thud crazily he opened the door behind him and moved back inside the supposed safety of the living room, slamming both doors shut and flicking the bottom lock. Damn that was scary he thought, it definitely sounded like a large dog of some kind.

As he scrambled back inside the phone had been ringing and then abruptly stopped. He walked quickly to the table beside his chair and hit the playback button. Damn, whoever it was didn't leave a message. Stupid, he hated these rings and hang-ups. Then he thought it might be Kathy so he picked up the phone and dialed her number again. On the first ring she answered.

"Dad, is that you? Where the heck were you at?" she frantically asked him.

"Why the hell didn't you leave a message?" he shot back at her

"Because I suddenly got worried when you didn't pick up so Johnny and I are on our way home now, I just pulled away from the Ridge. Where were you?" she asked.

"I heard a noise outside and stepped out onto the porch to see if I could see what it was. Rain is going crazy, can you hear her?" he shouted into the phone.

"Yes Dad, I can hear her. Listen to me very closely. Make sure the doors are locked and go upstairs into your bedroom and lock that door too from the inside. Don't open it for anybody but me or Johnny. Take Rain with you and do it now," she yelled into the phone.

Suddenly Carl saw two large shadows move across the ceiling. "Kathy, I think a large dog, or maybe two of them are on the porch."

"Dad, they may not be dogs. Please go upstairs," she shouted, "we'll be there in less than two minutes. Now go, hurry, you're in danger."

Rain was backing up and barking vociferously at the closed door and the shadows that were very visible. Carl had grabbed Rain by the collar again and was hauling her back. He placed the phone down on his chair, but left it on so he could yell if he needed to and Kathy would hear him. The dog was absolutely crazed, trying desperately to break free from Carl's tight grasp.

With a loud crash the window on the front door imploded in, glass and wood showering the inside of the living room. Through the damaged door hurtled the largest dog Carl had ever seen. It was impossible to hold Rain any longer, but he was deathly afraid to let her go. Then Carl realized that standing before him was no ordinary dog, it was massive beyond his understanding. Rain was not a huge dog herself, but she was big enough and solidly built. Yet she was dwarfed by the size of this beast. Carl had managed to get them both onto the small landing before the longer stretch of staircase began.

Rain then broke free and lunged at the slobbering beast, no concern for her own welfare, or the size of the fangs she was about to encounter. After all, this was no tiny, domestic cat that threatened her. Yet even though she was an extremely brave dog, Rain was clearly no match for the huge wolf standing amid a spray of broken glass littering the living room floor.

At that same moment one of the two large picture windows on the side of the house along the dining room wall crashed in as another equally large wolf landed atop the deep window sill and slid across the dining room table. If it wasn't so terrifying it would've been comical. The large gray wolf careened along the table cloth and landed with a heavy thud onto the floor, smacking up against a large stereo cabinet. Carl had lost his balance and was now sitting on the steps, scrambling backwards crab-like trying to get upstairs and possibly some modicum of safety. He was so frightened he could hardly breathe and worried about having a heart attack.

Rain had managed to sink her teeth into the thick mane of hair around the wolf's neck, hanging on for dear life. But it was like a puny, 175 pound defensive back trying to bring down a 260 pound full back running at full speed. The wolf, which had been at first stunned by the attack, angrily shook the dog and lashed out with a paw of massive strength. The claws struck Rain on the side and sent her flying through the air where she crashed against the television set. She immediately leapt back to her feet, snarling at the huge beast that consumed most of the empty space in the living room. Now Rain was more cautious, but equally intent on resuming the attack. The dog had no fear even though she was sorely overmatched.

In the meantime, Carl had managed to arrive at the top of the stairs and started to rise, but before he could stand up completely the other wolf had moved onto the steps and stared malevolently at him. He could feel the creature's hot breath against his own face and Carl knew he was about to die. Even when Kathy got here it would be too late. He could hear Rain downstairs attacking the other wolf, yet realized that as brave as the dog was, she was no match for what she was doing battle with. Carl began saying a prayer as the beast moved up a few more steps and now towered over him. Before the wolf struck though, Carl's heart had already ceased to beat. As long, sharp claws tore into his chest and fangs sank deeply into his throat Carl had already died from fright. His prayers had been answered and he did not feel the monstrous degradation of his physical being.

Downstairs Rain had leaped once more at the massive wolf before her. Strangely the wolf nearly stood up and caught the dog as she leaped. Rain found herself being held between two huge paws, her legs scrambling wildly in midair, lunging forward with her mouth and hoping to sink them into any piece of flesh she could.

Outside the screeching of tires filled the night. Johnny had already torn his shirt off inside the car and long before she came to an abrupt halt in front of the house he had already leaped from the moving vehicle, passenger door hanging open. Kathy jumped out with her gun pulled and raced towards the front porch. A menacing growl yanked her attention from the shattered front door to the side of the house. Coming around the corner of the stone porch, head held low and eyes centered intently upon Kathy came a third wolf. Without waiting for even a second, Kathy began firing, aiming for the head only. Before the wolf even had a chance to leap it was lying on the ground dead.

She raced for the splintered front door, hearing the sound of battle inside from two animals. Kathy knew one had to be her fearless Rain. She stopped and stared at the horrible scene of her beloved pet being held in the air by a semi-standing wolf which was just about to sink its fangs into Rain's exposed neck.

She shouted, "Let my dog alone you freakin' monster."

The wolf turned its head, large golden eyes glaring at this puny human female. It raked the dog down the middle of her chest with its claws and tossed Rain like a broken rag doll against the wall. At the same moment a large, massive black wolf leaped through the broken dining room window. Kathy knew it was Johnny so she began to empty her gun at the wolf which was now moving towards her. After three shots the gun clicked on empty chambers as the wolf continued to advance, only momentarily stunned by the impact of the bullets. She tossed the gun aside and reached down for the pistol she kept hidden in an ankle strap. But before she got the gun up the wolf was outside on the porch and she toppled back against a white plastic chair to land harshly on the cement floor. Cars were screeching to a stop on the street and then a loud bang as one unbelieving driver crashed into the back of another.

Kathy scrambled backwards until her head hit the stone wall with a thud. The wolf towered over her, hot slobber drooling down and landing on Kathy's pant legs and jacket. She pointed the gun towards the beast and began squeezing the trigger.

"Die you fucking monster, die," as the first three shots impacted the heaving chest and sent it sprawling backwards. She quickly jumped up onto one knee and fired into the beast's neck. Then standing she moved several feet and emptied the final two bullets into the wolf's brain. It was dead as the sound of another grinding impact of bumpers added to this nightmarish evening.

Inside the house another battle raged. Johnny, who was now Jaress, had leaped atop the back of the wolf on the steps. It was immediately clear to Jaress that Kathy's father was dead, his throat and chest torn open. The two massive wolves tumbled down the steps, splintering the wooden staircase and landing heavily upon the floor. Jaress lunged and sank his three-inch fangs into the other wolf's thick neck, massive paws holding him down and at the same time slicing through its enemy's chest to reach a beating heart. In seconds the wolf that had killed Carl lay dead as well, head literally torn from its body and heart lying exposed upon the floor. Jaress lifted his wide head and stared with a hungry, feral gaze at Kathy who stood aiming an empty gun at Jaress. He threw back his head and mournfully howled as she lowered her weapon, letting it fall to the floor.

Police sirens split apart the dark, horror-filled sky. She stared at this beautifully majestic and blood covered black wolf standing overtop another dead beast inside her destroyed dining room. It was the second time she had looked upon Johnny's wolf and both times his muzzle was painted with a deep crimson from some other beast's blood.

"Go Johnny, leave now before the police get here," but she didn't finish her statement completely. He lowered his head and within seconds had shifted back to human form, kneeling nude on the dining room floor.

Startled at the speed in which he changed shape, as if it was just nothing more than changing clothes, she shook her head in startled amazement.

"You'd better get upstairs then to my fathers room and put something on, the police will be here in less than a minute. Where is my father Johnny?" she asked, realizing after all that had transpired in no more than a minute or two that she hadn't seen him at all. She was terrified over what she would find.

"I'm so sorry Kathy, your father is gone. Please stay down here, I don't think you want to see him right now," as he moved quickly up the steps, trying to block her path.

"Screw you, where is he?" she said, following him onto the staircase and then stopping suddenly, hand moving to cover her mouth. "Oh my God...no...dear God not my father," she whispered, suddenly feeling very nauseous and dizzy.

"Please Kathy, don't come up here. I'll cover him up, go back downstairs," he told her, but she wasn't able to move an inch.

"Get dressed Johnny, I'm okay. Just get dressed," she was barely able to say, leaning against the wall and then slumping to the steps.

The sirens blared outside the house and she heard the slamming of car doors.

"Inside the house, put down your weapons and come out now with your hands up," one of the officers shouted. "Do it now, this is your only warning."

Kathy had already dropped her second gun onto the living room floor as she stared in a daze at the blood covered feet of her father. She wondered quickly where Rain was at and if she was still alive, but the numbness over losing her father kept her glued to the steps. She felt a hand upon her shoulder and glanced up into the eyes of Officer Ruiz.

"Detective Morello, are you hurt?" he asked her.

"No, I'm not hurt. Mr. Raven is upstairs, so please don't shoot him. He's checking the upstairs rooms for any other intruders. Just help me stand up," she said, lifting her arm.

"Who's lying on the floor up there detective?" he asked softly.

"It's my father. Did you see my dog downstairs?" she inquired.

"There's a large, reddish-brown dog lying in front of the television. Not sure if it's alive or dead, but it's not moving at all," he told her.

At that moment Johnny appeared at the top of the steps and the startled Ruiz raised his gun. "No, I told you that Mr. Raven was upstairs. Please put your gun down. The wolves are all dead," she instructed him.

"Detective Morello, what the hell is happening here? This is like a horror movie," he said in amazement.

"Ruiz, you don't even know the half of it," as she watched Johnny lay a white sheet over her father, which then became quickly saturated in places with his blood.

Out in the kitchen Romeo was going spastic. It seemed to be the only room that was not destroyed. His screeching filled the rooms, but Kathy was numb to all feeling and sound. She looked back as Johnny put his arms around her, pulling her towards his chest. Burying her face against his shoulder she began to cry. In the last week her life had been picked up, torn apart and thrown to the winds. Now her father was dead and possibly Rain too. Her own life was lost it seemed as well. The only stabilizing factor right now was leaning against Johnny's broad chest.

After a few minutes she looked up at him.

"Why? Why did they do this Johnny? My father never hurt anybody. Who are they?" she asked, her voice rising with each question.

"They are most likely from Victor's pack. You shot and killed his son the other night. I suspected you were in danger, but I didn't expect he would attack so fast. I'm sorry Kathy," he said, his voice fading to barely a whisper.

She stood back and glared hatefully at him.

"You knew they would do this and you didn't tell me? You're as much a monster as they are. Now my father and possibly Rain are dead because of you. Get out of my house Johnny," she hissed, pushing him roughly away from her.

"Please Kathy, listen to me. I thought there was time to get you and your father away from here. You're still in grave danger."

She moved off the steps and stared at him. "You're going to protect me like you did my father? I'm better off on my own. If I would not have been with you I would've been home and he might still be alive. Just leave Johnny, now," she said, wheeling and heading for the kitchen to try and quiet down a raving Romeo.

Outside the house and the carnage within, he stared at the dead bodies of the wolves on the porch and the front lawn. He turned and looked back through the open door, thinking he should close it to the cold temperatures and gawking onlookers, but then what was the use. Bright strobe lights from four police cars crashed against the nighttime sky. Several officers were taking statements from the drivers that had gotten into automobile accidents, their voices loud in disbelief over what they had seen, neither driver saying they were at fault. They weren't really!

Since Johnny hadn't driven his truck to Kathy's house he started walking up the hill as Captain Ganz screeched to a halt and jumped out.

"Hey Raven, where the hell are you going, I need to ask you some questions," he yelled over the noise. "You park your ass mister so I can talk to you. What the shit happened here?" he started shouting as he made his way to the porch, staring down at the dead wolves.

Johnny continued to walk slowly up the hill. He needed time to think and also to contact his father in order to tell him what had happened. His plans also included retrieving his truck where it was parked at the hospital and returning to this area. He had decided to change shapes and let his wolf guard over Kathy every second of the coming days. His father and the rest of the pack would come as well. The next time Victor planned to seek revenge against Kathy for killing his son they would be ready.

As he trudged up the hill, his heart heavy and torn, the frigid temperatures had zero effect on him. He was numb, aware that once again he had not been there when a woman he loved needed him the most. He made a pact it would not happen again, never! But at least Kathy was still alive. He vowed he would sacrifice his own life in order to see that she stayed alive and hopefully at his side forever.

Chapter 31

Victor paced back and forth like a caged lion. Well, okay, maybe an extremely agitated wolf. He was seething over the fact he had lost three more pack members to this very dangerous female detective and his enemy, Johnny Raven. This woman had become more bothersome than a parasitic flea or tick and without a doubt she had to die. He also knew that she had been infected by Quentin and would experience change under the next full moon's cycle. At least he had the foresight not to send any of his remaining sons to kill the woman detective, or they may very well be dead as well. Grabbing a wooden chair from the dining room table he flung it powerfully against the wall of this miserably small cabin they had fled to where it smashed, bringing down a large mirror and two pictures.

Tabitha sat on the corner of the couch relishing his anger. She had always loved her mate from the moment they first met so many years ago, but now that love had turned to hate. Her world had been turned upside down over the last few days and she was totally unsure of anything anymore. One thing she knew for sure though. Victor was not the man or weregune who she had idolized for so long and was definitely the reason her oldest son Barton was dead.

He turned and faced her, his face pained and angry. "I'm sorry for everything Tabitha. I should have told you about my past long ago. When we first met each other, you literally stole my breath away with your beauty and intelligence. I let my need for revenge against Johnny's father fade away and for many, many years it had. I have always, and will forever, love and treasure you. But this hate slowly began to grow once again like a cancer and consume me. I don't know why, but I do know it will not end until either I and/or Johnny's father is dead. I realize you blame me for Barton's death, but please believe me when I tell you I did not send him on a mission that night to kill Johnny. It is true I asked our son to follow him and report back to me where he was staying and how close Raven was getting to finding Quentin. I am as pained and grieved as you are with the loss of our first born."

Tabitha stood and walked to the window which looked out onto a small clearing that caressed the edge of a dark blue lake. She did love it here on this property they had purchased nearly thirty years ago. It sat nestled serenely in the beautiful palm of the Pocono Mountains. Her eyes, now filled with tears, gazed upon Barton's grave. It was easy for them to acquire his body from the police autopsy unit. In fact, there were very few places they could not make entry into and they're unique abilities for stealth and appearing invisible created those opportunities. Victor had already sent six of his most dependable pack members to fetch the three bodies slain at the detective's house. She turned to look at her mate, dabbing at her tear-stained eyes, yet standing ramrod straight nonetheless.

"Victor, tell me the truth. Did you have Johnny's wife slain?"

He had moved to the table and sat down heavily on one of the wooden chairs. Pouring himself a shot of whiskey he tossed it down his parched throat and let the burning liquid set fire to his insides. Closing his eyes he placed the small glass down gently on the table. A nervous tic began jumping crazily on his upper lip. He sat back and sighed heavily.

"It was a tragic mistake that went too far out of control Tabby. I sent three of the elders along with Quentin to Johnny's cabin that night with the expressed intent to bring him to me, and if not possible, then to kill him. My error was in not realizing how insane Quentin had gotten over the years. They lay hidden around the cabin for two days awaiting Johnny's return. It started snowing heavily and was extremely cold. His wife came out of the cabin to fetch some firewood and the elders had not noticed Quentin had moved behind the house. Even though it had started snowing the intense pull of the hidden, full moon was felt by all. When Samantha returned to the warmth of the cabin and closed the door she was confronted by Quentin who had completely turned. Since she was with child and what appeared to be only a few weeks away from birth then you know she was unable to shift. She screamed and ran outside where she was brought down from behind. Before the elders had time to react Samantha was on her back staring up into the rabid and crazed eyes of a most dangerous rogue werewolf. As she pleaded for her son's life he plunged his claws into her chest and ripped her open, digging his hands inside and removing the nearly born child."

His voice now a low, throaty whisper he grabbed the bottle of whiskey and took several long swallows. He slammed the bottle down onto the table, the sound echoing like a gunshot throughout the room.

"Tabitha, I have been haunted by her death. You know how strongly I feel about attacking unprotected females and children, whether they are weregune or human. The elders moved quickly, but it was too late. When Quentin removed the child he also tore her heart out. She was dead and the beast had run into the woods. They immediately followed him where they discovered the dead child cast tragically upon the blood-stained snow. Not truly knowing what to do, they then returned the child to where

Samantha lay. My brother Sha'fir stayed out of sight and waited for Johnny's return so he could report back to me. The other two followed Quentin where they found him inside a squalid hotel room three days later, lying in human form amid his own excrement surrounded by numerous empty liquor bottles. Johnny returned the next day to find Samantha and their un-born child lying in the melting snow. When my brother returned and related everything I was overly distraught. It was three years ago when my mood changed and I left you for a month. I never wished to harm her Tabitha, you must believe that."

She had moved to stand beside him and placed her hands on his slumped shoulder.

"You must stop this insanity now Victor. There has been enough tragedy and revenge. It is out of control and we must move on. I don't know if your guilt or anger can ever be appeased, but we have lost loved ones and so has Johnny's pack. We must move far from here, possibly to another country, start all over."

She knelt and took his face in her hands, wiping away his tears.

"Victor, we must leave and quickly before more die, not just weregune but human as well. Please Victor," she pleaded with him.

He stood and took her hands in his. "I can't Tabitha. Not only does my own revenge continue to tear away at me, but I am controlled by other factors as well."

She moved back and stared at him. "What other factors? This cannot continue and I will not be a part of it any longer."

"You have no choice. You are my wife and alpha female of this pack. As leaders we must do things we are not comfortable with and show strength. I don't know where this path towards confrontation will lead, but whatever happens will be destined and you will stand at my side," he told her, regaining his tone of authority, angry that he had shed tears in front of her.

"What other factors Victor? Who is controlling you?" she asked him, fearing what she might hear.

Silence between them was broken by a new voice behind her.

"I am controlling him," said a deep, guttural voice that sent chills up her spine.

Tabitha turned quickly and faced a very large, imposing and dangerous looking male who now filled the open doorway. That he was weregune was obvious immediately, but there was also something extremely menacing about him.

She whispered, "Who are you?"

"My name is Kahleel. I am the older brother of Jaress, son of Mandhar. It is I who controls your husband and you, as well as your entire pack," he said, moving gracefully and powerfully into the center of the room. His size and demeanor was overwhelming.

"Why?" Tabitha whispered, hardly able to speak at all.

"Revenge my dear. Sweet revenge against my entire family, especially my father and to avenge the wrongs they have wrought on your pack as well."

Colleen parked two streets over from her house and managed to get there undetected. No police in sight which was good, but she was certain they would be here very soon, especially over what had happened at her Washington Crossing home. The crime scene tape was broken, most likely by teenage vandals, and flapped along the ground in the chilly breeze like an angry, yellow serpent. She decided to sneak down the narrow alley that was behind the house and go through the rear door. Once inside Colleen quickly threw some clothes and essentials in a large gym bag, dumped some food in a brown paper ACME bag, and was back outside in less than five minutes, unseen as far as she could tell.

Sara was sleeping comfortably in the back seat. In checking the wounds across her neck, Colleen noticed they had already nearly closed. There would definitely be scars though. It was true that werewolves could easily heal themselves from injuries, some even from very serious ones as she had noticed with Quentin, yet those left no scars other than the initial one that infected you. That scar would remain for the rest of your life. Colleen placed her hand across her breast and knew that for a fact. Sara would have some very ugly scars around her throat, but with the proper make-up and scarves they could be hidden away nicely.

Colleen placed the bags on the floor and Sara moaned, opening her eyes.

"Hey Baby, what's happening? Where are we?" she asked, stretching and moving the blanket off her, sitting up. "Ooh, I'm stiff, and ouch, this hurts," she said, fingering her damaged neck.

Colleen placed her hand on Sara's and pulled it away from touching the very tender scars. "Let the wounds heal honey and the pain will fade fast enough. We're a few blocks from my house in Roxborough. I snuck in and got some clean clothes for us to change into, plus some food. Are you hungry?"

"Actually I'm starving," she murmured. "Hey, I love you."

"I love you too, so much," leaning over and kissing Sara on the lips.

"Was that monster dead when we left the other house?" Sara questioned.

"Oh yes, most definitely dead. The police will be happy they've caught their serial killer, but I'm sure they'll be looking for us as well. I haven't decided where we can go yet, any ideas?" asked Colleen, while opening the bag and handing Sara a large, green apple.

"Not really, though I do have a very close friend outside of York. None of my friends down here knows of her so we should be safe there for awhile."

"Sounds like a good enough plan to me. Do you need to call her first?"

"Not really, but I will. If anything hits the news before we get there, I don't want her to be worried or surprised when we knock on the front door. Do you have your cell phone with you?" asked Sara.

"Yes, but the cell phone can be traced. We'll stop somewhere as soon as we get out of Dodge so we can change into clean clothes and you can call her from a pay phone."

Both women moved into the front seat. If anybody did notice them, they were privy to a most interesting sight. Both Colleen and Sara had blood across the front of their clothes, with Sara's neck covered in white, blood-stained bandages. Colleen started the engine and headed for Henry Avenue. The thought crossed her mind that they should ditch the car since the police would most likely be on the look out for them, as well as both of their vehicles. However, if they got free of Philadelphia quick enough, then police in distant towns might not be as observant for awhile.

Colleen wondered if they would ever be able to come back and live in Philadelphia. She liked the city, born and raised, attended Temple University. Sara on the other hand was from Tennessee and when they met in college during their sophomore year, Colleen had become enamored with her gentle, southern accent, besides her extreme sensuality. They hit it off almost right away and it was only natural that a friendship ensued. It was just a lucky break when they were hired at the same law firm, making it easier to spend even more time together. The decision had been made that when they switched over to the new law firm after the first of the year, finally moving in together was something they looked forward to very much.

Now it seemed they would be spending all of their time together with a future completely uncertain. With Quentin dead, Colleen was very frightened about what would happen during the next phase of the full moon. As of yet, Sara was unaware she had been infected and Colleen had no idea how to tell her. First things first though since they had to safely get away from what would be an obvious police search. She smiled as they sped along Henry towards Conshohocken. She had always loved the movie "Thelma and Louise". Now it seemed that she and Sara would be living it for real, in more ways than one.

For three days Johnny watched over Kathy. He, along with his father and four other pack members, had concealed themselves around her house as wolves, undetected from human eyes, yet vigilantly prepared for another attack by Victor's clan. Kathy briefly came out of the house on several occasions during this mourning period and would look deeply into the woods, several times actually staring directly at the spot where Johnny lay camouflaged, as if she was totally aware of his presence. With her heightening senses he felt she knew he was guarding her. At least there was a constant influx of relatives, friends and numerous police. He wanted more than anything to go and comfort her, to hold her tight and whisper how sorry he was. He knew she was not yet ready to welcome him back though. Maybe she never would he thought.

Now he stood stoic in human form atop a hill overlooking a sea of gravestones in the cemetery where Kathy's father was being laid to rest. Johnny's own father stood silent within the quiet crowd that surrounded the coffin, close enough where he could immediately protect her if anything happened. Kathy sat in the front row upon a narrow folding chair dabbing at her eyes, the whiteness of the tissue stark against the blackness of her dress. Johnny wished he could be there at her side to hold her hand, but he was aware she detected his presence and that alone was some comfort.

The weather was overcast, typical for early November, and had a biting wind that stuck its teeth deep into your bones. He didn't mind though since it took his mind off the pain he felt for failing Samantha and now Kathy. Johnny glanced around the crowd and noticed Captain Ganz, her partner Tommy, and a number of policemen he had come into contact with in a short period of time since arriving in Philadelphia. He liked this city too and decided if he survived the battle which was sure to come shortly, then he may just settle down in this lovely town.

The service was relatively short and Johnny watched somberly as Kathy rose and walked towards the casket. She placed her right hand on the cold metal and set one red rose gently on its surface. Both Captain Ganz and Tommy Darnello flanked her in case she needed their support. Her partner didn't look well, wearing a neck brace around his damaged throat and a white cast on his arm from the savage ordeal with Quentin. There wasn't a doctor alive who could've kept him from being at Kathy's side today. As they walked slowly away from the graveside, Kathy seemed dwarfed by the size of Nathan Ganz. It would've taken an army to get through his protective embrace and Johnny was grateful.

As they walked towards the limousine Kathy looked up the hill where Johnny stood beside a large, imposing oak tree. She leaned over and whispered into Tommy's ear. He glanced up and spied Johnny as well. He said something to Kathy and she patted him on the shoulder, then broke away and began walking on the grass up the hill. Johnny pushed away from the tree and took a few steps, waiting for her to come to him.

"Thanks for coming Johnny. It means a lot to me," she told him.

"You know I couldn't stay away. How are you holding up?" he asked her.

"Okay I suppose. Thanks for asking. You've been watching over me, haven't you?" she questioned, looking up into his eyes.

"Yes, I've been around. I saw you come outside your house a few times and wanted so much to come to you, but I couldn't, not in the form I was in."

"You hid yourself well. You were not alone?"

"My father and a few others were with me, just in case Victor sent any more of his pack to try again where they failed," he said, pausing slightly. "Kathy, I am so sorry, I never wanted any of this to happen."

She reached for his hand and squeezed. "I know and I apologize for going off the deep end like that. It was the shock of seeing my father lying there and realizing how he died. I took it out on you and I shouldn't have."

"You had all the reason you needed. Victor is after me and my father. You became intimately involved when you shot and killed his son Barton. Kathy, you need our protection in more ways than just from him. He may very well try again and soon. We don't know where he is right now. It seems that when Barton died, he went and disappeared with his entire pack, but rest assured he's still near enough to try another hit.

Will you let us help you?"

She stared at him. "What choice do I have? I'm scared Johnny, but most of all I want and need to avenge my father's death."

"Vengeance is all encompassing Kathy, believe me I know. It seems that Victor has revenge against my father that is driving him, and I have mine for the loss of Samantha and my son. Now Victor has lost his oldest son and you have lost your father. It should all be settled very soon."

"So what's the next step?" she asked.

"How soon can you leave the house?"

"Right now I have to head for a restaurant where there's a lunch to honor my father and so I can thank everybody for coming. Then I'll need to go home and get out of this dress. Where are we going?" she asked.

"Not far, just north out of the city. My father will be very near you, as will several other members of our pack so you'll be safe."

She turned and looked at what was left of the mourners.

"Which one is your father?"

"There, the very tall man with kind of long, shaggy black hair, the one who looks most out of place wearing a suit," Johnny said, pointing and smiling at the same time.

"He's a very handsome man. I can see where you get your rugged features. Where will you be?"

"I'm going back to your house and scout around, make sure there will be no traps we might run into. When you're done at the lunch, let my father escort you back."

"If your father is a target, then how safe can I be?" she asked him.

"My father is an extremely formidable foe and he would give his life for you. Trust him completely and know that I will be nearby as well," he told her. "Also Kathy, we have to talk seriously about what your future holds if we all live through this."

"Yes, I suppose we do. It's been eating away at me and I have to tell you I've been feeling very strange inside the last day or so."

"As the full moon draws near it will get harder for you. We will talk about it, among other things."

She leaned into his chest and he put his arms around her, holding on tightly.

"Everything will be fine Kathy. We'll get through this. I'm not going to tell you that it will be easy, far from it actually. I just need you to trust in me and know that I will give my life for you."

She gently pushed away from his comforting chest and stared into those mesmerizing eyes with the golden tint. Finally, when she found a guy that really sent her head and heart spinning towards desire and all consuming lust, she ends up losing her father and has the unfortunate future of being a werewolf slap her rudely in the face. Hell, after dating a bunch of screwed up Neanderthals that were only a bunch of amateur werewolves anyway, not to mention at times she felt they were but a few steps higher on the human evolution chain than the creature they had been chasing, she herself was looking at slicing open a deer carcass with her own fangs and then howling at the moon.

"I do trust you Johnny and I know I need to believe in you as well. So, let me go do what has to be done, my family duty, and I'll meet you back at the house in a few hours," she said, standing on her tiptoes to kiss him on the lips.

He watched her walk down the hill and climb inside the limo. Both Nathan Ganz and Tommy Darnello stood staring up at him. For a second or two Johnny thought that Captain Ganz was going to charge up the hill to arrest him. Instead, they turned and walked to their respective cars. Johnny glanced over to where his father stood. With a nod signaling Johnny not to worry, he got inside his rental car and followed Kathy closely.

Johnny turned and started pacing stiffly across the cold, somber cemetery grounds to where he had parked his battered pick-up truck. As he walked, lost amid his own troubled thoughts, he wondered if Samantha was with him now. Avenging the deaths of her and his son was as vital as protecting Kathy, and then when it was all over, he would have to let her go. The last time Samantha had visited him in a dream was to say good-bye and ask him to finally continue his life without being haunted by her memory. It was as if she knew he would be meeting someone else that maybe would not take her place in his heart, but would be there to take away his pain and loneliness. Samantha had always been so much more intelligent than he was. Hell, for that matter, he knew most females were smarter than he was.

Stopping at the edge of the cemetery he glanced up at a dismal sky resembling a shroud of dirty gray concrete. He actually felt like howling soulfully right then, a lament for saying good-bye to a mate he would never stop loving, and welcoming a new mate he prayed would be at his side for many years to come. Instead, he jumped inside his truck and bounced roughly off the grass to merge into a steady flow of mid-afternoon traffic. Several angry motorists pressed down on their horns sounding like angry geese that had been rudely chased from a lush, green plot of real estate. Sure, they tasted good, albeit a tad oily, but then all they did was walk, shit, and eat. For a hungry wolf they were food, but as a frustrated human, geese left their mark all the way to their southern vacation spot.

He didn't let the trumpeting horns, or even the one-finger salutes, bother him. Much more important things weighed heavily on his mind, for he had to be ready when Kathy returned home in a few hours and then prepare for what he sensed would be an epic battle. It was a conflict that would be coming very, very soon. For one night reality would be wed with nightmares and Philadelphia might never be the same again.

Chapter 32

Kathy hadn't been able to eat hardly a bite of the delicious food at the wake. God, how she hated the word 'wake', feeling it should only mean a storm, or agitated turbulence, and not attached to the peaceful gathering of friends and relatives to honor somebody's life after their death. In fact, she hated viewings and burials as a whole, but she knew people really got upset when you didn't show up at the funeral so she always did her civic and moral duty. And yet, she was utterly overwhelmed at the outpouring of love, sympathy and support she received from all those who had come to pay their last respects to her father and offer heart-felt condolences.

The reason she wasn't able to eat much though was not completely because her father had died so violently. Sure, that was part of it, but the waves of nausea hitting from time to time were more due to internal changes. It was like she was a piece of cold metal being drawn towards a magnet and yet was constantly resisting the pull to something unknown. She was terrified her life seemed to not be her own anymore. The thought of running at night as a ravaging beast was a future Kathy could not accept and she would never welcome. However, she also knew there was an alternative she had to consider and would need to talk to Johnny quickly since time was running short. His father noticed her state of unease though, so he went to stand beside her.

He placed a comforting hand upon her shoulder. "Are you ready to leave? It's closing in on nightfall and we need to get you home and head someplace which will be much safer," he said.

"Yes, I'm just about ready. Let me say a few more good-byes and we can leave."

Most of the people had left anyway. So, after many tears and grateful smiles, she turned around to notice only three people remaining in the large banquet hall.

Captain Ganz enveloped her in a large bear hug with his huge arms pulling her into his massive girth. "How are you holding up kiddo? Did you cry enough today?"

"I'm okay Nathan," she said smiling, "though I miss him so much," a tear rolling quickly down one cheek and then joined by another.

He reached up and gently wiped it away with his broad thumb.

"Well, now that we found the body of the killer up in Washington Crossing hopefully all will be back to normal and we'll just go back to chasing and arresting regular criminals for a change," he chuckled. "Listen, I want you to take off as much time as you need. You've been through a lot, more than any of us. If you need a month, more even, you take what you have to and come back when you're ready. Got that?"

She nodded and smiled. "Thanks Cap, I just might take you up on that offer. Thanks for coming and being here at my side. But I'll be back as soon as I can, hopefully better and stronger than ever before."

As Nathan left, she turned and faced her partner Tommy. He looked like a train wreck and really needed to either get back in the hospital, or take off a month himself.

"Tommy, you look like hell," she said, kissing him tenderly on the cheek.

"Thanks a lot Kat, all compliments well received," he replied, smiling back.

"Listen Tommy, I'm going to be away for awhile. Not just from the job, but away from the city. Don't worry about me though, I'll be fine."

Tommy stood back and stared at her with a quizzical expression. She knew him very well since they had been partners now for three years and could tell he was more than just a tad curious. He also knew enough not to pry and let well enough alone, just as he knew that she wouldn't prod if he had told her the same thing. But, there was a fine line between prying and caring, so he just smiled at her like a mime on a street corner.

"So, you going away with him?" he asked her, deciding to pry anyway.

"By him, if you mean Johnny, probably. There are some things I need to take care of, as well as try and get my life into some kind of order again, if that will even be possible. But I'll be back Tommy, you can't get rid of your sidekick that easily," she said, smiling and touching his cheek, noticing how uncomfortable he looked in his neck brace.

"Well, you know how to get hold of me, day or night. You call and I'll be there," he stated emphatically.

She hugged her partner tightly and kissed him good-bye, grabbed her coat and purse before heading outside to join Johnny's father. A drab, gray afternoon had turned to a chilly, foreboding evening. She felt like she was saying farewell to an old life, one she had for the most part enjoyed. Her father was sadly gone now, with a future of uncertainty facing her upon a blood-red horizon, and an intense desire for a man who had come into her life only a week ago. She smiled when she realized this was certainly no ordinary man and was part of no ordinary lifestyle. A lifestyle she was soon about to experience whether she wanted to or not.

"It's good to see you smile," said a deep voice behind her.

She turned to face Johnny's father who was standing off to one side of the door.

"Well, my father once told me that if you look hard enough you can always find something humorous in most everything in life. Since this has been one helluva' week Mr. Raven, I'd better smile while I have the chance to," she told him, eyes glittering in amusement, her heart and nerves sensing something else. "Good philosophy, your father was a wise man. Sorry I never got a chance to meet him. Also, let's please dispense with the mister part, you can just call me Roland, or Mandhar, if you prefer."

"I rather like Mandhar if that's okay. So, what is the significance of the two different names?" she asked him.

"Well, since our very secretive world has been opened up to you by my wonderful son, Roland is what everyone refers to me when I'm in human form, and Mandhar is my weregune name when my wolf is present," he said quietly.

She studied him intently for a few seconds. He was an extremely handsome and distinguished looking male, tall and heavily built, but extremely muscular. She had no idea how old he was, but somehow felt he was older than she could even think about. Long, shoulder length hair, as black as a raven's feathers, caressed his broad shoulders, looking more natural on him than it should on any man. His eyes were deep and widely set with that same haunting, golden tint that Johnny possessed, with the eyes of a dangerous predator. Kathy got an immediate sense she would be safer with him and Johnny than with anybody else in or out of this world.

"We should be leaving Kathy, are you ready to go?"

"Yes, but I'd like to make a quick stop on the way if we have time?"

"Well, we should get you home as quickly as possible so if it's something that can wait....."

"No Mandhar, it cannot wait. I need to stop at the vet's office and check on Rain's condition," she said emphatically. "She's the only thread I have left to normalcy,"

Without saying another word they both slipped into his rental car and she gave him directions as they pulled out of the restaurant parking lot. Staring at her reflection in the window she wondered what that reflection would look like when the next full moon rose in the midnight sky. She couldn't imagine it would be a snarling beast.

They hit Main Street which knifed through lower Manayunk, Johnny's father remarking about what a yuppie feel this area had, with numerous boutiques and restaurants that had tables outside where you could sit and eat some lunch, have a beer or a glass of wine, as well as breathe in bus and truck exhaust fumes.

"Yeah, you should have seen it twenty years ago," Kathy chuckled. "You could've literally come down here on Main Street at any time of the day or night and found all the parking you wanted. It was named an historic district back in 1983 and in the 90's some upscale restaurants moved in with all the little boutiques and shops following closely. It was quite a renaissance really and good for the neighborhood in general. Originally, way back when, this area was known as Flat Rock, named for a part of the Schulykill where rapids raced and churned over rocks in this part of the river. The name was eventually changed from Flat Rock to Manayunk. It means "where we go to drink", from some Indians, I think the Lenape tribe maybe. The canal was dredged and actually runs up the river for quite a bit where at one point teams of oxen and mules hauled barges to and from the mills. This entire area became a huge industrial complex, kind of like the Manchester, England in this country. I believe it was a Captain John Towers who purchased a water right and erected the first oil-mill. After that, water-power and the influx of more mills helped to make Philadelphia the leading industrial city of the 19th century. During the Civil War the mills switched from cotton to wool and produced blankets, etc. for the war. There are still remnants of the textile industry here, but like anything, times change and this area has changed once again."

Mandhar looked at her and smiled. "Thanks so much for the grand tour. Quite interesting to be sure, I love history and Philadelphia certainly has its share of it."

"That it does, very much so. Maybe when this is all over and things are back to some degree of normalcy," she said, starting to laugh, "I can show you and Johnny around this city which I really love."

"I'd like that Kathy, thank you," he said, keeping his eyes on the busy street.

They drove the rest of the way to the vet's office where he parked and she walked inside. There were two young girls sitting behind the desk, one holding a small puppy.

"Hi, can I help you?" the cute little blond asked her.

"Yes, my name is Kathy Morello. Is the doctor in? I wanted to check on Rain's status, see how she's doing."

They both looked at each other questioningly and then back to Kathy.

"What's wrong?" she asked them, a nervous cloud in the pit of her stomach.

"Oh, nothing, Rain is stable and seems to be doing very well. The doctor is in with a patient right now, but if you want to wait he should be out shortly."

"No, I can't wait around. I'm in quite a bit of a hurry actually, but I would like to see my dog if that's okay," Kathy pressed, as nicely as she could before putting on the pressure.

"Well, I'm not sure that's possible unless the doctor okay's it," said the one with short black hair holding the adorable little golden lab pup.

"I'll repeat myself girls for the second and last time, I can't wait around and I want to see her. Now!!! So, either go and stick your head in the room to ask the doctor, or just take me to see Rain," she told them firmly, hoping a more authoritative and angry voice wouldn't be needed.

The blonde got up quickly and said, "I suppose it would be okay. She's back this way and then I'll get the doctor to talk to you before you leave."

Rain was lying inside a rather spacious cage, presumably asleep when Kathy entered the back room. As they closed the door behind them she slowly opened her big brown eyes and there was immediate recognition in her expression. Her bushy tail flicked a few times in back of the cage and she sounded a soft hello with a weak whine.

"Okay if I open the door?" Kathy asked.

"Yes, just be careful around her neck. There are quite a number of sutures there with a couple drainage tubes, along with some on her stomach as well. But she seems to be doing well and even ate a little bit today, though we had to feed her by hand."

Kathy opened the cage quietly as Rain tried to get up.

"No sweetie pie, just lie down. That's it honey, lie back and rest. Oh my Baby, my sweet little Rain, I love you so much," she said, her voice breaking as tears began to flow. It was all just too much, too damn much. She wondered how much more she could take before standing on the brink of insanity. Hell, she was nearly there already.

Kathy bent down and kissed Rain on her muzzle while placing a hand gently on the dog's back, softly rubbing an area that was still hard from cached blood.

Looking back at the nurse, she said, "Do you think that somebody could get some warm water and clean off this dried blood from her fur? It would make her feel better."

"Sure, I'll do it myself Miss Morello. We all love Rain and we're trying to be very attentive to her needs. In fact, right before you came I was sitting here and talking to her," the young blonde named Karen said.

"Thanks, I didn't mean for that to sound like you weren't. I remember back about fifteen years ago when I was in a traffic accident and the front part of my head was severely lacerated. After they shaved off a huge piece of hair and with this long row of stitches, I looked like Elsa Lanchester in the Bride of Frankenstein. But yet I kept putting my hand up to my head and feeling all this lumpiness, thinking it was additional stitches. When I asked one of the nurses aides, she told me that it was some dried blood and that she would come back later to wash it off for me. I felt a hundred percent better after that," said Kathy, stroking Rain softly on her rear leg."

"I'm sure you did so I'll clean her off much better after you leave. Trust me, I'll take good care of her," Karen said with smiling eyes.

"Okay my little Rainbow, now be sure and listen to the doctor and nurses, okay? Make sure you eat and get your strength back so I can get you out of here and we can go for long walks again. Things are going to be a little different when you're home, but we'll get by," she cooed, almost a whisper because there was just not enough strength in her voice to say it much louder.

She bent down and kissed her dog again and then stood up, closing the door to the cage. Rain let out a small cry and Kathy's heart broke.

"I'll be back real soon Rain, I promise," she said, walking out as teardrops ran down her cheeks in a non-stop flow. She wondered if that would be true, or Rain would end up being an orphan.

As she moved towards the very heavy front door, the doctor emerged from one of the examining rooms. "Hi Miss Morello, I see you went back to see Rain. That's fine, I'm glad you did, probably really picked her spirits up quite a bit. She seemed a little down in the dumps naturally. But, she seems to be doing really good. We've been giving her some heavy duty antibiotics to fight off any infection. She had some very nasty wounds and to be honest, I'm just surprised she was able to pull through at all. Rain is a very strong and courageous dog. I think the love and loyalty she has for you has been very instrumental in her recovery. Also, let me say that we're all so sorry about your father."

"Thank you doctor, I know she's in good hands," she replied. "Listen, for the next few days I'm not sure that I'll be able to get up here so if you need anything I left the phone number for Tommy Darnello, who's my partner. Either you or the nurses can call him if Rain is well enough to get out of here and he'll come to pick her up. But hopefully I'll be available and can do that myself."

"You do what you need to do Kathy and let us take care of Rain. She's absolutely no bother and is a delightful patient. All the girls love her and I'll have to guard against them killing her with kindness," he said, smiling.

"Thanks Doc," she said, closing the heavy outer door and walking to the car where Johnny's father waited rather impatiently.

"Everything okay with your dog?" he asked.

"Yes, she'll be fine. She's very brave and strong. I wish that I could be half of what she is," Kathy said, pausing to let that remark sink in. She smiled at the inside joke on herself. She would most definitely find out soon enough what it was like to be a beast.

Victor and Kahleel stood on the small, narrow porch of the cabin facing the majority of the pack. It was an interesting picture actually. Set amid the beautiful Pocono's with narrow rays of sunshine slicing their way through a dense layer of clouds and treetops, was a group of individuals in either human state, or several different stages of transition. Some preferred to stay in wolf form as much as possible, feeling that their beasts were so much more supreme to the human appearance. But being weregune, they were able to communicate telepathically with other pack members, a connection that came in handy more often than not when walking around on all fours.

Glancing around, Victor noticed Tabitha standing with her arms crossed within the tree line at the rear of the group. He was sorely frightened that he might be losing her, especially since the appearance of Kahleel late last night. It was easy to understand how his presence would intimidate anybody, including Victor himself. It wasn't so much he was uneasy about being with Kahleel, as a weregune that is, but rather his strong connection with Roberto, the Master Vampire of Seattle. Victor regretted the day he came into contact with that creature, but Roberto was also instrumental in helping his clan grow to the powerful size it had become. It was close to five years ago when Victor first met Kahleel and was soon made privy to the strange story he wove. Since birds of a feather flock together, it was not much of a stretch for both he and Kahleel to exchange their destructive paths for revenge.

Now they both stood silent and imposing, facing the anxious and nervous group in front of them. Victor was the first to speak.

"Thank you all for coming and it seems most of us are here. I know that some have been dispatched to keep an eye on certain individuals so we can plan accordingly. I also am aware from talking to some of you that you are concerned with being kept somewhat in the dark. The time has come for you to know what we are facing. There have also been murmurs among you as to who stands beside me today."

Victor turned slightly to face Kahleel, who moved forward to the edge of the porch. The man was extremely imposing. His dark, blonde hair was long and thick, hanging nearly to his waist. He easily stood 6' 7", maybe even taller, with expansive shoulders that would make an interior lineman from any professional football team look puny in comparison. But his face was the focal point, most noticeably those intense, amber-colored eyes. He was ruggedly handsome, highly-in-demand male model handsome, but his eyes grabbed you with a brooding, angry attitude that oozed from underneath darkly hooded eyelids.

He and Victor had already discussed how to approach the rest of the pack. If they knew the reason for stalking and attacking Johnny Raven, as well as Kahleel's intense need for revenge against his familial clan, then there might be difficult problems. A different reason was needed and the less they knew about vengeance the better.

"This is Kahleel from the Northern Cascade clan. A few among us may know who he is, but if not, most of you have heard of him. He has come to help us with this invasion of our territory," Victor spoke firmly to his followers.

At the mention of invasion, nervous murmurings began to snake throughout the pack. Kahleel moved forward another few steps and held up his broad hands for silence. He had to be forceful, yet make them believe what he was telling them.

"Your own Philadelphia territory is under threat of being taken over by those of the Crane Lake clan. You know that Jaress has been here for about a week, supposedly tracking a rogue werewolf. It was nothing more than a plot to get him here and infiltrate your clan. Even now as we speak, other members of his pack, including his father Mandhar, have recently arrived and are at this moment planning an all out assault against you. They are extremely dangerous, but you can and will repel them," he boomed out, his voice getting louder and more authoritative.

He continued. "We will be selecting a dozen of the more superior and stronger fighters to combat this danger on our own terms. Victor will contact those selected shortly and once you are told that you've been chosen, prepare to possibly fight your most difficult battle," he told them.

As he moved backwards and Victor stepped up to take his place, a voice echoed from the rear of the group.

"Kahleel, aren't you connected with Roberto, the Master Vampire of Seattle? I have heard things about you and quite frankly, none of them very good."

Both Victor and Kahleel stopped and faced each other, then turned to meet this verbal challenge.

"Yes, it is true I am Roberto's alpha weregune. I lead the Great Cascade clan with a strong fist and we have become extremely powerful. We have fought off takeovers from several neighboring packs and our intention is to help you as well," Kahleel answered forcefully.

The same deep voice rebounded against the dense envelope of trees. Two anxious squirrels, somewhat frightened due to the strange pack of wolves in their midst, scrabbled for the safety of higher limbs. An extremely large raven, its feathers blacker than the darkest sin, perched stoically on a low branch, beady eyes flicking from Kahleel to the weregune who dared challenge his power and reason for standing before them.

"So tell us all Kahleel, what are your real intentions here? Does Roberto, your evil Master, plan on relocating his base to Philadelphia?" the voice asked inquisitively. "We have our own Master Vampire in this region. Rest assured that he won't sit back quietly and have the malevolent presence of another dangerous predator in his midst."

Kahleel stared menacingly towards the spot where the voice seemed to come from, trying to pick out of the crowd the one who dared challenge him. His terrifying gaze zeroed in on one particularly rather large weregune, nearly a head taller than his wolfen brothers and sisters. He was one of those in partial transformation where his muzzle had elongated slightly, pointed ears sprouting from a mass of dense, dark brown fur that had begun to grow from his head and around his face. Muscled arms, already furry, were crossed against his massive chest, the shirt he wore beginning to bust the snaps which held it closed, like the popping from a bag of microwave popcorn. Snaps were a Godsend to almost every weregune and werewolf since it was less wear and tear on the wardrobe, especially if they began to change before disrobing.

Moving onto the open ground in front of the porch, Kahleel began snaking his way through the throng, parting it like Moses holding up his arms and staff to part the Red Sea. He strode purposefully amid a swirling aura of anger, somewhat surprised that someone would have the guts to defy him. As he moved towards the antagonist he called forth his own beast, fur quickly sprouting on his arms, already long fingernails beginning to burst forth into vicious looking claws.

He had suffered terribly at the hands of Roberto early on when he had first been captured. But his determination, resolve and courage displaced any fear and pain that he had experienced. Instead of sniveling like a weak puppy he grew to massive proportions, aided by some awesome gifts that Roberto eventually bestowed upon him. There was not a weregune alive who could rival him in ferocity and size, at least to this point. And his viciousness in dealing with others had become legendary in the great Northwest Territories. Kahleel stopped no more than two feet from the wolf who had disparaged him. The similarity in height was where any comparisons stopped. In fact, the member of Victor's pack, though misguided by his own false sense of bravado, now wished secretly he had kept his damn mouth shut.

"So my new friend, you question my reason for being here, as well as degrading Roberto, my Master. A very simple question to you is why?" he asked, his voice dropping just short of a frightening growl. "We have only the best of intentions to see that Victor's clan is not taken over by another invading pack. These particular weregune are quite vicious and deadly. I might think you would welcome assistance from any friendly direction."

"I meant no offense Kahleel, to you or Roberto," the other beast replied, seeming to have already shriveled a few inches in height. "It is just a surprise to me and others that somebody with your reputation would come so far to help us with a matter that Victor and his followers should be able to repel on our own."

Kahleel brought his right hand up with claws extended and ripped them across the other wolf's face, knocking him backwards into a large tree. Before he even had a chance to raise his own fist in defense, or even slide to the ground, Kahleel was upon him. Grabbing the stunned victim by the shoulders, talons digging deeply into exposed flesh and fur, he lifted the weregune up like he was nothing more than a stuffed teddy bear. Blood gushed from the six inch laceration that extended from left lip to the now severed ear that lay on the darkening ground beneath them.

Holding up the severely damaged creature by the neck with only one massive paw, Kahleel turned and faced the startled pack. His searing eyes, now a livid yellow, warned them all it was in their best interests to remain completely silent.

"Do any more of you dare question my reasons for being here to help you, or pertaining to the integrity of Roberto, my Master from Seattle? If you do then step forward and let's deal with it now. Otherwise, take a long, hard look at this wolf that had the misguided courage to challenge me."

With that said, Kahleel squeezed the other's throat like he would if he crushed an overly ripe tomato, then easily tossed him into their midst like a sack of Idaho potatoes. Lying in a cloud of dust, the partially transformed wolf gurgled loudly, gasping for air through ghastly slits across his throat.

Kahleel then strode through the stunned pack and entered the cabin, yelling for Victor to follow. As Victor did so, he looked in the direction where he had last seen Tabitha. She was no longer at that same spot. Glancing quickly around, he could not find her anywhere. His concern began to mount, but he desperately hoped she had just had too much with the loss of Barton and the sudden appearance of Kahleel, deciding to just find a quieter, safer place to pull herself together.

At least he prayed that was the case, heeding another violent call from Kahleel requesting his appearance inside the cabin. As he closed the door he glared back at the spot where Tomas lay sprawled, now surrounded by several concerned pack members. He would survive, albeit painfully, but Victor was now aware just how careful and wary he needed to be when dealing with Kahleel. Eating away at his mind was the realization that when this was all over he would most likely have to battle Kahleel to the death, thus remaining alpha leader of their pack. As intimating as Victor could be himself, the thought of facing Kahleel most definitely terrified him.

Kathy stood on the porch and stared at the new door which had been put up to replace the damaged one. She hesitated, not really wanting to enter the house. It was going to be so damn lonely without her father, and who knew how long it would be until Rain was able to come home, barring any unforeseen setbacks. She walked to the side of the porch and stared into the woods behind the house, trying to spot her protector.

"He's out there someplace isn't he, in wolf form, watching and waiting?" she asked Mandhar.

"Yes, he's there, halfway up the hill to the right side of that large, white oak tree. If there had been any danger then he would've alerted us before we arrived. Now, you need to go inside and get your things together. We have to move fast in order to join the rest of the pack," instructed Mandhar, as firmly and diplomatically as possible.

"Okay, I won't need much time. It's not like I'm going on a vacation or anything," she said, smiling back at him.

He returned the smile with a wide, wolfish grin of his own.

"No Kathy, I'm sorely afraid it will not be like taking a restful vacation where you can lie upon a beach on some island Paradise. After we're out of here and within the safety of the pack, both Johnny and I will tell you what we're most likely going to face. Be prepared my dear, it will be like nothing you've ever experienced or witnessed before."

"Why should I be surprised at that statement? Hell, this entire week has been nothing like I've ever been through in my life, especially three nights ago. My faith and everything I believed in has been destroyed. I highly doubt anything will ever be normal again," she sighed.

He placed his firm, confident hand on her shoulder and squeezed gently, letting her know she was not alone.

"Maybe not Kathy, but then you've only known one way of living. Let's get through tonight, or the next few days, and life could take on a whole new meaning for you, experiences that may have seemed not possible a week ago will become reality."

"I hope you're right Mandhar because I'm extremely frightened and have never felt so alone before with the loss of my father and Rain, this inability to reason out a problem and arrive at an answer," she told him, worry lining her eyes.

"You will never be alone again Kathy. I know you've lost your father which is a very tragic loss for anybody. I wish time could be rolled back, but sadly it cannot. We've all lost loved ones, some tragically like my son with Samantha. So now you have Johnny, me and our entire pack. We're your family now and we welcome you warmly if you wish to become a part of us," he said reassuringly. "Now young lady, no more talking. Plenty of time for that after we get the hell out of here."

He gently nudged her through the door into the gloom of the living room. She immediately glanced at her father's empty recliner and the air machine resting quietly beside it. Quickly tears began to form behind her eyelids which she quickly tried to suppress. The silence was even heavier because Romeo had been taken by a friend so he wouldn't be alone through this whole mess. She walked amid the thick stillness towards the stairs, dropping her coat and purse on the dining room table that only a few days ago had been splattered with broken glass.

She paused at the top of the steps, unable to move forward and get past the dark crimson stains on the already deep brown rug. She closed her eyes and saw her father lying there, slaughtered so violently for such a monstrous reason. Kathy began to feel dizzy and reel backwards. The thought quickly crossed her mind that maybe if she just let herself fall then she might break her neck and it would all be over.

But instead, a pair of strong and comforting hands caught her. Johnny had moved so quietly up behind her that she had not even been aware of his presence. He held her in his arms, feeling the rapid beat of her heart against his exposed chest. His desire for her was quickly overpowered by the knowledge he had to protect her, keep her alive, so that sometime soon such heated desire could be given its just reward. To be enjoyed by the both of them.

"You have a unique way of appearing when I most need you Mr. Raven. You also move so quietly that I would swear you were part animal," she murmured into the crook of his arm.

He chuckled in a deep growl of excitement, not anger. There was a big difference.

"I told you already, I will never leave you alone again. I'm here to protect you and hopefully show how much I want you, need you, and care for you," he said, his voice muffled inside her lush, auburn hair that smelled like freshly cut strawberries.

"So then, are you going to let me stand up so I can change clothes and we can leave?" she asked him. "Or, do you wish to practice crossing the threshold with me."

"It would be my utmost pleasure to carry you anywhere Detective Kathleen Morello."

He lifted her in his massively strong arms and held her tightly. She leaned her head against his chest, listening to the excited pounding of his heart. Kathy wanted to just melt into him, be overwhelmed with his scent and animal magnetism. She pressed her eyes closed, welcoming just the briefest moment of serenity, feeling him walking up the remaining steps and down the hallway to her bedroom.

Johnny placed her tenderly on the bed, gently brushing a lock of hair away from her forehead. She looked into his eyes, wanting only to be engulfed within their golden glow. To just sink into a pool of sweet, golden honey and let him take her to heights she had never experienced before.

He bent lower and brushed her lips with his, sending passion soaring through her veins. With a soft prodding, he opened her anxious mouth with the tip of his tongue, like an exploring bee wishing to drink from a vibrant orange and yellow wildflower awakening to a warm, summer morning.

She moaned, opening her mouth wider, to let him explore and caress her tongue, the dance of sensual serpents. His hands slipped underneath her back and lifted her gently from the mattress, all the time never letting their lips part. She allowed her own hands to slide around the back of his head and neck, holding on for dear life. Whatever future lay in store for her, whether death or that of a beast, it would be spent by his side.

Their lips parted and he whispered in the stillness between them.

"Kathleen, I need you so bad, but it can't be now, not like this. I want it to be special and have time to show you how much I've fallen in love with you," he breathed heavily into her ear.

She pulled back slightly, not wishing to break contact with his skin as the heat from him engulfed her with wave after wave of intoxicating passion. Tears trickled their way down her cheeks as she yearned to submerge herself within the honeyed sea of his eyes to ride the waves of his ocean.

"We may never have another time like right this minute Johnny," she sighed, "What happens if one, or both of us, die tonight or tomorrow? What happens when the moon is full and I change into some wild creature that you'll detest? I'm afraid about what will happen to me and that I may never have a life with you. I'm not afraid to die, but I am afraid of what my future will be like if I live through this."

He brought her tightly to his chest and gently stroked her hair as she sobbed against the warmth of his shoulder. The desire to make love to her at that moment and the realization they needed to seek the protection of the pack was overwhelming him. He could face any number of enemies and yet denying both of them the pleasure of each other's bodies was a war he was not doing well to win. But her safety was more paramount than his personal sexual gratification.

Tilting her head back, he rubbed away the tears on her face.

"We will have many times such as this, I promise you Kathleen, but I need to know that you'll be safe. Trust in me, if I pressed the issue of wanting sex with you then it's something we both might regret."

"But Johnny, I'm afraid, so afraid. I know that I'm infected and can only imagine the terror I'm going to face. Believe me, I won't face it, never," she said, shaking her head in defiance.

"It doesn't have to be that way, I've told you that. There is another option, but you have to realize what's at stake," he told her.

"What? Please tell me Johnny, because anything is better than becoming some insane creature like we've been chasing, and anything means death," she said.

He held her tightly and then stood, walking to the window where he stared out at passing traffic. Knowing what he had to do, what he needed to tell her, certainly didn't make it any easier. With a very heavy sigh he turned and walked back to where she was sitting on the edge of the bed, gently engulfing her hands within his.

"Kathy, there are only three options for you. One of course is death which you've already considered. The second option is to let the next full moon rise at which time you will change into a werewolf, a lycanthrope. Neither of those is what we want. Your third option is to become weregune, but that involves death as well," he told her.

She looked up at him, not knowing what to say. For some reason, none of the three options seemed very appealing.

"Don't stop, tell me more," she whispered.

He sat down and softly touched her flushed cheek. She was absolutely shaking.

"In order for a human to become weregune, you must die. Not necessarily slain by one of us, but that of course can happen. However, once your heart ceases to beat, I would need to put my fangs into your throat, opening it enough to allow a good portion of your human blood that has been infected to drain out. In the mean time, I must slice myself open and pass my own blood into you and then resurrect you with my kiss. This all must be done within only a few minutes so you do not suffer brain damage. At my kiss, your heart will begin to beat again. After a short period of time, you will regain consciousness with my blood running through your veins. You will then be weregune and will become my mate, bound in love and blood."

She was stunned by what he had revealed to her. Looking into his eyes, she reached and touched his cheek. Dying before she became a beast was what she had preferred. Now the thought of dying was desired in a completely new way.

"Johnny, to spend the rest of my life with you is what I most want and if that is what has to be done then I'm ready, but when would you do this? The full moon is only a few days away and I can already feel changes taking place inside of me."

"It will have to be very soon, tonight or tomorrow night at the latest. I will be as gentle as I can be Kathy. Please believe me when I tell you that I will make it as painless for you as I can."

She smiled and put her arms around him.

"Well Johnny, if I have to die, then let it be done by the one I love," she said, kissing him gently on the lips, wishing he would do it now, but knowing he would not do it here.

Suddenly a thought wiggled its way into his head, like an inquiring worm. He pulled away from her just slightly and stood up.

Johnny, we have a guest outside, an emissary if you will, and I need you here eside me.

Yes father, I'll be right there. Kathy is almost ready to leave.

"What is it Johnny?" Kathy asked, seeing the change in his eyes.

"It seems that we have a visitor, most likely from Victor's pack. The challenge will be made and we will know where the battle will take place," he told her. "Finish packing a few things Kathy for we'll be leaving here very shortly."

With that said he was instantly all business and quickly left the bedroom. She heard him running down the steps and wanted to go with him, but knew it was not her place to be there, not yet. Quickly she moved towards her closet to get other clothes to change into. She had an idea that whatever lay in store for her, wearing a short black dress was not the proper attire.

Johnny saw his father standing in the yard talking heatedly to several individuals. He quickly jumped off the side of the porch and hurried to stand by his father.

"This is my son, Jaress. These are members of Victor's pack who have come with word that Victor and up to a dozen of his strongest fighters will meet us tomorrow night in Valley Forge Park. It will be a fight to the death, no survivors left on the losing side. I've told them it doesn't have to be this way, but it seems there is something else directing us on this destructive path."

Johnny turned to one of the two weregune, knowing that it was one of Victor's younger sons.

"We are sorry for your brother's death, but it was not something which Detective Morello could've avoided without dying herself. She also has lost her father by members of your pack. There has been enough death over the last week, don't you think so?" Johnny asked.

"It is not our concern. You have come to our territory with the intent of taking over and we will not stand by to let that happen. It will be decided tomorrow night," Victor's son replied.

Johnny glanced at his father and raised his eyebrows.

"Invade your territory? That is not what we came here for. I arrived in this city chasing the rogue. My father came with members of our pack to support me after I was attacked by Barton. Your father is behind this, not us," he told him.

"It doesn't matter now. The challenge has been made and you know where it will take place. When tomorrow night ends it will all be decided," the weregune replied, as they both turned and walked to the car parked in front of the house.

In a screeching of brakes they peeled away from the house to the sound of honking horns. Johnny and his father walked slowly back to the house as Kathy came out the door to join them.

"So what's happening?" she asked them.

Johnny grabbed her hand and then hugged her tightly. "I'll tell you in the car. Lock up so we can join the rest of the pack and prepare. And Kathy," he said, looking into her eyes, "what we spoke about upstairs will happen. I want you beside me for the rest of my life. I hope you want it to come true as well."

"Yes Johnny," she said, squeezing his hand while turning to lock the front door, wondering if she would ever come back here.

It was funny to think that she looked forward to death, but in some insane way the possibility was exciting. Now she just had to make sure she survived the upcoming confrontation long enough to let Johnny perform his magical bite. That meant she would have to stay as close to him as possible because if she were to die far away, then he'd be unable to do what he needed in the small window of life they would have available.

Chapter 33

Colleen sat quietly on the edge of the bed and gazed lovingly down at the woman she adored. Gently caressing Sara's cheek, she tried her best not to wake her. Their lives had been so completely turned inside out, now staring into a future replete with fear and uncertainty. But, the most pressing issue for the moment was the need to tell Sara she had been infected and then try to explain the consequences. How do you tell the person you love they've become a werewolf? "Oh sweetie pie, by the way, pretty soon you won't have to worry about the little bit of hair on your legs and underarms."

Sara stirred and slowly opened her exquisitely beautiful green eyes, like small jade moons. It was a killer combination with her deep reddish, auburn hair. She smiled and stretched, reaching out from underneath the blanket to clutch Colleen's hand which still rested snugly against her cheek.

"Mmm, hi there darlin', been sitting their long?" Sara asked.

"No, just a few minutes. I was merely admiring how beautiful you are," Colleen replied, brushing aside a lock of hair which had fallen across her forehead.

Sara lifted the blanket and smiled invitingly, just a hint of tease along with a pinch of desire.

"Would you like to join me? It's really warm under here and I know how to make it quite a lot hotter," she said, sexuality dripping from her voice.

"I'd love to baby, but what would our hosts think?"

Extending her lip in a tiny pout, Sara replied, "Oh, Hillary and John are really cool. You don't have anything to worry about where they're concerned. Come on in here with me baby," Sara cooed, patting the bed beside her.

"Well, she certainly appeared to be surprised when we showed up at her front door, especially after relating as much of the story as we dared," said Colleen.

Sara slid back and sat up in the bed, leaning her head against some propped up pillows. She had removed the bandage from around her neck when they went to the bedroom after hours of talking to Hillary long past midnight, as well as polishing off two large bottles of wine. The long gashes running across her neck had completely healed, all but for the garish whiteness of scar tissue that would remain for awhile.

"Sara, there's something really important I need to tell you and I'm not sure how to because I have no idea just how you'll react," Colleen said quietly, her voice actually trembling.

Sara leaned forward and put her arms around Colleen, hugging her partner tightly. Leaning back she caressed Colleen's lips with hers, tender at first and then more urgent, tongue probing to deeply explore the passionate depths they had traveled so often, desiring more, loving this woman with all she could give.

With a murmur bordering on a sensual moan, Colleen broke free before she lost her will to tell Sara about the infection. Smiling, she kissed her on the nose, the forehead, and then whispered in her ear, "Not just yet my sweet, we have business to talk about."

Sara moved back with a quizzical look, knowing that at no time had Colleen ever been able to resist her sensual allure before.

"What's so important that you have such willpower?" Sara asked in a disbelieving voice.

"Because I don't want to feel that I welcomed your love with open arms and then smashed your life with what I'm about to tell you," whispered Colleen, a tear breaking away.

Sara tilted Colleen's chin up and could see the evident fear that lay there.

"Okay," she sighed, brushing a nervous laugh. "Now you have me worried and more than a little frightened. You'd better tell me before we both lose our nerve."

With a very long pause, way too dramatic in fact, Colleen finally asked, "Do you have any idea what Quentin was?"

Sara laughed and said, "Yeah, he was a sadistic bastard, a killer, a monster and I'm glad you blew him away, or he would've most likely killed us both. I'm not the least bit sad that he's dead."

"I agree with you honey, but you have no idea what kind of creature he really was," stated Colleen, searching for any sign of recognition in Sara's face.

"Tell me then, how much worse can it really be?" asked Sara, her eyebrows rising in curiosity.

"Sara, he was a werewolf, a lycanthrope to use a different term. He was not just a man who was a sadistic serial killer, but a real live beast that killed many people over many years when the moon was full."

Sara sat back against the pillows and stared for a very long minute at Colleen, trying to absorb this frightful bit of information.

"Well gosh golly gumpers, don't that beat all," she simply stated.

"That's all you can say? You're not frightened in the least?" asked Colleen.

"Shit yeah I'm scared, out of my mind in fact. But, I'm not sure what this all means other than it bit me and I'm alive. Is that what you mean by infected? You're not telling me that the crap you see in those horror movies is for real," Sara asked.

"Yes Sara, that's exactly what I'm telling you. We've both been bitten and infected by a werewolf. Do you truly know what that means for our future?"

Sara sat quietly for a long minute, staring into space, digesting this revelation like she was dissecting a frog in biology class before she answered. In her normally quirky, upbeat style in dealing with problems she began to laugh in order to counteract the serious side of Colleen. Small laughter quickly turned into a hysterical fit of amusement, her ample breasts jumping up and down as her eyes glistened with tears.

Colleen sat stunned, never expecting this type of reaction, wondering suddenly if Sara sat teetering on the edge of temporary shock, or maybe even insanity over all that had happened in such a short period of time. Finally, the laughter stopped as Sara tried to become somewhat composed.

"So my love, what's so amusing about this frightening revelation?" Colleen asked her, still surprised at Sara's reaction.

"I just thought it was funny because the picture of us sitting together in the woods around a slaughtered deer, or something more human, scratching at fleas came to mind," Sara replied, as seriously as she could.

"I think you're in a state of shock sweetheart, as I was. You always tackle everything with such a degree of levity, but I'm not sure it fits this situation," stated Colleen, standing and walking to the dresser where she grabbed a few tissues to dab at her reddened eyes.

"So, then tell me what's going to happen to us in a few short days when the moon is full?" inquired Sara.

"I honestly don't know baby. Quentin told me some details, but not many I'm afraid. He obviously planned on us staying at the house in Washington Crossing until the change took place for me. It was his intent to help guide me through it so to speak, even though he would be changing also. He was quite old and had been infected so long ago that he was more insane than anything, especially with so much death and destruction in his wake. I think he actually welcomed dying, grateful in his own way."

It became very quiet for a few minutes with Colleen moving back to the bed and taking Sara in her arms. They held each other tightly, knowing that whatever happened they would do it together, whether it be changing into beasts under a full moon, or helping each other to die through suicide.

"So what do we do now Colleen? I'm prepared to die if you are. Possibly if this change doesn't take place, just maybe we'll be okay," Sara asked, not truly believing, but hoping that her own hollow words rang true.

"Maybe honey, but I'm not ready to give up just yet. I can feel something inside me changing, but then I was bitten several days before you were. So if you're prepared to wait, then so am I," she said.

Sara kissed her and smiled. "Raving beast or welcoming death, I'm all yours," and they held each other some more in the early morning dawn.

Kathy stared at her reflection in the sliding glass doors that led outside to a large wooden deck. It had started snowing shortly after they left her house and headed for New Hope where the rest of the pack waited. By the time they arrived at the clan sanctuary the ground was becoming white even though the road surface still remained wet. An early November snow storm was not all that uncommon in the Philadelphia area and it appeared that the weather forecasters had finally pegged this forecast correctly. Estimations ranged from 2-4" up to 6-8" depending on what area you lived in. Out west of the city, where Valley Forge awaited, happened to be in the 2-4" range. Normally

Kathy loved the beauty of falling snow, especially late at night when you could just go outside and stand in the peacefulness of evening. No traffic, just the soft sifting sound of snow as it landed on the ground, tickling your nose and cheeks.

"Hey, nickel for your thoughts," said Johnny, as he came up and embraced her.

"Oh that's really funny to hear you say that, plus you're paying more. I wonder where you heard that expression from," she said, leaning her head back and letting him kiss her neck and ear.

"Some lady detective whom I happen to be really crazy about," he replied.

"So will this snow make it easier or harder tomorrow night?" she asked him.

"It doesn't matter really, a battle is a battle. There will be tracks of course, but either pack will know when the other is nearby so leaving paw prints in the snow won't hurt," he informed her. "What were you really thinking about?"

"Gee, nothing much to think about I suppose," she said smiling, "it's just another day in the life of any normal female detective in Philadelphia. I mean what girl wouldn't want to experience werewolves and weregunes running around her city, losing her father and almost her dog, and then knowing that she's going to have to die in order to live again?"

Johnny held her tighter with her hands grabbing onto his well muscled arms.

"Well, since you put it that way, I suppose it is kind of boring," he teased her.

She turned and broke out of his grasp, punching him in the shoulder. As he grabbed for her the cell phone in her pocket began to hum.

"Hello, Kathy Morello."

"Miss Morello, this is Dr. Stevens. I hope I'm not bothering you," he said.

"No, not at all Doctor Stevens, is it Rain? Is something wrong?" she asked, now worried that he would call her so soon.

"Actually it's the opposite. I tried calling you at home, not wanting to bother you on your cell phone in case you didn't want to be disturbed so I called your partner, Detective Darnello. He just left here with Rain and said that I should call you on this number to let you know he has her."

Kathy was stunned for a moment. "Rain is okay? She's recovered that quickly she could go home already?"

He began to laugh slightly. "Most unbelievable thing I've ever seen. This morning I was just happy she was alive and when you were here earlier today your visit seemed to raise her spirits quite a bit. When we were about to close, one of the girls came and told me I had to see Rain, that it was a miracle. When I went into the backroom she was standing up in the cage pawing at the metal screen, wagging her tail noisily against the metal sides. I opened the door and she jumped out of that cage like she was being freed from a jail cell. We managed to calm her down a little bit so I could do an examination and, as unbelievable as this may sound, her wounds are completely healed. Oh, there seems to be some tenderness of course and there is evidence of trauma on her neck and stomach, but for all intents and purposes she's healed. Since I couldn't get you at home I called Detective Darnello and he just left with a very happy dog. I'm assuming he's taking her to where he lives."

"Wow, that's all I can say other than thank you so much for all you've done for her," said Kathy.

"Well, I did my best and wondered if it was good enough. To be honest, I think there was something else at play here to heal her so fast, but I'm at a loss to say why. I hope you can be with her real soon and when you have time, call the office and make an appointment to bring her back for a follow-up. Goodnight," he said and hung up.

Kathy pressed the cell phone off and put it back in her pocket. Then turned and faced Johnny with a very odd look on her face.

"What's wrong? Is Rain okay?" Johnny asked.

"You knew, didn't you? You knew that Rain would be okay," she asked him.

Pausing slightly, he shrugged his massive shoulders. "I had a feeling that she would pull through this, yes I did."

"How could she heal so quickly? In fact, how did I heal so quickly?"

"It's an ability we have. Just as a werewolf can infect you with his bite, passing on his disease to you, we also have the ability to pass on something of us. In both situations, the saliva we insert into the wounds possess great healing powers. Don't be concerned though, Rain is not going to become a weredog," Johnny laughed. "However, she will be stronger and faster than she was before and most likely live beyond her normal lifespan. But an animal, even after being bitten and surviving, obviously cannot become human, and does not in effect become the type of animal that it was infected by. It doesn't work that way. Just be happy that Rain is fine and you'll be with her soon."

Kathy shook her head, not believing any of it, but so grateful her loving dog would be okay. Now the key question was, would she?

Johnny went and opened the door, stepping out onto the deck where snow was still coming down fairly heavily. She followed and slid the door closed behind her. They both walked to the railing and he put his arm around her.

"I'm not afraid of facing an enemy. I'm not fearful of dying, but I am afraid of turning into the kind of beast we were tracking."

She turned and looked into his eyes. "Johnny, can you do what you have to do tonight? I'm so afraid that something will happen to one of us tomorrow night. If you were killed and I survived, then living could not be possible for me. And yet if I end up being killed and you were no where around, then I would die and not be able to spend my life with you."

He turned and placed his hands on either side of her beautiful face, letting his right thumb caress her cheek.

"Yes, I can do it. Are you sure? Are you ready?" he asked.

"Hey, I'm not your red-headed sister Mr. Raven. Don't ask me again to make the hardest decision of my life. Just do it, please, and whatever happens will happen. I won't regret my decision and won't hold you responsible if I don't survive."

He kissed her hard, holding her as tightly as he could without breaking her.

"You'll come back, trust me and know that I'll always be with you, so don't worry about anything."

"Quit talking damn it, or I'm going to change my mind," she told him.

Taking her hand, he started back towards the house. "Not out here though."

"Where are we going?" she asked nervously.

"Just upstairs to our room, I want this to be as painless and comfortable for you as I can make it," he said.

On the way up the steps Johnny glanced over at his father and made a very imperceptible nod. Mandhar raised his eyes to let his son know he understood and that he was available to help if needed.

For Kathy, it was like 'dead woman walking', but not to have her life snuffed out by lethal injection. Rather to give her the chance of longevity beyond her wildest imagination. She was frightened of changing into a beast, after all who wouldn't be, but she always loved wolves anyway. It would be a lot better than transforming her body into that of a rat, or a groundhog, or maybe something worse like a pig.

However, then she realized what a prejudiced thought that was and silently berated herself for such a weak discretion. In a quieter moment, when they weren't chasing killers or fighting for their lives, Johnny had explained to her the difference between shape shifters, like the weregune, and were's in general, not just werewolves.

The weregune was the oldest form of shape shifter, the predecessor to all the Indian legends. Each clan had their own adopted animals, generally only two or three, and for the most part were larger predators like the wolf, bear, lion, tiger, or larger birds of prey like the eagle, hawk, raven, and great horned owl. When they shifted they became the animal in physical appearance and abilities, but also retained human thought. As a result, a weregune was hardly ever a smaller animal like a squirrel, chipmunk, rabbit, groundhog, or larger more docile animals like the deer, which of course were prey. The were-animal on the other hand was a human that had been infected by the bite, or clawing, from another infected creature. These almost always became wolves, bears, lions and tigers because of the wild and feral condition, the need to kill and feed on prey, though in the were-condition, it was possible to be a rat. That's where her prejudice came into play since she hated rats with a passion. It was all so damn confusing, but interesting nonetheless she supposed. Oh yeah, more than a little unbelievable too.

When they got inside the bedroom and closed the door, she was still smiling at her own reflective thoughts.

"What's so amusing?" he inquired.

"Oh, it's nothing, honest. Hell, I'm so damn nervous that if I don't smile or laugh, then I'll breakdown and you'll have to deal with a raving woman," she replied.

He took her hands and led her to the bed, guiding her to sit down as gently as he could. Leaning in, he placed his right hand on the side of her head and then kissed her long and deep, seeming to pull the breath right out of her body. If only dying could feel this beautiful, she thought, like floating on a blanket of clouds. Even after he let his lips leave hers, she still sat there with her eyes closed, not wishing to give up the pressing feel of him against her, that urgent need she had for this man/beast.

"You might want to remove your sweater. Sadly, the best area this can be done is the neck and it might get a little bloody," he said, trying to be as comforting as he could.

For a split moment she had second thoughts, but realized it was her only hope, so she slipped her head through the cranberry colored turtle neck and let it drop to the floor.

"Bra too?" she asked him.

"If it's a new bra I would say yes, but if it's not, then you'll most likely want to toss it out when you've returned to me," he replied.

"Oh sure, like my mother used to say, 'Make sure you always go out with clean underwear on dear, you never know when you'll end up in the hospital'," she countered, smiling and pulling down the straps from her shoulders at the same time.

"And I like the way you said return to me," she whispered up to him. "I hope I don't go so far away that I can't find my way back to you."

"It's only natural to be scared Kathy. I'm just as nervous about doing what I have to do, believe me," he said, more than she'd actually ever know.

Pushing back slightly, she looked at him and said, "How many times have you done this Johnny?"

"I've never done this if you must know. Samantha was my first true love and she was weregune from birth. Besides, if one is to perform this ritual then they need to know that when the two are united again, they will be mates. Unfortunately, and you must be aware of this, not all that many survive after they return. It does take a very special, extremely strong human to do this Kathy, but I think you can. Are you ready?"

She let herself fall back on the bed and smiled up at him, way too invitingly. Just lying there like that thrilled him down to his core, but he couldn't let himself become swayed by her sensuality from what he had to do.

"God, you're so beautiful Kathleen. I promise you that I'll make this as painless as I can," he told her.

"Damn Johnny, just get on with it or I'm going to lose my nerve. In a few more minutes I may just jump up and run screaming out of this room. Please, just do it," she urged.

He gently stroked her cheek and leaned over to kiss her one last time in this, her strictly human life. As his lips brushed hers he closed his eyes to call his beast forth and felt his teeth elongating into terribly sharp fangs. To alter just a portion of his body took only seconds as he opened his mouth to take her life in his.

"Wait, wait, hold it," she said, sinking as far back into the pillow as she could and pressing her hands against his more than normal hairy chest.

In a deep, gravely voice he asked, "What is it Kathy?"

"How long will I be dead?" she said in a shaky voice. "Damn, I can't believe I'm really letting you do this. What would my girlfriends think?"

"Do you have a lot of girlfriends?" he asked her, trying to ease the tension.

"None really, but being a detective doesn't leave you much time to cultivate friendships.

Seems my closer friends were other cops and mostly men," she replied.

"Well, when this is all over you'll have me, as well as the entire pack and we have plenty of females. Trust me, you won't be gone for long, only a few minutes, any more than that would be too dangerous," he told her with an audible lisp. Hey, it's not easy talking with one inch fangs sticking out of your mouth, and that was short since he only needed to puncture her neck, not rip it out.

"Look at me Johnny, please," she asked him.

"No Kathy, you don't want to see me right now. Just lie back and close your eyes, think good thoughts," he said, moving down onto her neck once again.

As his lips peeled back, his huge teeth caressed her skin sending chills throughout her body. How could she keep her eyes closed when she was about to die? Feeling the pressure of his sharp teeth against her throat she began to expel her breath in fear. There was a pinching as one of the fangs broke the skin above her carotid artery.

"Wait, wait, damn it, hold on a minute," she told him, afraid to push back or pull away, fearful that his fangs would catch on skin and rip out her windpipe.

He growled low and long. In a voice that was truly not his own, he asked, "Now what Kathy? It should almost be over by now."

"Do you mean that when I come back in only a few minutes, and I really find that so hard to believe, I'll be up and running around like nothing ever happened?" she started to chatter in nervous anticipation.

Keeping his face averted from her gaze, he sighed and let out a deep groan.

"No, you will return in a few minutes after my blood is mixed with yours, but then you will sleep for up to twenty-four hours, possibly longer. It will be a deep sleep, but at the same time not very peaceful. You will have dreams and nightmares, sometimes running together, but somebody will be with you the entire time. Now just lie back my love and let's get this over with," he said in a deep, gutturally strained voice.

"Wait Johnny, you said at least twenty-four hours, maybe more. That means I wouldn't be able to go with you tomorrow night if I'm sleeping," she said, pushing him roughly away from her. "No way Jose, I'm not missing that fight. Not on your life, or mine. They slaughtered my father and nearly killed my dog. I'll be damned if I'll miss this confrontation and you can bet your bottom dollar on that."

He rose angrily from the bed and walked to the window, releasing his moon and violently clenching his fists. Turning, he saw that she had already gotten up from the bed and began slipping into her bra.

"Kathy, you can't be there. It will be far too dangerous for a mere human, no matter how much firepower you may have with you. You'll stand a very good chance of being killed and I may not be near you," he told her angrily.

Looking at the blood on her fingertips after brushing her neck, she glared at him.

"You bit me. You actually bit me while I was lying there," she accused him, her voice beginning to rise more than just a little hysterically.

"What the hell do you think I was going to do? Lift my hands, wiggle my fingers and say 'You're getting very sleepy'?"

"Hey Mister Smarty Pants, back off and quit acting like the big bad wolf. I know very well what you were going to do. I didn't even feel you do this other than a slight pinch," she declared, more to calm herself down than from raw anger. "Seriously Johnny, I'm going tomorrow night and you can't stop me. I'll be okay and will stay near you the entire time, or close as possible. We can do this afterwards," she added.

"Kathy, you will not only be putting your own life at extreme risk, but mine as well. I will be a wolf, a beast among other beasts, and I can't fight with one eye on you and the other watching the enemy. It won't be pleasant and you will be unable to compete. As soon as Victor senses that you're in the vicinity he will make plans to assure that you die. I couldn't bear losing you. Please reconsider. We will win and I will come back to you. Let me avenge your father along with Samantha," he told her.

After slipping the sweater back on she started moving towards the mirror in order to comb her disheveled hair.

"Sorry Charlie, wild horses or a pack of wolves couldn't keep me away from this battle. Just forget it, I'm going," she stated emphatically.

Turning to stare out the window he looked up at the moon which would be full in two nights. Just then he felt his father's call.

Johnny, I don't know if you've started yet, but if you haven't then I need you to come downstairs. Seems we have another very interesting visitor.

I'll be right there, father.

Somewhat composed, his fangs now safely stowed away, he started walking towards the door, still steaming at her rebellious response.

"Where are you going Johnny?" she asked him.

"Father called me, we have a visitor downstairs," he told her, opening the door without looking back.

"Johnny, wait," she said, quickly moving towards him and placing her hands upon his face. "Please understand and don't be angry with me. I know how vital it is for us to do what we almost just did, and I know how dangerous it's going to be for me tomorrow night, but I need to be there. Please try and understand."

"I do Kathy. I more than understand how vengeance can rule your life. We'll talk about this more later on," he said, turning and disappearing through the open doorway.

She followed closely, watching his extremely strong body move in that graceful stride he had. He did excite her terribly, but no matter how hot she got when she was near him, no matter what would happen to her in a few nights if she did not become weregune, no matter if she died tomorrow night, her father would be avenged, one way or another. If she was going to die then she would send to hell as many murderous weregune that she could.

Chapter 34

When Johnny hit the floor at the bottom of the steps he noticed Tabitha sitting with her father in the den. Will surprises never cease, he thought. First though he desperately needed a beer so he made a detour into the kitchen. Hell, he needed more than one so he grabbed four figuring his father would want one as well.

By the time he got to the room Kathy had already reached the doorway and was standing there looking at a most extremely beautiful, dark-haired female. Even though she sat there seemingly very composed, Kathy noticed her hands never stopped fiddling with the keys she held tightly in her lap.

Turning as Johnny approached her she reached out and took one of the beers. Damn, only three left he thought so he put one to his lips and drank half of the contents down in three swallows. After going inside the room he offered his father and Tabitha the two remaining beers. They took them, of course. Now there was none.

"Hello Tabitha. Does Victor know you're cavorting with the enemy?" Johnny asked, trying to be relaxed, but knowing it didn't come across that way.

After taking a few sips from the ice cold beer she glanced up and smiled.

"No, he isn't aware. At least I don't think so, but I wouldn't put it past him to have had me followed, though I didn't feel anybody at my back," she replied.

Johnny glanced at his father who shrugged, saying only, "She came to the door and said that she needed to talk to you. I explained I was your father, but she was adamant in not speaking until you got here. So, now you're here," he said, returning his gaze to Tabitha.

She looked at Mandhar and then to Johnny before her gaze landed on Kathy.

"You're the detective who killed my son Barton," she stated quietly.

Kathy was unsure of what to say, wishing she had brought her gun along with her. However, it didn't appear this woman would be lunging at her to get the revenge it seemed everybody was hungering for these days.

"I'm sorry that was your son. In truth, I had no recourse. I was staring at a very large wolf that could've very easily turned on me and ripped my throat out. I had just a split second to react and I shot, more than once I'm afraid. I am sorry your son is dead."

Tabitha took another few long gulps of beer and placed the bottle on the table.

"I don't hold you responsible detective. I will admit I was angry at first and could've easily killed you if I had the chance, but things have changed. I know now that Victor was responsible for my son dying, not you," she said, her voice breaking and tears beginning to run down her cheeks.

With the emotional attachment most women have towards other women when they start to cry, she moved to sit beside Tabitha on the couch, handing her some tissues and placing a comforting hand on her shoulder.

"Thank you, but that's not why I came here," she said, glancing up at Johnny and then over towards his father.

"You of course know my husband has challenged you to do battle. That's not news and I'm certain that you are preparing.

However, something is driving him, a hate I never thought I'd ever witness in him," she said, looking straight at Mandhar. "You're the one he blames for his mate being killed by the trapper. I believe now that he never truly got over being rogue, he just hid it very adeptly from me all these years."

She looked at Johnny, her eyes glistening from the tears and sadness.

"I'm sorry for the loss of your Samantha and un-born son. It was Victor who sent members of our pack, along with that creature Quentin, to where you lived. They came for you, but you weren't there. Instructions were to bring you back to Victor and if that was not possible, then to kill you. However, you weren't there and after waiting so long, Quentin attacked your wife and before the others could react, she was dead. I am very sorry Johnny and if it's any consolation, I know Victor regrets that being done. He has never harmed a female, or a defenseless child, and I know for a fact it has caused him great anguish."

Johnny remained silent. Knowing for sure that Victor was the secretive part of his mate's death enraged him, fueling the vengeful fires that had consumed him for so long. He felt the wall slam down, hiding his emotions and letting the rogue part of him resurface. That part of him which had finally been tempered somewhat by his feelings for Kathleen. In a small way he welcomed its arrival. It would make him that much deadlier tomorrow night.

"There is something else you need to know," said Tabitha in a warning voice.

They waited for her to continue, wondering what else could make this situation even more enflamed than it already was. Mandhar leaned forward with elbows on knees, head bowed, realizing that his own sexual desires and discretions so many, many years ago had in fact been the reason for Samantha's death.

He began to make plans for the next evening, knowing it was up to him to meet Victor and settle this vendetta once and for all if that was even possible.

"Someone else is here and seems to be leading this confrontation over Victor. Have either of you ever heard of a weregune by the name of Kahleel? He's from the Seattle clan and is alpha werewolf under Roberto, the Master Vampire of that area," Tabitha informed them.

"I have heard the name. None of what I've heard was very good," said Mandhar.

Johnny could do nothing more than nod and murmur an assent.

"He arrived the other night and is quite an imposing, terrible individual. There appears to be some connection between him with the both of you. I don't know what it is, but it's most definitely there as part of his anger. Be very careful of him for I've never met a beast that terrifies me so much. I could also tell that Victor, who is afraid of nobody, was somewhat intimidated also. Do not put anything past this individual for it's my feeling he will not fight fair so beware. Also, I would prepare to be fighting more than the dozen warriors originally determined. They will not fight fair," Tabitha told them, finishing off the beer and placing the empty bottle back on the thick wooden table.

Johnny and his father looked at each other, searching for any recognition about how this Kahleel could be connected with them. Mandhar had his fears, but was not prepared to reveal them. Johnny let his mind go back in time and could not put a finger on it. However, with Tabitha's warnings he would be more than alert for anything.

"You realize Tabitha you cannot go back to Victor. Do you have any place to stay? Anybody you can go to until this is all over?" asked Mandhar.

"Not really, the clan is my life. You know that we don't make friends easily with humans. I suppose I could stay at a motel tonight and then possibly head back to my original family clan in Oklahoma. I still retain ties with them," replied Tabitha.

Mandhar shook his head and said, "No, it's way too dangerous. You'll stay here. Even when we leave tomorrow there will still be plenty of protection on these grounds. There is plenty of food in the kitchen if you're hungry and if you need some rest then a few of the bedrooms upstairs are empty."

She smiled and stood up. "Thank you, I am a bit tired. I'm also extremely upset over what has happened. I know you feel I don't need to make apologies for Victor. However, please know that underneath all the anger and hatred is a good man. Sometimes the measure of a man gets stretched so out of proportion that the person itself is lost. I think in his case, that's what happened, though there are no excuses."

Johnny spoke. "Tabitha, trust me when I say that we do not hold you responsible for any of this. But also please understand Victor will not live beyond tomorrow night."

He turned and started to stalk angrily out of the room. Kathy reached for his arm, Johnny turning quickly to stare at her with his once calm and loving, golden eyes now changed to a bright and terrifying silver. He placed his hand on hers and removed it from his arm before spinning and leaving the room. Kathy heard the front door slam shut and started to follow him, but was stopped by Mandhar.

"Let him go Kathy. He needs this anger to resurface now. It's the end of this horrible chapter in his life. It doesn't mean he loves you any less, just that now he's become somebody who is extremely dangerous. He knows from instinct that distance between you for the moment is what's best, especially for him. There are times when even we cannot control our beast completely."

After staring back at Victor for a few moments, she turned and concentrated her emotion at the still quivering front door, wishing she could help him with his sorrow and anger, but knowing that somehow after tomorrow night it would all be over, as well as life changing in several ways, that is, if she survived the night to see another dawn.

Colleen sat at the kitchen table hovering over a steaming mug of coffee, drowned in plenty of cream and sugar. For some reason she really needed something sweet to counteract the bitter feeling in the pit of her stomach. She stared out the large picture window as the early morning sun began to wash away the sleepiness in the shadowy back yard. It was nice of Hillary, Sara's friend, to welcome them, especially considering what had happened and part of the tale they decided to reveal. But in truth, nobody knew where they were. Their car was parked inside the garage and after watching the news broadcasts for several hours, nothing appeared about them on television in regards to what had happened in Washington Crossing. Oh, the discovery of Quentin's body in the house was reported as the number one story on all the stations, but evidently the police were keeping it a low profile as to who possibly had killed him. In a way, that worried Colleen, but on the other hand she was hoping the police early on were just happy to have the killer on a slab in the morgue, and that she and Sara were not their prime focus at the moment.

She heard a slight movement behind her. Before she had a chance to turn around Sara put her in a bear hug and kissed her lovingly on the cheek, the neck, the ear, working her way around to Colleen's anxious lips.

"Hey, you're up early, how long have you been awake?" Sara asked, tasting the sweet coffee from Colleen's lips.

"A few hours I suppose. I did get some sleep though, just had some damn nightmares that kept waking me up. So I thought it best to make a pot of coffee and stay awake. How are you feeling this morning sweetheart?"

Sara walked over to the pot and started pouring herself a large cup as well, only black, just one artificial sweetener.

"I feel great actually, really good. Best I've felt in a few days that's for sure. So what's up today honey? What's the plan for two deadly desperados?" she asked, the smile not really breaking the tension, or found amusing by her partner in crime.

Colleen pondered the problem for a few tense moments before saying, "I think we should head back to Philly. That's where I feel safest even after all that's happened. Home turf, you know? We'll be better at home than playing on the road. And, if something weird is going to happen to us in a few nights when the moon is full, then I'd rather it take place where I'm most familiar with. Plus, just possibly the police are not watching the house and if they are then it'll only be one squad car. They might be too busy eating donuts and drinking coffee. We should be able to get into my house easily enough. Your apartment might be tougher with all that damn security you have down there," she said.

"That's cool with me. Somehow we need to get some money too, I'm almost broke. Hey, I have an idea. Let's hit some different MAC machines up around here. That way, if they trace anything maybe it will send the police on a wild goose chase. In fact, let's even head out west towards Harrisburg and then just meander back into Philly while they start looking for us out here," Sara said, proud of herself.

Colleen smiled and placed her hand on Sara's cheek. "I knew there was something about you I loved. That wonderful brain of yours," Colleen giggled.

"Oh yeah, like that's the only thing you like? Couldn't be something else now could it?" she asked teasingly.

Colleen started to walk out of the kitchen and towards the stairs to the second floor. Looking back she winked at Sara and gave a suggestive nod. That was all it took as Sara jumped up and started chasing after her, the two women racing up the steps and towards the bedroom. Their roundabout trip to Philadelphia could wait for a little longer.

After storming out of the house Johnny started running as fast as he could, racing through the woods like he was demon possessed. While running, he pulled his sweatshirt over his head and tossed it on a passing bush. Shortly beyond that hung his pants, followed by his moccasins. Since he hated underwear and socks, his undressing was complete. Now he was free to let his wolf burst forth because he needed to let the beast run wild and howl. He was angry at everybody. Victor was number one due to the death and sadness he had sanctioned. His father was number two, because through his actions many years before, the house of dominos began to fall. He was pissed at Kathy also because she avoided letting him perform the change upon her and defied him when he said she could not join the confrontation tomorrow night. Females, so damn stubborn he thought.

Running as fast as his human legs would carry him, he let his eyes close and the bitterly cold wind wash over him as bushes and low lying limbs whipped and scratched his exposed skin. Pain meant nothing, but it would definitely be something he inflicted on others very soon. With his eyes squeezed tightly shut, he called out for his inner moon to appear. With the rising of his paramour in the dark, star-studded sky emerged the beautiful black wolf, long and sleek, powerful and cunning, wild and beautiful. As he ran, his body bent forward into a crouch. His legs curled into those of a beast and his arms elongated while his hands formed massive paws, long claws bursting forth. Hair sprouted along his body so quickly you could almost hear it growing, a steady sizzling sound like frying bacon. His mouth and nose pushed out to form a long muzzle, while thirty-two smaller human teeth were quickly replaced with forty-two longer, sharper, pointed teeth of a wolf. His ears began to take on that rounded, yet pointed shape of a predator, already twitching and listening to a myriad of forest sounds. As he ran, newly formed front legs touched the ground without missing a beat. He was complete now, racing wildly down the path and towards whatever dared stand in his way.

It felt wonderful, glorious, wild and feral. Running across a small open field the wind whipped his fur into a soaring cloud of darkness underneath an exploding full moon. At the top of a small rise he stopped, steam escaping his nostrils in big puffs of white, chest heaving from the exhilarating run. Looking up at the midnight sky he threw back his head and howled. It was a true song of the wild. There is not a more beautiful, haunting melody in all the forest than the call of a wolf. When members of a pack sing in chorus, they easily rivaled any large symphony orchestra in beauty and tone.

After he stopped howling, it seemed his voice continued to echo through the ceiling of swaying treetops. The Lord of the Forest was now on the prowl and he had no competition, whether it was on his own, or as part of the pack.

A normal wolf knew that obviously a much larger bear, especially the grizzly, was something to stay clear of. Even a much larger moose or elk was difficult one on one. But for a weregune such as Jaress, who was much larger than a naturally born wolf, there truly was no rival. Unless a bear he ran across just happened to be weregune also. Usually, but not always, they carefully avoided each other because it would most assuredly mean the death of one, or maybe both of them. There were many tales about just such encounters, extremely violent and bloody. Jaress and one of his brothers had come across the remains of two such unfortunate creatures, both most definitely dead and dismembered. Both he and his brother vowed that day to avoid such confrontations in the future. Better to be alive than bear meat.

After trotting through the dark, silent woods for about ten minutes he stopped abruptly. His nostrils flared excitedly as the succulent scent of deer tickled his hunger. And he was most definitely famished, not having eaten anything substantial for most of the day. He began moving towards the warm blooded feast that awaited him. Being weregune, he had such an unfair advantage in that he blended in to his surroundings so easy, appearing invisible to the wary eye until it was too late and he pounced.

A four point buck, large doe, and two younger deer stood in a small clearing, somewhat oblivious to his presence. The buck did have his head up, looking around, those black button eyes peering nervously around, sensing something, but not sure what. He was prepared to give a warning to his family and bolt for safety if he could just determine what danger was in their midst. He was obviously confused.

That moment of hesitation was fatal for one of the younger deer as Jaress lunged from the darkness. He was upon the animal before it had a chance to even take one full step and was smothered by the awesome size of the attacking wolf. The other three deer escaped the onslaught, sadness for their loss, but relieved they were not the victim this night.

Jaress held the struggling animal's neck completely in his mouth, exerting enormous pressure on the windpipe to stop air intake, his fangs sinking deeply into the warm flesh. Hot blood spurted down his throat while the deer's legs quivered in a final, desperate attempt at life. Less than thirty seconds later it was over, the surrounding forest completely silent, numbing in its stillness, quivering animals relieved they was still alive.

Releasing the dead deer, the massive black wolf stood and with bright crimson blood staining his muzzle he howled again, letting everybody know that this was his kill and to stay clear. A minute later, after easily opening the stomach from chest to anal cavity with claws sharper than any scalpel, the beast inserted his entire head inside the steaming body to dine on a recently beating heart. Nothing could be sweeter thought Jaress than a fresh kill. Sadly he remembered the times when he and Samantha would run down prey and dine under moonlight together. A few tears fell and merged with the blood for as much as he yearned to have Kathy as his new mate, he would never forget his beautiful Samantha.

Kathy awoke in a cold sweat, her oversized t-shirt completely drenched in fact. She lay there in the dark bedroom, listening to a host of unfamiliar sounds. Her hearing had become so acute, as was her eyesight. She had always possessed a wonderful sense of smell, but now it was at times more than she could handle. It was way too much incoming data to absorb, she thought. After a moment to escape her nightmare she realized she was not alone and that thought immediately terrified her. Not only was she lying on a strange bed in an unfamiliar house, someone or something was in the room with her. Should she reach for the bedside lamp and illuminate the room to see if danger surrounded her? Or should she just lie there and pray she was wrong, just an extremely over active imagination? She was too damn frightened to reach for the lamp, feeling that if it were an enemy then any movement would be fatal. Somehow though, whatever it was, she felt completely safe.

Then the odor assailed her, a metallic, pungent smell of blood which aroused her. It woke up an inner creature dying to spring forth. Kathy stirred noticeably, and when she did, a low growl came from the darkness. She froze, fearing somehow one of Victor's clan members, possibly that Kahleel character, had secretly entered her room. Angry at this incursion she decided to reach out for the lamp anyway, growl or no growl.

It wasn't a large lamp, but it threw off enough light that Kathy saw a large black wolf sitting near the door, staring at her with eyes of goldenrod. Instantly she knew it was Jaress and once again he had blood painted on his muzzle. Damn, she thought, how in the world did he ever expect her to get used to him when every time he appeared in wolf state he was covered in blood?

The wolf stood and moved towards the side of the bed, eyes centered upon her unmoving form. She was too petrified to move even an inch. Though she was positive there was nothing to fear, it was still an unsettling apparition which was all too real. And yet, she realized how magnificently beautiful he was. She suddenly had this intense desire to sink her fingers into the beast's lush black fur.

As if on cue he jumped onto the bed, giving her already pounding heart quite a start. Slowly he stretched out and lay down on the bed, his enormous size nearly taking up one complete side of the mattress. His eyes stared at her, urging her to reach out like she had desired. That's exactly what she did.

Her exploring fingers got lost in the thick mane of luxuriant fur around his neck. Closing her eyes she let herself sink back into the pillows with hand and fingers massaging the beast's massive neck. It had to be a dream, yet somehow she felt he would protect her from previous nightmares the remainder of the night and so she slept with a dream of her running wild and free beside her mate under a smiling moon.

In the morning, as sunlight scratched its way through an open window, Kathy opened her eyes and glanced at the thick, goose down comforter. She was now alone and pondered if it really had been a dream, a wolf lying in a woman's bed? Nothing new you might think. But not a wolfish Casanova type who thought he was God's gift to women. Rather the genuine item, the true beast, the shadow of your dreams, or nightmares. Her hand came up clutching a large clump of black fur between her fingers. A thrill of excitement raced through her entire body. She smiled, letting the incredible realization of what he had done blanket her in a sense of love like she had never felt before. He had presented himself to her in his wildest, most glorious state and in effect told her that he now belonged to her.

Glancing over at the nightstand she saw a small tray containing a small glass of orange juice, a large glass of milk, and a blue-flowered carafe of hot coffee. On the front part of the tray was a plate of fresh melon, two biscuits and fresh strawberry jam. Suddenly she was quite hungry and swung her legs over the side of the bed. Johnny just continued to amaze her. At one moment he seemed distant and dangerous. The next he was loving and attentive, extremely hot and desirous. She would get used to all his idiosyncrasies just as he would learn to enjoy all of hers.

Birds sang outside the window in the early morning dawn, adding their own version of music to her peaceful thoughts. She was so hungry she literally gulped down the sweet melon, and polished it off with the two biscuits lathered in jam. The coffee had somewhat of a bitter, chicory flavor so she added more cream and sugar to cover the taste. It was hot and that's all she wanted at the moment, to allay an icy chill seeping in through the slightly open window.

Pushing the tray away and issuing a slight, unladylike belch, she started to get up and head for the bathroom so she could shower and get dressed. But as she stood, the room began to spin and she immediately collapsed back down onto the mattress. That was funny she thought and tried it once again.

This time though the room really began to swirl and she let herself lie back down onto the comforter, feeling a little nauseous. Detective instincts quickly told her she had been drugged and she had only a few moments to be angry as total darkness enveloped her.

About ten minutes later the door to the bedroom opened slowly. Johnny quietly walked in, followed by his father. They stood on each side of the bed and stared down at Kathy. It was his father who gave him the idea to drug her, even though it was against his better judgment. She would be pissed off, really pissed. But as his father made him realize, it was better to be pissed off than lying dead somewhere in a field. He could not lose another mate, if she even wanted to belong to him after she awoke.

He gently pulled the thick comforter up to cover and tuck her in. Bending down he kissed her on the lips and whispered, "I do love you Kathleen Morello. Please don't be too angry with me, but I'm selfish and need to keep you safe."

Kissing her once more, he then stood and prayed he would return to her. In the event that he died in the upcoming battle, there would be pack members who would take very good care of her. But knowing how strongly Kathy felt, he also knew she would not desire to live as a beast, unless it was at his side. Simply stated, he had no choice. After he killed Victor and obtained his revenge, he and Kathy would then be together forever.

Chapter 35

The gently, rolling fields of Valley Forge seemed to run forever underneath a clear, crisp November night. Blanketed underneath a white, virgin snowfall, the awesome beauty of this scene was breathtaking. Pristine in its pureness, only broken by meandering footprints of browsing deer, the moon spread a glow that glittered like little sparkles tossed about by the loving hands of Mother Nature. An intensely deep, midnight blue hung over this unsuspecting landscape, dotted here and there by glittering, flickering stars and a moon softly embraced by a yellow haze that cast an eerie, haunting aura upon a picture soon to be interrupted with death and violence.

Dark, ominous shadows floated over the snow like predatory ogres, wrapping themselves in and around a stoic, silent phalanx of trees. Ghosts from winters past echoed eerily along the rolling hills. If one listened very closely it might just be possible to hear the moans and teeth chattering chills experienced by Washington's Continental Army that snowy, frigid, icy winter of 1777.

Soldiers limped and shuffled along on battle weary feet, sometimes shoeless or scantily clad, wearing nothing more than thread bare uniforms and thinly soled boots, shivering from bone chilling cold, stomachs angrily growling from hunger. The beleaguered army slowly and steadily flowed into a spoon shaped triangle of landscape known as Valley Forge, Pennsylvania. With Philadelphia approximately eighteen miles to the southeast, recently controlled by the British and Sir William Howe, the Continental Army wanted nothing more than to fall upon the frozen ground and sleep.

It was on December 19th underneath the gray, dismal cover of nightfall, when a steady snow and wind attempted to hinder their progress. But onward they came in brave determination. It would take approximately a month for nearly 12,000 soldiers to call this wild terrain home and build their winter quarters. After fighting the British in numerous battles and skirmishes over a mind numbing campaign, the recuperation time was welcome. But before they could rest, under orders by their leader George Washington, the men needed to build housing. Within a month's time they erected a small city of around one thousand log huts during a time when it snowed almost daily. Thomas Paine had once referred to them as a 'family of beavers'.

Even though the winter of 1777/1778 was severely brutal, with many soldiers suffering frostbite and succumbing to the cold temperatures, most of the men died early the following spring from a much smaller enemy called bacteria. Living conditions had become deplorable within this log city and disease was rampant. However, due to their bravery and determination, when the surviving army finally moved out towards New Jersey and Washington's eventual historic crossing of the Delaware, it was an extremely hardened Continental Army that marched onward to victory in the Great American Revolution. It was this horrible winter at Valley Forge that gave them the will to survive an even more brutal winter in 1778/1779 at Moorestown, New Jersey.

Tonight though wolves ruled this rural landscape which was bounded on the north by the Schuylkill River, the west by Valley Creek, a long ridge of low ground on the southeast, and a narrow ribbon of water on the east called Trout Creek. Route 23 wound like a loose New Year's Eve streamer through the park, but this late in the evening traffic was at a minimum. The battleground chosen though was far enough away from human eyes, a small postage stamp size field surrounded by tall trees. Earlier in the evening both packs had sent scouts ahead in order to select the area that would give them the greatest advantage to assure victory. Of course, both groups were keenly aware of the others presence. Protocol however kept anything from happening until both alpha weregunes were ready to meet each other first.

Veltar and Kahleel lay amid some sparse brush on a small rise overlooking the empty field, eyes on constant alert, just an occasional flick of a tail to signify their presence. Even their breathing had been purposefully slowed down in order to keep steam to a minimum from escaping their flared nostrils. For Veltar, it had been a long wait. He had dreamed so often and been assailed by nightmares for many years, hungry to avenge his previous mates death. Kahleel as well had revenge on his mind. Even though he was content with life as Roberto's supreme wolf, years of suffering had embittered him towards those who had failed to rescue him. Ten years of constant torture and degradation had created the hard, dangerous beast he had become, hatred now the only emotion that drove him onward. Maybe after tonight when this was finally over he would have enough room in his heart to let somebody inside. It was highly doubtful though.

On the other side of this nervous battlefield sat Jaress and Mandhar. These two magnificent black wolves were equally prepared for the fight of their lives, golden eyes staring intently at the spot where Veltar and Kahleel lay secluded. Both of them knew there was a possibility they might not survive, even though it was slim at best that they would both perish. Jaress had only one purpose and that was to destroy Veltar. Only then would he be at peace and be able to finally bury the vengeance he had carried within him for the past three years. And only then could he think of a future with Kathy and some form of happiness. Mandhar had other, equally dark thoughts running through him. Deep inside he sensed who Kahleel may be and that thought alone caused fear and trepidation to assault him for the first time in his life.

Around these four leaders hid their small, but powerful armies. They were not ruled by vengeance, or guided by hatred. It was law of the pack to follow their alphas, no questions asked and they did so without fail. But even then, it was difficult for them to not form opinions or have reservations, as much as they did not wish to. Within Veltar's pack had been the murmurings and concern of treachery, especially with the emergence of Kahleel as well as what had happened to Tomas back at the compound. They would've followed their leader, Veltar, to hell and back, but now it remained an open ended question. Other than six members of Mandhar's clan who had accompanied him, the rest were from the pack north of New Hope. As they sat quiet and edgy, it was not a stretch for them to wonder why they were present when it was not their fight. Yet there were family ties, as distant as they may be, and so now they faced the distinct possibility of death as well.

Speaking to a class of graduating cadets at the M.M.A., General William Tecumseh Sherman once told them, '*You don't know the horrible aspects of war. I've been through two wars and I know. I've seen cities and homes in ashes. I've seen thousands of men lying on the ground, their dead faces looking up at the skies. I tell you, war is hell!*'

But then, General Sherman did not have to face such a cunning and powerful predator like the weregune. His quote 'war is hell' definitely defined Satan's battlefield that was now surrounded by several dozen wolves who could easily fight as if possessed by the devil himself.

Kathy was really pissed off. Easily hitting ninety on the speedometer, she weaved in and out of late night traffic on the Schuylkill Expressway (otherwise known as the Surekill), deciding just to lay hard on the horn rather than hit the brakes. She was absolutely furious at Johnny for drugging her breakfast in order to keep her out of harms way, thus protecting her from the battle. Maybe he felt his intentions were those of love, but Kathy felt he had no right to make that decision for her.

After waking up in an extremely groggy state, it took only a few minutes to realize what had happened. Even though several of the female weregune's, including Tabitha, tried to calm her down and impress upon her the insanity of going to find Johnny at Valley Forge, she was unable to be swayed. Her purpose was final. Her emotions were of anger and betrayal. Her intention was to first avenge the death of her father and then to shove a pointed shoe up Johnny's you know what.

There was only one major problem. She was locked in the room and the only window had bars on it. Kind of like a comfy cell, but she figured it must be for those who were newly changing so it was for their own protection. After several minutes of screaming at the top of her lungs to let her out, she sat on the edge of the bed in tears, dizzy and exhausted emotionally. Johnny had no idea what kind of trouble he was in for when he returned.

However, not too long after she gave up on trying to escape there was a soft click at the door. Tabitha slipped in with a finger pressed to her lips for silence. Then, after sneaking a glance into the hallway, she motioned for Kathy to follow her. They crept silently through the back door and then managed to find Tabitha's car undetected.

"Why are you helping me to get away? You must hate me for what I did to your son," Kathy asked.

"I don't hate you Detective Morello. You did what you had to do in order to survive. I also think that what Johnny and Mandhar did, by keeping you locked away, was wrong. You have every right to be there even though you will be under extreme danger and most likely won't live through the night. However, it is your choice, not his," Tabitha answered.

"Thank you! Then would you please take me to my house so I can get to my car. There are weapons in the trunk I'll need and I can drive myself," she replied, already getting herself into battle mode.

"Certainly, you'll need all the protection you can get, believe me. It's very late though and by the time we arrive, it may be too late," Tabitha answered, following the directions that Kathy had given her.

"You're going along as well?"

"Yes, if Victor is still alive, he also has a number of questions to answer for," Tabitha said, her voice in a lower octave range, almost like a growl, that sounded so strange to hear coming from a female. Kathy realized that Tabitha would be quite a formidable foe herself.

Without slowing down at all, Kathy took the off ramp from the Expressway at King of Prussia and Rte. 202 nearly on two wheels and flew around the cloverleaf to merge onto Rte. 422. Tabitha held on for dear life in the passenger seat. She realized it had not been the proper decision for Johnny to hold Kathy at the compound against her will. Besides, she had unfinished business as well with Victor. There had been enough die already in the name of vengeance. Somehow it had to end tonight, even though she was positive more would die before the coming dawn.

Several minutes later Kathy spun her vehicle crazily onto Route 23. It was late, well after midnight, and small herds of browsing deer actually stood in the grass right along both sides of the road. After years of nearly becoming domesticated and used to people walking, jogging and riding bikes in the park, they had acquired a false sense of security, or at least until a time when one would venture nonchalantly onto the pavement and become road kill from the impact of a bumper doing forty or fifty miles an hour. Kathy prayed this would not be one of those times.

As she sped through the park, one eye was kept centered securely on the milling deer while the other searched for signs of Johnny's truck. Tabitha said they had taken several vehicles earlier that afternoon and drove out to Valley Forge in order to act natural and blend in so their presence would not be suspected by prowling police or park rangers. Also, of course, to gain some advantage over the enemy if at all possible. She could not tell Kathy where they planned to fight, but she felt it would be somewhere in the vicinity to where the vehicles were parked. New Hope was too far away from Valley Forge and it would've been impossible to travel that great a distance in wolf form during daylight hours without being detected. So they would park in different spots and then converge at a pre-designated place where they would stash their clothing and then transform sometime after nightfall.

Careening around a sharp S-turn she spied his vehicle parked quietly in the far corner of a small lot off to the left. Tires screaming, Kathy's car slid in a neck jarring stop just inches from the rear bumper of Johnny's battered truck. It didn't help that the recent snow from the night before, after melting somewhat during the day, had iced over when temperatures dropped below freezing, to become a treacherous ice skating rink. She was so damn mad at Johnny that for a few quick seconds of insanity she had the intense urge to smash into his truck and shove it down the small embankment it was parked in front of. Since that would've only damaged her own car, she decided to wait until she faced him before invoking her wrath.

She leaped out of her car and opened the trunk to gaze at the cache of weapons stashed inside. Pity the fool who was stupid enough to try and kill her. And shame on the idiot who decided to keep her prisoner. With lips pressed tightly together she reached for the large canvas duffel bag and yanked on the zipper. Spreading the opening wider she reached in to pull out the double shoulder holster containing twin, Smith & Wesson model 5906, 9mm semi-automatic pistols. After slipping it over her shoulders, Kathy took each gun out, checked the clips to make sure they were fully loaded and loudly clicked them back into place. Grabbing four extra clips, she shoved them in the side pockets of her vest and was beginning to feel a little better. Extreme firepower always made her feel a little more macho. It had been awhile since she had worn this much weaponry, but serious danger to life and limb called for drastic measures.

Beside the duffel bag rested a Mossberg 590 "Compact Cruiser" pump action shotgun. Kathy felt more comfortable with the pistol handle and handgun like trigger. She had always found it to be extremely powerful and easier for her to maneuver. Though it might not kill any of the beasts, it sure as hell would knock them on their furry asses, long enough for her to strategically place a bullet in their doggy brain from her Smith & Wesson. Grabbing some extra shells, she was ready to move. Kathy had a way of zeroing in on what had to be done, taking control of a situation and eliminating any fear or trepidation she might have. In battle mode now, she slammed the trunk down and took a deep breath. It was time to rock and roll.

As she did so a sharp jabbing pain pierced her stomach and raced down her spine. Trying to stifle a scream, she moaned louder than she really wanted to, almost bent over double now. For a few seconds it seemed like her insides were aflame and being stretched out of place like soft, salt water taffy. She felt like throwing up as a wave of dizziness almost took her to the ground. Strong hands grabbed her by the shoulders and helped her to lean against the trunk of the car.

"You've been infected haven't you?" asked Tabitha from behind, evident concern in her voice.

"How could you tell?" whispered Kathy, wanting to say some biting remark, but unable to come up with anything that was amusingly witty.

"Oh, maybe it's the fact your spine just performed a double pretzel-bend like a human's is unable to do. Or, it could've been the moan from your throat that sounded more like a growl. Of course, there's always the extra hair that seems to be sprouting on your hands," answered the female weregune, like they were having a nonchalant conversation over afternoon tea.

Kathy glanced quickly at the back of her right hand, startled in fact to see some long, snowy white hair growing on skin surface that had always been smooth as a baby's butt. Oh shit, it's starting to happen Kathy realized. Why now, why now she questioned.

"My arm and shoulder were clawed by the rogue. Johnny filled me in on everything, don't worry. It's not like I've started taking massive doses of progesterone in order to grow a beard. I'm not that macho, believe me. Oh shit," she cried, bending over and dropping to her knees. In a few seconds it passed and she suddenly felt a little better.

"Is it over for now?" she asked Tabitha.

"For the moment it is. You still may not change completely tonight, it doesn't always happen the first cycle of the full moon. However, you will feel some of the changes and, as you've already felt, some evident pain and discomfort. You can still back down from this insanity Kathleen."

"Not on the life of your beast, mine, or any of the creatures that are about to die," Kathy said, standing up and taking several long, deep breaths. "Do you have any idea where they might be?"

"Most likely they'll be deeper inside the park, like over towards that thick area of trees. They'll try to minimize exposure as much as possible, but it will sound like a battle for sure," Tabitha said. "Will you be okay on your own? I have to find a place to shift."

"Sure, go bring your little wolfie out for a walk. I'm going to head across that field towards those trees. If I were you Tabitha, I'd stay clear of my fire power. I won't be asking who anybody in particular is, and that includes Johnny and his father. Anybody is fair game out there if you're in my cross hairs."

Tabitha laughed as she started moving towards a small log construction, built to give tourists an idea of how Washington's Continental army lived during that brutal winter. All the original log huts had been destroyed, either on purpose or natural wear and tear over many years. Why not allow cover for a female to change from human to wolf? This entire night was going to be something straight out of your worst nightmare. The only major difference was this nightmare could be painful and very deadly.

The moon was invitingly alive, shining brightly off the white, snowy landscape. No mist, no fog, just small white puffs of feral breath breaking the tree line. All the wolves had stealthily maneuvered themselves into strategic positions and now just waited for the signal to attack. But initially, the leaders had to meet in the middle of the prospective battlefield.

First from the left came Kahleel, huge and imposing, eyes the color of simmering liquid silver staring across the field towards his enemies. Hatred seemed to melt the snow around his feet as he moved fearlessly towards the center of the small clearing. He had dreamed of this night a thousand times, to get his revenge against those who had spurned him. To his right, moving out from behind a tree appeared Veltar, equally as impressive in size as his jet black compatriot and propelled by his own hatred. The two awesome beasts stopped about five feet from each other and waited.

With massive, black head held low, mouth open and deadly fangs showing openly from peeled back lips, Jaress paced with a proud swagger towards the enemy. His eyes were mostly on Veltar, the creature who had dispatched Quentin to take his life, but instead stole Samantha from him. Kahleel looked distantly familiar, as if there was some familial connection, which he was unable to fully understand. This stranger had the black fur and small white blaze which ran underneath the muzzle and about an inch down the neck as Johnny and his father had, as well as another mark. Jaress felt it must be a coincidence, but there was a queasy feeling in his stomach nonetheless.

Mandhar followed his son closely, ever alert for a sudden attack. It was no slight that he was the fourth wolf to appear. His stature and age afforded him the protection of coming out last just in case of deceit happening. Walking stiff-legged and overly cautious he paced towards the center of the clearing. A sage, old owl, safely clutching precariously to a high perch somewhere off in the distance, broadcasted his warning to any unobservant wildlife that death was in their midst. But, it was only earlier that deer and other game had to worry about surviving the night since both packs had feasted quite well in pre-battle meals.

Jaress came to a stop at the same time Kahleel did, only ten feet separating them. Both massive, black wolves stared at each other, moonlight glittering off their hate-filled eyes. A low growl began to emerge from the chest of Kahleel while Jaress chose to merely stare and pull back his lips in a grimace showing large, gleaming fangs. Both Mandhar and Veltar had moved quietly to stand beside their younger counterparts.

Mandhar knew exactly who stood before him. No matter how much this beast had changed over the years, the unmistakable mark of their clan was present. It was like a fingerprint, a birthmark. A weregune could change packs, form one of their own as many younger males did, but that unique mark remained until the day they died. Sometimes it was extremely evident, even in human form, but more often than not could be detected only when in wolf form. In the case of their clan it was a tiny red teardrop shape in the lower inside corner of the left eye. Three of the four awesome wolves facing each other in the moonlit clearing possessed that tiny red teardrop. It was a sure bet that Veltar was not one of them.

Mandhar decided the best way to face this situation was in human form, so rather than try to speak through mental channels he shifted and now stood completely nude under the moon's accusing glare. Jaress was startled when his father performed the change and moved cautiously backwards several feet where he sat down warily on his haunches, looking about for any of Veltar's followers that may have slipped to the side or behind him. Obviously his father had a reason for altering shape and needed to be allowed his space to pursue that course.

Kahleel stared for several seconds and suddenly changed his shape to human as well. He was as magnificent in human form as he was in wolf shape, his long hair covering his broad shoulders like a velvet cape. His stomach muscles put the normal definition of sculpted abs to shame. Jaress knew instantly that this individual would be a most formidable foe in either shape. After he killed Veltar, then it was a strong possibility he would have to face the beast standing before him as well.

"Hello Bhetar," Mandhar said, referring to his son's original name.

Kahleel stared for a few moments, pondering what to say. Then his mouth formed into a sneer as he said, "I would call you father, but then you deserted me and thus lost that right when you ceased to care about me."

At the mention of son, Jaress perked up his ears, curious that Mandhar would refer to the huge man in front of him as son. Then he realized this must be the older brother who his father had searched so long for and never found. The bare flick of his bushy tail suggested that he was pleased and yet something told him this was not to be one of those loving, Hallmark moments.

"I searched for ten long, bitter years Bhetar. Each time when it seemed I was getting close, Roberto would keep you hidden, move you to another place and make it impossible for me to get near. I almost died several times in battle trying to rescue you. I'm so sorry if you thought I willfully deserted you," said Mandhar in a strained voice.

"Do you have any idea what kind of pain and degradation I had to endure? There were years of torture by Roberto and his evil brood, while my heart broke more and more each day wondering if you were coming. I would've gladly died just knowing you went through the pits of hell to find me," snarled Kahleel. "Instead of dying though, I got stronger, meaner and more vicious, doing anything and everything to stay alive for this very day when we would face each other again, and my name is now Kahleel."

Kahleel took two menacing steps toward Mandhar. Jaress quickly stood up, growling deeply, the hackles on his back standing straight up. Mandhar turned slightly and put out his hand to stop the younger son.

"No Jaress, stay out of this for the moment, Kahleel won't hurt me," he said, more as positive reinforcement than for his own nervousness.

His older son smiled and looked at his sibling. "So this is my younger brother, the one who was just a tiny pup when we went to war. He's grown up I see."

"This is Jaress, your brother. Unfortunately the two of you never had the opportunity to form a bond, but you're still brothers."

In a booming laugh, Kahleel moved a step forward. "Brother? Give me a break, I have no brother. I have no father or mother. I answer only to Roberto who has groomed and made me into who I am today. I'm here to make you regret the day you made the personal decision that I was lost. You will die because of that decision."

Kahleel knelt down, closed his eyes and called for the shift to wolf form. In seconds he stood tall on all four legs, lips pulled back in an unholy grin exposing long, curved teeth which were prepared to end his father's life. Veltar had slipped up beside Kahleel, head low and growling deeply as well. The surrounding woods erupted with snarling and quick movements, the small armies getting ready for whatever violence was about to take place.

Father, please shift while you have the time. You will die if you stay human, pleaded Jaress.

"No son, I won't shift. If Kahleel hates me so much then let him have conviction to kill me. It seems I've destroyed enough lives. Maybe it's time I sacrificed my own and all the vengeance ended here," replied his father, his human voice almost a whisper.

"But I hate you that much Mandhar for killing my Sasheen. You are about to die for that action," growled Veltar, before launching himself through the air, his mouth open and fangs reaching for his intended victim's throat.

Jaress did not wait and leaped at the wolf that was hurtling towards his father. The two massive wolves collided in a brutal collision in mid-air, their sharp teeth already imbedded in the other's throat, claws raking and tearing out large clumps of hair and skin. Only seconds slipped by, the speed of the attack and the protective stance happening with breath taking speed. Hitting the ground hard they rolled several times, each wolf trying to gain advantage over the other. Already the snow was splashed red with their blood.

Kahleel stared at his non-father with pure hatred glaring from his devilish eyes. If this man standing before him thought he would stay his deadly desire then the human part of the individual standing there was even crazier than he thought. Besides, it didn't matter if Mandhar was in human or wolf form, simply that revenge is so much sweeter the longer you wait.

Crouching, Kahleel launched himself at Mandhar, striking the older weregune squarely in the chest, propelling them both against a large tree. The impact shook the ground and caused Jaress to glance at his father even though Veltar had his throat securely held between powerful jaws. He realized that Mandhar had no chance against the beast as long as he stayed in human form.

Jaress bit down hard on Veltar's throat, trying desperately to maneuver so that he was on top. The move didn't work as he felt Veltar's claws plunge like white-hot pokers deeply into his shoulder and slice down towards his stomach. In terrible pain he released his hold on the other beast's throat, sinking his own rear claws into Veltar's softer underbelly, pushing upward with all his strength. Massive amounts of hot, steaming blood spurted out, melting the snow around them into a stream of crimson death. As Jaress pushed with all his strength he glanced over to see his father underneath the older brother who he had thought was dead, Mandhar's head with nearly lifeless eyes hanging from Kahleel's jaws.

Other fighting broke out around them as members of each pack converged not only within the clearing, but the surrounding woods as well. The growling and snarling sounded like thunder from a winter's storm. Each wolf was now engaged in their own death matches with only the possibility of one survivor. It was a scene unlike any other, for rarely do this many creatures wage war against each other on a snowy, moonlit field where vengeance is the reason.

Kathy came to an abrupt stop, nearly falling onto her butt in the snow. She stared into the clearing with unbelieving eyes. Hearing the fighting break out shortly after leaving the car she headed in that direction. Now she could do nothing but place a nervous hand to her mouth and gasp in disbelief at this bloody carnage. Surprise however only lasted a few brief seconds as she glanced to the left and saw a huge black beast straddling a nude male body hanging from its jaws. Realizing it was Mandhar, Kathy slipped one of the Smith and Wesson's from the holster and released the safety.

Crouching down, nearly on her knees, she crept into the clearing and was nearly bowled over by two rolling, snarling beasts. Lifting the pistol in both hands she pointed it directly at the beast that held Mandhar's seemingly lifeless body in his monstrous mouth. To hesitate would be a mistake. A wise old detective who had taken her under his wing told her that to hesitate for only a second could mean your life. The first bullet screamed out of the muzzle at over 1,000 feet per second and tore a hole in the beasts left shoulder. The massive wolf turned, not yet releasing the limp body of Mandhar, and searched for where the attack had come from. Spying Kathy almost sitting in a low crouch, aiming her weapon directly at him, he quickly moved to his right behind the large tree which he had previously crashed into, all the time never releasing the blood-covered body of his dying father.

Suddenly nervous about not seeing the beast clearly, she rose higher and slid a little to her left in order to get a better view. Very bad move! A sharp claw from a wolf fighting closely behind her got stuck in the base of her neck and yanked her backwards. Screaming in pain, she went with the motion until she felt the claw break free. She fell and rolled to her right, coming up with pistol aimed and fired once, twice, three times. After firing the first shot with the Smith and Wesson 5906 each one thereafter was easier to squeeze off. The explosion from the pistol merged with the loud snarling going on all around her.

Not giving it a second thought, she spun and continued to fire at anything that moved. It didn't matter really because if it was furry, then she could kill it. Shoot first and ask questions of the big bad wolf second, that was her motto right at the moment. The entire time Kathy felt this tickling, scratching sensation crawling over her own skin. She could only imagine what it was and decided not to check it out.

Instead she turned and saw two extremely large wolves locked in mortal combat right in the center of the clearing. Kathy instantly recognized the black wolf, even through all the blood, as being Johnny. It was a vision she was unprepared for because it clearly appeared he was in dire straights, lying on his back while the other wolf straddled him, murderous jaws locked on Johnny's ravaged neck. As she brought her pistol up to fire, a body hurdled past her and leaped upon the back of Johnny's enemy.

Kathy knew immediately it was Tabitha. Even amidst this hellish melee, she cracked a thin smile. It was kind of funny to think of this ferocious beast having a silly name like Tabitha. Here Tabby, come get your bowl of milk.

But the levity was short lived as Kathy was hit broadside with what felt like an out of control tractor trailer. All the air was knocked from her lungs in a loud whoosh as she was completely buried underneath a huge, black, hairy body. Shit, she thought, in all the uproar she had broken a cardinal rule. Never take your eyes off the more dangerous perp. Now it seemed she might pay the ultimate price.

She screamed as fangs buried themselves into her right shoulder, sinking all the way down to where she could hear the obvious crunching of shattered bone. The pistol had been knocked from her hand as she fell, but she wasn't completely defenseless. Even through the intense pain she reached for the Mossberg which had slipped from around her shoulder and lay only inches from her seeking fingertips. She screamed again as sharp fangs released their hold on crushed bone and sank into her throat, immediately cutting off her breathing. It was quite simple, shoot to kill or forever hold your peace.

Grasping the shotgun she let her finger slip through the trigger hold and maneuvered the barrel against the beast's side. Without hesitating she pulled the trigger at point blank range, the explosion knocking the beast off her, but unfortunately taking a large chunk of Kathy's neck with it. The creature howled in pain as it rolled free and landed on its legs, spinning and preparing to lunge back upon her sprawled body. Kathy used her one hand to hold her neck together and spun on her back, aiming the shotgun at the black devil which faced her. No hesitation, no thought, no feeling, only survival. She pulled the trigger as the barrel exploded into the face of Kahleel, sending him flying backwards into the sparse bushes where he disappeared, hopefully dead at last.

Kathy lay there, gasping for air, gurgling loudly on her own blood. She could feel life ebbing away, staring at a silver moon that seemed to be swimming in a black sea of forgiveness. Then she sensed a movement to her right. Using what little strength still remaining in her body, she turned her head slowly to see that Johnny had struggled painfully across the bloody snow to try and come to her aid, his own body ravaged by the fight with Veltar.

Kathy tried to crack a smile, but found it impossible to even move her lips. Whether she lived or died, it was enough to know that Johnny, even in wolf form, was trying to save her.

The black wolf moved to where he could position himself overtop of her. With his blood-stained muzzle he nudged her hand away from her throat, exposing the huge open gash. Without hesitating, Jaress closed his mouth around her thin neck and bit down, sinking his teeth deeply into her carotid artery. There was no pain for at this point she was completely numb with her final breath. Kathy was not sure if she would ever see the light of day again, but if she did then it would be at the side of the man and wolf who braved death to save her.

Chapter 36

Underneath the inquisitive glare of the sun breaking over the eastern horizon, two park rangers stood nervously at the edge of the clearing and stared at a sight which was impossible to describe. So they just stood quietly, trying to absorb the scene before them. Blood literally painted the once pristine snow red, but yet there were no bodies. One ranger moved towards a tree and bent down to pick up a large, bloody object.

"What you got there Ted?" asked the other ranger, his voice echoing through the light mist of early dawn.

"Don't rightly know Vinnie, but I'd swear it looks like the lower part of a dog's leg. A damn big dog too," he replied.

The other ranger chuckled nervously. "One helluva' dog fight I'd say by the looks of this place. Jesus, have you ever seen such a thing?" he said, shaking his head.

"Not on your life. Are you sure this was done by dogs and not something else?" Ted asked.

"I'm not sure of anything right about now. We should get the police out here to take a look, take samples of this blood and see if any is human, cast those tracks and try to determine what they're from. They've been having a pretty rough time of it in the City so I feel pretty confident they'll want to be advised of this."

Ted started moving towards Vinnie who still delicately held the bloody leg he had picked up. There was a loud cawing sound that sliced through the eerie, misty stillness. Vinnie looked up just in time to see the largest raven he had ever seen soaring straight down at him.

"Holy shit, what the ....." he yelled out as he began to duck out of the way.

Instinctively he held up his hands to ward off the surprise attack. The huge black bird extended its claws and latched onto the leg, ripping it from Vinnie's grasp and then flew off towards a break in the tree line, quickly melting into the swirling fog and sporadic shafts of sunlight. The park ranger lost his balance and fell backwards onto the ground which was still a bloody, muddy mess.

"Damn, did you see that Ted? What the hell was that?" Vinnie asked, trying to get up, but continuing to slip back into the mire.

Extending his hand towards his partner to help him up, Ted said in a voice barely above a whisper, "Biggest damn raven I've ever seen. It had to be three or four times larger than normal. Just what the hell is happening here buddy?"

Shaking his hands, trying to rid them of the muddy red goo, looking down at his soiled uniform, he shook his head.

"Not on your life. I'm getting the hell out of here in case whatever did this is still around. I can't believe we didn't know a pack of wild dogs was in the park," he replied.

"Same here, though we did hear howling the other night if you remember. It's obvious that something was slaughtered here and then taken away. The only large prey in the park happens to be the deer and I don't see any parts of bodies lying around," stated Ted.

"Well, good old Bambi didn't put up the kind of fight that obviously took place here. Maybe it was some kind of pagan ritual thing," murmured Vinnie, trying to wipe off some of the larger clumps of reddish-brown mud clinging to his pants.

"Come on, let's get out of here and call in the police. This is more than I can handle, let the big boys take over. Besides, I'm kind of nervous just being here," he said, moving off towards the direction of their jeep.

"Lead the way because I'm right behind you buddy. Crap, will you just look at this uniform?" Vinnie whined.

Laughing nervously, Ted replied, "Yeah, you look like Swamp Thing. Have to write you up for wearing a dirty uniform."

"Oh, look who's the big comedian. Very funny, very funny, but it wasn't you that got attacked by a giant raven and got knocked on his ass," growled Vinnie.

Kathy and Johnny slept and healed for nearly three days. It was the deepest sleep she had ever experienced. Of course, dying first will give you that feeling. She opened her eyes just a crack, but the light was too much and she quickly closed them. Moaning slightly she moved on the bed and was sorry she had. The wounds on her neck and shoulder screamed in her ears before realizing it was herself doing the crying. But the screaming hurt like hell so she stopped.

She felt a warm hand touch her arm and nearly jumped out of her skin.

"Easy Kathy, easy, I'm here," said a soft, soothing, masculine voice.

"Johnny?" she whispered.

"Of course, who did you think it would be unless there's somebody else in your life I don't know about," he said teasingly, enveloping her hand in his.

She tried to push back into more of a sitting position and grimaced in obvious pain. Not only did the wounds burn like hell, but it hurt to swallow as well and she was both thirsty and hungry. Opening her eyes slowly she let the light come back into her world a drop at a time until she focused on his handsome face.

"Hey Baby, nice to have you back," he said, his mouth cracking into a warm smile.

"It's nice to be back, I think. I am back, aren't I?" she asked him.

"Oh yeah, you're back Kathleen and I don't plan on ever leaving you again.

I'm sorry about drugging you the other day, but I didn't want you to get seriously hurt. You obviously didn't listen," he scolded.

"And you obviously don't know how close you came to getting your ass kicked for trying to keep me hostage. If I wouldn't have been attacked by that monstrous beast you might just have felt some of my bite," she replied.

He smiled and touched her cheek. "Hey, I said I'm sorry. I will now and forever know you have a singular mind and stubborn will of your own. It's just that I love you and didn't want you to die. Kathy, you realize that if I hadn't been able to crawl to you then you would not have survived. Kahleel would've killed you."

She closed her eyes in order to let the rough texture of his palm both comfort and excite her. His nearness was overpowering and intoxicating while emotions churned inside her like she hadn't felt in quite a long time.

Opening her eyes, she laid her hand upon the back of his, emitting a small moan with a contented smile.

"So, what the hell happened anyway? The last thing I remember was your mouth on my neck and then kind of just floating away. I thought I died," she whispered.

"You did die Kathy. In order to bring you back to me, I had to finish what Kahleel had started, though his bite was murder and mine instead was love and life sustaining. With my bite, I sucked away the infection you received from the rogue and could hear the final beats of your heart fade to nothing. It was extremely difficult for me and I prayed it was not too late. Then I replaced the bad blood with some of my own and within a few minutes you gasped for air with your heart beating once more."

She sat up and put her arms tightly around his neck, feeling the anxious throb and beat of his heart echo madly in her ears. Johnny encircled her gently with his muscled arms and whispered, "I will never let you go again. I do love you Kathleen Morello. Will you be my mate?"

She wondered if that was a proposal and what 'mate' meant, though she was sure it held the same connation as wife, or partner. For a minute she was unable to say anything, not normally speechless, but knowing her reply was important.

"Cat got your tongue? Or does that mean a no," he murmured against her cheek.

Leaning back, she gently placed her lips against his and applied pressure before both of their mouths opened to let their tongues madly explore depths of desire. God, his tongue was so long she thought, at first startled, and then allowed him to drive her wild.

They parted lips, gasping, breathing heavy and desiring more.

"I'd have to say the wolf got my tongue and the answer is yes Johnny Raven, I will be your mate, though you'll have to teach me since I don't know what is expected of a mate. Is it the same as a bride?" she said breathily.

"Mmmmm, much more so, but sweetheart we are human as well, just far beyond the normal human relationship. There will be a weregune ceremony that will match us together forever and, if you desire, we can also have a human style wedding, white gown and all. Whatever you wish my love," he told her, framing her face with his huge hands and kissing her lightly on the eyes, the tip of her nose, and then the lips.

"Johnny, make love to me now. I don't want to fall asleep again, I've slept enough. Just love me, please," she asked, pulling the oversized t-shirt over her head to expose breasts with nipples already excited and ready.

He stared with loving admiration and smiled. "Your wish is my command m'lady. You will never have to ask me a second time. I'll be gentle though because I know your wounds are still painful."

"I don't care about any pain. You just won't be able to tell if the moans or screams are from pain or pleasure, how's that?"

"Scream all you want my sweet, we're alone here," he said, standing in order to unbuckle his belt and let his pants slide down to the floor.

She looked at him in amazement, startled at his size. Immediately she wondered if she'd be able to survive having that awesome manhood plunge inside of her, but she was more than willing to take that chance. She tossed back the blanket and raised her hips to slide her panties down around her ankles, where he then completed the task and dropped them lightly on top of his jeans.

"My God, you're so beautiful, so awesomely beautiful Kathy," he said in a throaty voice.

"Look who's talking about awesome. I'm a little frightened now that I've seen how well endowed you happen to be," she said meekly, but excited anyway.

"Don't be frightened, we'll work this out together and it will be so much more pleasure than pain. And trust me, I will never hurt you. Kathy, you've excited me from the first time I saw you walk out onto that porch. We've been to hell and back, but know that through this entire journey, I've dreamed of this moment.

Now, I just want you completely, totally and forever," he said, moving down onto the bed and covering her with his massive body.

Her heart leaped wildly, banging inside her chest as if it were shock waves rumbling through the ground from an earthquake. The pain in her neck and shoulder was intense, but the pleasurable pain she experienced as he entered her overpowered everything else. My God she thought, so this is what true love means as they rode waves of passion and pleasure for the next several hours. It was sometime later in the afternoon when she awoke from a deep, contented sleep. She felt the back of his hand gently stroking her cheek as she opened her eyes and smiled.

"Hey, you ready for round two?" she giggled.

"Well now, aren't you just the wild, little wolf," he replied in a deep, sexy voice.

"Just wild for you my love and I'd have to say that beast of yours is pretty wild as well," she said, smiling and touching him, surprised to feel him already hard at her touch.

"Damn, you are a little vixen, but I have to decline as difficult as that may sound. Get dressed Kathy, you have a visitor," he said, standing up from the bed and handing her the panties they had discarded a few hours before.

"A visitor, who knows I'm here? Where in the hell am I anyway?" she asked, getting out of bed, slipping into her panties and then reaching for the t-shirt and jeans.

"It's a surprise, just hurry up. Are you hungry?" he said over his shoulder.

"Hungry enough to eat you up again, but I'll settle for a steak and a few eggs, sunny side, toast and orange juice. Oh, and lots of coffee," she replied.

He laughed. "Okay, just hurry. Your visitor is quite excited to see you again."

As Kathy quickly dressed, she realized the pain in her shoulder and neck had miraculously disappeared. She walked to the mirror and tilted her head. The ghastly wounds on her neck had healed nicely. There were still ugly scars, but they had closed and pain had vanished, as had those on her shoulder. She decided to take the t-shirt off and searched in her bag for a black turtle neck sweater. Straightening her hair as best she could, she then headed downstairs, curious and anxious to see who her visitor was.

Bounding into the kitchen under the intoxicating aroma of a steak sizzling in the frying pan, she went and encircled her arms around his rippled stomach.

"That smells so wonderful, absolutely heavenly. I am rather famished, see what you do to me?" she said.

"Well, I can't take all the praise for that. It's been three days since you've eaten anything. I'm making a few steaks because I think you'll eat more than one."

"Hey, I can't ruin this girlish figure now, one will be enough. So who and where is my visitor?" she asked excitedly.

Turning the burner down low, he turned and took her by the hand, directing them to the front door where he guided her out to the front porch. There was a car parked in the driveway at the end of the long yard and Kathy realized the car not only looked familiar, it was her partner Tommy's vehicle. Surprised, she turned to Johnny with wide eyes.

"How did he know I was here?" she asked.

"Your cell phone was ringing and I decided to answer it, thinking it might be important. It was Tommy and he said he needed to see you. So I gave him directions and here he is, though with a little surprise I think you'll like."

Kathy lifted her hand above her eyes to shade the glare from the sun and saw Tommy get out of the front seat and wave. Then he opened up the back door and Rain bounded out excitedly, jumping up at Tommy who then turned her head and pointed towards Kathy standing on the porch. Rain immediately started barking and leaped in the air towards the house. Stunned, Kathy walked down the few steps to the sidewalk, knelt and opened her arms wide.

A few feet away, Rain came to a sliding stopped and stood up on her hind legs, pawing the air in excitement. Kathy stood and put her arms around her magnificent dog, tears rolling down her cheeks.

"Oh Rain, my baby Rainbow, Mommy's so happy to see you," she crooned.

Rain just pawed and licked and jumped on her hind legs.

"She walks almost as good as I do," laughed Johnny.

"She's a magnificent dog Johnny. You'll come to love her. Hey Rain, come here, this is Johnny, you're new daddy," she said.

Rain stopped and lowered her head, a deep growl erupting from her wide chest.

"Hey sweetie, don't growl. Johnny's no threat," Kathy said.

Johnny knelt down on the ground, lowering himself so he wasn't so intimidating and extended his hand for Rain to sniff. Then she moved closer, head still held low, large brown eyes staring up at him.

"Hey girl, it's fine. I'm not stealing your mommy away from you. I love her as much as you do so don't be jealous," Johnny said, smiling and looking up at Kathy while he scratched the side of Rain's muzzle, her long, curved fluffy tail beginning to wag in contentment.

"I think you've stolen her heart like you have mine," she said.

"That's good, I think I can handle two wild females," he said laughing.

Kathy stood to greet Tommy as he slowly sauntered over. She moved and put her arms around his shoulders in a strong wolfish hug.

"Hey Kat, damn you feel like you're getting stronger," he said, hugging her back.

"Not really, at least I don't think so anyway. I've just slept a lot over the past few days so I'm probably pretty rested, raring to get back to work. Hey Tommy, thanks for taking care of Rain and bringing her to me," she told him.

"It was more than a pleasure. Rain is an amazing dog and I'm just glad she survived that ordeal, though it's just one more miracle on top of others. It seems that everybody is healing overnight anymore, or dying," he said.

"What's that mean, the dying part?" she asked.

"Just crazy, considering everything that's taken place over the past few weeks. Did you hear about what happened out at Valley Forge? It briefly went through my mind that somehow you were involved," he questioned her, squinting his eyes.

"No, we've been here for awhile, haven't we Johnny?" she asked, turning her head and glancing back at him with a 'what do I say?' look.

"Yes, we've been here. What happened out there?" Johnny inquired.

"Two nights ago, it seems there was some type of terrible fight waged in a small clearing surrounded by a bunch of trees. The entire ground was bloody, but no bodies were found. Appears it was a large pack of wild dogs since it was mostly paw prints that were found, though curiously enough, a few human prints were detected, small like a woman's boot," he asked, looking at Kathy, suggesting she wasn't telling him the truth.

"Wow! That is pretty weird," said Kathy, expressing surprise. "Maybe the woman was attacked and killed, drug off someplace. You didn't find any bodies at all with that much blood?"

"Nope, not a one, though the park rangers who discovered the scene had an eerie story to tell. Seems one of them found what appeared to be the lower part of the leg from a very large dog. As he held it out in front of him, a huge raven swooped down and snatched it from his grasp, knocked him on his ass," said Tommy chuckling.

Kathy glanced back again at Johnny who raised his eyebrows slightly with the barest hint of a shoulder shrug.

"Anything else happen?" Kathy asked Tommy.

"Yeah, there were a few more vicious murders last night. In fact, I just left one of the scenes a few hours ago and called you on my way home. A young couple taking a walk in a small park near their house was murdered, torn a part like those two boys were. Seems we have another sadistic killer on the loose. Oh yeah, you should give Captain Ganz a call sometime. I think these last several weeks finally pushed him towards retirement. But you know him, he's said that before."

"He sure has," grinned Kathy. "I'll call him later on. Would you like something to eat, we were just making a late lunch."

"Nah, smells wonderful though. I need to get back, no rest for the weary detective you know. So, are you coming back?" asked Tommy hopefully.

Kathy walked over and gave him another bear hug. "You bet I'll be back, but I'm going to take some of the sick time I've accumulated over the years, get my mind back to where it was. I don't think I'd be a very good partner right about now. Don't worry buddy, you can't get rid of me that easily," she said, lifting up on her toes and kissing him.

"That's good, took me a long time to break you in," he said, winking at Johnny who smiled back.

"Yeah right," Kathy said, punching him lightly in the arm. At least she thought it was a light tap.

"Damn Kat," Tommy said, raising his hand to rub the spot she just punched. "What have you been doing, getting Wheaties intravenously?"

"Oops, I'm sorry! You're probably just a little weak from your strangulation. How are you feeling Tommy?" she asked, truly concerned.

"Other than a deeper, sexier voice, sore ribs and a stiff wrist," Tommy said grinning, holding up his cast, "I'm fine, no real damage that won't heal with time. Captain Ganz wanted me to take sick leave, but I'd go bat crazy. I find myself drinking more though, especially in the morning when I wake up. It gives me the opportunity to drink more beer."

"Hey you boozer, don't turn into a lush," she said, avoiding the urge to give him a playful push, fearing she'd knock him on his butt.

"Not a chance Kat. Hey, I have to run. Bye Rain, watch out for your Mommy," Tommy said, turning to Johnny. "You take could care of her, she's very special to me."

"Me too, and I will for sure. We'll be back in a month or so," Johnny said, firmly grasping Tommy's hand in a very strong handshake.

After Tommy left, Johnny put his arm around Kathy's shoulder and guided her back into the house.

"You have to eat. I'm sure that Rain is probably hungry as well," Johnny said.

"What about you? Aren't you hungry?" she inquired, turning and looking up his wide, expressive face.

"You bet I'm hungry, but not for food," he said teased. "Now go sit down and let Chef Raven fix you the dinner of your life."

Two hours later they sat snugly on a large, overstuffed, brown corduroy couch in front of a fireplace that crackled with a warm glow. She let herself slide further into his embrace, smelling the wild nature of his beast, that alluringly strong masculinity that radiated from him like no man she had ever been with before.

She was quite content, but then some of that might've come after wolfing down two thick, very rare steaks, four sunny side eggs, a pile of hash browns, five pieces of rye toast, and she had lost count of how many cups of coffee she had drank. So not only was her tummy full, so was her love for this unique man.

"So tell me Johnny, what happened out at Valley Forge? I've been afraid to ask about your father and what happened to the others," she said against his chest.

There was a long, silent pause, giving Kathy an uneasy feeling, expecting to hear the worst.

"He's gone Kathy. He was no match for Kahleel in human form and he resisted changing. It was almost like he had given up. I think his grief over deserting his son and being somewhat the cause of Victor losing his mate, as well as Samantha's death, was just too much for him to handle. His long time wish was to be buried on our property in Maine so we'll be heading there later tonight so he can be buried at dawn," he said, his voice low and throaty. "Mother will join us there, along with most of the pack."

Kathy understood that pain, another connection they now had in common.

"What about the others?" she asked quietly.

"Victor's dead as well. I had wounded him gravely in our fight and Tabitha, who was strong and fresh, finished the job. She was injured very badly though and is recuperating right now. She should recover from the physical wounds, not sure about the mental. It takes awhile to go through internal grief like that, but she's strong and will most likely lead the Philly clan until she finds a new mate. As for Kahleel, you injured him badly as well, but he disappeared. That's not a good thing, we'll have to be on our guard because it's far from over between us even though he killed father."

"What about the dead, why no bodies?" she asked him.

"Kathy, we can't leave signs of who we are. There are obviously strong physical differences in our body structures and it would create upheaval within your society if they were to discover us as a species. That's why we need to remove all signs, as well as recover our own dead before any autopsy can be done," he instructed her.

"How about the raven sweeping down and grabbing that leg from the ranger?" she asked, wondering if he would get tired of all her questions.

"That was my uncle. He remained as a guard until the light came up for just such an event. Sometimes these battles are so vicious that limbs are thrown around and we need to locate those as well so no DNA can be done. Now, no more questions my love. Take a nap so we can be ready to leave later tonight," he said, kissing her on the top of the head and hugging her even more tightly.

She was so content being held within his arms, the fire warm and Rain lying at their feet. Yet there was so much more to happen in her life there was still a strong sense of trepidation. With Johnny at her side, any fears would be kept to a minimum and she felt confident he would teach her all the ways of the wolf.

Chapter 37

Roberto had been standing on the crest of a nearby hill in Valley Forge. Being a Master Vampire with all the unique and deadly powers that position held, he could literally hear the dead moaning from that cold winter of 1777/1778 calling out to him. Since he himself was one of the un-dead that was able to walk alive under the cover of darkness, he deeply felt their pain and loneliness. But, he was not a necromancer and thus could not be of any help in raising them from their long, breathless slumber, to let them feel the glorious softness of the moonlight.

Instead, he would offer assistance to Kahleel as he watched his magnificent alpha wolf struggle to sneak away after being shot several times by that pesky little female detective. It was the first time he had been able to lay his steely gaze upon her and without a doubt she was quite a tasty looking morsel. What a bloody battle it had been, the super bowl for werewolves. Oh, weregunes he thought amusingly. Well, even vampires needed to smile once in awhile.

Roberto was a vision of masculinity. His face and skin seemed like it had been cast from the finest Italian porcelain, almost to the point of being translucent. He was not overly tall, but the breadth of his shoulders made his height a moot point. Within his presence, nearly everybody seemed to be dwarfed, even those that were considerably taller. Around his head and shoulders was a thick mane of dark, reddish-blond hair, the kind of mane an

African lion would roar in delight for. But his eyes were the feature that reached out and could literally pull you underneath a rolling sea of aquamarine waves, changing from light lavender to a soft, greenish-blue. Eyes you could die for (and many had).

He decided to just glide over the moonlit ground rather than go through the hassle of changing to a bat. Sure, he could walk down the hill also, but gliding still gave him a thrill since not too many beings could actually glide over anything. Passing near the battlefield basically undetected, he could see the surviving weregune picking up the bodies of their dead brethren. It may have only lasted for about ten minutes, but during that time there was more blood shed and severed limbs flying through the air than debris from a category three hurricane.

Roberto paused to watch the large, black wolf crawl over to the lady detective and bite her on the neck. A soft, velvet thrill, like he was being touched by an experienced lover, flowed through his veins. His urgent hunger rose up like a river of bubbling lava. It was a ritual of the weregune he knew all too well, his own bite the kiss of death and then everlasting life.

Kahleel was bleeding quite profusely from the shotgun blasts. He would heal, of course. As ghastly as the wounds were, both the weregune and werewolf possessed astounding healing capabilities. In this case, however, Roberto decided to blend his own special powers with that of Kahleel and knelt beside the huge wolf that lay sprawled in the snow behind some thick, slightly frozen bushes. Turning the beast over onto his back Roberto spread the thick mass of fur as far away from the neck skin as possible and plunged his two, scissor-sharp teeth into Kahleel's throat, sucking blood out and injecting his own healing properties into the ragged edges of the wound.

The feeding served at least three purposes. First and foremost, Kahleel needed to heal faster than normal. Since Victor and over half of their small army happened to be dead or severely wounded, his alpha would not be welcome back at their compound. Second, in order for Kahleel to travel quickly he needed to heal while in wolf form and even with the morning sun several hours away, Roberto knew he needed to hurry so that his wolf would not be detected and the sun's hot kiss not burn his own lovely skin. And, of course, third was simply that he hadn't fed since before midnight and the blood from his own primo-serviteur was the absolute food he needed. As he sucked with a small slurping sound his memory reflected upon the young teenage girl he had seduced coming out of a bar in Phoenixville, a small community not far up Route 23. Her blood was simply the sweetest he had consumed for quite awhile and still, hours later, had left a pleasant after taste.

Kahleel moaned and began moving noticeably underneath Roberto. The wolf's silver eyes fluttered open and stared in surprise at the sight of his Master. The vampire stood and allowed the weregune to struggle up on all fours where he stood at first on shaky legs. Then he shook himself like a dog would just after getting a much needed bath. Even though his thick black fur was even darker, like a newly exposed oil spill, the wounds had indeed closed and he could now change back to human form. First though he had to head back to where his clothes had been stashed so he could become clothed after shifting. The massive wolf moved to stand at Roberto's side, his broad back nearly above his Master's waist and urged the vampire's hand to stroke him lovingly.

"I'm glad you survived that wild battle my son," said Roberto warmly. Of course, Kahleel was not Roberto's son, it was symbolic only. Hell, the Master Vampire was over eight hundred years old and had not fathered a child through sexual intercourse in nearly that long. But as evil and treacherous that he could be, those he had brought close to him like Kahleel were his children and he often referred to them as sons and daughters.

"Glad that lovely little detective didn't shoot you in the nether region. They most likely would not have grown back exactly the same," he said chuckling, while the wolf whined under the strong caress of his hand.

"Now, find your clothes and get dressed. You'll have to find shelter for the day so you can heal and come back here at nightfall. The dawn, with those damn burning rays, is too near. I need to seek a safe place quickly."

Kahleel stood on his hind legs, placing his front paws on Roberto's shoulders and actually grinned.

I will do that father. Please be careful for if you stay around here, the police will be all over this place soon.

"I will make sure I'm safe Kahleel. Now go before you're detected and we'll meet again when darkness calls," said Roberto, pushing the wolf away and watching the awesome beast limp slowly across a large open field towards where he had parked his vehicle in a secluded spot off a service road.

Finding a dark enough place where he could safely hide from the sun's glare, Roberto knew he needed to bring forth his bat. There was that large church he passed where in bat form he could get inside and find a dark enough place in the rafters. It was true that a vampire needed to be completely away from light during the day, but when he or she was in bat form, it wasn't totally necessary. They could stand some light touching their bodies, just not directly. The only problem was that once in bat form with the sun hanging high in the sky, they had to stay in bat form until nightfall.

Standing completely still, Roberto concentrated on altering shape, lifted his hands above his head and changed. It was that simple. His dark clothing was absorbed into the black skin of the bat and stretched over the fingers in his wings. With a screech he lifted into the air and began beating that wide wing span, propelling him higher and faster. He was huge and would most likely give anybody who saw him instant heart failure. Most humans were deathly afraid of bats and to see one of this size would be too much to handle.

He reached the church within several minutes and found an entrance high in the roof where he squeezed his large body through the smaller egress and discovered a secure spot in a far corner of the ceiling. Another misnomer was that vampires could not enter a church, being a holy place and all. Not true, at least for a Master Vampire that had the powers of Roberto. He closed his eyes and slept the sleep of the dead until such time when he could rejoin Kahleel and they could make their evil plans together.

Colleen held Sara in her arms, rocking back and forth like she was being carried along unmercifully by frothy waves in an angry sea, tears rolling down her cheeks as if the sky had erupted in tortured raindrops. Remembering shredded bits and pieces of last night was more than she could bear. Looking down at Sarah who lay cradled in her lap, she brushed away some hair and leaned down to kiss her cheek. Putting her head back against the pillows piled up behind her in this flea bag motel room, she closed her eyes and let the horrifying images come storming back.

Innocent daylight melting into terrifying nightfall as the moon reached down and seemed to tear them a part. Truth be told, that's exactly what it did. For a newly bitten, the first full moon is by far the worst, especially if you're alone. Yes, Colleen and Sara had each other, but they were both experiencing the coming change together and neither of the terrified women knew what to expect. Other than it would be horrifying which it was.

Intense waves of pain began late in the afternoon as the hungry moon began to sniff at lonely stars and cry out their names. They scratched at burning skin which seemed to be alive with a thousand scurrying fire ants, coarse hair attempting to escape through pores that were just simply not there. Their blood boiled like an out-of-control firestorm, bones stretching and going soft like liquid mercury, then hardening and expanding into shapes that were human, but then not.

Sara rolled into Colleen's arms and screamed, "Please let it stop, let it stop, I can't stand this."

Colleen grabbed hold of her partner and they cried, yelled, screamed together. At some point in this nightmare their once velvety soft, feminine voices became coarse, rough and deeper. Beautiful faces were stretched out of shape into ugly caricatures of a human turned beast. Clothes had been torn off long ago, even the touch of silk or satin against their burning skin was too much to handle. Hair began growing at an alarming rate on every square inch of their bodies, too much for a Lady Schick to take care of.

Who knows at what point in a living nightmare such as this that humanity is lost? Man or woman falls and is replaced by the beast. Right or wrong, good or evil, lust and passion, has no meaning for it is only the urge to run, to feed, and to kill. Sounds and senses literally came alive and called for them to race underneath a cold November night, searching for unsuspecting prey to quench their thirst for blood.

"Honey, you okay?" asked Sara, touching Colleen's arm, awakened by uncontrolled sobbing.

Sara moved up on the bed and they grabbed each other, feeling that closeness was all they had left to touch humanity. Two beautiful young women, once promising lawyers with such glowing futures, knew now without a shadow of doubt that life truly had turned into a real life, horrifying danse macabre. They fell asleep in each other's arms, searching for parts of their memories which were happy before those thoughts disappeared forever.

On a small table in the corner of the room rested a coffee stained newspaper, headlines screaming out, "Jogger Found Dead in Roxborough, Badly Mutilated Body Discovered on Towpath". The girls had been busy.

Kathy found the Maine woods which hid Johnny's cabin absolutely breathtaking. The wildness was overwhelming, especially for a city girl. Now, nearly ten days later, she couldn't get enough of it. Every day she walked or jogged along the many paths with not only Rain, but Johnny also, loping casually beside her.

They arrived at dawn, like Johnny had wanted. It was Mandhar's wish to be buried here and at dawn's early light so that they could put to rest the body of his father. Other weregune attended as well in what turned out to be a very moving ceremony. It was weird though for Kathy because it was the first burial she had attended where wolves lolled about and some of the seemingly humans weren't all that human looking.

That night Kathy and Johnny sat on the front porch, quiet and reflective, sad for their loss, but content in knowing they were together. Rain lay at Johnny's feet where he let his bare toes brush back and forth over her stomach. Kathy marveled at how quickly her dog had taken a shining to Johnny, but then it was understandable, Rain being a female and all, Johnny being such a hunk in whatever form he chose to take.

Reaching out to touch his hand, she asked, "So when does this big change take place? I thought you could change whenever you pleased."

"Soon, when the moon is full again, I will guide you through it. Before that, I'll prepare you on what you'll need to do in order for it to be as painless as possible. It's always easiest to change for the first time under the optimum amount of moonlight, but eventually you will be able to shift when you wish," he replied.

She squeezed his hand lovingly and said, "I know you'll be there and believe me I'm glad, kind of scary and unbelievable at the same time. I look at you when your wolf is free and I can see how happy you are. I want to feel that, but some part of me is afraid."

"That's a natural way to feel Kathy. Believe me, when you finally change you'll know what true freedom and power are."

"I hope so, but right now Mr. Raven, I'm tired and wonder if I could tease you to come inside to the bedroom and play around for awhile," she said, running her fingertips up his arm and behind his neck.

Rain growled at her touching Johnny. She glanced at the dog and said, "Hey, you be quiet, there's no jealousy here. Share and care, that's our motto, so get used to it."

Johnny laughed as he unwound his long, lean body from the old rocking chair on the porch. Taking both her hands, he helped her up and led her inside the cabin. The warm, crackling fireplace sang out and caressed their skin. He had a moment to reflect on how sad and lost he had been when living here the last time. And now, with his arm enwrapped protectively around Kathy, the cabin and these woods had a completely different melody to them. He had a brief image of Samantha in his head, smiling and nodding her approval as she walked away.

There was enough moonlight streaming through the open windows that there wasn't a need to turn on the small lamp on the nightstand. Besides, Johnny wanted to explore every curve and swell and mound of his new mate in the softness of darkness, the time he loved best.

Turning to face him, she looked up and smiled, laying her head against his chest.

"Mmmmmmm, you smell so good, like sugar maple on a crisp breeze. What do you have planned for me, my black wolf?" she asked alluringly.

He tilted her head back and let his mouth do the talking, covering her smaller lips with his, letting the thrill of passion take them to the edge of the bed where he softly placed her. For a man his size, with the urgency he felt for this woman, he showed considerable gentleness as he unbuttoned her blouse to let it slide down her back to the mattress. His hands went behind her and undid the clasp on her bra, sliding the straps smoothly over her shoulders to free Kathy's hungry breasts, nipples already ripe and anxious for his touch.

"My God, you are exquisite," he whispered in her ear, smelling the intoxicating aroma of strawberries in her hair. "You make me so happy just to know you're mine and that I belong to you. Are you happy?"

"More than you'll ever know, but talk is cheap my lord and master," she said in a soft giggle. "I'm lying here waiting to be ravaged by a beast so how long do I have to wait?"

He began to laugh and pulled the black sweatshirt with the face of a wolf (what else) over his head and then untied the sweat pants to let them fall to the floor. Kathy stared up at this awesome male, his chest and arms rippling like they were sculpted from the masterful hands of Donatello. Her gaze flowed from a slim waist to his more than adequate male endowments, his excitement seeming to grow as she continued to stare. Bending over her, he easily lifted her hips to anxiously slip the jeans from her legs. His beast captured the intoxicating smell of her, arousing him to levels possibly never reached before. Without waiting he easily ripped the thin satin panties from her waist, the last remaining body armor that kept him from her deepest, feminine world.

He stood back and just stared, admiring the beauty of her form, the artistic curves, the luscious swell of her breasts, the slim but exotic shape of her legs. His mind began to swim in a sea of desire, as if he was completely drunk. Of course he was, wishing now only to drink from her chalice.

Kathy smiled and reached up for him, not saying a word, her smile and extended arms said it all. Get the hell down her big boy! And he did, never one to wait for a second offering. He covered her with his much larger body, careful not to smother her. She didn't care really, wrapping her arms around his massive shoulders and pulling him tightly against her. They kissed and let their tongues explore depths that they had yearned to do from their very first encounter.

She moaned loud and long, the sound seeping out of the window and around the front of the cabin where Rain was lying in front of Johnny's rocking chair. She lifted her head and listened, wondering if her mommy needed her again. Then a slight movement from the bushes on her right brought her attention to a large, gray timber wolf that walked proudly into the soft moonlight. Rain whined, not sure if it was from sudden fear, or proverbial animal lust. Rasha, Johnny's old friend, walked nearer the porch and stopped, staring at Rain, a low growl blossoming from his wide chest. She stood up with some uncertainty and moved forward slowly, her head down, eyes glancing up and never leaving his deep, golden eyes. When she was only several feet from him, she dropped to the ground and rolled over on her back in a submissive pose. He quickly closed the short distance and dropped his head to smell every square inch of her. It was obvious to him that Rain was just a dog, but there was something else, something internal that made her wolf as well.

He stood straight and moved back, letting her scramble to her feet. Towering over the smaller, reddish-brown dog he moved forward and they touched shoulders, smelling each others muzzles in a wild kiss. He growled slightly and started loping towards the tree line. Rain wagged her tail, not sure if she should follow. Stopping, the wolf glanced back and growled again, louder this time. Rain turned her head to look back at the dark cabin, quiet now except for the occasional moans and groans that filtered from the window. She decided, what the hell, her mommy seemed safe enough in Johnny's arms. With a small bark, she turned and bounded towards Rasha who stood tall and waiting impatiently. A gray timber wolf and reddish-brown shepherd/chow disappeared into the dense Maine woods, ready to seek their own happiness.

Chapter 38

The following eight days seemed to fly by for Kathy. She had never been this happy, especially knowing Johnny seemed to be so much in love with her and happy as well. But tonight was the night of the first full moon since she had been changed from a human, who was to become a werewolf, who had been turned into weregune with his bite. She was frightened and excited, her nervousness building to where she would literally jump at his voice or touch.

He reached and gently caressed her cheek. "Hey, don't worry about anything. It's going to be fine. We've gone over all there is to know and it's just a simple matter of putting it into motion. Kathy, you will never experience anything more glorious than what is about to happen."

She smiled and tilted her head. He laughed and said, "Yes, even more glorious than that. Are you ready?"

"Yes, you'll shift with me as well?" she asked, beginning to take her clothes off.

"Oh, absolutely, but I'll stay human until you're changed and I know that you're okay. Now, just kneel down, close your eyes and concentrate on the moon that we now share as mates. Call out and let it come to you. There will be a moment of pain, but it won't last long. Just ride with it. Now close your eyes, I'll be right here beside you."

She leaned forward, kissed him softly on the lips and closed her eyes, calling out for their moon which she knew would come. It was the tie that bound them together. She felt the warmth and tugging that always accompanied its emergence. Keeping her eyes tightly shut, she felt her skeleton bending and twisting, a stretching of her face, the growth of hair on her limbs. Yeah, it hurt some, but it was more like the firm hands of an artist molding a lump of clay into something beautiful and glorious.

When she opened her eyes the world suddenly took on another meaning, sounds and sights and aromas assaulting her newly acquired senses. She looked up at the man who stood nude in front of her and wagged her long, bushy tail and whined in nervous anticipation. He knelt, closed his eyes and called forth the moon they shared to bring on his beast. In just a matter of seconds the transformation was complete.

Standing on top of an open hill, underneath the loving glare of an awesomely large moon, black wolf and white wolf smelled every square inch of the other. They began to prance and jump at each other, Jaress snarling with happiness, biting playfully at her rear legs. At Sheena's legs, because that was the weregune name they had decided upon for her. She turned and growled back, startled at the sound which burst from her chest. Surprises would continue for sometime to come.

Can you hear me my love? Just speak with your mind and I can hear you.

Yes, I can hear you Jaress. I don't know what to say actually. I'm stunned!

I know what it means to be weregune, man and wolf combined, but I was born his way. I can only imagine what it's like for you right now, so just let me lead you into a world you will come to love and embrace as I do.

I'm ready, lead on my alpha, she thought, her muzzle breaking into a wide grin with long tongue hanging out in front.

Come and let's run so you can get used to racing on four legs. First one to that large rock over there owes the other one something special, as he bolted away in long, loping strides.

At first she stumbled and kept getting her legs entangled, but eventually she got it right. After all, it was like riding a bike with training wheels and then being promoted to that first two-wheeler. She could only imagine what something special he had in mind for her as they raced along the crest of the hill towards the large rock.

Breaking from the tree line on their right was a large, gray timber wolf and reddish-brown dog anxious to join the larger black and white wolves that had begun to jump and cavort in happiness.

In their sheer enjoyment of being together however, none of them had detected the presence of something evil, a malevolent power that gazed at them from a distant cliff. It decided to let these pitiful, silly wolves enj0oy themselves, at least for a little while. Vengeance would be sweet and oh so terrible.

THE END

HAUNTED MEMORIES

Through crimson mist and icy fog
I share my tears to stand alone.
Tis raven wing and eye of dog
that rips my flesh down to the bone.
I clutch your hand within my fingers,
sweet womans touch now formed of claws.
The pain of love now lost...yet sadly lingers..

your name thus whispered from savage jaws.
This human skin now gladly shed
is cast aside like haunted memories.
Your throat exposed as once you bled
through frightful screams and tortured pleas.
I still love you now as I did then,
yet shutter while my beast roams free.
Forever lost upon this bloody path when...

fractured moon cries out to me
in dreams and fog of mystic beast.
Please share my haunted memories
if you so dare...

to share with me the stroll
up angry path of crimson tears.
Behind this mocking door
sobs the memory I most abhor,
the mark of beast upon
my breast to shatter my humanity.

Kerry L. Marzock

To shower at my feet the fears
that life has ceased to beat
with the beauty thus once held.
So come and take my hand,
or paw ....., or claw,
and let this wolf of mystic dreams
guide you up to stop and stand
before the altar where well share
the blood of beast and man.
Push wide the door that leads to me
and all my haunted memories.

About The Author

Growing up as a child, I immediately acquired a love of sports, animals, and horror, not necessarily in that order. My monster of choice was always the werewolf, simply because it represented change and stood for the most wonderful creature I loved from such a young age, the wolf. Life has certainly not always been easy and presented numerous challenges and difficult periods for me. However, I possessed an extremely strong will to survive and tackle all obstacles head on. Thankfully, I discovered all the many wonderful, talented authors who provided me the worlds of horror and science fiction which I escaped into, especially Laurel K. Hamilton whose work I have admired for a long time from the very first page I read. I have lived for the last 51 years in Philadelphia, a beautiful, historic, and wonderful city, so it was not a stretch to write this novel set here on the streets that I know so well. My first novel "Raven's Way" represented a lifetime dream, and also simply meant to never give up on your deepest desires. My life has certainly proven that fact. I sincerely hope you enjoy "Raven's Way", and then look forward to enjoying the continuation of his wild and crazy life in, "Raven's Rage - Order of the Claw". My third novel is titled, "The Reptilian Factor", which is about an angry alien in the Sonoran desert around Tucson, AZ. I also have written a book of poetry titled "A Sea of Emotion". It is simply a book of everyday life about the dreams we all possess of finding that never-ending romance or special friendship through sadness, love, loneliness and struggle adrift upon A Sea of Emotion. I followed that up with "Along A Burning Highway", comprised of both poetry and short stories.

You can check them out on my web site, www.kerrymarzock. com. Also, I would love to know your comments about Raven's Way so please feel free to send me an E-mail to kmarzock@ aol.com.

CPSIA information can be obtained
at www.ICGtesting.com
Printed in the USA
FSHW011546110222
88231FS